Rhythm of Deceit

by

Rachael Richey

The NightHawk Series, Book Two

Rhythm of Deceit

Contact Information: info@thewildrosepress.com

Cover Art by *Tina Lynn Stout*

The Wild Rose Press, Inc.
PO Box 708
Adams Basin, NY 14410-0708
Visit us at www.thewildrosepress.com

Publishing History
First Mainstream Women's Fiction Edition, 2015
Print ISBN 978-1-5092-0188-4
Digital ISBN 978-1-5092-0189-1

The NightHawk Series, Book Two
Published in the United States of America

"Mum," she whispered. **"Mum, wake up!"** With a grunt, Abi opened her eyes and stared up at her daughter. She frowned, brushed her hair out of her eyes, and pushed herself up onto one elbow.

"Wassup?" she muttered indistinctly, groping on her bedside table for her phone to see the time. "Is something wrong?"

"Dunno"—Natasha shrugged—"but Chris is at the door in a right state and said I had to get you. Now I must let him in."

She jumped off the bed, ran out of the room, and clattered down the stairs. At the bottom, she unbolted the huge front door and hauled it open. Chris was through the door before she'd finished opening it, going to stand at the bottom of the stairs and impatiently wait for Abi to come down. She appeared at the top, hair dishevelled, wearing only a long white T-shirt belonging to Gideon. She hooked her hair behind her ears and frowned at Chris.

"What on earth's the matter?" she asked in concern, starting down the stairs, her bare feet padding on the polished wood. Chris pulled the rolled-up newspaper from under his arm and brandished it at her.

"This is the matter," he said dramatically. "I take it you haven't seen it yet?"

Abi reached the bottom of the stairs and raised her eyebrows at him. "Until two minutes ago I was fast asleep," she pointed out, holding out her hand for the paper, "and besides, we don't usually read this rubbish."

Chris was watching her carefully as she unfolded it and looked at the front page. There was a long silence.

Praise for Rachael Richey and *STORM RISING*

"I didn't want to put it down….I loved the way the story flowed and the way it was written….Richey very cleverly weaves a beautifully crafted piece of work which had me laughing, cringing and crying in all the right places….A really good read and a nicely written and thoughtout book by a first time author!"

~Sharon Adetoro, British Paranormal Romance Author

"I loved this book….Rachael hasn't written stereotypical characters. The characters that she has created are true to life, with a narrative that is authentic. Her descriptions of the 1990's were spot on, and I was certainly taken back to that era. She has managed to make the whole book seem like we are reading about real people in real situations."

~Whispering Stories (4 Stars)

~*~

"Was I hooked? I read this book in one sitting, and I LOVED it. I'm looking forward to the next books in this series."

~Anna at A Wondrous Bookshelf (4 Stars)

~*~

"A real page turner with sympathetic characters. I liked how the plot was revealed with flashbacks to the past."

~Jill Rudge

~*~

"I love this! Was hooked from the beginning."

~Sophie MacKenzie

~*~

"Rachael Richey has perfectly captured the vitality, excitement (and awkwardness!) of youth."

~Alison Coote

Dedication

To Abi, Gideon and Natasha
for insisting I write the next part of their story

**The NightHawk Series by Rachael Richey
available from The Wild Rose Press, Inc.**

Chapter 1

Friday 18th July, 2008

"Tasha! Catch Ollie, can you? He's trying to climb the stairs again." Abigail Hawk covered the telephone receiver as she called to her daughter.

In a flurry of flowered skirt and long legs, Natasha shot past her mother and caught her eighteen-month-old brother just as he reached the third step. Grabbing him round the tummy, she swung him up in the air and around to face her. He chuckled his chubby baby laugh and grabbed a handful of her dark curls. Natasha grinned and, tucking him securely under her arm, carried him out into the garden, where she had been helping her father prepare the barbeque. Abi smiled to herself and uncovered the receiver.

"You still there, Judy?" she asked. "Oh, just Oliver trying to go upstairs again. He's getting far too adventurous." She paused. "Oh, I know they do…You must have had that all the time with your two…I was just wondering if there's any chance you could have the kids for a couple of days next week?" She listened again and grinned. "Oh, thanks, Jude, you're a gem. We're going to London to talk to the record company…Yes, it is about time, isn't it? He's been planning on releasing a solo album for the last year. Maybe it'll finally happen." She listened again and

1

laughed. "Yeah, well, I don't think that'll ever happen, do you? Not after what Simon did. No, I think he'll be going solo from now on. Anyway, see you on Tuesday, if that's okay? Bye for now."

Abi smiled as she replaced the receiver. Things had been going pretty well for them during the last two years, and she had to admit to being extremely happy. Wandering over to the French windows, she stared out into the garden, where her husband Gideon was attempting to light the barbeque, hindered by the attentions of twelve-year-old Natasha and baby Oliver. She looked fondly at them, marvelling to think that less than three years earlier none of them had been together. She closed her eyes for a moment and gave thanks for the life they now all had, then stepped outside and ran over to join them.

Gideon looked round and grimaced at her, his eyes harassed. "This bloody thing just won't light," he muttered, pushing his long dark hair back with a charcoal-blackened hand.

Natasha jumped in front of him. "Can I get the petrol, Dad?" she asked, her blue eyes dancing with mischief.

"No, you can't." Abi laughed, ruffling her daughter's hair. "Remember what happened last time?"

Natasha giggled and danced around the barbeque, blowing at it to try and help it light. Abi sighed and took the matches out of Gideon's hand.

"Here, let me do it," she said, and, leaning forward, rearranged the charcoal and the firelighters, then struck a match and pushed it in amongst them. Within seconds the firelighter caught and the flames began to lick around the charcoal. Abi stood back and surveyed her work, her hands on her hips. "You and fire are not good together, are you, Gid?" she said with a smirk. "Remember the gas fire in the caravan?"

Gideon reached over and took the matches out of her hand. "I'd warmed it up for you," he said, trying to keep a straight face.

Abi stood on tiptoe and kissed his smutty cheek. "'Course you had." She wandered over to the stone wall bordering the garden and gazed out over the long sweep of Sennen Cove. She sighed and smiled; life couldn't be better.

****

Simon was hung over again. He lay on his bed with the curtains closed against the strong morning sun. Manhattan in July was far too hot for his liking, and he was beginning to regret not leaving the city the day before and taking up the offer of a bed at the house of a friend in Vermont. He'd spent the last two and a half years travelling around America and making significant inroads into the fortune he'd amassed during his years with NightHawk. Such significant inroads, he'd recently realised, that he'd need to start earning again in the very near future if he was to be able to maintain his current standard of living. Even his fairly substantial royalties from their albums weren't keeping up with his expenditure. His dearest wish was to get the band back together and for everything to be as it had been before Gideon left. Simon formed his hand into a fist and pounded it hard into the bed beside him. He would never forgive Gideon for that. Or, more accurately, he would never forgive Abi. Quite irrationally Simon blamed Abi for the fact that Gideon had left the band so precipitously, even though she'd had no contact with him over the ten years prior to that. That they were now married, had discovered their lost child, and had another baby really rankled with Simon, and he had even managed, in his own mind, to conveniently play down his part in their original separation. The letters from Abi that he'd concealed from Gideon all those years ago still languished in his bag, and he was well aware that by now they would almost certainly know what he'd done. For that reason he appreciated that persuading Gideon to reform their band, NightHawk, was a lost cause. Simon would need to launch his solo career or join another band if he were to get his finances back on track.

Charles Bond, the erstwhile bass player of NightHawk, was in New York with his current band, Velvet Shackles, and Simon had arranged to meet up with him later in the day. He was hoping to be able to persuade Charles to form a band with him and then maybe rise to fame riding on the back of the previous success of NightHawk. If he were perfectly honest with himself, Simon should have realised that NightHawk without Gideon Hawk was a non-starter, but he was determined to get back out there and was relying heavily on the hope that Charles would help him.

With a grunt Simon swung his legs over the side of the bed and stood up. He closed his eyes for a moment, until the room stopped spinning, then made his way unsteadily into the shower. The cool water did a fairly good job of waking him up, and ten minutes later he was dried, dressed, and staring at himself in the mirror. The face that looked back at him was not a pretty sight. His curly blond hair was straggly and unkempt, and his ruddy face showed the ravages of time and hard living.

He leaned forward and peered more closely at his image. It was hardly the face of a rock star. He was thirty-two, no longer the fresh-faced teenager who'd first arrived in America with NightHawk thirteen years earlier. He found it hard to imagine the groupies thronging around him now. He stood back and looked down at his overweight body. Time to hit the gym and sort himself out. He doubted his ability to survive the rigours of one concert, let alone a whole tour.

With a sigh he turned back to the bed, hastily threw the covers over, picked up his jacket—despite the heat—and room key, and slammed out into the corridor. He was staying in the Western International Hotel on Central Park West, the same hotel the band had been staying in the day Gideon announced his departure in November '05. It was the first time Simon had been there since that day, and he felt the old resentment beginning to return. He rode the elevator down to the first floor and strode out into the stifling heat of a Manhattan summer day. The last time he'd stayed there he'd been mobbed by reporters and unable to leave his room without being approached. This time no one even registered his departure, and he crossed the busy street and entered Central Park without turning a single head.

Before meeting Charles, Simon had an appointment with a tour manager the band had used back in their heyday. He was hoping to get some positive response to his idea of starting a new band with Charles.

As he crossed the park he passed a newsstand and paused briefly to buy one of the English tabloid papers they had on sale. He carried it over to a shady bench and sat down to have a quick read. He grinned to himself when he saw the pictures of the dreadful weather most of Britain was experiencing and decided his decision to remain in the U.S. was a sound one. He flicked over to the next page and froze. A grainy black-and-white photo of Gideon, Abi, and the children arriving at some airport on their way back from holiday jumped out and gave him a mental slap across the face. Gideon was carrying the baby, and Abi had her arm protectively around the older child's shoulders. They all looked happy, healthy, and—to Simon's mind—smug, and he was tempted to tear the paper to shreds. He resisted and glanced at the caption beneath the photo.

"Former NightHawk guitarist and front man Gideon Hawk and his family arriving home from their holiday in Greece on Wednesday. It's rumoured Hawk is due to start recording a solo album later this month. When asked about the possibility of re-forming the band, Hawk immediately dismissed the idea."

Simon closed the paper and tossed it into the nearest bin, then got to his feet and set off across the park towards the office of Seth Cotterill, the former tour manager. Simon had had no contact with Seth since shortly after the band split, and he was a little unsure of his reception. As he rode up to the third floor he rehearsed what he was going to say, and when the elevator doors opened he ran a hand through his hair, took a deep breath, and marched up to the door. He tapped sharply and after a moment received permission to enter. Seth Cotterill, a solidly built dark-haired man in his late forties, got to his feet as Simon entered.

"Simon," he said in his East Coast drawl, extending his hand. "Good to see ya. Take a seat." The two men shook hands briefly, and Simon took the seat opposite Seth's desk and crossed his legs. "What can I do for you, man?" the tour manager asked, narrowing his eyes at Simon's rather dishevelled appearance.

Simon wiped the sweat off his brow with the back of his hand and sat forward in his seat.

"I need to get back into the business, Seth," he said. "I want to get a band going again with Charles Bond. Maybe get another guitarist and follow on from NightHawk. What d'you reckon? Will you help us?"

Seth leaned back in his chair and pursed his lips. "Nice idea, Si," he said, "but NightHawk is nothing without the Hawk."

"It won't *be* NightHawk," interrupted Simon, "but we could ride on the back of our earlier success. Bill us as former NightHawk members. That's gotta stand for something surely?"

Seth got to his feet and walked over to the window, keeping his back to Simon.

"The thing is, Simon," he began, "no one's interested in you or Charles." Simon flinched. "If you can get Gideon to re-join you and actually get NightHawk back, then I'll give you all the help you need." He turned round and grinned. "Not that you'd really need any help if that happened." He saw Simon's face and sighed. "Look, man, you and I both know Gideon *was* NightHawk. Without him no one's even going to remember who you and Charles are. Get him on board and we can talk again." He paused. "I heard he's about to do some solo work, so he's clearly ready to get back in the saddle. Maybe now's the time to ask him?" Simon was silent, and Seth looked at him inquiringly. "Simon? Is that possible? Or did you two fall out? I never really talked to any of you after the breakup."

Simon got to his feet. "Thanks, Seth," he said with a wry grin. "That makes me feel much better." He held up his hand as Seth started to speak. "No, don't worry, not your fault. I'll talk to Charles and see what he thinks. Maybe enough time has passed and we can find a way to get Gideon back. I'll call you." With a wave he left the room and slammed the door behind him.

Back in the corridor Simon leaned against the wall and closed his eyes. The heat of the city was intense, and sweat was running down his chubby face and staining the neck of his shirt. He ran a hand through his damp hair and took a deep breath. Time to approach Charles. Maybe if he could persuade him to ask Gideon, they might get somewhere. Holding on to that thought, Simon took the elevator back down to the bottom and emerged out of the building onto the crowded Manhattan pavement. As he wove his way between the mix of hurrying locals and slow-moving, camera-clicking tourists, he once again cursed the day Gideon had met Abi at the school dance. If only they hadn't agreed to play that night then none of this would have happened. The band would still be together and he and Gideon would still be best friends.

Ten minutes later Simon arrived at the apartment Charles was sharing with another member of Velvet Shackles and pressed the buzzer on the intercom.

"Yeah?" came a voice.

"It's Simon," he said tersely. There was a loud buzz, and the door opened smoothly. Simon hurried inside and puffed up the single flight of stairs to apartment number two. As he approached the door it opened, and a small, slight figure with a shock of messy black hair stepped out. Charles held out his hand, a huge grin spreading across his face.

"Si!" He grabbed Simon's hand and pumped it furiously. "It's amazing to see you, man. Come on in, have a beer." And he stood aside to allow Simon to enter the apartment.

The air conditioning was on. The room felt almost cold after the heat of the city, and Simon immediately began to relax. Charles shot over to the fridge and retrieved two beers, one of which he thrust into Simon's hand, then indicated they should take a seat in the large, sparsely furnished living room. Simon sank down into a deep, cream-upholstered armchair, and Charles perched on the edge of the one opposite him.

"So what gives?" he asked, snapping open his can and grinning at Simon. "It's brilliant to see you. Are you working, or just visiting?"

Simon took a long swig of his beer and stretched his legs out in front of him. "Just visiting so far," he said cautiously, "but I was hoping to be working soon."

"Cool. Are you with a band?" Charles asked, sliding down into the armchair and crossing his legs.

Simon made a face. "Not yet." He watched Charles as he spoke. "But I was rather hoping you might be interested in getting NightHawk back together."

Charles stared at his friend in amazement, then threw his head back and roared with laughter. "Simon, you kill me. You're kidding, right?" he glanced at Simon and saw his face. "Oh, right. You're not kidding. God, Si, surely you know that'll be impossible? Did you see the paper today?" He indicated the English newspaper lying open on the coffee table. The picture of Gideon and his family at the airport taunted him, and

Simon turned away in annoyance.

"Yeah. So what?" he demanded. "He wants to get back in the business, so why not with us?"

Charles leant back in his chair and surveyed Simon thoughtfully. "The fact it says Gideon dismissed the idea of re-forming the band means nothing to you, then?"

"Well, he *says* that"—Simon shrugged—"but who knows what he actually means? I thought maybe you could ask him."

Charles raised his eyebrows. "Why don't you?" he asked in surprise. Simon was silent, and Charles watched him closely for a moment. "Si, was there some trouble between you two? I was surprised you weren't at the wedding, but I didn't like to ask why."

"You went to their wedding?" Simon's head shot up. "I had no idea." He got to his feet and walked over to the huge window overlooking Central Park, then rested his head against the glass and closed his eyes.

"What happened between you?" Charles asked again. "It must be something bad if you didn't get invited to the wedding. You're his oldest friend."

"Abi fucking happened!" Simon swung round to face him, venom in his voice.

Charles frowned and held up his hand. "Steady on, man." He shook his head. "That's a bit steep. He and Abi have been in love for…like ever. Do you really want to deny him his happiness? They were parted for ten years 'cause of her mother hiding his letters—let 'em be happy now."

Simon gave him a look of mild dislike. "Might've known you'd take her side," he muttered, flinging himself back into his chair again. "Gideon'll never come back to us while she's around."

Charles leant forward, concern in his eyes. "I don't think he wants to re-form the band anyway," he said. "Remember, he'd had enough back in '05, when he left. It wasn't just Abi, you know. You can always go and ask him, but you'll have to get used to Abi being around." He paused. "If you can get him to agree to re-form the band, then I'm in. But I don't think much of your chances. Go and clear up whatever went on between you and see how it goes."

Simon nodded and got to his feet. "I'd better get back to England, then." He forced a smile. "See if I can work some magic."

Charles gave his friend a quick hug and a pat on the back. "You do your best, mate," he said cheerfully. "But remember—Abi's here to stay. Better get used to it."

****

Half an hour later, as he lay on the bed in his hotel room, Simon's mind was working overtime. He knew Gideon would never agree to re-forming the band and would probably never speak to him again. He knew the reason for that was Abi. If only he could find some way to split them up. Some way to discredit her—to make Gideon realise that he, Simon, had been right all those years ago when he'd withheld her letters. If he could find some way to make Gideon lose trust in Abi, then maybe he stood a chance of rekindling their friendship. He sat up thoughtfully and pulled his old sports bag towards him. Reaching into an inner pocket, he pulled out a bundle of letters and sat with them in his hand as a plan began to form.

Chapter 2

Tuesday 22nd July, 2008

Natasha crawled across the conservatory floor and placed her train on Tommy's beautifully constructed track. She pushed it over the bridge and let it come to a stop at the station. Tommy pushed his train into the station from the other direction and crashed into hers. Natasha sat back on her heels and laughed.

"You always make them crash," she said, ruffling his fair curls. "Some trains travel safely, you know."

Tommy regarded her seriously. "Some do," he agreed, "but some cwash. An' I like mine to cwash. It's more fun." He continued to ram his engine into Natasha's until they both fell off the track and landed on the carpet. She laughed again and crawled over to the opposite corner of the room, where Tommy's little sister Sabrina, aged three, was attempting to teach Oliver how to build a tower with her bricks. Each time she balanced three bricks on top of each other, Oliver's little hand came out and knocked them down. Natasha watched them for a moment, a grin on her face.

"You're fighting a losing battle there, Sabby," she said, smiling at the little girl. "He's very determined." Then she got to her feet and wandered back into the kitchen, where Judy was preparing the children's dinner. She perched on the edge of the cluttered table and folded her arms. "Judy? You know you said Robert has a squash match and will be late tonight."

Judy turned and raised her eyebrows. "Yes?"

"Well, I was wondering," went on Natasha with an engaging smile, "could we—you an' me—maybe have a bit of a girly evening? You know, have nibbles an' stuff, and you can tell me all the stuff you an' Mum used to get up to when you were my age."

Judy laughed and turned back to the stove. "Yeah, why not?" she said easily. "Sounds fun to me. Your mum and I used to do that a lot. Not sure I should tell you everything we got up to, though! Might give you ideas." She grinned over her shoulder at Natasha. "Now go and round up the little ones for tea, there's a good girl. The sooner we get them to bed, the sooner this girly night can begin."

An hour later, when all three small children had been fed, bathed, and safely tucked up in bed, Judy and Natasha curled up on the sofa in the cosy living room, surrounded by bowls of crisps, bars of chocolate, and a large pile of photograph albums. Natasha gave a little wriggle of pleasure. She was fond of cosy evenings, especially on a one-to-one basis—possibly a hangover from her early years in the children's home—and she was really looking forward to this one. She had formed a very close attachment to her mother's best friend and often found she could ask her things she might find awkward asking Abi. Judy poured herself a glass of wine and handed Natasha a can of cola.

"Would you like to see pictures of your mum when she was little?" she asked, a twinkle in her eye.

Natasha grinned and nodded vigorously. "Yes, please," she said. "We don't have many at home at all.

Did she look like me?"

Judy picked up a brightly coloured album and flicked it open. "See what you think," she said with a little smile.

Natasha leaned forward and peered at the picture in the book. Two smiling twelve-year-old girls stared back at her, one with long blonde hair tied in a high ponytail, the other with messy dark auburn hair escaping from its ineffectual hair band. Both girls were wearing jeans and wellies and were covered in mud.

Natasha caught her breath. "She looks just like me!" she exclaimed with a giggle. "And you haven't changed a bit. You still tie your hair up like that, and you've still got the freckles on your nose."

Judy rubbed her nose ruefully. "Think I'm stuck with those," she said with a chuckle.

Natasha shook her head. "Oh I like them. They give you character." She flicked the page over and chuckled at similar photos. She pointed to one of Judy on her own. "Your hair is down in this one. It looks nice."

Instinctively Judy put her hand up to her hair and released it from its large tortoiseshell clip. It swung down over her shoulders as she gently shook her head.

Natasha nodded with approval. "That's better. No need to keep it tied up when the kids are in bed. No little hands to pull it." She continued to flick through the album, picking at the crisps as she did so. Eventually she stopped at a large picture of the two girls together again. "When was this taken?" she asked curiously.

Judy leaned forward to take a look. She grimaced. "That was at our school Christmas dance in 1994," she said, watching Natasha's face.

The girl nodded. "The night Mum and Dad met," she murmured. "So that's what she looked like then." She studied her mother's rather sulky face with its overdone mascara and very messy hair. "You both look very…" She searched for the right word, finally deciding on "tatty."

Judy laughed. "That, my dear girl, is grunge fashion. Take a pretty dress and add clumpy boots and tatty accessories. We thought we looked really cool."

Natasha surveyed the photo dispassionately. "I guess you do," she said at last. "I think I like the style, actually. Are there any pictures of Dad in here?"

Judy picked up the next album and turned to the middle.

"There you go. That was on your mum's sixteenth birthday. We went to the New Forest for the day." She showed her a picture of Abi and Gideon sitting on the grass beneath a huge yew tree, munching on large pieces of chocolate cake.

"Oh, I know where that is." Natasha smiled. "Grandma and Grandpa have taken me there. It's nice. Lots of ponies."

Judy grinned. "Abi and I kept calling them horses, and your dad kept correcting us," she said with a laugh.

Natasha tutted. "Don't you know the difference?"

Judy laughed. "Your mum and I both grew up in the town. Your dad lived in a big house with stables and horses and all sorts of stuff. He knew all about horses and ponies."

Natasha looked pensive for a moment. "I've seen lots of pictures of Dad as a child, 'cause Grandma has them all over the house, but I've not seen many of Mum at all. I guess her father has them all."

Judy frowned. "Well, I know your mum has some in a box. Her father gave them to her when her mother died. Has she not shown you those? There are quite a lot from when she first met your dad."

Natasha shook her head. "No. Well, she showed me a couple, but none with her parents in or anything. I know it was them that put me in the children's home and told Mum I was dead, but I'd still like to know what they look like." She paused for a minute, then looked at Judy under her lashes. "Does Abi's father still live in Newbury?"

Judy hesitated before nodding. "Yes. Yes, he does. Same house, too." She flicked open another album and held it out to Natasha. "Here, this is the house. Your mum grew up there."

Natasha snatched the book from Judy and peered intently at the picture. It showed a very plain, red-brick, 1930s semi-detached house, in a tree-lined suburban road. The garden was neat and tidy, and a large, rather old Saab stood in the drive.

Judy pointed to the car. "He still has that car, would you believe it?" She chuckled. "He's always had it, as far back as I can remember."

Natasha glanced up at her. "How d'you know he's still got it?" she asked curiously. "Mum never has any contact with him."

"My mum lives just round the corner," Judy explained. "She keeps me updated about everything."

Natasha leaned back on the sofa. "So could you show me where it is on a map?" she asked. "I'd like to imagine Mum there. I can't ask her to show me, 'cause she gets too upset thinking 'bout her parents." She paused and frowned. "They were really quite nasty people, I think. I'm glad her mother's dead, even though it means I've got less grandparents." She nodded to herself. "But Roger and Caroline are very nice grandparents. I don't need any more, actually.''

Judy watched her carefully for a minute, then nodded. "Okay, I'll show you where his house is. Can you pass me my laptop? There's a love.''

Natasha leapt to her feet and retrieved Judy's laptop from where it resided on her desk in the corner of the room. Judy turned it on and waited for it to load, then quickly called up a map website and found the correct area of Newbury. Her fingers flying over the keys, she located the map of the requisite roads, and pointed to the screen.

"There," she said, "that's where my parents live, and just around the corner here—this is where Arthur lives.''

"Arthur." Natasha tried out the name on her tongue. "So I have a grandfather called Arthur. No one told me his name before. What was his wife called?" her voice became slightly brittle as she said the words.

"Her name was Joan," Judy said. "She died nearly three years ago now." Natasha was silent as she studied the map on the screen, trying to imagine the people who lived there and trying to make sense of what she knew they'd done twelve and a half years ago.

She looked at Judy. "Why did they do it?" she asked, almost inaudibly.

Judy shook her head sadly. "I really don't know, darling," she said. "No one does. Not even your Mum.''

Natasha's eyes hardened. "I want to meet this Arthur," she said sharply. "I want to ask him why they did it. I want him to see me. To see that I'm real."

Judy reached over and took her hand. "Yeah, I'm sure you do, but I don't think Abi's ready to talk to him yet. He hurt you all a great deal."

Natasha wriggled in frustration. "But *I'm* ready," she objected. "It was me he hurt most. I want to know why." Judy held out her arm and, after a moment's hesitation, Natasha moved a little closer and snuggled up to her. Her big blue eyes were wet with tears as she looked up at Judy. "You understand, don't you, Judy?"

Judy nodded and sighed. "Of course I do, Tasha, and I'm sure one day you'll all get closure for this. Give it time, eh?" and she dropped a kiss on the child's curly head.

Natasha nodded and snuggled closer. "I guess," she conceded. "Can I have a glass of wine?"

Judy laughed. "Certainly not!" She grinned down at her. "You make do with your cola. Plenty of time for wine in a few years. Now, d'you want to see some really bad photos of your Mum and me? Our worst fashion disasters?"

Natasha raised her head and gave a watery grin.

"'Course I do!" She sat up expectantly, rubbing a hand impatiently across her eyes. Judy grinned at her and heaved a large album onto her knee.

****

"Abi, stop worrying." Gideon lay back on the sofa and stretched his long legs out in front of him. "Judy can cope fine. They'll be having a great time." He looked over his shoulder to where his wife was standing at the window of the flat, staring out over the houses towards the back of Buckingham Palace. "I bet you anything Ollie is safely asleep in bed and Tasha is bombarding Judy with questions about you when you were a child."

Abi turned to face him and managed a reluctant grin. "You're probably right," she admitted. "I just worry so much about Tasha. I'm never too sure what she's thinking." She moved quickly across the large room and sat next to Gideon. "Does she really like us, Gid? Has she accepted us as parents?"

Gideon put out his arm and pulled her towards him. "Of course she has, Abs," he said quietly. "She loves us. She just needs a bit of careful handling, and at some point very soon she's going to need some answers." Abi looked up at him. "Well, I think we all need to know exactly why your parents acted the way they did. You and Tasha really need to get closure on that." He paused and gently stroked her head. "I think it might be time to go and see your father."

Abi shook his hand off and sat up abruptly. "No," she stated firmly. "No, not yet. I can't." She turned anguished eyes to him. "Gideon, I can't imagine what he'll say…I'm scared."

"I bet you're not half as scared as he is," Gideon retorted. "He's been waiting for you to ask him ever since we found Tasha. It won't be an easy conversation for any of you, but it must be done…and soon." He raised his eyebrows at her. "How about we go and see him when we pick the kids up on Thursday?"

Abi wrapped her arms around herself and shivered. "Maybe," she conceded. "I guess Tasha needs to know. She's old enough now. Not that I can begin to imagine what they were thinking. The whole thing is still like a nightmare we're only just waking up from." She lay back in the curve of Gideon's arm again and rested her head on his shoulder. He leaned over and gently kissed the top of her head.

"I think today went well, don't you?" he asked, changing the subject.

Abi nodded vigorously. "Oh, yes. I told you it was time to launch you back on to the music scene, didn't I?" She smiled smugly and snuggled up to him. "I reckon you'll be bigger than ever."

Gideon grinned. "Sure you won't be jealous of the groupies? Of the adoring teenagers that will follow me everywhere? Of the—" He tailed off with a yelp as she wound her fingers into his hair and pulled his face down to hers.

"They'll have to get past me first," she said balefully.

Gideon laughed. "And that will be scary," he agreed. "They're still wanting me to get the band back together, of course. But that ain't gonna happen."

Abi closed her eyes. "Well, not with the original drummer, anyway." Her nose wrinkled. "Simon wouldn't dare show his face again, would he?"

Gideon shrugged. "Hmm. You say that, but he's a strange one. He probably still thinks he did what he did for the good of the band."

"Does it bother you that we still haven't talked to him about the letters?" Abi narrowed her eyes at him. "I hate that he might think he's got away with it."

"Yeah." Gideon frowned. "Yeah, it does. We do still need proof, though, and to be honest, we've had far more things to take up our time than worrying about him these last two years." He paused. "Don't worry, he'll get his comeuppance one day."

Abi nodded. "He'd better. I know it was him. We'll

get proof somehow."

Gideon smiled grimly. "We will. But I certainly won't work with him again. I'd work with Charles again, of course. Not that he'd want to, I'm sure. He's playing with Velvet Shackles now."

Abi sat up and stretched. "They're not a patch on NightHawk," she said dismissively. "I bet he'd come back like a shot if you asked him."

Gideon shook his head. "Doubt it. Now, d'you want another drink, or shall we just go to bed?" he asked, his eyes twinkling.

Abi smiled. "Oh, bed, I think," she said at once. "I love the bedroom in this flat. Let's make the most of it."

They were staying at the London pied-à-terre Gideon's father kept, in Wilton Crescent in Belgravia. Abi still found herself slightly fazed by the curious world of Gideon's family. His father, Roger, had worked for MI5 and had government connections who could make almost anything happen. Gideon took it all in his stride, but to Abi it was rather like a fairy story— or possibly a spy novel. They hadn't brought the children to the flat yet, but Abi was sure Natasha would love it as much as she did.

"Okay." Gideon got to his feet. "I guess we should get a fairly early start tomorrow; we need to finalise stuff with the record company, and then I reckon we should try and do some touristy stuff. Just have a bit of time to ourselves…" He held out his hand to her, and together they made their way into the master bedroom and closed the door behind them.

****

Natasha lay in bed in Judy's tiny guest room in the

attic and stared at the night sky through the skylight set in the sloping ceiling. She had really enjoyed her evening with Judy and loved seeing the photos of Abi as a child, but something was gnawing away at her and she couldn't get to sleep. She really wanted to go and see Arthur. Confront him and find out why he and his wife had kept her and her mother apart. She scowled to herself in the darkness. He wasn't going to get away with it. She was going to demand more than just an apology. A tiny idea began to form in her mind. She'd made a note of the road name when Judy showed her on the computer where he lived. She'd already known it was in Newbury. How hard could it be to find? She grinned. That was it—she'd go and see him on her own. Tomorrow she'd find some way to get away from Judy, catch a bus to Newbury, and take it from there. She knew she could find a bus timetable on the Internet, so she'd get up really early and sort that out. She had enough money for the fare, so the only problem would be escaping Judy without making her suspicious. She wriggled with pleasure as her plan began to come together. Maybe tomorrow she would finally get some answers.

Chapter 3

Wednesday 23rd July, 2008

When Natasha awoke the next morning, the first thing she was aware of was the heavy rain lashing down on the window above her head. She sat up carefully so as not to bang her head on the sloping ceiling, swung her legs over the side of the bed, and shivered. It really didn't feel like July, and she thought back fondly to the previous week, when she'd been on the beach in Greece. She reached for her dressing gown and padded downstairs to the living room. It was only six thirty, and although she could hear quiet voices coming from Judy and Robert's room, no one was up yet. She hurried over to Judy's laptop and turned it on. Within minutes she had located a bus timetable for the local area and made a quick note of all the possible buses she could catch to Newbury. It all looked fairly straightforward, she thought, frowning at the screen in concentration, and she only had to walk about a mile to the main road to catch it. She smiled to herself and turned the computer off just as she heard footsteps start down the stairs. She jumped up and made it into the kitchen just in time to be filling the kettle when Judy entered the room.

"My god, Tasha! You are up early. Couldn't you sleep?"

Natasha grinned at her. "No, I slept fine, thanks.

Just felt like getting an early start." She paused and shrugged nonchalantly. "I thought I might go out and walk down to the village shop this morning. Unless you need me to help with the kids, that is?"

Judy shook her head. "No, not at all. Not the best day to walk anywhere, though, is it?" she asked with a grimace, indicating the lashing rain that thundered on the conservatory roof.

Natasha giggled. "I actually quite like the rain," she lied. "I'll get dressed up for it and go after breakfast. I am allowed, aren't I?"

Judy hesitated for a second, then nodded. "I don't see why not. So long as you only go to the village, and you take your phone with you. Does Abi let you go places on your own?"

Natasha raised her eyebrows at her. "Of course she does," she said. "I am twelve and a half, you know. I go all over the place at home."

Judy looked momentarily doubtful, then nodded again. "Okay, then. But you must come straight back," she said seriously. "No deciding to go somewhere else afterwards."

Natasha nodded vehemently, a slight qualm of guilt pulling at her conscience. "'Course I will," she promised ducking her head to let her hair conceal her face. "The kettle's boiled. Shall I make tea?"

"Yes, please. One for Robert, too. Thanks, pet." Judy popped some toast into the toaster and cleared a space on the ever-crowded table. Natasha watched the kettle until it boiled, unable to bring herself to face Judy while she was feeling so guilty about planning to deceive her. She didn't want to go behind her back, but she knew she'd never be allowed to go on her own—or even go at all—if she told her what she was planning. She carefully poured the hot water into the mugs, added the milk, and carried them to the table. Judy looked up at her with a smile, her long blonde hair swinging over her shoulder.

"Thanks, Tash, you're a gem. Any chance you could go and see if the little ones are awake yet?" Natasha nodded and skipped out of the room and back upstairs to the large bedroom shared by Tommy and Sabrina, and currently by Oliver, as well. She opened the door quietly and found Tommy sitting up in bed reading a Thomas the Tank Engine book, his lips moving and his brow furrowed in concentration. The other two were still asleep, so Natasha waved to Tommy, then slipped out of the room again as quietly as she'd entered. She ran up the stairs to the attic room and shut the door behind her. She was feeling positively dirty about her proposed deception but was determined nonetheless to go through with it. She pulled a piece of paper out of her dressing gown pocket and unfolded it. The first bus she could conceivably catch was at nine fifteen, and it would take her about twenty minutes to walk up to the main road. If Judy objected to her going out so early, the next bus was half an hour later, so she could get that one. She delved into her bag and pulled on a pair of faded jeans, a white NightHawk T-shirt, and a blue checked shirt. She tugged a hairbrush through her thick dark curls and tied them back in a high ponytail with a blue scrunchy. She shoved her bare feet into her navy blue baseball boots and ran back down the stairs again.

Robert had joined Judy in the kitchen, and the three of them sat at the table and had tea and toast. When

Robert left for work at seven forty-five, Natasha ran back up to see if the children were awake. This time Sabrina had climbed into bed with Tommy and was attempting to turn the pages of his book while he tried to read it. Oliver was standing up in the cot, shaking the bars and shouting to Sabrina. The best he could manage was "Seena," which he kept repeating over and over despite the fact that she was paying him no attention whatsoever. With a grin, Natasha ran over to the cot, lifted her brother out, and gave him a big cuddle. He beamed at her, grabbed a handful of her hair, and put it in his mouth. Natasha untangled his fingers, then hoisted him onto her hip, called to Tommy and Sabrina, and set off down the stairs. Judy had put the highchair ready at the table, and Natasha slotted Oliver in and did up the straps. Tommy and Sabrina erupted into the room and took their places, waiting expectantly for their breakfast, while Natasha went over to the kettle and flicked it back on.

"More tea, Judy?" she asked.

Judy shook her head. "Coffee this time, please, Tasha. Need waking up this morning!"

Natasha rummaged in the cupboard, found the coffee, then made a cup for Judy and a mug of hot chocolate for herself. She joined the children at the table and sat warming her hands on her mug.

"Are you sure you can manage without me, Judy?" she asked taking a sip.

Judy grinned as she fastened her hair back with a large clip. "Yes, thanks. Have to manage on my own most days," she said serenely.

"Yeah, I guess. But you've got Ollie as well, this time," Natasha pointed out.

Judy smiled at her. "I'll be fine, Tash, and you're not going to be long, after all. Oh, and can you pick me up some eggs while you're there, please?" She glanced out of the window. "I think the rain has eased a bit. You might like to go early while it's not too bad. The forecast for later is dreadful," she said, playing directly into Natasha's hands.

Natasha drained her mug and put it in the dishwasher. "Shall I go now, then?" she asked.

Judy nodded. "Sure. Go and have fun. Just be careful, and do take your phone. And turn it on!" she added with a laugh.

Natasha nodded, waved to the little ones, then skipped out of the room. In the hall she pulled on her green waterproof and pushed her phone and purse into her deep pockets. She opened the front door and stepped out into the damp July morning. The path was dotted with large puddles, and Natasha skipped agilely over them and let herself out of the gate, pulling her hood over her head against the gently falling rain.

The walk to the main road took slightly longer than she'd anticipated, and she finally reached the bus stop just as the nine-fifteen hove into view. She stuck out her arm, and it slowed down and pulled up alongside her. Mounting the steps, she paid her fare and took a seat near the front of the bus. Taking off her waterproof, she folded it up on the seat beside her, then took out her phone and held it for a moment. She knew she needed to let Judy know she'd gone somewhere else and had decided that sending her a text when she was well on her way was probably the best option. She took a deep breath and pressed Messages. She located Judy's number and started to type: *Sorry, Judy. Be back a bit later. Gone on a mission. Don't worry, I'm fine. Be back for tea.* She hesitated for a moment, then pressed Send. The phone bleeped as the message sent, and then Natasha turned it off and put it back in her pocket. She was feeling very guilty about her behaviour but managed to convince herself the end result of her deception would be worth any trouble she was going to get into. It didn't occur to her that Judy might panic and phone her parents, or that Judy herself might get into trouble for not looking after her properly.

Thrusting her hand into the pocket of her jeans, she pulled out a folded piece of paper. She opened it out and stared at the unfamiliar address, reading it several times to see how it sounded. To imagine it had been her mother's address for the whole of her childhood seemed really strange. Her mother had lived at that address when she'd met her father; when she'd discovered she was pregnant; when she gave birth and was separated from her baby. Natasha's face hardened as she thought about the man who still lived in the house. She was going to make him pay for what he'd done. She'd told Judy she was glad her grandmother was dead, but in fact she was feeling a little cheated she wouldn't have the opportunity to make her pay too. It sounded, from what she'd heard, like her grandmother had been the driving force behind the events that separated Natasha from Abi, and her grandfather had just gone along with it. She scowled to herself. Not that it made him any less responsible, in her eyes.

The journey to Newbury took nearly three quarters of an hour, and Natasha spent most of the time staring out the window at the unfamiliar countryside. She couldn't help thinking how glad she was she now lived in Cornwall, and she could completely see why her mother had moved there after finishing college.

As the bus finally drew up in Newbury, Natasha took a deep breath and walked out into the dreary, drizzly day. She looked around her and, to her satisfaction, saw there was a large street plan of the town fixed to the wall of the bus station. She moved over to it and peered at it closely. The large arrow proclaiming her current location appeared to be about a mile away from the residential area in which Arthur's house was situated. She pulled her waterproof back on, checked her pocket for her phone and purse, and, still clutching the piece of paper with his address on it tightly in her hand, she set off across the town.

****

Judy didn't find the message on her phone until Natasha had been gone for over two hours. She had begun to wonder where the child had got to after an hour, but she didn't actually start to worry until an hour and a half had passed. She had tried to call her using the landline, and it had gone straight to answerphone. Judy wasn't too surprised; the signal in the village was not the best, and at first she assumed the child had got chatting to someone and forgotten the time. However, when two hours had passed, she began to feel a little knot of dread in her stomach. She ran upstairs to where she'd left her mobile on charge, with the intention of texting Natasha in the hope a text might get through where a call did not. Failing that, she was going to put the children in the car and drive down to the village. She picked up her phone from beside the bed and immediately saw she had a message. Her initial feeling of relief turned to near panic when she read it. She sat down on the bed and stared ahead of her. What on earth was the child up to? She quickly pressed Reply on her phone and typed fast: *Where are you? Call me immediately.* The phone bleeped as the message sent, and Judy put it down on the bed beside her. Where could Natasha have wanted to go that she wouldn't have been allowed? Judy racked her brains. What would she and Abi have been up to at that age? Suddenly realisation dawned on her, and she snatched up her phone again. She dialled Natasha's number and listened. Straight to answerphone again. The wretched child had turned it off, thought Judy in frustration. She considered for a moment. She was fairly sure Natasha had gone to see Arthur, and she needed to decide what best to do about it. Her first instinct was to put the children in the car, drive to Newbury, and pick her up. She paused and considered how Natasha would react to that. She shook her head, then picked up her phone again and dialled a number.

"Hello? Mum?" she said a moment later. "Yeah. I need your help…no, they're okay…it's Tasha." She paused. "She's gone off on her own, and I think she's gone to see Arthur…" She stood up and walked over to the window as she listened. "Yes, Mum, I know. It's all my fault. I showed her where he lived—long story. Seemed like a good idea at the time." She paused again. "I know I should. But she told me she was going to the village shop this morning and then sent me a text to say she'd gone somewhere else and she'd be back for tea. Mum, what should I do?" She paced the room as her mother spoke. "Really? You wouldn't mind? I'll call him first, to make sure she's there. That would be brilliant if you could. I'll call you back." She terminated the call and ran back downstairs to use the landline.

****

Natasha edged past the old Saab and walked slowly up the path to the front door. She swallowed, took a deep breath, and pressed the doorbell. Nothing happened for a long time, and she pressed the bell again. Still nothing happened, so she stepped back a little and looked up at the house. There was no sign of life, but an upstairs window was slightly open, and she fancied she could hear the very faint sound of a television or radio. She stepped up to the door again and this time raised her hand and knocked loudly on the frosted glass panel. Within seconds, she heard sounds from within, and a shadowy figure approached the door slowly. She licked her lips and took a step backwards, suddenly nervous as the moment of confrontation drew close. The door slowly opened, and Natasha found herself face to face with a short elderly man with very sparse greying hair and lifeless grey eyes. They stared at each other for a moment.

Arthur spoke first. "The bell doesn't work," he said quietly. "Did you ring the bell? It doesn't work."

Natasha stared at him, taking in his cowed stance, his shaking hands, his old flannel trousers and green cardigan. She took a step forward.

"I'm Natasha," she announced, her voice sounding hollow and overloud in her own ears.

Arthur surveyed her silently, then gave a small nod. "Yes," he said at last, "you look like Abi."

They stared at each other again, and then Arthur slowly stood aside and indicated that Natasha could enter the house. She stepped forward with no hesitation and walked into the dark narrow hallway. Arthur closed the door behind her and led the way into the kitchen.

"Would you like a coffee?" he asked politely.

Natasha looked at him scornfully. "I'm twelve," she said. "I don't drink coffee. I'll have hot chocolate." She sat down at the kitchen table and rested her elbows on it.

Arthur looked slightly lost. "I don't have any," he said at last, standing with his hands by his sides.

"I'll have milk then," said Natasha flatly, staring at him. He turned away, took the milk from the fridge, and poured her a tall glass. He placed it on the table in front of her and sat down facing her. She took a long swig, wiped her mouth with the back of her hand, and replaced the glass on the table.

"Why did you do it?" she asked bluntly, her piercing blue eyes as hard as flint. "Why did you and your wife keep me from my parents? Why did you hate us?"

Arthur flinched at her words, and his shoulders sagged still further. "I didn't hate you," he said at last.

Natasha leaned forward. "Well, you must have hated Abi, then. How could you hate your own daughter that much?" She didn't take her eyes off his face.

Arthur sighed and leaned back in his chair. "No," he said at last, his voice tired, "no, I loved—I love—Abi. I never meant her—or you—to get hurt. I should have been stronger."

"So it was all *her* idea, was it?" asked Natasha, carefully holding her emotions in check. "Her idea, but you went along with it?" Arthur's head moved slightly in acknowledgement. Natasha went on. "But that still makes you guilty. And why did *she* hate us?"

Arthur pushed back his chair and stood up. "Come with me," he said nodding to Natasha. "Let me try and explain why I acted the way I did." He paused and looked her straight in the eye. "But no one hated you, or your mother. It was all done with the best intentions, however misguided they turned out to be."

Natasha's eyes flashed. "So putting your only grandchild in a children's home for ten years was in whose best interests?" she asked sharply. "Lying to your only daughter, making her think her boyfriend had abandoned her and making her think her baby was dead—that was all in whose best interests?"

Arthur shook his head. "No one's," he admitted quietly. "No one's. We were very wrong. But I never knew she'd hidden the letters from Gideon. That was all her."

"You can't use that as a defence," stated Natasha, staring at him coldly. "You did all the other stuff. And I don't see how you can explain it."

He beckoned to her to follow him and led the way into the small square living room. The furnishings were heavy and old-fashioned, and everything was covered in a thin layer of dust. Natasha wrinkled her nose and followed him in.

"Look around you," Arthur said gesturing with his hand. "What do you see?"

Natasha stared around the room. "A smelly, old-fashioned, dirty living room."

Arthur nodded. "Yes. Old-fashioned. And that's what we were, Joan and I. We had Abi very late in life, and we—especially Joan—never really took to parenthood." He paused, reached out, picked up a framed photograph that was on the mantelpiece, and went on. "We couldn't relate to a teenager. In our day, everything was different. We obeyed our parents, we dressed nicely, we were...different."

Natasha reached over and took the photo out of his hand. It was of Abi, aged about thirteen, standing on a pier somewhere. She was smiling broadly. Natasha handed it back.

"She looks happy here," she commented.

Arthur nodded. "Yes. When she was a child, it was better. Okay, we—particularly Joan—may have been rather strict, but things were all right." He stopped talking and looked away from her. He was silent so long, Natasha reached over and jogged his arm.

"What changed?" she asked impatiently.

"Abi grew up," he said sadly, "and neither Joan nor I understood her any more. Looking back, she did nothing different from any other teenager at the time, but Joan in particular couldn't take it. She got very controlling, and consequently Abi rebelled, and all the problems started." He looked guardedly at Natasha. "And then she met your father."

"Did you hate him too?" she asked with a scowl.

Arthur sighed. "I didn't hate anyone," he said patiently. "I actually thought Gideon seemed quite a nice boy. Looked dreadful, of course, but was very well spoken and polite. But Joan had a big problem with Abi having a boyfriend. It seemed to particularly bother her that he was eighteen. I never really knew why." He stopped again and frowned. "There was something that happened in her past that coloured her judgement, I believe. I don't know what it was, though. And when Abi become pregnant, Joan completely lost control.

When it was too late to terminate the pregnancy"—he glanced at Natasha as he heard her sudden intake of breath—"she insisted that the baby—you—be adopted at birth. Abi refused even to consider the option, and that was when Joan came up with the plan that was carried out."

Natasha stared at him, her blue eyes sparking dangerously. "Why wouldn't she let Mum keep me?" she asked quietly.

Arthur looked desperately unhappy. "She said she was too young to look after a baby. She seemed to think Abi would take you and go to America to find your father, and that something dreadful would happen to you."

"Something dreadful did happen to me!" shouted Natasha. "I was kept from my parents for nearly ten years! They thought I was dead. That's really, *really* dreadful! How much worse could it have been?"

Arthur's shoulders sagged, and he shook his head. "I don't know, Natasha," he said, his voice shaking. "I really don't know."

"Don't use my name," she snapped. "You don't deserve to." She wrapped her arms around her thin body and walked away from him towards the window, where she stared out into the neat front garden and took a deep breath. "What you did was evil," she said at last, "and I still don't really understand why. It still doesn't make sense to me. I need to ask your wife, but she's dead." Arthur opened his mouth as if to speak, then changed his mind and closed it again. Natasha turned round to face him again. "D'you have photos of her?" she asked at last. He stared at her in consternation, and just as he seemed about to answer, the telephone rang.

They both jumped, and Arthur walked slowly over to answer it.

"Hello?" During the pause that followed, his face registered resignation. "Yes, Judy, she's here. She just turned up…All right, that sounds like a good idea. Do you want to speak to her?" He paused, then held out the phone to Natasha. She shook her head and took a step backwards, fear in her eyes. Arthur took pity on her. "Judy? She's scared to speak to you. Thinks she'll be in trouble, I expect." He listened for a moment. "Okay, I'll tell her. Bye." He replaced the receiver in its cradle and turned to face Natasha. "Judy has asked her mother to come and pick you up and take you back to her house." He saw her face and gave his head a slight shake. "Don't worry. I think she'll be so pleased you're safe she won't be too cross. I'm sure she'll understand why you came."

Natasha stared at him. "She'll tell Mum and Dad," she said at last. "They'll be mad."

Arthur looked at her closely. "If I know my daughter, I expect she'll understand too," he said reassuringly.

Natasha scowled at him. "But you don't know your daughter, do you?" she said cruelly. "Or you wouldn't have done what you did twelve years ago."

They stared at each other across the room: The child standing straight and stiff, her hands balled into fists at her sides, and the man, his shoulders sagging and his face reflecting all the pain and guilt he'd been carrying for the last twelve years. Arthur took a tentative step towards her. She stepped backwards and knocked over a small coffee table. As she bent to pick it up, there was a sharp knock at the door. Arthur crossed the room and took the table from her. She straightened up and looked at him, chewing on her bottom lip.

"You didn't show me the photos," she said.

He looked from her to the door and back again. "You could come back…" he began hesitantly.

Natasha pushed past him and walked over to open the front door.

"Oh, I'll be back," she said ominously, scowling at him. "I haven't finished yet. I still need answers. So then you can show me the photos." And with a flounce she pulled open the door to reveal Judy's mother standing on the doorstep, dripping umbrella in hand.

Chapter 4

Thursday 24th July, 2008

Abi awoke to the tantalizing smell of coffee wafting into the bedroom, accompanied by the telltale sound of sizzling bacon. She pulled the duvet up to her chin and wriggled with pleasure. She liked nothing better than breakfast in bed, and breakfast in the luxurious four-poster bed in Roger Hawk's flat was the best of all. She pushed herself up onto one elbow and strained to see out of the window. The sky was clear and blue, and the day was promising to be warm. She pushed her pillows up behind her and wriggled into a sitting position just as Gideon kicked open the door with his bare foot and entered the room, balancing a loaded tray on one hand and holding his mobile to his ear with the other. Abi reached up and took the tray from him just before it landed precipitously on her knee. She raised her eyebrows at him, but he shook his head and grunted down the phone.

"Uh-huh…mmm…really?" he said doubtfully, sliding into bed beside his wife. "He really suggested that?…That's most bizarre." He paused and tucked his long legs under the covers. "Of course I will…always happy to work with you, mate…No, definitely not. It's not the sort of falling out that can be sorted, I'm afraid." He paused again, glanced at Abi, and rolled his eyes.

"Okay then, mate, be lovely to see you. Call when you get back to England. Bye for now." He disconnected the call and placed his phone on the bedside table. Abi looked at him enquiringly, a piece of bacon protruding from her mouth. Gideon grinned at her, leaned over, and kissed her on the top of her head.

"That was strange," he said thoughtfully, picking up his coffee mug from the tray that was now balanced on Abi's knees. "That was Chas. He's in New York touring with Velvet Shackles, and apparently a few days ago he had a visit from Simon."

Abi's eyebrows shot up, and she hastily swallowed her bacon. "Really? I wondered when he'd surface again," she said with a frown.

"Yeah, and here's the best bit…" Gideon paused for dramatic effect. "He wants to get the band back together."

Abi's mouth dropped open; she stared at him in amazement. "You've got to be kidding," she gasped. "What did Chas say to him?"

Gideon grinned. "Apparently he told Simon he was up for it but that he'd have to ask me himself. Chas asked him if we'd fallen out, but didn't get a decent answer. He thinks Simon's on his way to England to see me."

"Did you tell Chas why you fell out with Simon?" Abi asked curiously, picking at the bacon.

Gideon shook his head. "No, We're still only surmising he was the one who took your letters. We have no proof, do we? I'm not going to tell others until we have proof."

Abi gave him a look. "I think the way he just vanished as soon as we found each other again speaks for itself, don't you? He couldn't risk sticking around until we put two and two together and confronted him. He's guilty, Gid, and you know it," she said. "He never liked me anyway. He's probably been thinking of ways to get rid of me so he can have you all to himself again."

Gideon raised an eyebrow. "You sound like my father," he complained, picking a piece of crispy bacon off the plate. "Simon isn't gay, and he isn't in love with me! You didn't see how many girls he got through when we were touring."

Abi slapped his arm. " 'Got through'?" she repeated, screwing up her nose. "What a nasty way to put it. But that doesn't mean a thing. He might just be in denial. Overcompensating, even." She leaned back and sipped her coffee, watching him over the rim of her mug.

Gideon shook his head. "No," he said emphatically, "he's straight. You remember the condom?" Abi looked at him in surprise. "You know, the out-of-date one? The one I got when I was fourteen?" She smiled, and nodded. "Well, Simon had the other two from that packet, and he used them by the time he was fifteen. With girls!" he added seeing Abi's face.

She grinned at him. "Okay, you're probably right. But that doesn't change the fact that he has a big problem with me. He must realise you wouldn't want to work with him again."

Gideon sighed and leaned back against the pillows. "I'm sure he does." He frowned. "Which makes me wonder what he's up to. He has a strange mind—I wouldn't trust him an inch." He paused and looked at her seriously. "I think we should be on our guard."

Abi stared at him in surprise. "Why?" she asked. "What on earth could he do to us now? He did his damage thirteen years ago."

Gideon shook his head. "If he could do that then, imagine what he could come up with now," he said darkly. "I have no idea what he could do, I just think we should be prepared for trouble." He turned to her again and grinned. "Now, put down that tray, wife, and let's make one last use of this wonderful bed."

****

As his plane touched down on the runway at Heathrow Airport, Simon's mind was busily working on his plan to discredit Abi. He had the purloined letters safely stored in his luggage, and he'd already made his approach to the editor of a very downmarket tabloid that focused on the misdemeanours of the rich and famous. Simon knew very well that the story he told them would not be checked too closely for "mistakes" but would be printed pretty much verbatim, and he smirked to himself as he imagined how it would look. He could visualize the front page already. He closed his eyes and imagined the tiny niggle of doubt that would begin to eat away at Gideon when he read the article. Even if he dismissed it as sensationalism, the seed would have been sown, and Simon would help it to grow.

He got to his feet, pulled his bag down from the overhead locker, then followed the other travellers down the steps and out onto the tarmac. The weather was fine but cool, compared to the temperatures he'd left behind in New York, and he breathed deeply, taking the fresh air into his smoke-battered lungs. He passed through customs with no problem and headed out towards the taxi rank. He jumped into the first one he saw and slid over into the corner of the seat.

"Take me to the Ritz," he said to the driver, then leaned back and closed his eyes. His money may be beginning to dwindle, but he was not prepared to compromise on his accommodation and had called ahead and booked himself a suite. The driver grinned at Simon over his shoulder.

"The Ritz, eh? You staying there, or just visiting someone?" he asked curiously.

Simon answered without opening his eyes. "Staying there." he said shortly.

The driver whistled. "That'll set you back a pretty penny," he said, studying his ride in the mirror.

Simon opened his eyes and shifted in his seat. "So?" he said rudely, uncomfortably aware of his dishevelled appearance and flushed sweaty face. "I can afford it."

"So, you famous or what?"

Simon scowled. "Yeah. I'm famous," he said.

"Who are you, then?" persisted the driver. "Rock star? Film star? Royalty?" he ended on a laugh.

Simon sighed. "Rock star." he said. "I'm the drummer with NightHawk."

The cab driver grinned. "Oh I remember them!" he said. "That Gideon Hawk, he was something else. Saw him in the paper the other day. Very pretty wife. Nice family." He glanced in the mirror at Simon again. "You getting the band back together, then?"

Simon gave the man a look of intense dislike. "Just drive the cab," he snapped, leaning back in the corner again and wiping a chubby hand across his damp face.

The driver watched him in the mirror for a moment, then shrugged and wove his way through the traffic in the direction of Piccadilly.

The superior suite Simon had taken was on the second floor of the hotel and had an amazing view over Green Park. He threw himself down on the huge bed and lay with his eyes closed enjoying the solitude. After the claustrophobic atmosphere of the plane and the smells and noises of the London streets, the cool silence of the opulent room was a real luxury. He had ordered a meal to be brought to his room at noon, but until then he decided to try and sleep off some of his jet lag.

He kicked off his shoes, undid the button at the top of his jeans, and made himself comfortable. The afternoon would be time enough to continue with his plans.

****

Natasha stared out the window, nervously hugging her arms around her body. It was rapidly approaching midday, the time her parents had said they'd be arriving to pick them up. She knew they'd need to be told about her actions of the day before, and she was fairly sure she'd be in trouble. Judy had totally understood her need to go and see Arthur but had given her a severe telling off for going off without informing anyone. Natasha had to admit the telling off had been justified, but she was still glad she'd done it. She now needed to persuade her mother they should both go back to see Arthur in an attempt to get more answers. She'd been quite shocked by the old man's appearance and demeanour and began to understand how he could have been so controlled by his wife. She had no respect for him and, despite the fact he'd clearly been bullied, still held him responsible for her earlier plight and for all the heartbreak he'd caused her parents.

She turned away from the window and began to pace around the room. Judy was upstairs changing the beds, and the three little ones were all playing in the conservatory. As she circled the room for the third time, Natasha heard the doorbell ring. She bit her lip. Then, taking a deep breath, she walked slowly over and pulled open the door. Abi and Gideon were standing on the doorstep, both grinning at her, and at the sight of their happy faces Natasha burst into tears as she ran forward and buried her face in her mother's chest. Abi exchanged a glance with Gideon, then gently put her arm around her daughter and led her back into the house.

"What's the matter, sweetie?" she asked gently, pushing Natasha down onto the sofa and sitting beside her. Gideon hovered in front of them, his face concerned. Natasha shook her head and clung even tighter to her mother, the tears still pouring down her cheeks.

"Abi! Gideon! You're here." Judy appeared in the doorway and took in the situation at a glance. She walked over to them and sat down on the other side of Natasha. "We had a little…incident…yesterday," she began with a crooked smile, "and Tasha is scared you'll be cross with her." She paused as Natasha raised her tear-streaked face and looked desperately at her. "We've had a chat about the thoughtlessness of her behaviour, and she understands she must never act like that again, but the most important thing is why she did what she did."

Gideon frowned. "But what did she do?" he asked,

impatiently. "Judy, you're not really making much sense."

Natasha sat up straight and rubbed her eyes. "I'll tell them, Judy," she said with a sniff. "I went to see Arthur. On my own. Without telling Judy where I'd gone." She paused and looked cautiously from Abi to Gideon, and back again. "I had to know why they did what they did. I needed to see him, but I thought you wouldn't let me, so I just went, and I know I should have told Judy, but…" The words all came out in a rush before tailing off as she sat staring down at her hands in her lap. There was a short pause, and then Abi put her arm around the child's shoulders and pulled her close.

"Oh, darling, I'm sorry," she whispered. "I should have let you see him much, much sooner." She glanced up at Gideon. "In fact, your father mentioned it only two days ago. He said we needed to get closure over this."

Natasha raised wet eyes and gave a tiny smile. "So you're not mad at me?" she asked tentatively. "'Cause I'd do it again if I had to."

Gideon covered his mouth with his hand and gave a muffled snort. Abi frowned at him.

"Well, you really shouldn't have gone off without telling Judy where you were," she said firmly. "That wasn't fair on her. But I can understand why you did it and also why you thought you wouldn't be allowed to go." She paused and turned Natasha's face to hers. "We should have taken you to see him ages ago, and I suggest we go again now that you've…opened up communications, *but*"—and she looked severely at her daughter—"you must promise *never* to go off on your own again like that. And you must apologise very strongly to Judy."

Natasha nodded and flung her arms around her mother's neck. "Okay. Thank you. I'm sorry." She looked up at Judy. "You know I'm sorry, don't you, Judy?"

Judy put out a hand and stroked her curly hair. "Yes, Tasha, I do," she said simply.

Natasha sat up and rubbed her eyes impatiently. She looked at Abi. "So will you come and see him with me?" she asked.

"Yes, I will," Abi said with a nod. "It's a bit late to go today and still get home, so I've got a suggestion." Natasha looked at her expectantly. "Dad has to go back to London next week to get started on his album, so how about you and I come back here and go to see Arthur then? If Judy would be prepared to have Ollie again, that would be even better," she added with a grin at her friend.

Judy nodded emphatically. "Of course I will," she said at once. "You and Tasha will have to share the spare room, though."

Abi pursed her lips. "Well, actually," she began slowly, "I was thinking that maybe Tasha and I could stay at the motel near Newbury where I stayed after my mother's funeral. We could have a girly night and chat about whatever my father tells us."

"I'm sure we could find you somewhere better than that to stay," Gideon murmured.

Abi shook her head. "No, that's the point," she said. "It was there I started to read your letters. I just thought it might be fitting."

Gideon smiled at her and gave a slight nod. "Okay, I see your point. That okay with you, Tasha?"

The child nodded her head vigorously, causing her dark curls to fall over her face. "Yeah, that'd be great," she said enthusiastically. "Which day can we come?"

"I've arranged to get started on Monday, so I suggest we all leave really early in the morning so you can get in a full afternoon with Arthur," suggested Gideon.

Natasha wrinkled her nose. "Hope we don't need that long," she said with a frown. "I didn't like him. Or his house. It smelled bad."

A look of pain crossed Abi's face, and she dipped her head to allow her hair to conceal it. Gideon watched her closely. She had had no contact with her father since soon after they'd discovered Natasha living in the children's home in Kent, and he knew this was going to be quite an ordeal for her. He perched on the arm of the sofa and gently put his arm around her shoulders.

"D'you want me to come too?" he asked quietly.

Abi raised her head and smiled at him. "No, it's okay. I guess Tasha and I should do this. Your presence might make him less forthcoming." She leaned her head against his strong arm. When Natasha curled her legs up under her and wriggled closer to them, Abi put her arm around her, and the three of them clung together.

Judy got to her feet and tactfully withdrew into the conservatory where the three smaller ones were busily involved in their own little worlds. She stood for a moment watching Tommy with his trains, Sabrina attempting to dress her doll, and little Oliver systematically taking all the blocks out of one box and putting them into another. She smiled to herself. She really was very lucky. She glanced back at the trio in the living room and crossed her fingers that they managed to get some answers from Arthur. It was high time they were all able to get closure and move on with their new happy family life.

****

Natasha's visit had left Arthur feeling very dirty. He'd spent the rest of the day on edge and been unable to settle to anything constructive. Seeing her standing on his doorstep had been like stepping back in time, and it had given him a very nasty shock. As he pottered in the kitchen the following morning, he found himself debating what to do about it. He realised the child—quite rightly—was not going to let the matter lie, and she would be back again, probably with Abi in tow, for a final showdown. With a sigh, he carried his morning coffee to the kitchen table and sat down heavily. Instinctively he reached for the biscuit barrel and took a chocolate digestive without even realising what he was doing. He dunked it in his cup and slowly raised it to his mouth. The warm sogginess of the biscuit felt strange in his dry mouth, and he took a single bite, then left it to one side. He sat motionless for several minutes, his hands cupped around his hot coffee and his eyes glazed and haunted.

Finally he seemed to come to a decision, drained his cup, fastidiously washed it up, put it away, then made his way slowly up the stairs. At the top he paused to get his breath. Then he grabbed a long pole from the corner of the landing and reached up to open the loft hatch. It swung down, and Arthur hooked the pole under the bottom of a metal ladder that he pulled down to rest on the landing. He replaced the pole and started slowly up the ladder, pausing at the top to reach in and flick on a light. The dimly lit attic space was floored with sheets of chipboard and neatly organised with everything in boxes. Arthur hadn't been up there since Abi had helped him sort out Joan's things after the funeral and discovered the letters from Gideon packed in a box. He sighed deeply again and hauled his spare frame up into the roof space. He crawled across into the far right corner and stopped in front of a large, very old, battered leather suitcase. He took a deep breath and pulled it towards him. He'd been avoiding investigating this suitcase ever since Joan died, but he now realised it most probably contained the information Abi and Natasha would be looking for.

Joan had brought the suitcase with her when she married Arthur, back in 1965, and she'd never allowed him any access to it. All she'd said was that it contained things from her past she would rather not revisit but that must never be destroyed. Arthur had complied with her wishes, but he had long realised the suitcase probably held the secret to the darker side of Joan's character, and now that Natasha had forced his hand, he decided to take a look for himself. He heaved the heavy case over to the open hatch and lowered himself stiffly back onto the ladder. Holding the case in one hand, he flicked off the light and made his way carefully back down to the landing. He pushed the ladder back up and reached up with the pole to close the hatch. Then, carrying the heavy suitcase, he slowly descended the stairs and took it into the kitchen.

He heaved it onto the table and sat down with a sigh. The case had been a shadowy part of his life for the last forty-three years, and he was a little nervous about opening it. Arthur gently ran his hand over the worn leather, removing a thick layer of dust, then reached behind him for the paper towel roll, tore off a piece, and continued to wipe off the remaining dust and mould. When he'd done that to his satisfaction, he placed both his hands palm down on top of the case. Finally he could put off the moment no longer, and he gently opened the catches. The old fasteners had rusted, and he had to prise them open with his thumb before he could gently lift the lid. He found himself staring down at a motley collection of books, albums, loose photographs, and trade journals. He frowned and picked up the top book. He opened it cautiously, and his tired eyes widened in surprise. He quickly scanned down the page, then laid it to one side and picked up a very old photograph album. The contents caused his stomach to do somersaults as he finally realised just how little he'd known his wife. He spent the next couple of hours picking through the rest of the contents, then sat back in his chair, a very haunted and deeply disturbed look on his face.

Chapter 5

Friday 25th July, 2008

Simon's head was pounding when he awoke the next morning. He struggled into a sitting position and cursed the several too many cocktails he had imbibed the night before, He'd spent the evening in the hotel's bar, sampling the champagne cocktails and generally drowning his sorrows, and his heart sank when he remembered just how many drinks must have been added to his bill. He could hear the voice of his accountant ringing inside his head, and he scowled as he swung his legs out of bed. The sooner he sorted out the NightHawk issue, the better it would be for his bank balance, and getting rid of Abi was the only way forward. He stumbled unsteadily into the bathroom and splashed his ruddy face with cold water, then lifted his head and stared in the mirror. His eyes were bloodshot, his hair greasy and matted, and his skin looked an unhealthy dull grey colour. He shook his head in frustration. How could he ever expect to be taken seriously if he didn't begin to look after himself? He pulled off his T-shirt and boxers and stepped into the shower.

Twenty minutes later he was relaxing on the sofa, coffee in hand, waiting for his breakfast to be delivered to his room. His blonde curly hair was now clean, although still damp, and he was dressed in a crisp blue shirt and a pair of cream chinos. As he sipped his coffee, his headache began to subside and he started to feel more human. He had arranged an appointment to meet with Richard Morrison, the editor of *The National Crier*, at eleven, and he was determined to make his plan work.

Over the years Simon's hatred for Abi had grown and by now had reached such immense proportions that it included her children, as well. He saw them all as a barrier between Gideon and himself, and as such they had to go. If he could discredit Abi in Gideon's eyes, maybe things could get back to how they used to be. Simon nodded to himself with satisfaction. Things could get back to the way they were when NightHawk first went on tour in the summer of '95. He was loathe to admit to himself just how much he missed Gideon's friendship, and would never acknowledge that it had in fact been foundering during the last couple of years they were touring. Had he been prepared to admit it had been, Simon would have found some way of blaming that also on Abi.

A knock on the door heralded the arrival of his eggs Florentine, and he settled down to enjoy his breakfast, safe in the knowledge he was about to take control of events and get his life back where he wanted it.

****

Natasha stood in the conservatory staring out at the spectacular thunderstorm raging over the sea. She knelt on a chair and pressed her nose up against the glass. As she did so, a fork of lightning shot across the sky from left to right, and she jumped back from the window. A chuckle behind her made her turn to find her father grinning down at her.

"Dad, this is amazing!" she said, grinning back. "I've never seen such a good storm before. D'you think the house will get hit?"

"It'd better not!" Gideon laughed, ruffling her hair. "We're not the highest building, so we're probably safe."

Natasha looked a little crestfallen and turned back to the window just as a huge rumble of thunder shook the whole house. From under the table in the dining room came a whimper from one of the dogs, and she ran in and crawled underneath to comfort her.

"It's all right, Lilt," she said soothingly, gently stroking the collie's head. "It can't hurt you. I'll protect you." Lilt raised her head and nudged Natasha's face with her long nose. The child laughed and put her arms around the dog, holding her close. Another nudge on her side made her turn her head to find Flora, not wanting to be left out, trying to join them under the table. Natasha put her arm out and pulled the other dog to her, then wriggled into a better position and sat with an arm protectively around each of them. "There," she said with a smile, "that's better, isn't it? You'll be safe with me. The thunder can't get you now."

Gideon watched his daughter, a smile playing about his lips. He loved seeing her with the dogs, and loved the way it brought out her selfless attitude. He turned and walked into the large bright kitchen, where Abi was attempting to bake a cake, hindered by the ever helpful Oliver. She glanced up as Gideon entered and brushed a strand of hair off her face with a floury hand. She rolled her eyes.

"He really thinks he's being helpful," she said ruefully, indicating where Oliver was very carefully making a ring of paper cake cases around her feet. The little boy looked up and grinned at his father.

"'Ook, Daddy!" he said proudly, pointing to his work. "Help Mummy."

Gideon grinned as he bent down, swept the child up in his arms, and swung him in the air. Oliver chuckled with glee, and a line of dribble trickled from his floury mouth and landed in Gideon's hair.

Abi giggled. "Nice," she commented. "Baby dribble—excellent conditioner," and she bent down and slid the cake into the AGA. Gideon swung Oliver back down to the floor and rubbed ineffectually at his hair with his sleeve.

"You are gross," he said affectionately to the little boy, who giggled and toddled across the room in search of something else to be helpful with.

Abi straightened and rubbed her hands on a tea towel, then pushed her hair out of her eyes and smiled at Gideon. "Are you excited about recording again?" she asked, winding her arms around his waist.

"I guess." He looked down at her and shrugged. "Bit odd to be doing it alone, though. Could be tempted to restart the band."

Abi pulled back and stared at him in surprise. "Really?" she asked doubtfully. "But you said definitely not, the other day. What's changed?"

"I guess it was chatting to Chas," he admitted, pulling her back against him and resting his chin on her head. "It made me remember just how much fun we had. To start with."

"Yeah, to start with," said Abi sagely. "You

weren't enjoying it by the end, though, were you?"

Gideon sighed. "I wonder how much that had to do with my obsession with you," he said, "or the fact that I really wasn't getting on with Simon at all by then. If we did re-form, it would be with a new drummer, of course."

"Well, you know what you're doing, I guess," Abi said, then tilted her head back and looked up at him. "You do know if you go on tour again we're all coming with you, don't you?"

"I wouldn't have it any other way." Gideon grinned. "It's going to be bad enough to be away from you next week in London. You must bring the kids up once I've got going."

Abi nodded vigorously. "Absolutely! Try stopping me. We can stay at the flat again, can't we?"

Gideon nodded. "Of course. Dad hardly ever uses it now, and anyway they're still away on the cruise."

"They'll be back on Wednesday," Abi pointed out. "I may take the kids there first, actually, before we come and join you." She paused for a moment and thought. "Yeah, we'll go to Judy's on Monday, and go and see Dad, and then I'll take them to the New Forest for a couple of days, and then come and join you. That sound okay?"

"Perfect," Gideon planted a kiss on the top of her head. "Now, how's that cake coming along? I want to see if it's as good as my mother's this time."

Abi sniffed. "The last one came close," she said a little sulkily, moving over to the AGA to take a quick look at how the cake was doing. "It's rising," she said hopefully, opening the door a crack. "Maybe this will be the one."

Gideon laughed and shook his head. "I doubt you can do it," he teased before turning to run as the oven gloves sailed across the room towards him.

****

There was the slightest hint of thunder in the air when Simon left the hotel and headed off to Canary Wharf to meet with the editor of *The National Crier*. He jumped into one of the cabs waiting in line just around the corner from The Ritz and barked out his directions, then sat back in the corner and rehearsed his approach. The plan he'd been formulating for the past week had finally come together in his mind, and now all he had to do was persuade Richard Morrison to run it as an exposé. He patted the pocket of his light brown suede jacket to make sure the letters were safely in place, and a little smile played on his full lips. If his plan worked, it would plant seeds of distrust in Gideon's mind, hopefully eventually leading to his breakup with Abi. After that it was only a matter of time before he, Simon, could make his move and approach Gideon as a concerned friend, worried for his welfare.

Simon rested his head on the back of the seat and closed his eyes. He was so caught up in his fabrication he could not see any of its pitfalls and completely failed to comprehend the bond between Abi and Gideon. He opened his eyes as the taxi was moving slowly along Victoria Embankment and watched the activity on the river with little interest. He had got so enmeshed in his plans for the band that his thoughts very rarely strayed beyond his hatred of Abi or his disappointment in Gideon's behaviour. Had he discussed his plans with anyone else, they might have shown him how his obsession was leading him down a very unsavoury path, but Simon was not one to share his thoughts, even if he'd had any friends left to confide in.

The trip across London took longer than Simon had bargained for, and it was five past eleven before the taxi drew up at Canary Wharf. He leapt out, thrust a twenty-pound note at the driver, and hurried through the huge glass doors of the towering building that housed the offices of *The National Crier*. Simon went straight to the main desk, and, after informing the receptionist where he was headed, he was directed up to the twenty-sixth floor.

The journey in the lift was not one he wanted to repeat on a regular basis, and he breathed a huge sigh of relief when he finally reached his destination and the doors slowly opened. He pushed his way through the hot sweating bodies of his travelling companions, out of the confining space and into a cool, air-conditioned corridor. As the lift doors closed behind him, he got his bearings and headed for a pair of double doors clearly marked *The National Crier*. Patting his pocket to check once more that the precious letters were in place, Simon took a deep breath and pushed the doors open.

The busy newspaper office was a hive of activity, and after announcing himself to a pretty girl seated at a desk just inside the door, Simon was taken to a glass-fronted office at the far end of the huge room. Richard Morrison was talking, or rather shouting, on the phone when Simon entered, and he was impatiently waved into a seat on one side of a large mahogany desk covered with piles of papers, magazines, cuttings, and photographs. He sat down carefully and pulled his chair slightly closer to the desk. As he waited for Morrison to finish his call, Simon's eyes flicked across the sprawling papers on the desk and assessed the type of story the paper was looking for. He smiled to himself as he realised his story was almost certainly one that would be picked up. He leaned back in the chair and crossed his legs, forcing himself to relax and subtly taking deep breaths. After about three minutes Richard Morrison barked an oath, disconnected his call, and flung the phone back onto the desk.

"Fucking stupid idiot!" he snarled, throwing himself into his deep leather swivel chair and knocking a pile of papers to the floor. Simon stayed silent, watching the newspaper editor closely. The man was in his early fifties, tall but solidly built, with closely cropped greying hair and curiously pale green eyes. He ran a stubby hand across his head and looked directly at his visitor. "You're late," he said shortly. "I said eleven, not quarter past."

Simon sat forward. "Yeah, sorry about that," he apologised with a nod. "Traffic was dreadful."

"This is sodding London," Morrison replied dismissively. "What d'you expect? Now, get on with it. What you got for me? You mentioned Gideon Hawk on the phone."

"Yeah. I was the drummer with NightHawk"— Simon shifted his position again—"and I have…acquired…some information that might be of interest to your readers." He paused, and Richard Morrison waved for him to hurry his story along. "You may remember the story a couple of years ago about Gideon finding he had a daughter with his old girlfriend…?"

"Yeah, yeah, yeah, that's old hat," Richard

interrupted impatiently. "So bloody what?"

Simon swallowed nervously and went on. "Well…suppose I had some evidence that suggested the child was not actually his…?" he said, watching the editor carefully.

Richard Morrison leaned back in his chair and frowned.

"Go on," he said, crossing his legs.

"I have some letters written to Gideon by the mother of his supposed child"—Simon couldn't bring himself to say Abi's name—"in which she tells him of her pregnancy." He paused for a moment and licked his lips. "My suggestion is…if it was his baby, why didn't she tell him before he left? Why wait and then write to him about it? That seems a bit slap happy." He swallowed again. "I believe this girl got pregnant by someone else and decided she would rather have a famous father for her child than just some kid from school."

There was a long silence while Richard Morrison looked dubiously at Simon. Eventually he sat forward and rested his arms on the desk.

"Potentially a good story, if you can back it up," he said slowly, narrowing his eyes at Simon. "I assume you have an agenda here." He held up his hand. "No, I don't want to know what, but if you can let me have some of these letters to print, and give me the outline of a believable story, then I'm sure we can come to some sort of arrangement." His brows came together and he leaned across the desk. "You realise, of course, it's the girl who'll be hit hardest in this?" Simon nodded, a small smile playing on his lips. Richard Morrison raised his eyebrows and sat back, holding out his hand.

"Right. Right. Let me see these letters, then."

Simon reached into his pocket and pulled out the first of the letters Abi had written to Gideon. He passed it across the desk and watched as the editor carelessly unfolded it and quickly scanned the page. He pursed his lips thoughtfully.

"Hmmm. Sounds quite a genuine letter to me," he said at last. "What's the angle here, Simon? How d'you propose we make it seem suspicious?"

Simon wiped some beads of sweat from his brow and licked his lips again.

"That's your fucking job," he said, beginning to sense the plan slipping away from him. "Distort the facts, change the dates... I don't fucking care. Just discredit that bitch and get her out of his life!"

There was silence while Morrison surveyed him through narrowed eyes. Then he tossed the letter onto the desk and sighed. "Okay. I get that you have a problem. I'm not averse to a bit of minor twisting of the facts, but there's not that much to go with here. Give me some more. When did she get pregnant? When did he leave? When did she give birth? Help me out here."

"She had the baby in January '96, which means she got pregnant in April '95." Simon paused. "I thought we could suggest the baby was premature, thus implying she didn't actually get pregnant until June, which was when Gideon left to go on tour. She didn't write that first letter till the end of July. Why would she wait that long if she'd been pregnant since April? In fact, why didn't she tell him before he left? Come on, man, surely you can do something with that?" He looked imploringly at the editor and ran a sweaty hand through his damp curls.

Richard Morrison picked up the letter and read it again. Then he nodded slowly. "All right," he said at last. "Maybe we can do something with this. We'll print this one as it is, most of it, and you get some good bits from later letters that we can add." He drummed his fingers on his desk as he considered. "You give me the background to their story—what sort of girl she was, did she sleep around, that sort of thing—and we'll see what we can do." He grinned at Simon. "Should sell a few with that. People love to see the beautiful people brought down. Gideon Hawk has been far too happy lately."

"So you'll do it, then?" Simon smiled. "How much'll you pay me?"

Richard Morrison gave a snort of laughter. "Reckon I'm doing you a favour running with this, lad. Maybe you should be paying me." He raised his eyebrows.

Simon's face turned a livid puce, and the sweat started to run down his neck. He reached out to grab the letter back off the desk, but Morrison caught his wrist.

"Calm down, kid. I'm only joking. This'll sell papers. You'll get paid, don't worry. Now get the rest of the details, including photos of the girl, and the baby if possible, to me by Monday morning, and I'll run it on Wednesday. I heard that Hawk's starting to record his solo album next week. Good thing to coincide with." He paused and scowled at Simon. "I don't know why you're trying to split them up," he warned, "but from what I've heard, they're 'the perfect couple' and your plan might not work."

Simon shrugged. "I know," he said, "but anything's worth a try."

The men shook hands briefly, and after promising to deliver the rest of the information on Monday morning, Simon took his leave and made his way back out to the lift, a slight spring in his step. He'd taken the first step towards bringing about the destruction of Abigail Hawk.

Chapter 6

Saturday 26th July, 2008

Caroline Hawk stretched out in her deckchair and tilted her sunhat over her eyes. She had just read the weather forecast for England and was giving thanks for the umpteenth time that they'd decided to take a cruise. They were at present travelling along the coast of North Africa and due to anchor at Tangier within the hour. Caroline was keen to go ashore and visit the markets of the Medina, in the old town, and was determined to get Roger to accompany her. He was quite happy to stay on the ship playing deck quoits or generally relaxing, but Caroline believed in getting her money's worth, and had gone ashore at each stop. She sighed and adjusted her position in order to catch the best of the sunshine. They had set off from Southampton nine days earlier, and so far had cruised around the Canaries, with a stop off at Lisbon on the way past, and were now having a day in Tangier before starting back towards Southampton, with another stop on the way, this time at Cadiz.

Caroline became aware of another presence and opened her eyes. Roger was standing next to her holding two tall glasses of Pimms. Caroline smiled and pulled herself into a more upright position. She held out her hand.

"Thank you, darling." She pushed her sunhat further back on her head. "Are we nearly at Tangier?" She peered over the balcony, looking towards the coast. The town was now clearly visible, and the ship was drawing ever closer inshore.

"Should be docked in about fifteen minutes." Roger sat down next to her, wiping his glistening brow with his handkerchief.

Caroline looked at him over the top of her sunglasses. "If you took off some of those clothes, you wouldn't get so hot," she observed, smiling slightly at his long-sleeved shirt, grey flannel trousers, and sturdy brogues. "Honestly, Roger, you look ridiculous in those shoes. What happened to the deck shoes I got you? And surely you could wear your shorts. It's not as if anyone actually knows us here. We're never going to see any of these people again."

Roger fixed her with a baleful look. "I'm not comfortable in shorts, Caroline," he said firmly, "but I suppose you may be right about the shoes. I'll change them in a minute. I was planning to play deck quoits anyway."

Caroline sat up straighter. "Not this time, Roger," she said sternly. "You're coming ashore with me."

"Do I have to?" Roger sighed. "I'd really rather stay here. You'll only want to go shopping for more trinkets for Abi and Tasha, and I'm no good at that haggling thing you do."

Caroline smiled, remembering the one time Roger had tried to haggle. They'd ended up paying more than the starting price.

"But it's not safe for me to go into the old town alone," she objected. "Someone might try to buy me.

That happens here, you know."

Roger sighed again. "Caroline," he said patiently, "who will they buy you from if you're on your own?"

She frowned, then shook her head impatiently. "Well, it's not safe. I might be kidnapped and sold into slavery." She glared at him, adding darkly, "It always happens in books."

"Okay, you win." Roger laughed and stood up. "I'll come this time. Now knock that drink back, and we can go and join the merry throng." He indicated the crowd of passengers already congregating near where the gangplank would be lowered.

Caroline drained her glass and got to her feet. She stretched her arms above her head, then turned and walked back into the cabin. She and Roger were lucky enough to have a suite, and the rooms were light and airy and very well serviced. They even had the services of a butler if they so wished. A selection of the English papers were brought to them each day, and their room was continually supplied with baskets of fruit, chocolates, and flowers. Caroline picked up a copy of *The Guardian* as she passed by and quickly flicked through in case there was anything of interest.

"Good lord, Roger!" She fumbled for her glasses. "Gideon and Abi are in *The Guardian*!" Roger joined her and peered over her shoulder. " *'Gideon Hawk and his wife Abigail caught leaving the offices of PTW Recordings, where it's rumoured Hawk will be recording his upcoming solo album,' "* she read. She peered more closely at the picture, murmuring, "He could do with a haircut, but they both look really well. That holiday in Greece must have done them good."

"You go and get ready." Roger leaned over and

took the paper out of her hands. "You know what your son looks like," and he sat down in one of the armchairs and began to read the rest of the article.

Caroline shook her head as she disappeared into the bathroom to freshen up before they ventured onto dry land.

Half an hour later, Roger, still wearing his brogues and with the addition of a panama hat, and Caroline, much more suitably attired in a loose, floaty, flowered dress, sandals, and a floppy sunhat, were walking slowly through the streets of the old town. Caroline had already managed to haggle a good deal on a pair of leather sandals for Abi, a brightly coloured bag for Natasha, and a necklace of bright blue stones for herself, and she was feeling very satisfied. The streets were hot, smelly, narrow, and lined with a motley assortment of dark grotto-like shops and rickety market stalls, all selling a multitude of gifts, leather goods, clothes, and a whole Aladdin's cave of treasures designed to excite the tourists. Caroline smiled as she noticed Roger being drawn into a quietly ambivalent price war with a swarthy stall holder.

She gazed around her, fanning herself with her guide book, and leaned back against a rough stone wall while she waited for him in the shade of an overhanging building. It really was almost unbearably hot, and she couldn't help but feel sorry for Roger in his heavy brogues. Suddenly a vaguely familiar figure caught her eye. She moved a little closer and gave a gasp of surprise. The plump middle-aged lady currently haggling for a bright pink patterned scarf with a harassed-looking shopkeeper was, without a doubt, Josephine Dean, Simon's mother. Caroline chewed her lip. She had had no contact with Josephine since moving to the New Forest shortly after NightHawk had gone on their first tour in '95, and she felt rather awkward approaching her now. She was also acutely aware that Gideon believed it was Simon who had concealed Abi's letters from him, and Caroline felt understandably antagonistic towards any member of his family. She was just deciding whether or not to approach the woman when Roger appeared beside her, grinning broadly and brandishing a leather-bound book.

"I did it!" he announced triumphantly holding it aloft. "I actually haggled." At the sound of his voice, Josephine turned and stared directly at Caroline. The two women stood motionless in the oppressive heat, and all the sounds of the market seemed to fade into the distance.

"Caroline?" Roger frowned at his wife. "Did you hear me? Are you okay?" Caroline nodded and patted his arm vaguely.

"Yes darling, well done," she said absently, beginning to move towards the other woman. Josephine remained rooted to the spot, her face beginning to flush an unbecoming red and her eyes taking on the look of a hunted deer. "Look who it is, Roger," said Caroline, catching his arm and pulling him with her. "It's Simon's mother, Josephine Dean." By this time she was within a yard of the other woman and stopped in front of her. "Good afternoon, Josephine," she said formally, inclining her head.

Josephine nodded jerkily. "Good afternoon, Caroline—Roger. How…curious to see you here," she replied, equally formally.

"Are you on a cruise?" Caroline asked politely,

licking her drying lips. Josephine shook her head.

"No," she said with a slight smile, "just a package tour to Cadiz. This is a day trip." She looked around her. "I'm here with my sister. She's around here somewhere."

"Oh, that's nice." Caroline nodded. "We're on a cruise. We're stopping at Cadiz next." She frowned slightly. "I was sorry to hear about your husband."

Josephine nodded. "Thank you," she said quietly. "It was for the best at the end. He'd suffered enough. I'm just glad…" She looked away across the market. Caroline glanced at Roger for support, but he was engrossed in the book he'd just bought and didn't notice. She turned back to Josephine and took a deep breath.

"How's Simon?" she asked.

Josephine paused before answering. "I have no idea," she said at last. "I haven't seen him for over two years. I…I…asked him to leave after he told me…something." Her face was a fiery red by this time, and the sweat was beginning to run down her cheeks. Caroline took pity on her.

"Let's go and get a cool drink," she suggested, moving closer and taking the other woman by the elbow. "Roger, find us a safe café."

Roger looked up in surprise. Then, taking in the situation, he led the way down a narrow street and found them a table in the shade, outside a small restaurant. After they were seated and had ordered a jug of lemonade, Caroline leaned back in her chair and surveyed Josephine closely.

"What did Simon tell you?" she asked bluntly.

Roger frowned at her, but she shook her head at

him.

Josephine sighed. "I expect you've guessed," she said sadly. "He told me he'd concealed the letters that Abigail Thomson wrote to your son when they were on their first tour. The letters in which she told him she was expecting his baby." She went silent and stared down at her hands resting on the table. "I told him he was no son of mine…and he left. I haven't had any contact with him since."

Caroline reached over and patted her hand gently. "I'm sorry. Gideon guessed it was Simon, but he had no proof. Did you know Abi's mother hid the letters Gideon sent to her? It seems everyone was trying to keep them apart." She paused and smiled. "At least they're finally together."

Josephine raised tear-filled eyes to Caroline. "I'm so sorry," she said emphatically. "I just couldn't believe my son could behave like that—and to his best friend. I still don't understand his motives."

Beside her, Caroline felt Roger shift in his seat. She deliberately stepped on his foot to prevent him from speaking his thoughts, then smiled at Josephine again.

"It's not your fault," she said immediately. "In no way do we, or Gideon, blame you. I shall tell Gideon what you've told me, though. They need to know the truth."

"Yes, of course." Josephine nodded sadly. "I just hope Simon comes to his senses and realises just what he did."

"Well, yes," Caroline said, "but it's a little late for that, I think. I doubt if Gideon would want to see him again anyway. Now, are we keeping you from your sister? She may be looking for you."

Josephine pulled her mobile out of her pocket and dialled a number.

"Hello? Yes it's me…I know, sorry. I met some old…friends. I'll be back in the market in just a moment." She put the phone back in her pocket and stood up, tentatively holding out her hand. "Goodbye," she said. "It was nice to see you both. And very nice to be able to tell you what Simon did. It's quite a relief, actually."

Caroline took her hand and squeezed it firmly. "It was good to see you, too," she said sincerely. "I hope things go all right for you. And I hope you can be reconciled with Simon one day."

Josephine shrugged and shook hands with Roger. "Not sure that'll ever happen, but who knows what the future will bring?" Then she waved her hand and bobbed off down the winding street back towards the hustle and bustle of the market.

Just before she disappeared around the corner, Caroline called out to her, "Wait, did Simon read the letters?" she asked, her brow furrowing. "Did he know about the baby?"

Josephine stopped suddenly and turned to face them.

"No," she said at last. "No, he didn't read them at the time. He only read them after Gideon left the band." She raised anguished eyes to the Hawks. "At least he didn't know about the baby all along. I'm not sure I could have lived with that."

She turned and vanished into the thronging crowds of the market.

As they watched her go, Roger muttered to

Caroline, "Why didn't you tell her what Gideon told you? About Simon going to see Charles?"

Sadness in her eyes, Caroline replied, "She doesn't need to know that. He probably won't go to see her, so it's better she doesn't even know he might be back in the country. I'm not convinced he has Gideon's best interests at heart anyway. No need for his mother to suffer any more." She took her husband by the hand, and together they made their way back to the ship. "But now we know he kept the letters," she added thoughtfully. "I think Gideon needs to know that."

****

"Are you sure you don't mind looking after the dogs again?" Abi placed a mug of tea on the kitchen table in front of her friend and former neighbour, Chris. He looked up at her and grinned, his thick blond hair flopping across his forehead.

"'Course not, sweetie. You know I love them." He glanced around the room. "Gives me a chance to hang out in your gorgeous house again, too."

Abi grinned, looking at him affectionately. For nearly four years she and Chris had been neighbours, and he still lived in the little row of terraced cottages about half a mile away. The two of them had become good friends during that time, and Chris was still their primary dogsitter. Abi joined him at the table and offered him a slice of chocolate cake. He took a piece and examined it closely.

"Well, did this one come up to scratch?"

Abi shook her head and gave a rueful giggle. "No. Still falls short of Caroline's. I like it, though. At least it's edible, not like that one last week." They sat in a companionable silence for a few minutes while each munched on their cake and drank their tea. Then Abi got to her feet and patted him lightly on the shoulder. "Not being anti-social, but I've still got loads to do before we go off on Monday. You sit and enjoy the cake. I must go and put a load of washing in." She left the room and ran up the stairs to gather up the dirty linen but met Gideon on the landing, staring intently at his mobile, a deep frown on his face.

"What's up?" she asked, stopping beside him and attempting to read the screen.

He looked down at her. "Text from Mum." he said slowly. "Seriously weird, actually. Apparently they bumped into Simon's mum in Tangier." He paused at her sudden intake of breath. "I know, hard to believe, isn't it? Anyway, she told Mum that Simon had confessed to her he stole your letters all those years ago."

"I knew he had," Abi said with satisfaction. "Did she say anything else?" Gideon nodded.

"Apparently Mum asked if he'd read them, and Mrs. Dean said he hadn't at the time, but that he did just after I left the band." He looked intently at Abi. "You realise what that means, don't you?"

She looked at him blankly for a moment, then gasped as realisation hit her. "Oh, god! He still has them!" she exclaimed, her eyes wide. She wrinkled her nose. "Oh, I don't like the thought of that."

Gideon leaned back against the wall, and his frown deepened.

"Neither do I," he growled. "Damn him. I told you he could be trouble." He put an arm around Abi's shoulders and pulled her to him. "Not sure I want to leave you and the kids on your own," he said, resting his cheek on her head.

Abi slid her arm around his waist. "We'll be fine. We won't really be alone much anyway. Going to Dad's on Monday, Judy's on Tuesday, then on to your parents for Wednesday. No time to be murdered by Simon!"

Gideon raised his eyebrows and stared at her. "Well, I doubt he'd go that far!" He grinned. "But he might try to upset us. Really don't know what his problem is, though," he added, shaking his head. He paused for a moment, then pushed Abi slightly away from him and looked down at her seriously. "We do have a more pressing issue to deal with, though."

"What?" Abi stared at him in slight surprise.

Gideon pulled her down to sit on the top step and fixed her with a stare.

"Where are you going on Monday?" he asked patiently.

"Dad's," she said, frowning.

"And who will he have photos of that he'll probably show to Tasha?"

Abi sucked in her breath. " 'Nan,' " she said with a sigh. "We have to tell Tasha who Nan was."

When Abi and Gideon had first discovered Abi's mother had visited Natasha in the children's home but had not revealed her true identity to the child, they had been both shocked and disturbed. They had decided not to tell the child immediately because she had grown to like and trust her visitor—known only to her as Nan— and they felt that knowing the truth could destroy her trust in anyone. Now the matter was being taken out of their hands. On Monday Natasha would discover who Nan really was, if they didn't tell her first.

"How the hell do we tell her?" Abi whispered.

"No idea." Gideon shook his head. "However we put it, she's going to freak. And quite rightly so. There never could have been a good outcome from this." He paused and glanced at her. "No chance you can stop her seeing any photos, is there?"

Abi shook her head vehemently. "Not a chance. Apparently she'd already asked him if she could see a picture of my mother. Then Mary arrived to fetch her. We have to tell her, Gid. We can't let her just see the photos. That would be too much of a shock."

"Tell her what?" asked a suspicious voice from the bottom of the stairs. Natasha stood in a pool of water that was draining off her wetsuit and spreading out across the polished wood floor. Her hair was hanging in rats' tails over her shoulders, and her bare feet were covered in sand.

"Tasha!" shrieked Abi. "How many times have I told you! Take your wetsuit off in the garden! You're going to flood us!"

"But it's raining," the child objected, standing on one foot in an attempt to lessen the flow of water.

"So? You're already wet! Go outside and take it off." Abi began to walk downstairs in a threatening manner. Natasha giggled and ran back out through the conservatory, leaving a trail of sand and water behind her.

"Then you tell me what ever it was," she called back over her shoulder.

Abi turned at the bottom of the stairs and looked back up at Gideon.

"Guess we have to now," she said, biting her lip.

"Guess we do," Gideon agreed seriously.

They both jumped as a figure emerged hesitantly from the kitchen.

"I think I'll leave you alone now, Abs," said Chris, with a crooked smile. "It looks like you've got some family stuff to deal with."

Abi gasped and stepped forward. "Oh, Chris, I'm so sorry! I forgot you were still here. How rude of me. Please, don't feel you have to go."

"It's fine, you have stuff to do." Chris grinned, his eyes gleaming. "Anyway, I've got a date to get ready for."

"Not George?" Abi asked suspiciously.

Chris laughed and shook his head. "Not George," he agreed. "I'm not going there again. However much he wants to. No, this is someone new. I'll keep you posted." With a wave he skipped out the door and headed off across the cliff top towards his own cottage.

Natasha came running back in through the conservatory, dressed now in her dark blue swimming costume. She stopped in front of her parents and shivered.

"So? What you gonna tell me?" she asked through chattering teeth.

Abi tutted and shoved her towards the stairs. "Shower first," she ordered, "and then get dressed and come back down. Then we'll talk. And dry your hair," she added as Natasha started up the stairs.

Fifteen minutes later, Natasha reappeared in the living room, showered, dressed in a red T-shirt and stripy pyjama trousers, and rubbing her hair with a towel.

"I meant use the hair dryer," Abi observed mildly.

Natasha tossed her head. "Oh, Mum! It's nearly

dry. I'll finish it later." She bounced down onto the sofa opposite her parents. "So, what's up?" she asked expectantly.

Abi glanced at Gideon and took a deep breath. She faced Natasha again and sat forward on her chair.

"Tasha," she began hesitantly, "there's something you need to know about your grandmother before we go to see my father on Monday."

"Don't call her that," Natasha interrupted sharply. "She doesn't deserve to be called that. Call her Joan."

Abi inclined her head. "Okay," she agreed, "there's something about Joan that we need to tell you—" She stopped as Natasha interrupted again.

"No," she said, holding up her hand. "Not now. I want *him* to tell me stuff, not you two. I don't want to hear bad things now, in this house. I want to keep the bad things for the bad house." She set her lips in a determined line and stared at her parents.

"Are you sure, Tash?" Gideon asked gently, leaning forward. "We think it might be easier for you on Monday if you knew this one thing beforehand."

Natasha pulled her feet up onto the sofa and hugged her knees. She shook her head violently.

"No," she repeated. "Keep all the bad stuff for the bad house. Whatever it is, it will keep till then."

"It's something that might come as a bit of a shock to you," Gideon tried again.

Natasha stared at him in surprise. "It came as a bit of a shock to suddenly get parents," she said bluntly, "and to find out what went on when I was born. Anything else can't possibly be as weird." She paused and looked at both of them. "It's okay. I know we'll find out some bad stuff. I'm okay with that. But not now. Not here. D'you understand?"

"Yeah, I guess we do, Tasha." Abi nodded slowly. "I'm not sure you're right, but we'll respect your wishes." She paused. "But be prepared for some surprises, okay?"

Natasha nodded and gave a slight smile. "That's fine," she said. "Monday's going to be weird anyway. Now can I have tea? I'm starving." She looked expectantly at her mother.

Chapter 7

Monday 28th *July, 2008*

Simon awoke to the sound of rain tapping on the window. He muttered a curse about the English weather and got out of bed with surprising alacrity. A speedy shower later, he was choosing his attire for the day. As he pulled on his cream chinos and a dark blue polo shirt that was just that little bit too tight, he couldn't help feeling slightly queasy. He was due to deliver the rest of his information to *The National Crier* office that morning, and he was experiencing the tiniest niggle of conscience about what he was doing. He looked in the mirror and ran a hand through his hair. At least his eyes looked less bloodshot. He had stopped drinking at a more civilised time the night before and consequently had a pretty good night's sleep.

He moved over to the coffee table where he'd piled several photos, a couple of letters, and some handwritten notes. He sat down and picked up the first photograph. It showed Abi at age fifteen, the night she first met Gideon. Simon smiled as he congratulated himself on acquiring the picture. He had had to trawl through a lot of old pictures on the Facebook sites of his old friends, eventually finding the perfect one. Abi was shown leaning against the wall talking to a couple of boys, her long hair falling half across her face. It wasn't very flattering, and Simon was confident he could use it to give the impression she spent time with other boys. The second picture was also of Abi. It had been taken by his mother at the New Year's party Judy's parents had held a couple of weeks later. Abi had been drinking some wine that she and Judy had concealed in the understairs cupboard, and her face was red and her eyes looked distinctly glazed. The picture had originally shown Judy, as well, but Simon had cut her off so as not to further complicate the story he was fabricating. The next photo he picked up was of Natasha. He had had that in his keeping since it had appeared in a magazine several months before. She had been captured riding her pony in the New Forest and was scowling fiercely at the camera. He placed the picture next to the one of Abi and marvelled at just how alike they were. That she clearly took after her mother made his job a little easier. He smiled to himself and gathered up the papers. He was choosing to ignore the fact that Natasha had inherited her father's piercing blue eyes, something that thankfully didn't show in the black-and-white photograph. Thrusting the papers and photos into a canvas bag, Simon snatched up his jacket, phone, and wallet, and headed for the door. He wanted to get the rest of the information to the newspaper office as soon as possible to ensure the story made it into the Wednesday edition.

****

"If we don't leave right now, you're never going to make it to your father's by one!" Gideon bellowed up the stairs where Abi was still randomly throwing items into her bag. "Come on! I've strapped Ollie into his car seat in your car, and Tash is already waiting in mine."

79

At that moment Abi appeared at the top of the stairs, three bags slung around her shoulders and her arms full of books and magazines. She grinned at Gideon and ran down to join him.

"Ready!" she said, shaking her hair back. He gave a short laugh and shook his head at her.

"One day you'll be ready on time and I won't know what to do," he commented, ushering her out the front door and carefully locking it behind them.

They were travelling in tandem to Judy's house, where Gideon would take his leave of them and carry on to London. Abi pulled open the back of the 4x4 and tossed in the remaining luggage, then slammed it shut and turned back to Gideon. She reached up and gave him a quick kiss on the lips.

"See you at Taunton Deane services?" she said as she opened the car door. Gideon nodded and moved over to get into his new sports car.

Natasha was already in the passenger seat, a huge grin on her face. "Dad, can we have the top down?" She nodded her head hopefully.

Gideon laughed. "Not a chance, kid," he said, sliding into the driver's seat. "It's about to pour with rain. If you think I'm getting the inside of this beauty wet, you've got another think coming." He grinned at her. "Just think yourself lucky I'm even allowing you in here. You're not to touch anything, and definitely not to eat anything!" He paused and raised his eyebrows at her. "Still want to come with me?"

Natasha nodded vigorously. "'Course I do," she said, carefully pressing the button to open the window and waving at her mother and brother as they drove past them and out onto the road. "Are you going to let them get ahead and then take them, Dad?" she asked, her eyes gleaming.

Gideon started the engine, then turned to look at his daughter.

"That's the general idea," he said with a grin. "Let them think we're just going to potter behind them, and then once we're on the dual-carriageway I'll open her up and leave 'em standing."

Natasha chuckled and clapped her hands. "This is going to be an awesome journey," she said with satisfaction, leaning back in the soft leather seat and giving a little wriggle of pleasure.

Apart from the stop at Taunton Deane Services, where Natasha and Gideon had to wait nearly fifteen minutes for Abi and Oliver to arrive, they all made good time and arrived at Judy's cottage just before midday. Abi pulled the 4x4 up alongside Judy's little car and turned off the engine with a sigh. She twisted round to smile at Oliver.

"There we go," she said. "We made it. You've been such a good boy!" She opened the door and stepped out onto the shiny wet concrete.

Gideon had managed to pull the Mercedes into a gateway just along the lane and was currently offloading Natasha, fastidiously brushing invisible crumbs off her seat. She looked at him in amazement.

"Dad, how can there be crumbs?" she asked patiently. "You wouldn't let me eat anything!" and she skipped off down the road to join Abi and Oliver, jumping over the puddles as she went.

As Abi lifted the little boy out of the car, Natasha held out her arms for him. She cuddled him tight, then hoisted him onto her hip and set off up the path to the house. Abi heaved Oliver's luggage out and closed the door with her foot. As she started towards the house, Gideon fell into step beside her.

"Going to miss you, babe," he said seriously, taking one of the bags from her. "Don't be too long till you come and join me, will you?"

"'Course not." Abi smiled up at him. "Just a few days to let you get started, and for us to sort out the Dad stuff. Then we can come to London and annoy you."

"Good." Gideon pushed open the gate with his knee. "I had far too many years not being annoyed by you—I can't get enough of it now." They exchanged little smiles. Natasha was hammering on the door when they reached her, and Abi laughed.

"Not so hard, Tasha! Judy'll wonder what on earth's happening," she said, dumping her bags on the doorstep. At that moment the door flew open and Judy stood there, flour on her nose and her hair in a tangle.

"Hi, guys," she exclaimed with a grin. "Sabrina and I were just making a cake to welcome you. Come on in."

Gideon hung back slightly. "I won't come in, Judy," he said. "I really need to get on to London. Meeting at the recording studio this afternoon, and I need to get my head in the right place."

"Of course." Judy nodded approvingly. "Well, I'm sure I'll see you again soon. Have fun in London. It's about time you did some more music."

Gideon grinned and held out his arms to his children. Natasha lifted Oliver off her hip and handed him to her father, then put her arms around Gideon's waist and gave him a hug.

"Bye, Dad," she said, her voice muffled by his

tummy. "Have fun and behave yourself."

Gideon laughed and dropped a kiss on her curly head. "Cheeky monkey," he said. "I always behave myself." He gave Oliver a big squeeze, then set him down on the floor and turned to Abi. "Bye, darling," he said quietly. "Hope it all goes well this afternoon. Call me later, yeah?"

Abi nodded silently. Putting her arms around his neck, she pulled his head down and fastened her lips on his. They clung together for a moment before she loosed her hold and stepped back. Gideon winked at her, then turned and walked back down the path towards his car, with Abi watching him go until Judy closed the door and ushered them all into the kitchen.

"Abi, take a seat," she ordered, gesturing towards the ever-crowded table. "Tasha, take Ollie to the conservatory, pet. The playpen is up if you think he needs it." She flicked the kettle on and leant against the worktop with her arms folded. "So, everything set for this afternoon?"

"Yeah, I think so." Abi nodded cautiously. "Dad's expecting us at one, so we can't really hang around, and I've booked the motel for tonight." She paused and bit her bottom lip thoughtfully. "We tried to tell her about Nan on Saturday, but she refused to let us." Judy looked surprised, and Abi went on. "She didn't want any 'bad things' being talked about at home. She said she wanted Dad to tell her the bad things in the 'bad house.'" She looked helplessly at Judy and shrugged. "What could we do? We told her we really thought she should listen to what we had to tell her, but she was adamant." She paused and grimaced. "You know how strong-willed she can be."

Judy surveyed her friend thoughtfully. "D'you want me to try?" she suggested tentatively, wrinkling her brow.

"I s'pose you could, but don't hold your breath."

Judy pursed her lips. "I'll try." She wandered over to the door of the conservatory. Natasha was sitting on the floor watching Oliver and Sabrina attempt to build a train track. Sabrina was carefully laying the track, and Oliver was just as carefully taking it up again. Judy squatted down beside Natasha and smiled at her. Natasha looked at her suspiciously.

"That's the sort of smile Mum does when she wants me to do something."

Judy laughed. "You're far too savvy," she said, and wriggled into a sitting position. "I think there's something you need to know about your grandmother before you go to see Arthur," she began carefully.

"Don't call her that," Natasha snapped. "And don't you start. I told Mum and Dad I don't want to hear it till I get to the bad house. He can tell me. I don't want it to spoil nice places!" She got to her feet, walked to the opposite end of the conservatory, and stood looking out the window. Judy watched her for a moment, then got up and re-joined Abi in the kitchen.

She shook her head. "Sorry, no go," she said with a shrug.

Abi gave a crooked smile. "Oh, well. Didn't think so. Thanks for trying." She paused. "I'm just really worried how she'll react when she finds out."

****

At five past one, Abi parked her 4x4 a few hundred yards down the road from her father's house. She didn't feel comfortable parking directly outside; she knew just how nosey the neighbours could be. Arthur wouldn't have told them she was coming, but she was fairly sure the net curtains would start twitching if such an ostentatious vehicle suddenly appeared in his drive. As they walked along the road towards the house, Natasha slipped her hand into Abi's, and her steps slowed. Abi looked down at her and smiled encouragingly.

"It's okay, sweetie. We'll face this together. You did brilliantly on your own last week. Don't be afraid now." She gave her daughter's hand a squeeze. Natasha looked up at her solemnly.

"Okay. I'll be okay," she said with a decisive nod. "I just suddenly felt a bit"—she searched for the words—"a bit…like I don't know who I am. Like I used to feel at the children's home sometimes."

Abi stopped walking and bent down in front of her. "You are Natasha Storm Hawk," she said firmly. "You're the very loved daughter of Gideon and Abigail Hawk and the adored big sister of Oliver Hawk. Hold on to that, and you need never feel alone or lost."

Natasha stared at her for a moment; then her face broke into a watery grin.

"That sounds nice," she said simply, and pulling her mother up she led the way along the road until they reached Arthur's house. As they turned up the drive and squeezed past the Saab, Natasha glanced back at Abi. "I still find it hard to believe you actually lived here," she said with a frown. "It just doesn't look like you."

Abi pursed her lips and looked up at the red brick house. She found it hard to believe it herself these days, and yet at one time this house had been the most familiar place in her life. Natasha walked up to the door and knocked loudly on the glass.

"The bell doesn't work," she explained to Abi as they waited. After a moment or two Arthur's silhouette appeared behind the glass, and the door creaked open slowly. He stared at them for a second, then stepped back to let them into the hallway. Abi took a deep breath and followed her daughter into the house of her childhood.

"Hello, Dad," she said quietly, looking him up and down. He had shrunk even more since she had last seen him and had very little hair left. His skin was almost the same grey as his remaining hair, and he was very sloppily dressed in old grey flannel trousers and a baggy maroon cardigan.

"Hello, Abi," he said in his tired voice, "and... Natasha." He hesitated to use her name, remembering her last visit. She stared at him, but remained silent. "Come on through. I've just boiled the kettle." They followed the old man into the kitchen and each took a seat at the table. Arthur went straight over to the kettle for a moment, then turned to the table and placed a cup of tea in front of Abi and a large mug of hot chocolate in front of Natasha. He looked at the child.

"I bought it specially for you." he said, his eyes daring her to refuse it. Natasha picked up the mug and took a sip.

"Thank you," she said, without looking at him. Arthur poured himself a cup of tea and joined them at the table. He looked at Natasha.

"After your visit last week," he said, "I did a bit of detective work, and I found some things in the attic I think you may be interested in." He paused for a moment. "They may help to explain why your...why Joan acted the way she did."

Abi looked at her father in surprise. "What did you find?" she asked, frowning at him.

He shook his head. "Finish your tea," he said. "Then we'll go into the living room and I'll show you."

Natasha drained her mug and put it down noisily on the table.

"Do you have that photo of her you were going to show me?" she asked shortly. Arthur glanced at Abi nervously. She shrugged and glanced at Natasha. She made one last attempt.

"Tasha, remember what I tried to tell you at home?" she began, but Natasha pushed her chair back and stood up.

"No, Mum," she said, pointing at Arthur. "He's got to tell me all the stuff. Is it something to do with the photo, then? What? Does she look like me or something?"

Despite her worries, Abi couldn't help a slight smile.

"No, Tash, it's not that," she assured the child, then pushed back her chair and got to her feet. "Come on, then, let's go and see the stuff you found, Dad." She led the way out of the kitchen, across the dark hall, and into the dingy living room. Abi was rather taken aback by just how dirty and uncared for the room looked, and she had to restrain her instinct to plump the cushions, tie back the curtains, and turn on the table lamps. Arthur turned on the main overhead light, whose weak bulb did nothing to improve the feel of the room, before he plodded over to the sofa, where a large leather suitcase was lying with the top open.

"It's all in here." He gestured to the suitcase. "Your mother brought it with her when we got married, but she'd never let me look in it. She told me it contained things from her past she didn't want to revisit but that must not be destroyed." He paused, and a look of great distress passed across his face. "Now I understand why. I think you should take the suitcase and spend some time looking though it. Some of the contents are extremely disturbing and shocking, but they may help you to understand why she was like she was." Natasha stared at the suitcase, then looked back at Arthur.

"But why did you do what you did?" she asked bluntly. "You don't have a suitcase full of bad memories as an excuse."

Arthur flinched, and his grey face showed a tiny hint of pink in the cheeks. "I was weak, Natasha," he said with a sigh. "That's my only excuse. Joan was a very strong-willed woman, and she nearly always managed to persuade me that her way was the right way."

"She was a bully, then," stated the child flatly. She turned to Abi. "And she bullied you, too, didn't she?" she added quietly.

Abi nodded. "Yes, she did. Maybe because I stood up to her…maybe that was part of why she did what she did. If I'd given in to her and had you adopted, then she wouldn't have had to pretend you were dead."

Natasha gasped. "No! You were right to stand up to her. She was completely in the wrong to do what she did. No one in their right mind would do that. Mum, it wasn't your fault!" She grabbed Abi's hand. "And if you had given in, we wouldn't be together now, would we?"

Abi squeezed Natasha's hand and smiled at her. "Does that make it worth it, then?"

"Yes," Natasha said simply. "'Course, I wish I'd been with you all the time, but as I wasn't, at least you found me, and these last two years have been so happy. I love you and Dad, and I'm just so glad we're all together now." She glanced over at Arthur and scowled. "That doesn't mean I forgive you, though," she added.

Arthur inclined his head. "I don't expect you to," he said sadly. "I don't deserve it. But if you read the things I found in that suitcase—It will shock you beyond anything you might be imagining, but it might help you to understand a bit more."

Natasha walked over to the case and picked up an old exercise book that lay on the top. She opened the front cover.

"It's a diary," she said, then hesitated a moment before dropping it back into the case. "Shall we take it to the motel, Mum?" she asked. "I don't think I really want to stay here after all. Except to see a photo. Show me one now," and she stared at Arthur, her blue eyes flashing. Slowly Arthur walked over to the bureau. He pulled open the top drawer and brought out a large framed picture. He held it with the photo pressed to his chest for a moment.

"This was taken about six months before Joan died," he said quietly. "On our fortieth wedding anniversary." He hesitated again, then held it out to Natasha. Abi took a step forward.

"Tash, remember what I said…"

Natasha had turned the picture over and was staring at it. Abi held her breath and took another step forward. A tiny sound came from Natasha's throat as she tried to speak and failed. She raised enormous eyes to her mother and stared at her mutely. Abi moved to her side and put her arm around her shoulders. Natasha remained motionless, the picture still in her hand. Eventually she licked her lips and spoke to Arthur.

"Did you know?" she asked croakily. "Did you know she was visiting me?"

Slowly he nodded, his arms hanging limply by his side.

"Then why didn't you come too?" she asked. "Didn't you want to see me? Didn't you care?"

Startled by Natasha's reaction, Abi gently took the picture from the child's hand and placed it on the coffee table.

Arthur was completely lost for words and stared at his daughter for help.

Abi put her arm around Natasha and led her over to the sofa. She pushed her down onto it and sat beside her.

Natasha turned to face Abi. "This is what you tried to tell me? You didn't want me to find out like this."

Abi nodded silently.

"But why didn't you tell me before? You must have known for ages."

Abi nodded again. "Yes, we found out the same time as we found out you were alive." She paused as she tried to find the correct way to put it. "But you liked Nan; you enjoyed her visits. I think you trusted her. We couldn't bear to tell you that the one person you thought was your friend was in fact the same person who put you in the home in the first place. We had no idea what that might do to you." She paused again and looked Natasha directly in the eyes. "We always planned to tell you sometime, but when you first came to us you were very…vulnerable. You had been hurt, and it just seemed that if you found this out right then it would hurt you even more and you might never trust anyone again."

Natasha sat silently for a moment staring down at her hands in her lap. Eventually she looked up at Abi.

"Okay, I think I get that," she said slowly. "I think you should have told me sooner, but I do see why you didn't. You were thinking of me, so I guess that's okay. But you..." Her head snapped up and she fixed Arthur with her piercing glare. "Why didn't you come with her?"

Arthur stared back at her. "She went the first time without telling me," he said eventually. "Then when I found out, she didn't want me to go with her. I think she was actually feeling guilty by then but couldn't change what she'd done. I think the visits were somehow meant to make up for it."

"To make her feel better," said Natasha with a wisdom beyond her years.

"Yes, I rather think so," Arthur said sadly. "But she wanted to go alone. I suppose I should have insisted I go with her, but to be honest I thought it was rather strange that she went at all. It all seemed wrong to me. I'm sorry," he finished inadequately.

Natasha watched him for a minute, then turned to Abi. "Mum, can we go now?" she asked, standing up. "I don't want to be in this house any more."

Abi got to her feet and turned to pick up the large suitcase. The catches were stiff to close, but she forced them shut, then heaved the case off the sofa. With her other hand she held Natasha's shoulder and steered her towards the front door.

"Goodbye, Dad," she said to the old man. "I'll let

you have these back when we've had a look at them."

"No need," Arthur shook his head with a sigh. "They only serve to remind me how little I knew my wife. You deal with them. And I strongly suggest you destroy them so they can't hurt anyone else."

At the door, Natasha turned and looked at him again. "Thank you for the hot chocolate," she said politely, "and thank you for being honest." Then she stepped out onto the path and headed down towards the road. Abi paused a moment longer and turned to her father.

"Thanks, Dad," she said. "I'll call you when we've looked at this stuff. Can't imagine it will help us understand Mum any better, though."

Arthur's face took on a haunted expression. "Don't be so sure, Abi. I nearly destroyed the whole lot when I found what was in it, but I decided you really needed to know the truth. There's some deeply disturbing stuff in that case. Take care." He reached out and patted her on the arm before shuffling back inside and closing the front door.

Natasha was half way back to the car when Abi caught up with her. Her head was down and Abi could see she was trying hard not to cry. She put her free arm around the child's shoulders, and together they walked the last few yards back to their vehicle.

Chapter 8

Monday 28th July, 2008

By four o'clock, Abi and Natasha had booked into their family room at the motel and were both sitting on the double bed deciding what to do.

"We could go out for a meal if you like," suggested Abi doubtfully. "Or maybe get a take-away and bring it back to the room. What do you fancy?"

Natasha cocked her head to one side thoughtfully. "It would be cosier if we got a take-away," she said at last, "and lots and lots of chocolate and crisps and stuff, of course."

"Of course," Abi agreed immediately. "And wine and fizzy drinks." She stood up and looked around the room. "It certainly doesn't look cosy at the moment. Maybe if we pop out now and get the stuff, we could come back, draw the curtains, have bubble baths, and then tuck up and get started on the suitcase while we eat. What d'you think?"

Natasha jumped up and nodded vigorously. "Yeah, that sounds great fun! Did you bring bubble bath with you?"

"Never travel without it," Abi said serenely. "Now, come on, let's go and get the goodies." Catching Natasha by the hand, she picked up her bag and they headed out the door together.

There was a fast-food restaurant right next door to their motel, and they decided to get their take-away from there rather than drive anywhere. They each chose and ordered their food, and then while they were waiting popped into the shop at the petrol station and stocked up with fizzy drinks, chocolate, crisps, and a bottle of wine. By the time they'd done that, their food was ready, and they collected it all and made their way back to their room. Once back, Natasha ran round, drew the curtains, put on all the small lights, and turned off the main overhead light.

"That's better," she said with a satisfied nod.

Abi popped her head out of the bathroom, which was rapidly filling with steam. "Your bath's nearly ready," she said with a grin, "or would you rather eat your burger first?"

Natasha shook her head. "Bath first," she said firmly, and began to pull off her jeans and T-shirt. Leaving them in a heap on the floor, she padded into the bathroom and waited while Abi swirled the bubble bath into a lather for her. She stepped carefully into the hot water and sank slowly down into the bubbles, leaned back against the end of the bath, and closed her eyes.

"You stay and talk to me, Mum," she ordered, opening one eye slightly to make sure Abi acquiesced to her demand. With a smile, Abi sat down on the toilet and looked fondly at her daughter. "You know I'm very cross, don't you?" continued Natasha, still with her eyes closed.

"I'm sure you are," Abi said sadly. "And I'm really, really sorry."

Natasha opened her eyes and stared at her. "I'm not

really cross with you or Dad," she said, "although you should have told me about Nan, but I understand why you didn't—no, I'm most cross with Arthur. He should have come to see me too. He shouldn't have let her bully him like that." She paused and considered for a moment. "He's very weak, isn't he?" she said at last. "You're not like that."

"Sometimes I don't feel very strong," Abi admitted. "Especially when you were born. I felt totally beaten—I couldn't even think for myself properly."

Natasha wriggled into a more upright position with much splashing.

"Of course you felt like that," she said firmly, "but you're normally very strong. I don't think you take after Arthur." The unspoken words hung between them, and Abi dipped her head forward to let her hair conceal her face. The thought that she, in any way, took after her mother was totally abhorrent to her, but she could understand how it might seem that way. Natasha spoke again.

"I think I'm strong," she said carefully. "I think we might be very alike."

Abi looked up at her and gave a little smile. "Is that a good thing?" she asked tentatively.

Natasha nodded. "Of course it is," she said in surprise. "I really admire you—and Dad. I just wish I'd known you all my life."

Abi got up from the toilet seat and dropped to her knees beside the bath. She took one of Natasha's soapy hands in hers.

"Oh, darling, I wish you had! I don't go a moment without regretting the years we were apart. But now I treasure every minute we're together. The last two and a half years have been amazing."

Natasha looked at her solemnly for a moment, then reached out her soapy arms and wound them around her mother's neck.

"Yeah, they have," she agreed. "Totally amazing. I've gone from thinking no one wanted me to living in an amazing house by the sea, with wonderful parents, a baby brother, two lovely grandparents, and lots of money!"

Abi laughed. "The lots of money is quite fun, isn't it?" she agreed, her eyes gleaming. "That's new to me, too! What d'you think of having a famous dad, too?"

"That's pretty cool." Natasha considered, her head on one side. "Can be a pain, though, when everyone at school wants to be my friend just to meet him. I have to be very strict with them." She paused for a moment. "An' I'm not too keen on when we get followed by the paparazzi whenever we go anywhere interesting. But I guess it's more fun than most of my friends' lives!" She grinned up at Abi, her blue eyes shining.

Abi sat back on her heels and smiled in return. "I remember the first time that happened to me," she said, a twinkle in her eye. "It was the day after your dad turned up at my cottage, back in '05. First time I'd seen him for over ten years, and he just appeared. He spent the night on the sofa, and I got up the next morning to find a helicopter hovering outside, taking photos through my bedroom window!"

Natasha, who had heard the story before, giggled. "Was that when you threw coffee over a photographer in the garden?" she asked.

Abi nodded. "Yes," she said with a grin. "As you know, I have a pretty short fuse, and he annoyed me! I couldn't understand how your father kept so calm. He was just used to it, I suppose."

Natasha reached out, grabbed a towel, and stood up in the bath.

"I s'pose it'll get worse now he's making another album," she commented as she began to towel herself dry.

Abi wrinkled her nose. "Yeah, probably," she said with a sigh. "What I'm dreading is the groupies. As soon as he starts touring, they'll all come crawling out of the woodwork. Nasty little scrubbers, trying to crawl all over him." She scowled, her mind flitting back to the summer of '95 when she had seen Gideon on the news with a girl draped over him and had thought he was being unfaithful to her. She gave a little shiver and tried to put the memories of that dark time out of her mind. She turned back to Natasha and smiled. "But this time I'll be there," she said firmly. "No girl is going to get within ten yards of him."

Natasha stepped out of the bath and padded back into the bedroom to find her pyjamas. "I pity any who try," she said with a giggle. "I wouldn't want to get on the wrong side of you, Mum." She delved into her bag and pulled out a pair of check pyjama trousers and a pink T-shirt. She pulled them on, then bounced onto the bed and investigated her take-away packet. She pulled out her burger and took a large bite. Abi had stayed in the bathroom and, having decided a bath would take too long, was having a quick shower before joining her daughter.

When she finally emerged into the bedroom, she found Natasha sitting cross-legged on the bed, the remains of her take-away lying beside her, avidly watching the television.

"Look, Mum! Dad's on the news!" She waved the remote in the direction of the screen.

Abi gave a short laugh. "Bit of *déjà vu!*" she said. "Last time I stayed here I watched him on the news the day he left the band." She turned her attention to the screen, where her husband was pictured going into the Savoy Grill with a couple of record company people Abi recognised but couldn't put names to. She laughed. "There he is, living it up in one of London's best restaurants, and we're having take-away in a motel in Newbury!"

"I think this is fun." Natasha giggled. "But I think Dad should take us there when we're in London. D'you think he will?"

Abi nodded vigorously. "Absolutely. We're going to go everywhere," she promised.

Once cosily wearing her Jack Wills pyjama bottoms and an ancient NightHawk T-shirt belonging to Gideon, Abi joined Natasha on the bed and made short work of her own burger. The child had opened the big bar of nut chocolate they had purchased at the garage and was rapidly washing it down with a can of diet cola.

Abi squeaked. "Leave some for me! That's the best bit of the meal!" She hopped off the bed and went to pour herself a cup of wine to go with it.

Natasha watched her. "Is wine really nice?" she asked, her head tipped. "I asked Judy for a glass last week, but she wouldn't let me."

Abi raised her eyebrows. "I should hope not!" she said with a grin. "You're twelve. Judy and I drank a bottle on New Year's Eve one year and got rather tiddly. That was really my first experience of it. I was fifteen, and she was just sixteen. And I don't recommend the way we felt the next day. However, once you're grown up there's nothing better than a glass of dry white with your dinner. Or with chocolate," she added, breaking a piece off the large bar and popping it into her mouth.

Natasha grinned and pushed her hair out of her eyes. "Shall we look in the case?" she asked tentatively.

"Yep, I guess we should. You turn the TV off and I'll fetch it." Abi hopped off the bed again and retrieved the large suitcase from where they'd stored it in the corner of the room. She heaved it onto the bed, and the two of them climbed up beside it. They stared at it for a moment, and then Abi gently released the catches and lifted the lid. The exercise book Natasha had looked at back at the house lay on the top. Abi picked it up and opened the first page.

"It's a diary," she murmured, "for 1950."

Natasha crawled closer and peered over her shoulder. "That's really old," she said. "Whose is it? Is it Nan's?"

Abi raised her eyebrows at Natasha's use of the name and looked more closely at the book. "Not sure," she said, shaking her head. "Let's look at some other stuff first." She laid the book to one side and turned her attention back to the case.

Natasha pulled out a large, very old photograph album. The pages were black and all the remaining photographs were held in place with photograph corners.

Natasha grinned. "This should be in a museum," she said, gingerly turning the pages.

"It's not that old," Abi objected with a laugh. "Look, there's my mother. She looks about fifteen or sixteen." She gently removed the photograph from the book and turned it over. On the back in very faint pencil had been written "Joan—July 1949." Abi nodded. "Well that would make her...fourteen, nearly fifteen. D'you think she looks like either of us, then?"

Natasha took the picture off her and peered at it closely.

"A bit," she admitted. "Let's see the others. Did she have brothers and sisters?"

"Just Auntie Margaret." Abi grimaced. "Dreadful woman. She's about five or six years younger, I think. Let's see if we can find her." She turned the next page of the album. A large photograph of three girls was fastened in the centre of the next page, and Abi studied it. "There's Mum again, and I think that little girl must be Auntie Margaret. She actually looks quite sweet. I wonder who the other girl is?"

Natasha looked at the photo. "One of Nan's friends?" she suggested. "They look about the same age." She peered more closely at the girl and frowned. "Are you sure she didn't have another sister? 'Cause that girl looks a lot like Nan...in fact she looks just like you, too!"

Abi looked back at the picture in surprise. "Hmm. I guess she does. In fact, if their hair was done the same they'd be almost identical. Let's look on the back; maybe it says. She's probably a cousin or something. I don't really know my mother's family very well." She removed the photo and turned it over. It was labelled like the previous one, in very faint pencil, "Pauline, Joan and Margaret— July 1949."

Natasha sat back on the bed. "Pauline," she said thoughtfully. "I wonder who she is? See if there are any more of her."

She watched as Abi turned to the next page. The next few were empty, with just the photograph corners remaining, but the next picture they found was of Pauline and Joan again, this time just the two of them. They were both wearing what looked like party dresses, and they had ribbons in their hair.

"Looks like they were off to a party," remarked Abi as she eased the picture out of its fastenings and turned it over. The pencil writing had almost faded beyond recognition, but Abi just managed to decipher it: "Pauline and Joan—17th August, 1949—15th Birthday." She frowned and held it out to Natasha. "That's odd. 17th August was my mother's birthday, but why is Pauline there too? Who is she?"

Natasha took the picture and looked at it closely. "She really does look just like Nan," she said again, "and like you used to look when you met Dad. Bit like me, too, really. Are you sure she didn't have another sister?"

Abi flicked over the next couple of pages to reveal random pictures of a variety of people, but no more of the strange girl. She laid the album to one side and searched deeper in the suitcase. After a moment she pulled out another even older-looking album, and brushed the dust off. She opened the first page, and there was a very faded photograph of two almost identical little girls of about six, their curly hair tied back with ribbons, smiling broadly into the camera and supporting a baby of about six months old between them. All three children were dressed in pretty party dresses, and the picture had clearly been taken in a studio. Abi carefully removed it from the page and turned it over. Once again, in faded pencil, it had writing on the back. "Pauline, Joan and Margaret—May 1941." Abi turned the photograph over again and stared at the little girls. Her mouth was beginning to feel dry, and she took a deep breath.

"Tash, I think you're right. Pauline is another sister," she said at last. "I never knew anything about her."

Natasha wriggled nearer to her mother and stared at the photograph over her shoulder. "1941?" she said in surprise. "That's during the Second World War. Your parents are very old."

"Yeah, they are," Abi nodded absently, murmuring, "But where is Pauline? Why have I not even heard of her?"

Natasha took the photo out of her hands. "She looks about the same age as Joan," she remarked, "and just like her—maybe they were twins?"

Abi sat back on the bed cross-legged and stared at the suitcase with a puzzled frown.

"How could my mother have had a sister—possibly a twin—that I knew nothing about? It's not like she lost contact with her family. Auntie Margaret was always coming over. They were really quite close. As much as my mother got close to anyone..." She chewed her lip thoughtfully.

Natasha crawled over to the case again and started to rummage. After a moment she pulled out a brown-edged trade magazine. It appeared to be a periodical dealing with the footwear industry, and she waved it at Abi. "Did your mother have anything to do with shoes?" she asked.

"I think I remember her telling me her father did. I think he had a shop—or a factory, or something to do with shoes. He died before I was born, so I never really knew much about him." She took the magazine from Natasha and thumbed through it. It was dated 1948 and was full of suggestions for making clothes rations go further. Abi shook her head. "This is very strange," she said. "It all seems so alien and so incredibly long ago. How can this have anything to do with my mother and her more recent actions?"

Natasha was still rummaging in the case and emerged with several more notebooks similar to the one she had found first. She held them aloft.

"I think these are more diaries," she said, sneezing as the dust went up her nose. "Maybe there'll be clues in these?"

Abi took them from her and blew the dust off them, away from the bed. With the one they'd found earlier, there were four books altogether, and on investigation Abi found them all to be handwritten accounts of events during 1950, all four written in the same handwriting. Abi opened the first book and looked to see if it contained the name of the diarist. In tiny writing inside the back cover, she eventually found: The Diary of Pauline Forrester, aged 15. She turned to Natasha.

"Well, it looks like Pauline was the owner of these." A cursory glance told her that the first book ran from January to March, the second from April to June, the third from July to October, and the last from the middle of November through December. The early part of November was missing. "I guess we'd better read these. See what happened to my mother's twin sister."

Natasha had gone very quiet and Abi glanced around at her. She was kneeling in front of the suitcase holding a long piece of paper in her hand. Abi gently touched her arm.

"Tash? What have you found?" she asked with a frown.

Natasha turned round, her blue eyes huge and her face ashen.

"It's a birth certificate," she whispered and held it out to her mother. Abi took it and quickly scanned it. It registered the birth of a baby girl, Sarah Forrester, to Pauline Forrester aged 16, on October 29th 1950. There was no father named on the certificate and the birth had been registered by Joan Forrester on 30th October, 1950.

"Pauline had a baby, Mum," Natasha said, her voice barely audible. "She had a baby when she was sixteen, just like you. D'you think Nan took her baby away, too?"

Abi stared at the birth certificate, her mind racing. Surely it was no coincidence that her mother's sister— almost definitely her twin sister—had given birth at the age of sixteen, and that when she, Abi, had done the same, her mother had reacted in such a strange way. She carefully placed the birth certificate and all the photograph albums back in the case, keeping the four notebooks to one side. She closed the case and put it back in the corner of the room. Then she turned to Natasha and took a deep breath.

"Okay, Tasha, time to find out what this story's all about, I think. Have you got a drink? Right. Let's find out what happened in 1950."

Chapter 9

Friday 27th January, 1950—Luton, Bedfordshire

"Come on, Pauline, we'll be in dead trouble if we're late for tea!" Joan called impatiently to her twin sister, who was running towards her across the debris of the old bomb site just around the corner from their house. It was beginning to get dark, and Joan couldn't help worrying her sister was going to trip and break her ankle, leaping across the rocky terrain. Pauline reached her and bent forward to catch her breath, her long hair escaping from its ribbon and falling across her face. She looked up and grinned at Joan.

"Stop worrying," she said. "Dad won't be home yet, and I can wind Mum round my little finger. You know that. Come on." She caught her sister's hand, and they ran off down the road towards their home. The large four-bedroomed red brick house stood at the end of a row of similar properties at the better end of Luton. The girls' father, Walter Forrester, was the proprietor of Forrester's Shoes, a small footwear manufacturer located on the edge of the town, and he was providing very well for his family. The twins were fifteen, and their younger sister Margaret was nine. Pauline was the dominant twin, lively, popular, and very mischievous. Joan was much quieter, more level-headed, and had rescued her more flighty sister from any number of scrapes over the years. Pauline looked sideways at Joan and grinned.

"I saw him again," she said, her blue eyes sparkling.

"You're going to get caught," Joan chided, rolling her eyes but unable to conceal a small smile. "I really don't know what you see in him anyway. He's so old."

"He's eighteen." Pauline tossed her head. "I'll be sixteen in…seven months. That's not too big a gap." She giggled and added in a whisper, "I told him I was sixteen already, actually."

Joan snorted and pulled her sister up the path towards their back door.

"Well, you be really careful, Pauline," she admonished. "If Dad finds out you're seeing one of his employees, he'll be livid. He won't think he's good enough for you. He probably won't think anyone's good enough for us. You know what he's like."

"It's all right, Joanie," soothed Pauline as they let themselves in through the kitchen door. "I'll be really, really careful. I want to marry him anyway. When I'm sixteen, we'll tell Dad, and run away if we have to. I've already told Jimmy I love him." She flashed a wide grin at her sister as they entered the house. Joan sighed and followed Pauline into the kitchen. She couldn't help wondering if Jimmy had told Pauline he loved her, too.

The two girls squeezed past the large wooden kitchen table and made their way through the dark narrow hallway into the living room. The heavy red velvet curtains were drawn, and the coal fire in the tiny tile-surrounded fireplace was crackling merrily. Their mother was working her way through a pile of ironing in the middle of the room, while nine-year-old Margaret was curled up on the sofa looking through a picture book. She glanced up as her big sisters entered, and smiled at them.

"Look, Joan! Look, Pauline! Gran'ma got me a new book!" She held her latest acquisition out to show them.

The older girls exchanged glances. Their grandmother had a tendency to spoil the baby of the family and shower her with gifts. Luckily so far she'd remained a very kind and thoughtful little girl, and Joan and Pauline sat down beside her to look through the book with her.

"You're late back, girls," said their mother, eyeing them with suspicion.

Pauline looked round and smiled at her. "Had to stay late at school," she lied blithely. "They want us to help with the Valentine dance."

Janet Forrester narrowed her eyes at her but nodded briefly and continued with her ironing. Pauline was fairly sure her mother had her suspicions about the activities of her daughters but had decided it was probably better to leave well alone. If their father thought they were up to anything, all hell would break loose, and Pauline guessed her mother had decided to keep the peace. As she watched, Janet sighed, brushed a strand of faded auburn hair out of her eyes, and carried on with her chore, her tired pale blue eyes watching her girls as they laughed together on the sofa.

Pauline, with her long brown wavy hair tied up in a high ponytail, was wearing a bright red full-skirted dress, pulled in at the waist with a black belt. She had bare legs and quite unsuitable high-heeled court shoes on her feet. Joan, in contrast, was still in her school uniform, her hair neatly braided in a single plait down her back.

"Pauline?" Janet raised her eyebrows at her daughter. "Why are you not in school uniform? And where on earth did you get those shoes?"

Pauline hesitated a moment before answering, ducking her head so her mother couldn't see her face.

Joan answered on her behalf. "She got changed at school, Mum. She wanted to show people what she might wear to the Valentine dance."

Janet pursed her lips. "Hmmm. Well, I'm not sure it's entirely suitable. You're only fifteen, Pauline. You may draw unwelcome attention to yourself dressed like that. In future you're to come home in your uniform."

Pauline's head shot up and she turned round to face her mother. "But Mum," she started, stopping as Joan pinched her hard on the arm.

"It's all right, Mum. We stick together. Nothing will happen to her," Joan assured her mother with a smile.

****

Friday 10th February, 1950

"Pauline, hurry up!" Joan called up the stairs, exasperation in her voice. "If we don't leave now we're going to miss the start."

As she finished speaking her twin appeared at the top of the stairs, resplendent in a figure-hugging, lime green, short-sleeved jumper, a tight black pencil skirt, and high-heeled black court shoes. She posed for a moment on the top step grinning at her sister, before she teetered down the long flight and arrived safely in the narrow hallway. She had tied her hair into a very high ponytail, and her lips were liberally coated in bright red lipstick.

"Well?" she asked, spinning unsteadily on one heel. "How do I look, Joanie?"

"Okay, I guess." Joan surveyed her critically, a twinkle in her eye. "But you still look fifteen trying to be eighteen. Now come on, or we'll never get there." She caught her sister by the wrist and propelled her out the front door and down the path.

The school Valentine dance was being held on the Friday prior to Valentine's Day itself, and both girls were very excited. It was the first year they'd been allowed to attend, and they were determined to make the most of it. Like Pauline, Joan had dressed up for the occasion, but she had been more conservative in her clothing choice and had gone for a simple full-skirted blue polka-dot dress and flat black patent court shoes. She too had her hair in a ponytail, but her application of lipstick was a little less obvious. As they hurried down the path, Pauline still pulling on her winter coat, a couple of other girls passed the gate, and they all joined forces and walked the half mile to the school together.

The hall was decorated with masses of huge pink hearts and long trailing pink ribbons crisscrossed the ceiling. As the girls entered, the band were just starting up, and they quickly disposed of their coats and found a suitable place to lean nonchalantly against a wall in order to be seen yet still be in a good position to see the band in action.

Pauline leaned towards Joan and whispered in her ear, "I've got some cigarettes. D'you want one?"

Joan looked at her in amazement. "Pauline! Where on earth did you get them?" She stifled a giggle.

Pauline pulled them surreptitiously out of her

pocket and showed them to her sister. "Jimmy gave them to me," she said with a smirk. "Shall we go outside and try one?"

Joan hesitated for a moment, looking around nervously, then nodded and followed her sister out of the back door of the hall. Outside in the cold February night air, the girls fumbled two cigarettes out of the packet and finally managed to get them lit. Giggling, they both took tentative drags and tried to look as though they were enjoying it. Pauline leaned back against the wall and crossed her ankles, holding the cigarette casually in her right hand and taking occasional puffs. Joan watched her with admiration. One puff and she had collapsed with a fit of coughing, so her sister's ability was most impressive—and suspect.

"Pauline, have you done this before?"

Pauline cocked her head and raised her eyebrows. "May have done," she said casually, then grinned widely and giggled. "Yeah, Jimmy gave me some last week. First one nearly made me sick, but it gets better. You'll get the hang of it." She put the cigarette back up to her lips and took a long drag, eventually puffing the smoke back out of her mouth. She glanced across the playground and smiled with satisfaction. "Oh, look, here comes Jimmy."

Joan looked up in surprise. "Jimmy can't come here! He doesn't go to school. He won't be allowed in."

"He's not coming in, silly," Pauline said patiently. "We're going for a drive in his car."

"I didn't know he had a car!" Joan gasped.

Pauline shrugged. "Well, it belongs to his brother, but he can borrow it whenever he likes."

She started to walk carefully across the playground towards the young man. Jimmy was very smartly dressed in a dark grey suit, pale blue shirt, and narrow tie. His blond hair was slicked back, and he was strolling towards them with his hands thrust casually into his pockets. He stopped in front of Pauline and immediately bent his head to kiss her full on her bright red lips. Her left arm went around his neck while she held the right arm, with the cigarette still clutched between her fingers, out to the side.

Joan hurried after Pauline. "You can't just go off like that!" she protested. "Someone will notice you've gone."

"Cover for me, there's a pet," said Pauline with a winning smile before linking her arm in Jimmy's and heading off towards the school gate where he'd left his brother's Austin Seven. He pulled open the passenger door and waited while Pauline attempted to slide in elegantly, then went round to the driver's side and got in next to her.

As they drove away from the school, Pauline glanced round and had a momentary qualm of guilt when she saw her twin standing alone in the playground, the glow of the cigarette still showing in her hand.

"We mustn't be too long, Jimmy," she said, turning to face him.

He kept his eyes on the road as they turned left and headed out of town. "Stop worrying, Pauline," he said smoothly, reaching over and patting her knee. "We don't need to be long. Are you still ready for this?" He glanced sideways at her.

In slight confusion, Pauline dipped her head

forward and let her ponytail swing over her shoulder to partly conceal her face. She knew perfectly well what Jimmy was referring to, but now the time had come she was beginning to feel both nervous and faintly embarrassed.

"Pauline?" he repeated impatiently. "You still want to do this, don't you?"

"Of course I do, Jimmy," she said at last, raising her head and forcing her lips into a smile. "I love you. Of course I want to do it. I'm just… It's just… Well, I'm…" She sat miserably looking down at her hands in her lap.

Jimmy patted her leg again. "You're nervous," he said with a nod. "It's all right. I'll be gentle. You don't need to worry about anything."

Pauline looked up at him. "Anything?" she asked cautiously.

"I'll deal with everything," Jimmy said with confidence. "You don't need to worry." He turned off the main road down a small country lane, coming to a sudden stop by the side of a lake.

"I didn't know this lake was here!" Pauline looked around her in surprise.

"That's because you never go anywhere." Jimmy laughed, turning off the engine and swivelling round to face her. "You and that sister of yours never leave the town. There's a whole world out here, you know."

Pauline smiled at him. "Can you take me to see the rest of the world, Jimmy?" she asked, staring adoringly into his eyes. "Can we explore the whole world together?"

Jimmy hesitated, then nodded his immaculate head. "Sure, why not? Now, come on, let's get in the back. It'll be more comfortable."

He opened the driver's door, stepped out, then moved the seat forward and slid into the back. Pauline took a deep breath and followed suit, pulling the door closed behind her. Jimmy pulled her towards him along the seat and wrapped his arms around her, his wide mouth coming down on hers. After a moment she felt herself relaxing and allowed his probing tongue to enter her mouth and his skilled fingers to slide under her jumper and cup her breast. She caught her breath as he flicked his thumb expertly across her nipple and pressed her body hungrily closer to his.

****

Friday 24th March, 1950

Pauline was sitting curled up on the window seat in her bedroom, staring out at the street below, when Joan found her.

"There you are. I've been looking *everywhere* for you," she said, plumping down onto the bed and grinning at her sister. "You left school really quickly tonight. Did you go and see Jimmy?" Pauline shook her head and leaned her forehead against the window pane. Joan looked at her in concern. "Pauline? What's up? You look dreadful. Jimmy hasn't broken up with you, has he?"

Pauline turned to face her twin. "Shut the door," she whispered.

Joan jumped up and gently closed the bedroom door, then went straight back and sat down on the bed again. "What's up?" she repeated urgently, watching her sister like a hawk.

Pauline chewed on her bottom lip and looked at her under her lashes.

"I…think…" She cleared her throat and started again. "I think I may be having a baby."

There was a moment of total silence and the loud ticking of Pauline's alarm clock dominated the room.

Eventually Joan spoke, her voice crackly with emotion. "You're pregnant? Oh, Pauline, no! How did it happen?"

Pauline looked at her in surprise. "The normal way," she said, widening her eyes.

Joan shook her head impatiently. "No, no… I mean, surely you used…something?" she asked in desperation.

Pauline nodded emphatically. "Oh, yes, Jimmy took care of all that. He told me not to worry."

"But did he put a…you-know-what on his…you-know-what?" Joan asked, blushing furiously.

Pauline looked confused. "I don't know," she said at last. "I s'pose he must have. He told me it was all okay and not to worry," she repeated, with a little less confidence.

Joan stared at her sister in consternation. "Oh, Pauline, I think he's used you. I don't think he took any precautions. I don't think he cares." She narrowed her eyes. "Have you told him yet?"

Pauline shook her head miserably. "No. You're the first person I've told. Only I missed the curse last month, and now it's due again and it's not come, and I feel sick." A large tear rolled down her flushed cheek. "But Jimmy does care. He loves me. I'll tell him tonight. We can get married."

Joan sighed in exasperation. "No, you can't. You won't be sixteen till August, and even then you need permission."

Pauline stood up and wrapped her arms around herself. "Well, we'll run away if we have to. I know he loves me. We're going to explore the world together. He said so." The words sounded hollow even to her own ears.

Joan stood up and put her arms around her sister, hugging her close. "Don't worry. We'll get through this together," she assured her.

Pauline clung to her tightly. "Thanks, Joanie. But if Jimmy says we can get married in August, there's nothing to worry about, is there?" she said, forcing a cheerful tone. "Don't tell Mum, though, will you?"

Joan gave a short laugh. "'Course not, silly. Now you go and see Jimmy and tell him. D'you want me to come with you?"

Pauline hesitated for a second, then shook her head.

"No. I must do this alone. Thanks, though. I'll come to your room for a natter when I get back," and she turned to her wardrobe and pulled it open, muttering, "Now, what should I wear?"

An hour later, dressed in light blue slacks, a bright red jumper, and sneakers, Pauline was making her way across the bomb site towards her normal meeting place with Jimmy. As she approached the remains of the small building where they habitually met, her steps slowed and she chewed on her lip nervously. Although she'd told Joan she was sure Jimmy would be pleased she was pregnant, she was beginning to feel a lot less confident as the moment of confrontation loomed.

He was standing in the shadows, leaning against the wall, a cigarette hanging out of his mouth and his hands in his pockets. As Pauline approached, he pushed himself upright and started to walk slowly towards her. He caught her wrist when she got close enough, and pulled her to him, his mouth coming down roughly on hers. When she didn't respond with her usual alacrity he pulled back and looked down at her.

"What's wrong, babe?" he asked with a frown.

Pauline swallowed nervously, but held his gaze. "Umm...I've got something to tell you," she began. Jimmy waited expectantly, a guarded look on his almost handsome face. "I think...I might be having a baby," she finished in a rush, and looked up at him in mute appeal.

Jimmy stared down at her silently, his face darkening. "What?" he demanded shortly, his brows coming together.

Pauline swallowed again. "I'm pregnant, Jimmy," she whispered. "D'you mind? We can get married in August."

With a sudden movement he flung her away from him and took several steps backwards. "Well, it's not mine," he said harshly. "We used precautions. You can't prove it's mine."

Pauline went pale with fear and took a step towards him. "Of course it's yours," she said, her mouth dry and her voice cracking. "I haven't done it with anyone else. It's all right. We were going to get married anyway, weren't we?" A tone of desperation leaked into her voice.

Jimmy took another step backwards, a look of terror on his face. "You fucking stupid bitch," he said savagely. "How could you let this happen? Of course we're not getting married. And why August?" he added, shaking his head as if to rid it of the news.

Pauline felt her knees begin to give way and reached out to lean against the remains of a wall. "But you said you had everything sorted. You told me not to worry. And you love me." She began to sob quietly as she spoke, and felt her whole life slipping away from her.

"It's not my responsibility," Jimmy spat out. "Little sluts like you should know that. And why August?" he repeated impatiently.

Pauline looked up at him, her now-terrified eyes full of unshed tears. "Because that's when I'll be sixteen," she whispered.

Jimmy swore loudly, swung round, and slammed his fist into the wall. "You fucking stupid bitch," he repeated. "I could go to prison for this! D'you realise that? You're under age!" He walked menacingly over and stared down at her. "If you breathe a word of this to anyone," he threatened, "if you tell anyone it was me, you'll regret it for the rest of your life. I'll deny it all." With a final snarl, he turned on his heel and stumbled back across the bomb site towards his car.

Slowly Pauline slid down the wall and sank to her knees on the rubble-strewn ground. A cold drizzle was just beginning to fall, but she stayed where she was, her brain and body numb with despair. Jimmy didn't love her. He blamed her for the pregnancy and had refused to take any responsibility. She felt a tiny qualm that she'd let him believe she was sixteen, but his behaviour had still been unbelievably cruel and heartless. Tears trickled unheeded down her cheeks, mingling with the rain that was gradually soaking into her jumper. A gentle hand on her shoulder made her start and look up in fear. Joan stood looking down at her, pity and concern on her young face. She held out a hand to help Pauline to her feet, and then the two sisters clung desperately together as the rain fell heavily all around them.

Chapter 10

2008

Abi put down the notebook and stared at Natasha. "Wow," she said at last. "Poor Pauline. Although she was rather naïve to think that Jimmy would've been pleased about the baby and want to marry her."

Natasha nodded slowly. "She was very young," she pointed out, frowning. "Even younger than you were when you got pregnant with me. She was rather silly to lie about her age, though. I guess Jimmy was right to be cross about that. Though he was a right pig. He treated her really badly. I don't think he ever cared about her; he was just using her."

Abi was silent for a moment, then cleared her throat apologetically. "I lied about my age the first time I met your father," she admitted, her face flushing. "I don't really know what I was thinking."

Natasha stared at her in surprise. "Were you wanting to have sex straight away?" she asked rather sharply.

"I don't know, really," Abi admitted. "I think I just wanted to appear older. But he already knew I was only fifteen. I felt quite ashamed to have tried to lie to him."

"I should think so." Natasha nodded approvingly. "I'm glad he knew already. But you waited to have sex till you were sixteen, anyway."

"You make it sound rather sordid," said Abi, her cheeks beginning to burn with shame. "It was actually very beautiful. We really were in love, not like Pauline and Jimmy." She paused and looked carefully at her daughter. "But it's too young. Much too young."

"Well, I know that," Natasha said scornfully, with a toss of her curls. "I'd never do it that young. I'm not stupid." She leaned forward and picked up the second volume of the diary. "Shall we see what happened next?"

"Not now." Abi shook her head. "It's getting very late. Let's save that for tomorrow."

Natasha nodded and put the book carefully back in the suitcase. "Can we go home tomorrow?" she asked suddenly. "Instead of staying here or going to Judy's? Let's take the suitcase home and look at the rest there."

"Are you sure?" Abi asked doubtfully. "You were very set against finding out any 'bad stuff' in our own house."

Natasha nodded. "I know, but this is different. It's not like that. This is sort of, well, sort of like learning family history. It doesn't seem bad. Not bad like I was expecting. I'd be okay to be at home." She frowned again. "And maybe stay home for a few days instead of going to see Grandma and Grandpa on Wednesday."

"I was already thinking that wasn't such a good idea," Abi admitted. "They only arrive back on Wednesday, and I think we should give them some time to settle back home. All right, then, tomorrow morning we'll go and pick up Ollie from Judy, go back home for a few days, and then maybe go and join Dad on Friday. How does that sound?"

"That's great." Natasha nodded enthusiastically. "I

want to learn about Pauline and Joan at home. It just feels right." She paused for a moment and chewed on her bottom lip. "Don't be cross, Mum, but I think Pauline sounds a lot like you were at that age."

"And Joan is a lot like Judy"—Abi gave a little smile—"always trying to keep her out of trouble!"

Natasha nodded wisely. "I wonder if Nan realised you were like her sister and that's why she was so strict with you?" she suggested.

"Could be, I s'pose." Abi shrugged. "Joan sounds really nice when she was a teenager, doesn't she? It's hard to believe she was the same person who bullied Dad and me all those years."

Natasha nodded again and reached over to give Abi a hug. "Don't worry, Mum. I'm never going to do anything stupid like that," she said firmly.

Abi squeezed her back. "I know, sweetie. You have far more sense than I ever did! Now, I'll just give your dad a quick call, and then I think we should get into bed and maybe watch some TV to cheer us up."

****

Gideon put down his mobile thoughtfully and leaned back on the bed. He'd had a long and very tiring afternoon with the record company, ending, as Abi and Natasha had seen, at the Savoy Grill for dinner with a number of the executives, and he was looking forward to starting recording in the morning. But the news Abi had just told him on the phone had left a very unsettled feeling in his gut. That her mother could have had a twin sister Abi had never heard of seemed almost too bizarre to be true, and he couldn't help wondering how the rest of the story was going to pan out. The tale seemed to have caught the imagination of both his wife and his daughter, and he hoped the ending wouldn't prove to be too harrowing. That Natasha had elected to return home to Cornwall to continue their investigations surprised him. The child had originally been so vehemently opposed to any 'bad stuff' being told to her at home. Gideon feared she may have got so caught up in the romance of the story that she'd lost sight of the reason they were reading about it.

He picked up the remote control and flicked on the TV. He really needed to relax before the rigours of the studio sessions began. It was already feeling strange to be starting an album on his own, and he was beginning to have qualms about the wisdom of pursuing a solo career. He'd loved his time in the band, right up until the last year, and he'd loved to feel part of a close-knit group. He now had that with his family, but he was beginning to think he might also need it in his working life. The chat with Charles had stirred something in him he thought had long gone, and he realised he could very easily be tempted to re-form NightHawk, but with a new drummer. He needed to discuss it with Abi before he made any final decision, and he decided to call her again first thing in the morning to see what she thought.

****

Simon had had a very good day. His meeting with Richard Morrison had gone well, even better than he'd hoped, and between them they'd concocted a story that would be bound to raise Gideon's suspicions and paint Abi in a very bad light. Simon smiled to himself and stretched his legs out in front of him. He was relaxing in his suite at the Ritz prior to popping down to the bar for a nightcap, and his only frustration was that he was unable to have a cigarette, either in his room or in the bar. He had spent so much time in the USA over the last couple of years that he was finding the smoking ban in England very difficult to cope with.

He was beginning to get twitchy, so he wandered over to the window overlooking Green Park and opened it wide. The rain was still falling silently in the dark streets, and Simon peered out into the gloom. He groped in his pocket, brought out his Rothmans and lighter, and, leaning on the windowsill, he lit up and took a long thankful drag. He closed his eyes and leaned back against the wall, gently letting the smoke drift out of his mouth towards the open window. A few good puffs later he began to feel more like himself, and glancing at his watch he realised if he was going to catch the bar before it closed he should get down there. He chucked his cigarette stub out the window, which he then pulled closed and fastened securely, then snatched up his jacket and room key and made his way out into the corridor.

He headed straight for the lift, not even considering the stairs as an option, and rode impatiently down to the stylish Art Deco bar. He ordered a champagne cocktail, with a Lagavullin to follow, and then, taking his drinks, he slid behind a small table in the corner of the room. He downed the cocktail in a couple of gulps, relaxed, sipped more delicately at the malt, and thought back over his day. The story that would appear in the Wednesday morning issue of *The National Crier* was even better than Simon had originally imagined. He smirked to himself as he predicted what Gideon's reaction would be. And the thought of Abi's discomfort as her dirty linen was aired for everyone to see gave him immense satisfaction. If all went according to plan, he would turn up to see Gideon on Thursday or Friday in the guise of a caring friend offering support. From that meeting he hoped to be able to gauge the success of his plan, and when it would be prudent to approach the idea of re-forming the band. Such was the twisted state of his mind it never occurred to him Gideon might not believe what he read in the papers and still might not welcome Simon with open arms.

Aware the barman was watching him intently, Simon drained his glass, pushed the table forward, and left the bar without even a nod of thanks. He took the lift back up to his room, taking care to resist the temptation of venturing out to a club until the early hours. He was keen to keep as low a profile as possible until after Wednesday. Consequently, apart from his trips to Canary Wharf he had stayed in the hotel, alternating between sleeping, eating, and drinking. There was a faint smell of stale smoke lingering in the room, so he immediately opened the window again in an attempt to dispel it. The last thing he needed was to be ejected from the hotel for smoking in his room. He'd never been thrown out of a hotel, even during the wilder years of NightHawk, and he wasn't in the mood to start now. He wafted the window for a moment or two until he felt confident the odour had dissipated, and then he tossed his jacket down on a chair, kicked off his shoes, and poured himself another whisky from the bottle he kept by the bed. He downed it in one, immediately topped it up again, then carried it over to the seating area and lounged back on the sofa with his feet up. He was planning to spend Tuesday making the most of the facilities the hotel had on offer, including a good workout at the gym, and working on his plan to get back into Gideon's good books.

He finished his second whisky, paid a quick visit to the bathroom, then slid into bed and stretched out, luxuriating in the soft sheets. If he was going to be able to sustain such an extravagant lifestyle, he really needed to succeed in his plan. He smiled to himself as he drifted off to sleep, and such was his confidence that his dreams that night were all concerning the re-forming of NightHawk with the original line-up.

Chapter 11

Tuesday 29th July, 2008

When Gideon awoke the following morning, his first thought was to call Abi and tell her his concerns about his solo career. He glanced at his watch, noted it was still only seven o'clock, and hopped out of bed with an agility that surprised even himself. His dinner at the Savoy had been long and mainly liquid, and he had not been expecting to feel quite so human in the morning. He wandered into the kitchen and flicked the kettle on for a much-needed cup of coffee, then padded into the bathroom for a quick shower.

Ten minutes later he was back in the kitchen, rubbing his long dark hair with a towel. He had pulled on a pair of ripped and faded jeans and a blue-and-white-striped rugby shirt, his feet still bare. He made the coffee, popped a couple of pieces of bread into the toaster, and walked over to the window to inspect the weather. Peering down onto the already busy street below, he pushed the window open a crack to determine the temperature. Although it was fairly overcast, the air felt warm and slightly heavy, and Gideon wondered if they might be in for more thunderstorms. He closed the window again and rescued his toast as it shot out of the toaster and landed on the worktop. He shook his head, a slight grin spreading across his face. Why did his parents always have things that didn't quite work properly? He spread some butter on the toast and then began a fruitless search for something more interesting to go on the top. Inwardly cursing his disorganisation in not remembering to bring the Marmite, he sat down at the kitchen table and made short work of the toast and coffee. His hangover had begun to kick in, and it wasn't until the third cup that he began to feel like himself again.

Leaving the dishes on the draining board, he wandered into the living room and lit a cigarette. He had cut down dramatically but found he still craved one when he was in an unusual situation or under any kind of stress. He classed this morning as a bit of both. He was both excited and nervous about beginning the recording, he was missing Abi and the children dreadfully, and he was more than a little disturbed by the information Abi had given him the night before. He wished he could be with them when they went through the diaries, but he also realised it was something they needed to do on their own. Natasha's early childhood in the children's home, believing herself to have been abandoned, had obviously had a huge effect on her, and Gideon hoped the information she and Abi were discovering might go some way towards helping her understand how and why it had happened. Nonetheless, he had a nasty little niggle in the pit of his stomach that the story wouldn't be all that straightforward. He sighed and ran his hand impatiently through his hair. He would have to trust Abi to deal with the situation the right way. He knew she would and had to stop himself worrying about them all the time. These last two years, being part of such a perfect family, had left him very possessive of his wife and children and all they stood for, and he was finding it even harder than he'd expected to be apart from them.

Glancing at his phone to see the time, he decided it was late enough to call Abi, and quickly pressed on her number. He held the phone under his chin while he lit another cigarette and made himself comfortable on the chesterfield. Eventually Abi answered, and Gideon smiled to himself at the sound of her voice.

"Morning, darlin'," he said, taking a long drag. "Did you sleep well in your wonderful motel?"

Abi's disembodied voice echoed in his ear. "Don't start!" she said with a giggle. "Tasha and I shared a bed, and she took all the covers and slept diagonally across it. I was scrunched up in one corner—so, no, I didn't sleep well!"

Gideon chuckled. "Still prefer sleeping with me, then?" he asked, then carried on without waiting for her reply. "Wanted to run something past you, babe. You got a minute?"

"Sure, what's up?" came Abi's concerned voice.

"Nothing to worry about. It's just ever since I spoke to Chas I've been thinking. It seems really weird doing this album on my own. D'you think I should consider getting NightHawk back together after all?" There was a long silence at the other end of the line, and Gideon could just discern his wife's breathing.

Finally she spoke. "That's a hard one, Gid. Part of me screams yes, go for it—the part that missed out on your touring years; but another part keeps remembering that you really seemed to have had enough—or maybe that was just because of Simon? Maybe it would be okay now he's out of the picture."

"That's another issue," Gideon replied. "Remember what Chas said about Simon wanting to get the band back together? He thought Simon was on his way to see me. He could still turn up and make things difficult." There was another long silence from Abi's end.

"Well, now we know for sure that he hid the letters, he can't really expect you to take him on again, can he? He doesn't have a leg to stand on. You hold firm, Gideon. Don't let him get to you."

"I'm more worried I might do him some damage," Gideon muttered darkly, viciously stubbing out his cigarette in the cut-glass ashtray.

A chuckle came down the phone line. "Well, that's up to you," said Abi smoothly, "just don't get arrested. You're too old for that sort of behaviour." She gave a little sigh. "I guess you should get together with Chas and discuss it. That can't do any harm. You know I'll support whatever you decide."

Gideon grinned to himself. "Thanks, baby. You always make things seem easier to deal with. I'll call Chas and get him over here. Could be good to see him again anyway. It's been too long." He stretched his long legs out in front of him and yawned. "What're you girls up to today, then? Are you heading straight home?"

Abi's voice echoed down the line again. "Pretty much, just popping to Judy's to pick up Ollie, and then we're off. Aiming to get home early afternoon. Wish you were coming too," she added wistfully.

Gideon's eyebrows came together. "Oh, me too. I'm missing you guys so much. You will be up on Friday, won't you?"

"'Course we will. Try stopping us," said Abi at

once. "Now I really must go, or we won't get home till this evening. Love you, Gid. Be good."

"Love you too, babe, and the kids. I'm always good. See you soon."

He disconnected the call and placed his phone thoughtfully down on the arm of the sofa. Abi had helped him make up his mind, and he would call Chas and get him over to the recording studio as soon as possible.

****

Abi and Natasha arrived on Judy's doorstep at exactly nine thirty, to be welcomed by a very exuberant Tommy brandishing a bow and arrow. He hauled the door open to let them in and promptly aimed a rubber-ended arrow at Natasha's head. Judy appeared behind him, Oliver in her arms. She handed the little boy to Abi, then lifted her son up, turned him around one hundred and eighty degrees, and sent him off in the direction of the conservatory. She grinned at her guests and pushed a straying strand of blonde hair out of her eyes.

"Morning, girls." She ushered them into the kitchen. "How did yesterday go? Did you find anything out?" She waved them into seats at the table. Natasha carefully pushed a pile of washing out of the way and sat down at one end, resting her elbows on the slightly sticky surface. She looked expectantly at her mother. Abi sat down with Oliver on her knee and raised her eyebrows at her.

"Well," she began with a slight smile, "it was very enlightening, actually. We discovered my mother had a twin sister called Pauline"—she paused briefly as Judy gasped—"who had a baby when she was sixteen."

Judy hastily put three mugs on the table, slid into the chair between Abi and Natasha, and nodded encouragement. "That's amazing!" she breathed. "And you had no idea of any of this?"

Abi shook her head. "No, none. As far as I knew, the dreaded Auntie Margaret was her only sister. It's all rather a shock."

"We found some diaries Pauline had written in…1950." Natasha took up the story, "An' we read the first one. She's in love with a horrid person called Jimmy, who works for her father, an' she had sex with him when she was fifteen but told him she was sixteen, an' then when she was pregnant he was really, really horrid and left her." She finished all in one breath, her cheeks looking slightly pink, then dipped her head forward and let her hair fall over her face.

Judy glanced at her and stifled a smile. "Well…" she said with a long intake of breath, "that all sounds fascinating! Is there more to read, or was that all of it?"

Natasha looked up with a frown. "No, as I said, that was the *first* book. There's loads more."

"Yep, so now Tasha wants to go home and read the rest," Abi said, raising an eyebrow at Judy.

"Today?" asked Judy. "That's a bit of a change of plan, isn't it? I thought you were going to Roger and Caroline's tomorrow and then on to London on Friday."

Abi nodded. "We were. We'll still go to London on Friday, but we're going to give the grandparents a miss just now. They only come back from the Med tomorrow anyway. We just came by now to pick up Ollie, and then we'll get on our way."

"If you'd like some more time, just the two of you to read the stuff, I'm more than happy to have Ollie for a couple more days. You can pick him up on your way to London," Judy suggested.

"Oh, no, we've imposed on you far too much already," Abi protested. "You've got your hands full with your own two."

Judy gave a lopsided grin. "It's no problem. It would be good practise for me."

There was a moment's silence before Abi clapped a hand over her mouth.

"Judy!" she squeaked. "Are you pregnant?"

Judy nodded silently, her cheeks flushed.

"Wow." Natasha giggled. "That's cool. When's it due?"

"Oh, not till March," said Judy airily. "We've only just found out. It's very exciting."

Abi carefully placed Oliver on the floor so she could jump up and hug her friend.

"That's brilliant," she said, grinning widely. "You're such a good mother. Do you really want to keep Ollie for practise, then?"

"Well, I'm more than happy to, if it would help you two to concentrate on the investigations!" Judy laughed.

Abi glanced at Natasha, who nodded. "Might be easier to concentrate," Abi conceded, "but I'll really miss him. Maybe we'll come back on Thursday night, if that's all right with you?"

"'Course it is. Now, if you are going to get home this side of dinner time, you'd better get going!"

****

Gideon paced the room impatiently. He had called Charles just after he'd spoken to Abi, and they'd arranged to meet at the recording studio at eleven. It was already ten past, and Gideon was not renowned for his patience. He'd had a hurried conversation with the record company about the possibility of re-forming the band, and they'd been enthusiastic. They tried to persuade Gideon to get Simon back, as well, but he'd held firm on that score, although he refused to tell them the reason. All they needed to know was that he and Simon had fallen out and there would be no reconciliation.

He glanced at the clock for the umpteenth time and scowled to himself. He'd made a start at laying down the first track, but his heart wasn't in it, and he'd petulantly ordered the sound engineers to take a break until he'd had his meeting with Charles. That meeting was now nearly fifteen minutes late, and Gideon lit a cigarette in frustration. One of the engineers tapped on the glass and indicated he should extinguish it, pointing to the very large *No Smoking* sign on the door. Gideon cursed and, crushing the cigarette in his hand, strode to the door and flung out into the corridor. At that precise moment, Charles appeared through the double doors at the end of the hall and started towards him. Gideon visibly relaxed and held out his hand to his friend.

"Chas! Good to see you, mate! Glad you could make it." The two men clasped hands and shook firmly. "Let's get out of here for a bit and grab a coffee. Easier to talk."

Gideon stuck his head around a door marked Private, muttered something inaudible, then caught his friend by the arm and ushered him out into the street. He turned right and strode off along the busy road, Charles almost running to keep up with him.

"Hold on, Gid," he panted, falling into step

alongside his friend. "We're not running a race. Not sure I'm as fit as you are! I've just been touring, remember."

Gideon slowed his pace a little and had the grace to grin at Charles.

"Sorry, mate," he said, indicating they should cross the road. "Been a bit stressed this morning. Not quite sure why, but I reckon a good coffee will help. You can't get one of those in the studio." They dodged across the road and headed off in the direction of St. John's Wood. "There's a pretty good coffee place about half a mile away. We can talk there."

Charles fell into step beside him, and they hurried through the crowds towards the café.

Ten minutes later, seated at a secluded corner table, each with a latte and a *pain au chocolat* in front of them, Gideon sat back and sighed.

"Sorry for the rush, Chas," he said with an apologetic grimace. "Been getting rather stressed about the Simon thing. Was hoping you might have some more info about him."

Charles took a long slurp of coffee and shook his head. "Sorry, mate, nothing more. I got the impression he was coming to England and was going to try persuading you to re-form the band. I knew you two had had a falling out, but he didn't elaborate, and I felt he thought it could all be sorted out."

Gideon sighed again and put down his mug. "That's one thing it can't be," he said firmly. "Simon crossed the line, and there's no going back. If he really is coming to see me, he must not be in his right mind. Did he seem normal to you?"

Charles considered for a moment. "A bit stressed,

sweaty, cross…you know Simon. Nothing particularly different; I got the impression he hadn't worked for a while. He did seem a bit desperate." He paused and looked at Gideon cautiously. "He does seem to have it in for Abi, though. Any idea why?"

Gideon's dark brows came together, and he tore his croissant apart savagely.

"That was always the problem," he said through clenched teeth. "Remember when I brought her to that gig in Reading?"

Charles nodded, grinning. "Yeah, he hated that. But we were only kids then. He used to think girlfriends ruined a band. Surely that's not still an issue, is it?"

"Even more so, if possible, mate," replied Gideon darkly. "Look, I may as well tell you what happened. You will have heard the story that Abi's mother hid my letters to her back in '95?" Charles nodded. "Well, Abi wrote to me, too, and Simon hid those letters from me." Gideon paused and watched Charles' face. "Apparently he managed to keep them all from me, and—we only found this out recently—he kept them, and as far as we know he still has them."

Charles leaned back in his chair and stared at Gideon in horror. "Jeez, Gid! That's fucking awful. He's supposed to be your friend. What the hell was he thinking? Does that mean he knew about the baby all the time, then?"

"No, according to his mother, he only read them after the band broke up. That's how we know he still has them—his mother." Gideon paused again and ran a hand through his hair. "So he's clearly always had an issue with Abi, and from what you say, he still does. He worries me, Chas. I feel he's unpredictable, and I don't like the idea that he's back in England."

Charles wiped pastry crumbs from around his mouth and frowned. "But what could he really do?" he asked. "He could piss you off, sure, but I don't see how he could hurt you or Abi."

At the suggestion that Abi could get hurt, Gideon's face darkened, but he spoke quietly. "If he fucking goes anywhere near her or the kids, I will not be held responsible for my actions," he muttered. "I don't like that we're not together just now, but they have some stuff to sort out, and then they're coming up to London on Friday, so I guess that's not too long."

Charles smiled encouragement. "Don't worry, Gid. He's not a lunatic. He may turn up to ask for his job back, but I'm sure that's as far as it'll go." He glanced up at his friend. "So if you do get NightHawk back together, I take it we need to find a drummer?"

"Yeah. Know anyone suitable?" Gideon asked hopefully.

Charles shook his head. "Sorry, all the good ones I can think of are already working. Mind you, so am I— until next month anyway," he said with a short laugh.

"Yeah, great that you could come over this week, though. When are you off again?"

Charles considered. "Got a gig in Seattle on Tuesday next week, then Vancouver on Wednesday, Montreal on Friday, and New York the following Tuesday. That's it, then. After that, if you want me, I'm yours!"

"If you want to, that'd be great. When I started on the solo album it just didn't feel right. I really do want to get the band back together," Gideon said with a grin.

Charles leaned back and surveyed him

speculatively. "So, back to Simon… What is his problem with Abi? Is he jealous?"

Gideon rolled his eyes. "According to my father he is. He thinks Simon wants me for himself. I keep telling him that's not the case, but he's not convinced!"

Charles made a face. "Hmm… He could have a point. I mean, Simon never has serious relationships with girls, does he? He just has one-night stands. Always has. And with as many as he can. Maybe he's overcompensating?"

"Oh, god, not you too!" Gideon groaned in exasperation. "I've known the guy since he was eight! He's not gay. He doesn't fancy me. I think he just thinks girlfriends and wives break up bands."

Charles looked unconvinced but shrugged and finished his coffee. "So what now? Do we need to go and talk to the record company or anything? D'you want to start recording anything? We could get a session drummer for now."

"Yeah, let's go and lay down a track or two. Can you stay for a few days?"

"Yeah, I was going to book in at the Ritz." Charles shrugged.

Gideon grinned. "Very nice. But if you don't mind roughing it, you can stay at my father's flat with me, if you like. Abi and the kids are coming on Friday, but we could have it to ourselves until then. Get some stuff worked out?" he suggested.

Charles nodded. "That'd be great. And if I know your dad, the flat will not be roughing it." With a laugh, they left the café, pausing only to sign a couple of autographs on the way out, and headed back to the recording studio.

****

Simon was frustrated. He was finding his self-imposed incarceration very boring and was ready to break cover and go out on the town. He had started the day very virtuously with an hour in the hotel gym, followed by another hour in the pool, and had then spoilt all the good work he'd done with a large lunch washed down with far too many pints of lager. He had then retired to his room and was guiltily hanging out of the window with a cigarette, wondering how on earth he could pass the rest of the day. He wasn't planning on going to see Gideon the next day, either—he wanted to leave at least one day after the story broke—but at least on Wednesday he would have the paper to peruse and the news to watch for any developments. He took a long drag on his cigarette, then tossed the butt down into the street below and pulled the window closed again. The air was heavy, and Simon idly wondered if a thunderstorm was threatening. At least that would be something more interesting, he thought to himself, as he idly flicked through some magazines that had been provided for his entertainment. Nothing caught his eye, so he flicked on the television and slumped down on the sofa. He channel-hopped for a while, until a familiar figure caught his eye. He paused on Sky News to see a shot of Gideon and Charles leaving a coffee shop. He sat forward and swore under his breath.

The newsreader's voice faded in. "Former NightHawk guitarist Gideon Hawk, seen in St John's Wood this morning accompanied by former band member Charles Bond. Rumours that Hawk is planning to re-form the band have been circulating for some time, and the sighting of him with another band member…" Simon muted the sound and swore again. So Charles was in London too. He couldn't decide whether that would make his task easier or more difficult, and fell back against the cushions running a distracted hand through his rather greasy hair. Charles had been perfectly friendly when they'd met in New York, so maybe his being there would be to Simon's advantage. He closed his eyes and gave his head a slight shake. Nothing to do now but wait until the shit hit the fan the next morning.

Chapter 12

Abi and Natasha arrived back home just before five, having enjoyed a trouble-free journey broken only by a brief stop near Bristol for a quick lunch. Natasha had chattered most of the way, speculating on the outcome of the Pauline and Joan story, seemingly quite excited at the prospect of finding out, and not at all apprehensive, as Abi herself was feeling. Still reeling from the news that her mother had had a twin sister, Abi was far more nervous of investigating the diaries further, and as they drew up outside the house, she felt compelled to warn Natasha the story would probably not have a happy ending.

Natasha tossed her head impatiently. "I know that," she said, rolling her eyes. "If it had been a happy story, Nan wouldn't have kept it secret, would she? An' it wouldn't have made her into the nasty person she was." She opened the door of the 4x4 and slid out onto the driveway. "I'm 'specting it to be sad, but I just want to understand Nan better, and I hope I will after this."

She skipped over to the front door and waited for her mother to open it. Abi shook her head, fished her key out of her bag, and followed Natasha into the house. As they entered the large hall, they were bombarded by the two dogs, who launched themselves on the returning travellers with a great deal of howling and excited barking. Within seconds, Natasha was rolling on the floor with them climbing all over her, and Abi stepped over them all, laughing as she made her way into the kitchen and deposited her bag on the table. She quickly checked around the downstairs rooms for any sign of a break-in, then ran upstairs to do the same. Natasha eventually disentangled herself from the collies and ran outside again to bring in the bags from the car. She was just struggling to haul the large leather suitcase out of the back when Abi came out to join her, and together they carried it through into the house.

"Where do you want it, Tasha?" Abi asked as they entered the hall.

Natasha nodded to the large living room. "In there," she said without hesitation. "We can get cosy in there best. Maybe we could light the fire?"

"Tash, it's July!" Abi laughed, shaking her head as they heaved the heavy case onto the sofa. "It may be wet and a bit miserable, but it's still pretty warm. I think we may be in for some more thunder later."

Natasha's face lit up. "Ooh, goody!" she squeaked, clapping her hands. "Maybe we'll get hit this time."

Abi chuckled and ruffled her daughter's unruly hair. "Or maybe not," she remarked. "Now, d'you want something to eat? I'm going to have a cup of tea and some cake, and then I think we should give the dogs a run."

Natasha opted for some cake and a glass of lemonade, and they partook of their snacks at the large pine kitchen table, the dogs sniffing around their feet. They ate in silence for a while before Natasha glanced up at Abi with a slight frown on her face.

"Mum," she said, "when did Nan marry Arthur? How old was she?"

Abi thought for a minute. "It was 1965," she said, nodding. "In May. She would have been...thirty. Nearly thirty-one. Why d'you ask?"

Natasha looked serious. "Just wondered if Pauline's experience with Jimmy put her off men. If she didn't get married for another fifteen years, then maybe it did." She paused thoughtfully for a moment. "And Arthur looks a pretty safe man, doesn't he? She wasn't going to get any surprises there."

Abi smothered a smile behind her hand, amused at her daughter's attempt at maturity, and nodded.

"I guess you might be right," she said, just managing to keep her face straight. "My father is rather boring."

"And yet he still managed to make some very bad decisions," added Natasha, glowering at the cake in front of her.

"Yes, they both did," Abi agreed, and, reaching across the table, she gave her daughter's hand a squeeze. "Now, come on, let's take these animals for a run, then come back, get some dinner on, and get stuck into the next bit of the saga."

Ten minutes later, both dressed in shorts and T-shirts, Abi and Natasha were running along the cliff top, the two collies bounding alongside them. Since it was summer, the dogs weren't allowed on the beach, and Abi had to content them with long treks around the countryside or on the cliffs or coast path. Natasha stopped and stared out to sea, shielding her eyes against the glare of the sun.

"Some big clouds out there, Mum. D'you think it'll thunder?" she asked with a gleam in her eye. "Imagine what fun it would be if it was thundering while we read the diaries. That would make it really spooky!"

Abi laughed. "Guess that's one word for it," she said, studying the sky. "We may get some thunder. Not sure yet, the weather changes so rapidly here. It's certainly muggy enough."

They continued their walk, chatting idly about the weather, the holidays, and their forthcoming trip to London, until the dogs finally tired and trailed along beside them, panting heavily. Abi turned for home and led the way back across the fields and into the garden. Natasha filled up the dogs' water bowls while Abi sorted out their food, and then the two of them set about deciding what to have for dinner. They finally settled on macaroni cheese, and Abi rustled up a large pot while Natasha made the living room cosy and started to rifle through the suitcase again. When Abi brought in the food, she found her daughter sitting in the middle of the hearth rug, the case open beside her, flicking through one of the photograph albums.

"Let's save it until after we've eaten, Tasha," she said with a smile, placing the loaded plates on the coffee table and sitting down on the large sofa. Natasha jumped to her feet and slid into the seat next to her mother, her blue eyes flashing with anticipation.

"I can't wait to read the next bit," she said, tucking into her dinner with gusto. "It's kinda weird, but I just looked at some more photo albums, and I can't find any more pictures of Pauline after 1950."

Abi munched on her pasta thoughtfully, watching Natasha closely. "Well, as I said earlier, I doubt there's a happy ending to this story," she pointed out eventually.

Natasha waved her fork in the air. "I guess. D'you

think her parents throw her out when they find out about the baby? Or maybe she runs away and no one ever sees her again," she speculated, her eyes gleaming. "Maybe you've got a long lost cousin somewhere, Mum, just waiting to be found." She took another forkful of macaroni and frowned. "A very old cousin, actually. That'd be really weird…" She stared into the distance.

Abi watched her covertly, keeping her own ideas on the subject close to her chest. She was fairly sure there was no long-lost elderly cousin waiting to be found, but she decided to let Natasha have her fantasies. They would find out the truth soon enough.

A distant rumble of thunder took Natasha's attention, and the two of them watched the storm clouds gather out across the sea. Abi glanced at her daughter.

"Shall we close the curtains to be cosy, or leave them open in case the storm gets going?" she asked, a twinkle in her eye, already knowing the answer.

Natasha grinned widely, "Leave 'em open," she replied promptly, abandoning her dinner and running to the window. "Oooh, look, lightning!" and she pressed her nose to the glass, staring out over the sea, anticipating the next flash.

"Come on, finish your dinner. I want to get reading." Abi chuckled.

Natasha reluctantly dragged herself away from the scene and gobbled up the last of her macaroni, washing it down with her diet cola. Then she collected the plates and almost ran with them to the kitchen. She returned a minute later clutching several packets of crisps and a large bar of chocolate.

"I have got you well trained," Abi commented with

approval, curling her feet underneath her and taking a sip of her wine. Natasha grinned and deposited her armful on the table, then got down on her knees and pulled the suitcase across the floor towards them.

"D'you want to look at any other stuff first, or shall we just read the next diary?" she asked, beginning to rummage in the case again.

Abi pursed her lips. "Up to you," she said at last. "Apart from the photo albums and the birth certificate, have you found anything else interesting?" She leaned forward to peer down into the case. Natasha was sitting cross-legged on the floor in front of it, her hair swinging loose in front of her face as she bent forward. She suddenly pulled something out and stared at it closely.

"This might be interesting," she said slowly. "Look, Mum, it's another notebook, a bit like Pauline's diaries but a different colour. I hadn't noticed it before—it was right at the bottom." She opened the book and peered at the writing. "The writing isn't quite the same as the others. I don't think it's Pauline's." She looked up at her mother, her eyes sparkling hopefully. "Maybe it's Joan's?"

Abi reached out and took the book. She opened it and quickly scanned a couple pages. Her eyes widened slightly, then she closed it again and put it to one side.

"Yes, I think it is my mother's," she said, biting her lip. "It seems to be mostly from November 1950, so we shouldn't read it until we've read Pauline's and reached that date. Are there any more of these?"

Natasha rummaged again and shook her head. "Doesn't look like it," she said. "There's loads more

145

photos…and a couple of letters. No more diaries, though."

"Pass me the latest photos of Pauline that you found." Abi leaned forward again. "Let's see if she looks pregnant."

Natasha giggled and pulled out a large dark red album and handed it to her mother. She scrambled up onto the sofa next to her and curled her feet under her. Abi opened the book and flicked over the pages until she found a picture of the girls. It showed Pauline and Joan, dressed in school uniform and looking very alike, standing in the garden on a summer's day. Joan was smiling, but Pauline had a rather sulky look on her face.

Abi peered closely at the photo. "Hmmm…difficult to tell," she said at last. "She does look a bit fatter than Joan, but those uniforms are pretty shapeless. They could hide a multitude of sins!" She turned the photo over to see the inscription on the back. "Pauline and Joan, June 1950, last day of exams," she read, frowning. "June… She must have been at least four and a half months gone by then," she said in surprise. "Well, she certainly doesn't look that big. Still, I managed to hide it that long, so I suppose anything's possible."

Natasha had returned to the floor and was rummaging again. "Look, Mum, this is an album from a bit later. Pauline isn't in it at all." She held the book out to Abi. Abi took it from her and opened it carefully. The first picture was clearly taken at Christmas time and showed Joan, Margaret, and their parents, posed rather formally in front of a large Christmas tree.

Abi turned it over and read the back. "The family at Christmas 1950." She looked at Natasha, her eyes sad. "The family," she repeated. "No mention of Pauline. She would have had the baby by then. Oh, dear, I think this is going to be sad. Joan doesn't look very happy, does she?"

Natasha peered over her shoulder, her face serious. "No, she doesn't," she agreed. "She must be really missing her twin." She handed yet another album to her mother. "This one is a very old album. Just see how alike the twins were when they were little. You can hardly tell them apart." Abi looked down at the photo of the much younger twins and caught her breath. The little girls, probably aged about four or five, were dressed the same, had their curly hair tied back with ribbons, and either one of them could have been Joan or Pauline.

Abi whistled softly. "They really were identical," she breathed. "They don't look it in the later pictures. That just shows how different hair and clothes can make you look." She laid the book down and raised her eyebrows at Natasha. "Are you ready to read some more now?" she asked. Natasha nodded, picked up the second of the diaries, and sat back on the sofa next to Abi.

"Okay," she said with a nervous smile. "Let's do it."

Chapter 13

Thursday 20th April, 1950

Joan stared at her sister with dismay. "But you have to come to school, Pauline," she said in desperation. "Otherwise they'll know something's up. Mum will come snooping and then maybe tell Dad."

Pauline raised red-rimmed eyes and stared back at her. She shook her head violently. "I can't, Joanie," she whispered, her voice cracking. "I still feel sick, and I keep wanting to cry. People will notice."

Joan sat down on the bed beside her and put her arm around her shoulders.

"They'll notice far more if you're not there," she pointed out sensibly. "And if you tell Mum you feel sick she'll call the doctor, and then there's no way you can keep it secret." She shook her twin gently. "We have to go back to school and take our exams. Once they're over, we'll be free and we can work out what to do. You just have to keep it secret until June." She paused. "Unless you want to tell Mum and let her take control."

Pauline's head shot up, and she stared at Joan in terror. "No," she shouted. "Then they'll make me give it up. They'll treat me like I've done something dreadful and never let me forget it. I'm going to keep my baby, Joan, and no one is going to stop me."

Joan got up and pulled Pauline to her feet. "Right. In that case, you're coming to school, and you're going to behave normally. Can you manage that?" she asked, looking intently at her. Pauline slowly nodded her head, then pulled her blazer on and picked up her brown leather satchel.

"All right, you win. Let's get it over with." She smiled a watery smile and rubbed her hand impatiently across her eyes.

Joan smiled back and led the way downstairs. Janet was waiting in the hallway, ready to see her daughters off the premises, and handed them each a paper bag containing lunch.

"Straight home after school, girls," she said severely. "Your exams are starting in a few weeks, and you'll need to be revising every night from now on. No more gallivanting in the evenings." She fixed Pauline with a beady stare. "If you two are going to work for your father, you'll need to pass your School Certificate. He won't employ anyone in his offices unless they finish school properly." She ushered the girls out of the door and watched as they went down the path and onto the pavement. They waved to her and made their way in the direction of the school.

Pauline snorted. "Work for Dad!" she said. "I was never going to do that anyway. Were you?"

"Don't really know," Joan said vaguely. "I hadn't actually thought about it. I probably will. At least it's a safe job with prospects."

Pauline looked askance at her sister. "Safe job with prospects!" she repeated in astonishment. "Joanie, how boring are you? Don't you want excitement? Don't you want to live, to travel, to see the world? I'm going to do

149

that. I shall take my baby with me. We'll be inseparable. She'll come everywhere with me."

"She?" Joan repeated. "It's going to be a girl, is it?"

"Yes," said Pauline firmly. "She's definitely a girl. I can tell. She's called Sarah."

Joan gave a little smile. "And how do you propose finding the money to travel the world with your daughter?" she asked curiously.

"Well, I don't know yet." Pauline tossed her head impatiently. "But I'll find a way. I can do anything I want." She set off down the road at a very fast pace, leaving her sister standing. Joan finally caught up with her at the school gate.

"Wait up, Pauline," she puffed, catching her sister's arm. "Why are you rushing?"

Pauline spoke without turning round. "If I have to be here, let's get it over with. Let's pass these stupid exams and get out of this awful place. Come on." She caught Joan's hand, and together they walked into the school to start the new term.

****

Saturday 20th May, 1950

Pauline and Joan lay on the grass in the back garden, their French books open in front of them. The examinations were looming ever closer, and they were spending every waking moment studying for them. Pauline's belly was beginning to swell, but by clever arrangement of her school uniform and carefully forged letters to excuse her from physical training class, no one had yet noticed. Both girls were well aware Pauline would get found out eventually, and had more or less decided to tell their mother once the exams were over.

Pauline groaned and rolled onto her back. "I can't take much more of this, Joanie," she moaned, her arm across her eyes shielding them from the hot afternoon sun. "I'm beginning to dream in French... I even dreamt I named the baby Françoise!"

Joan looked up and giggled. "*Tu es trés drôle*, Pauline," she said in an exaggerated French accent.

Pauline groaned again. "*Et tu, Brute?*" she muttered, "See, now I'm getting French and Latin mixed up. I'm never going to pass anything." She carefully rolled onto her side, avoiding lying on her bump.

Joan watched her with concern. The bump was becoming more difficult to conceal, and she was wondering how they were going to manage it for much longer.

"D'you think Mum will insist on telling Dad?" she asked, not needing to elaborate.

Pauline rolled her eyes. "If she does, then I'm dead!" she said dramatically. "I don't think she will. She's pretty scared of him, and I think she'll know he'll be furious. She'll probably send me away somewhere until it's born."

Joan looked stricken. "Not without me!" she gasped in horror.

"Don't be daft." Pauline giggled. "I'm not going anywhere without you, silly." The sisters smiled at each other, and Pauline reached out and squeezed Joan's hand. "I couldn't do any of this without you, Joanie. You're my rock. I'd have done something stupid by now if it wasn't for you."

"I think you did something stupid anyway," Joan remarked tartly, her eyes flicking to the well-concealed bulge of her sister's belly.

Pauline flushed and dipped her head. "Yes, well, all right, that was a bit stupid," she conceded, "but you've stopped me doing anything even more stupid since."

Joan looked doubtful but shrugged and squeezed Pauline's hand. "Well, make sure you keep listening to me," she said. "We're going to need to be pretty vigilant if we want to keep this quiet until after the exams."

Pauline grunted and struggled into a sitting position. "Maybe we could not tell anyone ever," she suggested brightly. "We'll just tell them we both got jobs miles away, and we'll go and live in a flat with the baby."

Joan sighed and ran a hand through her hair. "Pauline!" she said in exasperation. "Do you honestly think Mum and Dad would let us do that? And that they wouldn't want to visit us to make sure we were all right? Honestly, you do have some silly ideas sometimes." Pauline had the grace to look embarrassed. "No, we really will have to tell Mum as soon as the exams are over. Hopefully she'll come up with a plan that works."

Pauline was silent for a moment, her long fingers gently picking the petals off a daisy. Eventually she raised her head and looked mournfully at Joan.

"Mum's going to hate me, isn't she?" she murmured, her blue eyes filling with tears. "She's never going to forgive me for letting the family down. And she'll be horrified about Jimmy."

The tears began to trickle down her pink cheeks, and Joan crawled quickly across the lawn to sit beside her. "Pauline, no one must know about Jimmy," she said urgently. "You lied to him, remember. You told him you were sixteen, but you were underage. He could go to prison." She paused and gently shook her sister's arm. "I know he behaved like a real rotter, but I don't think you want him to go to prison, do you?"

Pauline rubbed a hand across her eyes and shook her head. "'Course not," she muttered. "He didn't love me, but he didn't know he was breaking the law. That was my fault. But Mum'll ask who it was. What do we tell her?"

Joan frowned in concentration, then shook her head. "Nothing," she said at last. "We tell her nothing. We just refuse to say. She can't actually force you to tell her." She looked at her sister thoughtfully. "She'll probably ask if you were raped—you do know that, don't you?"

Pauline's head shot up and she looked at Joan in horror. "What d'you mean?" she asked, her eyes wide.

"Well, if you won't tell her who the father is, she might think someone forced you to do it," she said patiently. "In fact, she might prefer to think that, rather than think her daughter did it because she wanted to."

"But he didn't force me," said Pauline, concern on her face. "I did want to do it."

"Yes, I know." Joan patted her arm. "But Mum won't know that. Just be prepared for her to ask you. And she'll be very embarrassed about the whole thing. I mean, she's never even talked to us about…that sort of stuff, has she?"

"Maybe I should say a stranger forced me," suggested Pauline doubtfully. "Then no one gets into trouble."

"I really don't think that's a good idea," Joan said at once. "They'd ask all sorts of questions, and it could still lead back to Jimmy. No, just don't tell her, that's all we can do." She sat silently for a moment, and then an idea came to her. "I really don't think Jimmy should be allowed to get away with this scot free, though," she said thoughtfully.

"What d'you mean?" Pauline sniffed miserably. "We can't tell on him—you said he'd go to prison. What else could we do?"

"Get him the sack," said Joan with a wicked grin. "Make it look like he did something bad at work, and then Dad'll sack him. That'd serve him right for being such a nasty piece of work."

Pauline looked admiringly at her sister. "Very clever," she said with the ghost of a smile. "Any idea what we can do?"

"I'll give it some thought," replied Joan. "Leave it with me."

****

Wednesday 21st June, 1950

"I can't believe we never have to do exams or school work again," Pauline said with a sigh as the two sisters walked home enjoying the intense heat from the midsummer sun.

"We're supposed to go back in to school until the end of term…" Joan stopped what she was saying as she saw her sister's face.

"By the end of term we'll probably be miles away. Locked up with some old relative until the day arrives," Pauline said morosely. "Oh, Joan, what do you think Mum'll do?"

Joan caught her hand and gave it a squeeze. "We

won't know till we tell her," she said sensibly. "Let's go and get it over with."

Pauline pulled her hand away in horror. "Today?" she gasped. "No, no, Joanie, let's wait a bit longer. Let's have a couple of days' holiday before it all begins."

Joan sighed and smoothed her hand down her sister's belly, revealing the ever-increasing bulge.

"You're getting huge," she said bluntly. "I think you must be more than half way. We have to tell her now; otherwise Dad might find out. You don't want that, do you?"

Pauline shook her head violently. "No. He'd kill me, or throw me out on the streets, or…or something else dreadful!" She sighed and pushed a strand of hair out of her eyes. "Okay, let's tell Mum, then. What time is it?"

Joan glanced at her wristwatch. "One thirty."

"Good. Margaret will still be at school. We can't do it if she's there."

Pauline picked up her pace and led the way back to the house. Joan fell into step beside her, and hand in hand they turned up the drive and approached the house.

Janet was in the kitchen when they let themselves in the back door.

"Hello, girls," she greeted them with a smile. "How was the last exam?"

"Hmm. Glad it's over," Joan grimaced. "It was only geography. Not really important."

Janet shook her head. "They're all important," she chided. "Now come and sit down and have some lunch. I've cooked us some nice haddock."

Rachael Richey

Pauline shuddered and slid into one of the chairs that were arranged around the kitchen table.

"I'm not really hungry, Mum. Can I just have some bread and butter, please?" she said nervously.

Janet frowned. "Now, Pauline, you mustn't waste food. Try some. And you can't have any butter. You've already had this week's ration." She placed a plate of haddock, peas, and boiled potatoes in front of her daughter.

Joan sat down next to Pauline and smiled sympathetically at her. She knew that even the smell of fish made Pauline feel sick, and she felt very sorry for her. She gently kicked Pauline's ankle and raised her eyebrows at her. Pauline looked scared and shook her head imperceptibly. Janet placed a similar plate in front of Joan, then sat down opposite them to eat her own lunch.

"Do you have to go back into school at all?" she asked, scattering pepper on her food.

"We're meant to," Joan said, "but I doubt if we'll be doing any work."

There was silence for a few minutes while Joan and Janet tucked into their lunch and Pauline moved hers gently around her plate, her face pale and her eyes downcast.

"Come on, Pauline," Janet chided. "Try and eat some of it, please. Otherwise your father'll make you eat it for supper."

Pauline raised tear-filled eyes to her mother and pushed her plate away.

"I can't eat it, Mum," she said, her voice cracking. "I'll be sick."

Janet looked at her in concern. "Are you ill? Why

didn't you say before?" she asked. "I'll take your temperature in a minute and see if we need to call Dr. Jones."

Pauline looked at Joan in desperation, then back at her mother, and cleared her throat nervously. "No, don't do that," she said quietly. "I'm not ill." Janet stared at her in surprise. "I'm pregnant."

There was a long silence. Joan held her breath and watched her mother closely. Eventually Janet laid down her knife and fork and licked her lips.

"What did you say, Pauline?" she finally managed, her hands clutching tightly onto her napkin and her eyes deep pools of sorrow. Pauline's face drained of all colour and she swallowed audibly.

"I'm pregnant," she whispered. "I'm having a baby."

Without a word Janet stood up, carried her plate to the sink and laid it on the draining board. Then she left the room, closing the door behind her.

Pauline stared at Joan in terror. "She's gone to tell Dad," she hissed, her eyes filling with tears. Joan leapt to her feet and followed her mother out into the hallway. She was nowhere to be seen, but the telephone lay undisturbed on its table by the front door.

"She's not calling Dad," whispered Joan as Pauline joined her.

"Maybe she's gone out to see him?" Pauline suggested, hugging her arms tightly around her body. Joan quietly opened the door to the sitting room and discovered their mother sitting silently in the dingy room, her hands clutched together on her lap. Pauline ran over to her, knelt down beside her and grabbed her hands.

"Mum, I'm so sorry," she gasped, tears beginning to flow down her pale cheeks. "Please don't tell Dad. It was an accident."

"Did someone force you?" Janet asked quietly, without looking at her daughter.

Pauline hesitated, then shook her head. "No. No one forced me," she said.

"So who is…the father?" asked Janet, anguish sounding in her voice. Pauline was silent. "Pauline? The father. Who is he? He must marry you."

Pauline let go of her mother's hand in shock. "No, he can't," she said abruptly. "I'm too young, Mum."

"You'll be sixteen in two months," Janet said, her voice shaking. "You can get married then. When is the baby due?"

Pauline stared at Joan in desperation. Joan sat down next to her and put her hand on her mother's knee.

"I think it's due in November," she said cautiously. "It takes nine months, doesn't it?"

Janet shifted uncomfortably in her chair and glanced down at her daughters.

"She can get married in August, then," she said decisively.

Pauline grabbed her hand again. "Mum, I can't," she said in panic. "He doesn't love me. We're not seeing each other any more."

Janet looked at her, her face softening. "Do you love him?"

Pauline hesitated for a moment, then shook her head sadly. "No. I thought I did…but no. I don't."

Janet bit her lip, a strange look in her eye, and then she took a deep breath and shook her head. "Well, he has responsibilities now," she said firmly. "He caused this, he can sort it out. Who is he?"

Pauline glanced at Joan again and bit her lip. "I can't tell you," she blurted out. "You can't make me. Please don't make me marry someone I don't love."

Janet's pale eyes glistened, and she turned her head away.

"And he's married to someone else," Pauline said in a rush, blushing furiously, and dipping her head forward to hide her face. Beside her she felt Joan stiffen in surprise. Cautiously she raised her head and looked up at her mother. "Mum, please don't make me say who he is. Can I go and stay somewhere until it's born, so Dad doesn't need to know?"

Janet frowned and stared into the distance. "You could go to Maureen's," she mused to herself. "That might do for now. I could say she'd offered you work for the summer." She turned and faced her daughters again. "Yes, I'll call her later. My friend Maureen in Norfolk. She lives on a farm. You met her when we stayed in Norfolk at the beginning of the war. You can go there until the baby's born, and then we'll arrange for it to be taken away, and you can come home. Your father need never know."

"What do you mean, taken away?" Pauline stared at her in horror. "I want to keep my baby. I don't want to give her away!"

Janet stared at her sadly. "Of course you can't keep it," she said gently. "You're a child. Walter—your father—wouldn't tolerate it in his house. It must go to be adopted."

Pauline burst into tears and shook her mother's arm. "Mum, no!" she cried. "You can't take her away. I want to keep her. I'll get a flat to live in. I'll look after her. Dad never needs to see her. Me and Joan can look after her."

Janet gently shook Pauline's hand off her arm and stood up. "I really don't see how you could keep it," she repeated, her voice shaking. "I shall go and telephone Maureen and see if she can take you. Then maybe…"

Joan jumped up and caught her mother's hand. "Mum, please can I go with her to Norfolk? She needs someone to look after her. Please."

Janet paused, her hand hovering over the door handle. "All right," she said at last. "That would probably be sensible. I can trust you, Joan." She left the room, closing the door quietly behind her.

Joan ran to Pauline and hugged her tightly. "It's okay, Pauline. We'll sort it out. Once we're in Norfolk we can come up with a plan for you to keep the baby. Maybe these people will be nice. Maybe you can stay there and work for them afterwards."

Pauline nodded miserably, and sniffed. "Oh, Joanie, how would I manage without you?" she wailed. "You always know what to do."

Joan moved away and stared out of the window thoughtfully.

"We'll need some money," she mused. "If you're going to have any chance of looking after a baby, you'll need some money. And I think I know how we can get some," she grinned. "And kill two birds with one stone, as well."

Pauline frowned at her in confusion and opened her mouth to speak just as the door opened again and Janet walked back in.

"I've spoken to my friend," she said quietly. "She's prepared to have both of you to stay with her and work on the farm until the baby is born." She paused and looked sadly at Pauline. "She will then organise someone to take the baby and see it gets put with a suitable family. You girls will return home and get jobs. I shall explain to your father that this will be a worthwhile experience for you both and get you used to some hard work. He's a great believer in hard work, so I'm sure he'll agree without being suspicious." She regarded her daughters thoughtfully. "Pauline, I want you to know how very disappointed I am, but I do partly blame myself, and I want you to know I'm not totally unsympathetic. I had no idea you were ready... You're so young. So much younger than... I should have talked to you, explained things better. But if Walter ever found out..." Her pale face blanched still further, and a look of intense pain appeared in her blue eyes. "Joan, I hope you've learned a lesson from your sister." She turned to leave the room again.

"When are we going?" Joan asked tentatively.

Janet didn't turn her head. "On Saturday," she said, closing the door behind her.

Joan caught Pauline's hand. "Okay," she said, her eyes gleaming, "we don't have much time. We need to get this money now. Come on!" She left the room and ran up the stairs, followed more slowly by her sister.

In her bedroom Joan pulled off her school uniform and began to drag some casual clothes out of her wardrobe. Pauline sat on the bed and watched her dismally.

Joan smiled at her. "Come on," she encouraged. "Get changed. We're going out."

"Where to?" Pauline asked wearily, not moving off the bed.

"To give Jimmy his comeuppance and get some money at the same time," was the surprising reply. Pauline frowned but got to her feet and wandered into her bedroom to get changed.

Ten minutes later, both dressed in flowered summer dresses and tennis shoes, the two girls let themselves quietly out of the house, without Janet hearing them, and walked quickly down the road and across the old bomb site.

Pauline looked miserable. "This is where I used to meet Jimmy," she said mournfully, her steps slowing.

Joan caught her by the hand. "No time for that now," she said. "We need to get on."

Pauline rolled her eyes and struggled to catch up with her sister.

"But where are we going?" she whined, brushing her hair out of her reddening face as she trotted after Joan. Joan led the way across the bomb site and onto the main road.

"To Dad's factory," she said, pausing for a moment to let Pauline catch up, then setting off along the road at a brisk pace.

Pauline gasped and fell into step beside her, catching her hand. "Joan, we can't," she cried. "Jimmy works there! I can't see him."

Joan glanced at her without slowing her pace. "Don't worry, you won't have to see him," she assured her. "You're going to be my lookout." Pauline stared at her in surprise, but said nothing and puffed along beside her until they reached the large iron gates of the shoe factory, located on the outskirts of the town.

Joan stopped and pulled Pauline into the shadows just outside the gate. "Right. Here's what we're going to do." Her eyes glinted. "Dad keeps lots of money in the safe in his office. I happen to know the combination to the safe…" Pauline gasped and stared at her wide-eyed. "First, we're going to cause a distraction that will draw Dad out of his office. Then, I'll go in and take lots of money while you keep watch outside. And then…" She paused dramatically. "Then, we're going to plant some of the stolen money in Jimmy's pockets. Dad will have everyone searched when he discovers the money is gone, and when he finds it on Jimmy, he'll give him the sack!" She grinned triumphantly at her sister.

Pauline went pale. "Joanie! That's so dangerous! Suppose we get caught? Dad would kill us. And suppose he doesn't just sack Jimmy… He might call the police," she whispered.

Joan wrinkled her brow. "Hmm. You do have a point. He might call the police if the safe's broken into." She leant against the hot brick wall and considered for a minute. "I know. I won't take the money from the safe, I'll take some from his desk. He always keeps some in there, too. Ooh, yes, and I won't plant money on Jimmy, I'll plant some papers."

"What d'you mean…papers?" Pauline asked with a puzzled frown.

Joan chewed on her bottom lip thoughtfully. "Well, something secret. I don't know yet. I'll see what I can find."

Pauline looked at her with admiration. "I'm impressed," she said with a small smile. "This is the sort of stupid plan I usually come up with and you stop me from doing. How come?"

Joan flushed. "This is a desperate situation," she said seriously. "You'll need money for when the baby comes, and Jimmy needs to be taught a lesson. I know I wouldn't normally do anything so risky, but this is for you. I'll do anything for you; you're my twin. You're part of me."

Pauline's eyes filled with tears, and she flung her arms around her sister's neck. "Oh, Joanie, I don't deserve you!" she sobbed, rubbing her wet eyes on Joan's shoulder.

Gently Joan pushed her away and smiled at her. "'Course you do," she said. "Now come on. If we go now, everyone'll be having their afternoon tea break. Listen, hear that hooter? That's when they all go to the canteen for fifteen minutes. That's our chance. Dad doesn't go, of course, but we can easily get him out of his office. Come on!"

She caught Pauline's hand and pulled her through the gate, and together they ran along the wall, keeping in the shadows until they reached the huge red brick building. Joan dodged to the left and ran lightly along the building and then turned down the side, heading towards the back. Pauline puffed after her, beads of sweat beginning to appear on her forehead. When they reached the back corner of the building, Joan stopped suddenly, and Pauline cannoned into her.

"Look," Joan whispered, pointing round to the right. "That second window along is Dad's office. The one with the window open. Now, see that old bin just to the left of the window?" Pauline peered around her and nodded dubiously. "Well, I want you to set fire to something in the bin and make lots of smoke. That should bring Dad out to investigate, and then I can run in and get the money and stuff."

"I thought I was the lookout, not the diversion," Pauline said crossly, wiping her forehead with the back of her hand. "How do I start the fire?"

"With these, and this." Joan grinned, producing a small box of matches and a piece of folded paper from the pocket of her dress. "Sorry, but I just realised I need to be round the other side of the building, so there wouldn't be time for me to do the fire and then get into Dad's office and out again before he returns. You'll be okay. As soon as it's smoking well, run back this way and hide in that gap in the wall over there." Pauline looked round and noticed a space between two walls, just large enough for a person to slip into. She walked over and peered in cautiously.

"Okay, I guess," she agreed. "When shall I set it alight?"

Joan grinned and squeezed her arm. "Just give me time to run back to the front and get in place outside his office door—about a minute should do—and then you can light it. Stay in your hiding place until I come and get you. Okay?"

Pauline took a deep breath and gave a brief nod. Joan smiled and patted her arm, then turned and ran quickly back towards the front of the building, disappearing in a flash of flowered skirt. Pauline licked her lips nervously. She glanced down at her wristwatch and stared at it until the second hand had completed its journey around the face. Then she ran across the back of the building, making sure to duck down below the level of the windows. She reached the old oil can that was serving as a bin, and peered inside. It was approximately half full of a mixture of paper and cardboard rubbish and old oily rags. She smiled to herself. They should catch fire very well. She carefully set a lighted match to the edge of the paper Joan had given her and lowered it gently into the bin on top of the other rubbish. She watched for a moment to make sure it was going to keep burning, and then as the first plume of smoke started to rise she bent down and scurried back to her hiding place.

Slowly the smell of the burning oily rags began to filter across the back of the building towards her, and she grinned and hugged her arms around herself tightly, taking care to remain concealed. About a minute later she heard the sound of hurrying feet, and her father ran past her hiding place, heading towards the now heavily smoking bin. Pauline giggled quietly to herself. To see her usually smart, clean, and very proper father bending over a smoking bin attempting to quash the fire was very amusing. He managed to extinguish the flames by covering the top of the can with a metal tray that he found propped up against the wall, then wiped his hands fastidiously on his handkerchief, a look of fury and distaste on his face. When he hurried back past Pauline and headed round to the front of the building again, Pauline held her breath. She crossed her fingers Joan had had enough time to complete her task, and she peered cautiously out again. At that moment Joan appeared back around the corner of the building, running fast. She caught sight of Pauline peeping out of her hiding place and beckoned furiously to her. Pauline squeezed out and ran to join her.

"Did you manage it?" she asked in a loud whisper.

Joan nodded, her eyes shining. "Yep. I got thirty pounds for you and the baby, and some financial records or something to plant on Jimmy. Come on. We might just have time before they all get back from the canteen."

She caught her sister by the hand and pulled her along the front of the building until they came to a door marked Private. Joan pushed the door open cautiously, then beckoned to Pauline to follow her. They ran lightly down the long corridor until they came to some double doors at the end, leading into a large cloakroom.

"Everyone hangs their coats here," whispered Joan. "We just need to find Jimmy's and hide the papers in his pocket."

Pauline looked impressed and began to investigate the numerous coats hanging on the line of pegs.

"How on earth do we find his?" she asked, wrinkling her brow.

Joan called quietly from the other side of the room. "Over here," she said. "Each section is for a different department. Jimmy works in the orders department. One of these must be his." Pauline joined her, and they scanned along the line of coats. Three obviously belonged to women, and of the other three one was clearly for a much fatter gentleman than Jimmy, so they only had to choose between two. Joan looked hopefully at Pauline. "Well? Do you recognise either of these?" she asked. Pauline lifted one of the coats off the peg and held it up. She frowned, hung it back, and picked up the other one. This time she felt something in the left pocket and pulled out a silver cigarette lighter.

She nodded. "This one," she said decisively. "I recognise this lighter." She held out the coat, and Joan carefully placed the folded papers in the inside pocket. Then she replaced it on the peg, caught Pauline by the hand, and pulled her back into the corridor just as the other door to the cloakroom opened and two girls walked in, giggling. Joan and Pauline sped back along the corridor and out into the hot sunshine. They ran along the wall towards the large gate and didn't stop until they were well out of sight of the factory. Then Pauline stopped running and leaned against a lamppost, panting.

"Can't run any more, Joan," she gasped. "It slows you down, having a baby inside you."

Joan stood next to her, her face red and shiny with sweat and her hair escaping from its ribbon. She grinned at her sister.

"We did it," she said with satisfaction. "We got enough money to keep you and the baby going for ages, and hopefully we've got Jimmy into trouble. A very good day's work."

"I'm very impressed." Pauline smiled, pushing her hair out of her eyes. "How on earth do you know so much about Dad's factory?"

"Well, we are supposed to be working there after the summer," Joan said. "I thought it might be useful to learn about the place that was going to be my workplace. If I work hard, Dad might make me something important. I could even be the boss one day."

Pauline gaped at her. "You *want* to work there?" she asked in amazement. "I can't think of anything worse! I'd been trying to think of ways to get out of it even before the baby."

"Well, it's not really your thing, is it?" Joan agreed with a grin. "But I quite like the idea of being a successful business person. It's not easy for a woman, but if your father owns the factory, there's a better chance of success." She held out her hand to Pauline. "Now, come on. We'd better get back before Mum sends out a search party. We need to get packed for Saturday, too."

Chapter 14

Tuesday 29th July, 2008

"Joan was pretty resourceful, wasn't she?" said Natasha, unable to keep the admiration out of her voice. "And she really loved her sister."

"She did." Abi nodded. "It's so hard to believe it's the same person I knew. Something really bad must have happened to change her. I suppose it'll be something to do with Pauline's baby." She reached over and poured herself a glass of wine.

Natasha jumped up and went over to the suitcase. She pulled out a large photograph, clearly taken in a studio, showing the whole family posed and dressed in their best clothes. She studied it closely.

"This must be one of the last photos of the whole family," she said holding it out to Abi. "It says Easter 1950. Pauline and Joan are really alike in it—look." Abi took the picture and stared at it. The family were arranged in a group, posed very like the old-fashioned Victorian photos. Janet sat on a chair in the middle, Walter standing proprietarily behind her, his hand on her shoulder. Margaret was sitting at her feet, and Joan and Pauline on either side, leaning in towards their mother. Both were dressed in full-skirted cotton dresses and had their long hair held back with hair bands. Everyone except Walter was smiling, albeit rather falsely, and they looked like the perfect family group. Abi took a sip of her wine and looked up at Natasha.

"They look identical here, don't they?" she agreed. "Funny how matching clothes and hairdos can do that. You can't tell Pauline's pregnant here." Her face took on a sombre look. "I've got a very bad feeling about her, you know," she added, laying the photo down on the sofa beside her.

Natasha sat down on the floor in front of her. "Me too," she admitted. "You can't imagine she was allowed to keep the baby, can you? And why haven't you heard of her before? D'you think her father threw her out when he found out?"

"Maybe." Abi shook her head sadly. "People did that sort of thing in those days. My mother almost did it with me, and that was in the nineties! Maybe this is what gave her the idea."

Natasha wriggled closer and rested her head on her mother's legs. "I'm so glad I found you," she said quietly.

Abi reached down and gently stroked her head. "Oh, me too, sweetheart," she said. "Me too."

"Shall we read the next book?" asked Natasha, straining her neck back to look up at Abi.

Abi shook her head. "Let's leave it till tomorrow. It's getting late, and we've had a long day. Let's get to bed now. Then we can start again fresh in the morning." Natasha nodded, and together they packed the photos and the notebooks back into the suitcase, finished their drinks, and headed upstairs to bed.

****

Gideon lay back on the sofa and crossed his long legs in front of him. He was dressed in old faded jeans, a white T-shirt, and bare feet, his long hair still wet from the shower and his face showing the exhaustion of his first full day in the studio. He ran a hand through his hair and grinned across at Charles, who was sprawled out on the well-stuffed armchair opposite.

"That was fun today," he said. "If you really are up for it, then I think it's definitely time to get the band going again."

Charles yawned, and took a long swig of his beer.

"Oh, I'm up for it," he said with no hesitation. "I didn't want to disband in the first place."

Gideon looked a little embarrassed. "Yeah. I guess that was just me," he said, rubbing his nose awkwardly with his thumb. "It had to be done, though. I wouldn't be with Abi now if we'd just carried on as we were. You do understand, don't you?"

"'Course I do." Charles nodded at once. "You had to do it. But now we can get it going again. With a new drummer, of course." He looked around him and yawned again. "This place is fantastic, Gid. How long has your dad had it?"

"As long as I can remember." Gideon shrugged. "He used to use it a lot for work, but now he's retired—well mostly—and he doesn't use it much, so he said Abi and I could. We did think of getting one for ourselves, but there's really no point when we can use this pretty much whenever we like."

"How are your parents?" asked Charles, remembering them with affection.

"Oh, fine," replied Gideon with a grin. "On a cruise right now. Due back in Southampton tomorrow, actually. Think Mum may have enjoyed it more than Dad—he really doesn't do all the touristy stuff very well. I can imagine him being dragged around markets against his will, probably still wearing his suit and tie."

Charles smiled and snapped open another can of beer. "How do they get on with Abi?" he asked curiously.

"Oh, I think they like her better than me!" Gideon said with a laugh. "With my sister all the way over in New Zealand, my mother was desperate for another girl to do female stuff with. They get on really well. And they adore the kids." He paused and looked over at Charles with narrowed eyes. "How about your love life, Chas? Anything interesting there?"

Charles snorted. "Not a chance," he said dismally. "All I ever meet are airheaded groupies wanting a quick shag. More Simon's cup of tea than mine. Last time I had anything approaching a proper relationship was that girl in Seattle, back in '99. D'you remember her? We lasted about six months, I think, and then we went off on tour, and she didn't bother to keep in touch." He grinned ruefully. "I really envy you."

"Well, it was a long time coming." Gideon smiled. "But I do feel really lucky now. Sometimes I just can't believe it's true. It was like a fairytale finding Abi and then finding Tasha... Pretty unbelievable, actually." He frowned as he remembered everything that had led to the near-perfect existence he had now.

Charles watched him, a small smile playing on his lips. "Never thought I'd see the day," he said, "that the wild man of grunge, Gideon Hawk, had settled down in the country with a wife and kids."

"Settled down, my ass!" Gideon snorted. "I've just been enjoying a couple of years of peace before the next onslaught." He raised his can to his friend. "I love the life in Cornwall with Abi and the kids, but Abi has been the first to encourage me back into the business. One day I'll be ready to settle down for good, but not yet. I just enjoy the odd bit of time away from things now and again." He paused and frowned. "The only thing that worries me a little is the media attention the whole family will get once I'm properly back in the public eye. It's been bad enough the last two years…whenever we go on holiday, there they are waiting to snap us at the airport, but it's not been too bad. I reckon it's going to be a whole lot worse now. Not sure how the girls will deal with it."

"D'you think it might upset them?" Charles asked.

Gideon laughed out loud. "Hardly. I'm more worried what they'll do to the reporters! Both Abi and Tasha have short fuses, and neither of them think before they act or speak. Could be interesting, actually. The day after I found Abi again, you know, back in '05, the paparazzi followed me to her cottage and had us besieged. Abi was ready to—her words—machine gun the lot of 'em! And she actually did pour coffee over one of them out of the window. My girl can handle herself."

Charles laughed, then yawned and stretched. "Think I might hit the sack, Gid," he said, carefully putting his empty can on a coaster. "We've got an early start tomorrow."

"Yeah. Okay, mate. You know where everything is, I think. Help yourself to anything from the kitchen, if you're up before me. And give some thought to another drummer, eh? We really need to get that sorted ASAP."

Charles nodded and stood up. "Sure. We'll think of

someone. Let's just hope Simon has decided not to come and see you. That would make things awkward."

"I just hope he doesn't bump into Abi," Gideon said wryly. "I don't rate his chances if he does. Although I do still have a bad feeling in my stomach about him. I wouldn't put it past him to try to make things difficult for us. I feel I'm just waiting for him to show his hand, but to be honest I have no idea what he could actually do."

"Don't worry," said Charles heartily. "The Simon I saw in New York was a bit of a mess. Apart from his obvious dislike of Abi, I didn't really get any sense of danger from him. He was a bit pathetic, actually." He raised a hand and made his way to the guest room, letting the door swing shut behind him.

Gideon watched him go with a thoughtful look on his face. He ran a hand through his still damp hair and picked up his mobile. Time for a quick call to Abi before he turned in.

****

The hotel bar was quiet, even for a Tuesday night, and Simon was beginning to get very stir crazy. He'd spent the whole day in the hotel, and having watched at least four groups of people leave the bar heading for night clubs, he was feeling very disgruntled. He pushed his chair back with a crash and stalked out of the bar towards the lift, a dark brooding look on his face. He only had to hang on until the story was in the paper, and then he could venture out into society again. As he rode up in the lift, he went over the conversation he'd had earlier in the day with Richard Morrison. The editor had subsequently e-mailed him a copy of the story as it would appear in the paper the next morning, and Simon had been almost shocked at its audacity. It ticked all the boxes he had aimed to fill, but nonetheless, reading it in black and white had made his already rather queasy stomach turn over, and he had broken out into a cold sweat.

When the idea of discrediting Abi had first come to him, he had conjured up a vague idea of the story which would hint at the idea that Natasha was not Gideon's child. The story that would appear in *The National Crier* the next morning was much, much more. It not only implied that Natasha was not Gideon's, but it also delved far deeper into Abi's background, dredging up old stories about her that, to the fairer side of Simon's mind, were probably wholly untrue but made her look very unsavoury.

The lift doors opened on his floor, and he made his way along the richly carpeted corridor to his suite. He flung his jacket onto a chair, kicked off his shoes, and poured himself a whisky. He downed it in one gulp and lay down on the bed with his eyes closed. Maybe he'd gone too far. His eyes snapped open again almost immediately, and he sat up. No, the little bitch deserved it. She had destroyed the band, and consequently his livelihood, and for that she had to suffer. His re-admittance to the band would be the icing on the cake. He rolled off the bed, walked over to the sofa, and sat down, flicking on the television as he did so. He channel-hopped for a few minutes, finally deciding on an old episode of one of his favourite shows to take his mind off things. He groped in his pocket for his cigarettes and was about to pull one out of the packet when he paused, changed his mind, and abandoned the packet on the coffee table. Instead, he walked over to his jacket and extracted a small packet from an inner pocket, along with some rizla papers. He carried them over to the window, flung it open, and rolled himself a joint. He lit it and leaned his elbow on the windowsill, blowing the smoke out onto the street. The sounds of revellers heading out for a night on the town floated up to his ears, and he slammed his hand into the wall in frustration. He was not used to being cooped up in one place for days on end, and he was almost wishing he'd gone to visit his mother for a few days. At least he could have gone out for a walk.

He cast his mind back to the last time he'd seen her. He had a vague recollection she'd thrown him out for some misdemeanour or other. He couldn't remember what and felt sure she would have forgiven him by now. He wondered if he should call her in the morning and maybe spend the next day in Berkshire until the initial hoo-ha about the story had died down. He didn't plan to go and see Gideon until Thursday, or possibly even Friday, so maybe a trip out of town would be a good idea.

He took a final toke on his joint before tossing it outside and pulling the window shut again. He slumped down on the sofa, watched the rest of the programme, then flicked off the television and got ready for bed.

Chapter 15

Wednesday 30th July, 2008

Natasha awoke on Wednesday morning to the sound of a loud hammering on the front door. She lay in bed for a moment or two, the covers pulled up to her chin, wondering what on earth was happening. Then she pulled herself together and jumped out of bed. Running to the window, she peered out. Chris stood on the doorstep, a rolled-up newspaper under his arm and a look of frustration on his face. He lifted his hand to hammer on the door again just as Natasha opened the window and grinned down at him.

"Hello," she said. "What on earth's the matter? It's very early, you know." Chris stared up at her, his eyes full of concern.

"Get your mum," he said briefly, "and let me in."

Natasha's eyebrows shot up, but she withdrew her head, closed the window, and ran down the passage into Abi's room. Her mother was still asleep, her long dark auburn hair spread out across her face and one arm hanging off the edge of the bed. She was snoring gently. Natasha stifled a giggle and crawled onto the bed beside her. She shook her shoulder gently.

"Mum," she whispered. "Mum, wake up!" With a grunt, Abi opened her eyes and stared up at her daughter. She frowned, brushed her hair out of her eyes, and pushed herself up onto one elbow.

"Wassup?" she muttered indistinctly, groping on the bedside table for her phone to see the time. "Is something wrong?"

"Dunno"—Natasha shrugged—"but Chris is at the door in a right state and said I had to get you. Now I must let him in."

She jumped off the bed, ran out of the room, and clattered down the stairs. At the bottom, she unbolted the huge front door and hauled it open. Chris was through the door before she'd finished opening it, going to stand at the bottom of the stairs and impatiently wait for Abi to come down. She appeared at the top, hair dishevelled, wearing only a long white T-shirt belonging to Gideon. She hooked her hair behind her ears and frowned at Chris.

"What on earth's the matter?" she asked in concern, starting down the stairs, her bare feet padding on the polished wood. Chris pulled the rolled-up newspaper from under his arm and brandished it at her.

"This is the matter," he said dramatically. "I take it you haven't seen it yet?"

Abi reached the bottom of the stairs and raised her eyebrows at him. "Until two minutes ago I was fast asleep," she pointed out, holding out her hand for the paper, "and besides, we don't usually read this rubbish."

Chris was watching her carefully as she unfolded it and looked at the front page. There was a long silence.

"Shit," she muttered, her eyes rapidly scanning the page, then turning to the next one. Natasha peered round her and looked at the front page.

"That's me!" she shrieked in dismay. "What on

earth's going on? Mum, what's it say?"

Abi glanced at her, her eyes glinting dangerously. "Chris, put the kettle on. Natasha, get me the phone."

She strode into the conservatory and flung the paper down on the coffee table. Natasha ran up to her, clutching the phone, then snatched up the paper and scurried to the other end of the room with it. She curled up in a chair and started to read the front page. The picture of her riding her pony in the New Forest dominated the page, and underneath the headline ran: *Is this child really the daughter of Gideon Hawk*? She gasped and started to read the body of the text, her mind beginning to reel as the lies jumped off the page and danced in front of her eyes. She nervously turned the page and was confronted by a series of pictures of Abi. aged about fifteen, in various different locations. None of the pictures were flattering, and in one she looked decidedly drunk. Natasha quickly read to the end of the article, then turned anguished eyes on her mother.

Abi was pacing the room, her phone clasped to her ear, talking very fast, and getting louder. Natasha got up and went to join her. Abi glanced at her and put her free arm around her shoulders.

"Yeah, I know," she was saying to the person at the other end. "They even used that picture of New Year's Eve '94 when Judy and I got drunk. They're trying to make out I was a dirty little drunken slut who slept with anyone! How could anyone do this, Gideon? Why would anyone want to hurt us like this?" She paused and listened impatiently, her arm tightening around her daughter's shoulders. "Yeah, but listen, they also got hold of one of my letters to you...I know...They just printed bits of it, so it sounds really suspicious that I hadn't told you I was pregnant before you left." She listened again and then caught her breath. "No...D'you really think he would?...I guess so, but why, Gideon? Why does he hate me so much?" Her voice caught as she held back the tears. Natasha put her arms around her mother's waist and gave her a squeeze. Abi looked down and gave her a watery smile. "I don't know, Gid, what d'you think? You won't be able to go anywhere without being mobbed today...I guess they will. It'll be just like that day in '05..." She managed a grin at the memory. "Maybe Tash and I should get away somewhere for a day or two?" She listened again, her free hand stroking Natasha's tangled hair. "Nice idea... I'll call Judy...It'll mean we won't get to you on Friday. Maybe you can get down to join us?...Yeah, I guess. They'll follow you everywhere, won't they? Is Chas still there?" She moved over to the sofa and sat down, pulling Natasha down beside her. "Oh, good, at least you'll have someone to play with if you get besieged," she said with a chuckle. "Look, I'd better go. Chris is making faces at me. I think he has an idea. Talk to you later, baby. Love you."

She ended the call and tossed her phone onto the sofa beside her. Chris placed a mug of tea in front of her and sat down in the chair opposite.

"You have to get away, as soon as possible," he said emphatically. "The press will be here just like they were last time, only this time it'll be worse. Can you go to Wales again?"

Abi nodded and picked up the phone. "Hope so," she said grimly. "Just going to call Judy." She dialled Judy's number and put the phone up to her ear.

Natasha stared at Chris wide-eyed. "Were you here

when Mum and Dad got besieged before?" she asked curiously.

"Yeah, don't you know the story?" Chris nodded. "Your mum and dad pretended to be me and Judy, and then we pretended to be them, and they managed to get away."

"Oh, yes, of course. I think I did know. I'd forgotten." Natasha looked at him nervously. "Will we have to pretend to be other people this time?"

Chris shook his head. "Not if you're quick enough. The paparazzi aren't here yet—surprisingly—so if you get going soon you'll be okay."

Abi had wandered down to the other end of the room and was deep in an animated conversation with Judy. She picked up the paper Natasha had abandoned on the chair and glanced again at the photo on the front. Her eyes darkened in anger, and she turned round to face her daughter, mouthed "I'm sorry," and then continued her conversation with Judy. When she had finished, she marched purposefully down the room and stopped in front of the other two.

"Right. Judy says we can have the caravan. Luckily, no one's using it this week. She says we're okay until Sunday. Hopefully things will have died down a bit by then." She smiled encouragingly at Natasha. "Let's go and pack some stuff, and then we can get going."

"What can I do to help?" Chris got to his feet, gathered up the mugs, and headed towards the kitchen.

"Keep watch for any strange cars heading this way," Abi said at once. "Although at this time of year that's not so easy. Still, I expect you'd recognise the press, wouldn't you?"

Chris raised a neat eyebrow at her. "Yes, darling, I would. You and Tash go and pack, and I'll keep watch. Would you like to take my car so they won't recognise you so easily?"

Abi paused for a moment. "That's a nice idea," she said thoughtfully, "but I think we'll stick to the 4x4, thanks." She grinned at him over her shoulder as she started up the stairs. "I reckon you just wanted a few days driving my car, didn't you?"

"Got me!" Chris laughed gaily and, following her up the stairs, positioned himself at the landing window, which commanded the best view of the road and any approaching traffic.

****

Caroline Hawk walked out onto the balcony and stretched her arms above her head. They had just passed The Isle of Wight and were about to start the last leg of their journey up Southampton Water to the dock. It had been a lovely two weeks, and she was determined to persuade Roger to make a cruise an annual affair. She was pretty sure that even he had enjoyed most of the trip, especially since he'd got the hang of haggling so well. She sighed and turned back into the bedroom to finish her packing. The morning papers had just been delivered, and she wandered over to the table to glance at them.

"Honestly, Roger, the quality of the newspapers on this boat has taken a nosedive!" she said in surprise, as the first one she picked up proved to be *The National Crier.* "I wouldn't even use this rubbish to line the cat's litter tray." Nonetheless, she glanced at the front page curiously—and emitted a strangled cry. Roger appeared from the bathroom, toothbrush in hand, wiping his face with a towel.

"What're you gabbling on about, Caroline?" he asked with an amused smile, which faded when he saw his wife's ashen face. "Caroline? What is it? Is something wrong?" He moved quickly over to her. She held the paper out to him mutely and groped behind her for a seat to slide into. Roger swore under his breath, and his dark brows came together.

"What on earth... Where did they get this rubbish?" he exploded, scanning down the page and onto the next one rapidly. "This is outrageous, quite preposterous! Heads need to roll!"

Caroline swallowed. "Who's done this, Roger?" she asked, her voice almost a whisper. "Who hates them that much?"

"I rather think it's Abi this is directed at." Roger regarded her solemnly. "Someone who hates Abi. And I think I have an idea..." His mouth compressed into a thin line.

Caroline looked at him, a frown creasing her forehead. "Who? Who could hate Abi that much?" she asked emphatically. "Some ex-girlfriend of Gideon's? He hasn't really had many, has he?"

Roger raised his eyebrows at her. "Think, Caroline," he said patiently. "Who tried to sabotage their relationship?"

Caroline gasped as realisation hit her. "Simon," she said softly.

Roger nodded. "And look—they've actually printed part of one of her letters to Gideon from all those years ago." He scowled at the paper. "Misquoted, probably, and we know Simon still has the letters, don't we?"

"Oh, poor Abi." Caroline jumped to her feet. "She'll be distraught! They're not even together at the moment, are they? Gideon's in London and Abi's at home. Oh, Roger, we must go to her." She caught her husband's arm imploringly. Roger patted her hand and looked down at her affectionately.

"Don't fuss, old thing," he said calmly. "Abi can look after herself. If she has any sense, she'll take the kids somewhere out of reach of the press. That caravan in Wales they used last time should be good. They never did track them there, did they?"

"Yes, that would be good," Caroline agreed. "Do you think she's thought of that? Will she even have seen the paper, do you think? Shall we call her? Shall we call Gideon…?"

"Yes, I expect she's seen the paper." Roger smiled at her. "I expect she'll think to hide, and of course you can call them both if it will make you feel any better. Not much more we can do from here anyway," he said, wandering back to the bathroom to finish cleaning his teeth.

Caroline snatched up her mobile and hurriedly began to dial.

****

Gideon replaced his phone on the table and angrily ran his hands through his hair. He still hadn't seen a copy of the offending paper, but from what Abi had told him, it was a direct assassination of her character and was designed entirely to throw doubt on the paternity of Natasha. His daughter Natasha, whose photograph now apparently adorned the front cover of one of the most obnoxious tabloid newspapers of all time. He went to the window and peered down into the

185

street below. As expected, several vehicles, clearly media-related, were parked opposite, and a number of individuals strung around with cameras were lounging near the entrance to the flats. He muttered an oath, flung out of the room, and burst into the spare bedroom where Charles was still asleep. He grabbed the end of the quilt and pulled sharply. The cover fell to the floor to expose the sleeping Charles, clad only in his boxers, his arms flung across his face and his mouth open.

"Chas," said Gideon loudly. "Get up. We have a problem."

Charles stirred and slowly opened his eyes. He blinked a couple of times, when he saw his friend standing at the end of his bed with a face like thunder, and sat up suddenly.

"Dude," he said in consternation. "Whatever is it? You look dreadful." He swung his legs out of bed and reached for his jeans, which lay abandoned on the floor. As he struggled into them, he stared at Gideon. "Tell me, what's happened?"

Gideon strode over to the window and looked out. "See down there?" He jerked his head sideways. "See those photographers? Those are waiting for me."

Charles joined him at the window and looked at him blankly.

"So?" he asked, confused. "You're bound to be news. You're re-forming the band. The news has probably got out..." He stopped as he saw Gideon's face. "It's not that, is it. What's happened?"

Gideon ran his fingers through his hair again and scowled. "Apparently that cesspit of a tabloid, *The National Crier*, has printed a story about Abi." He paused as Charles gasped. "The object of the story is to

186

throw doubt on the fact that Natasha is my daughter, and to discredit my wife's name."

"Jeez, Gideon!" Charles went pale. "That's awful! Why would they do that? What's Abi ever done to them?" Gideon regarded him silently for a moment, his eyebrows raised. Charles sighed and rolled his eyes. "Simon," he stated simply. "Christ, I never thought he'd go that far. What have they said?"

Gideon turned on his heel and paced the room. "Don't know for sure, but apparently they printed part of one of the letters Abi sent to me back in '95. And we know who has those." He balled his hands into fists and swung round to face Charles. "What really fucks me off," he added through gritted teeth, "is the fact they've put a picture of my daughter on the front of their sodding comic. And pictures of my wife in unflattering poses." Charles raised his eyebrows in surprise. Gideon elaborated. "There's one of her when she and Judy got drunk at New Year's, when we had just started going out. In context it's funny, but in their fucking paper it's…" He viciously kicked the leg of the bed. Charles snatched up his shirt and shrugged it on, rapidly buttoning it up.

"I'll slip out and get a copy of the paper," he offered, sliding his feet into his trainers.

"You'll get mobbed," Gideon said doubtfully, indicating the crowd in the street below with a flick of his head.

"No one'll recognise me," Charles said with confidence. "They'll be looking for you. They don't know I'm staying here, and I'll wear a hat." He suited the action to the word and pulled a tweed deerstalker out of his bag.

Gideon stared impassively at it for a moment, then shrugged. "I won't ask," he said with a shake of his head. "I'm not sure I really want to know. Okay, then, but try not to be seen. My dad's going to be pretty pissed off that they've tracked me to this flat, actually. It's supposed to be off limits."

Charles raised his eyebrows. "Why?" he asked in surprise.

"Oh, just stuff to do with dad's job," Gideon muttered vaguely. "But I don't think it counts so much now he's retired. Pity."

Charles stared at him for a moment, then pulled the deerstalker on, grabbed his leather jacket, and left the flat with a quick wave.

Gideon wandered back into the living room and flung himself down onto the chesterfield. He reached for the remote control and flicked on the television. With a sigh he went to Sky News and prepared himself for the possibility of being confronted by pictures of his wife and child. None was forthcoming, so he changed over to the BBC News channel and was unpleasantly rewarded. Filling the screen behind the news reader was the picture of Natasha that currently adorned the front of *The National Crier*. Gideon caught his breath and his eyebrows came together in a dark scowl. He turned up the sound.

"Natasha Hawk, aged twelve, is the daughter Gideon Hawk only discovered just over two years ago. Until that time Natasha had been living in a children's home in Kent, apparently unbeknownst even to her mother Abigail. This morning information published in *The National Crier* throws doubt on the paternity of Natasha, claiming her mother had numerous sexual partners in her teens. The article also suggests that Abigail did know Natasha was in the children's home and that she had in fact put her there herself..."

In a fit of temper, Gideon hurled the remote across the room, smashing it against the wall, then lunged towards the television and pulled the plug out. He snatched up his phone and viciously punched at the keys.

****

Simon stared at the paper in horror. What on earth had he done? His original idea had spiralled out of control and had now appeared in the gutter press as a sordid, nasty little story about his best friend's wife and child. He rephrased the thought in his mind. His ex-best friend. His idea had been to get Gideon to begin to doubt Abi's integrity and thus be more amenable to Simon's re-entry into his life. Having read the finished article, Simon began to feel a touch of sympathy not only for Gideon but also for Abi. Even he had to admit she didn't deserve that. The paper had completely assassinated her character by using and misusing the information he'd provided. They had only quoted parts of the letter she wrote, taking them out of context. They'd published the photographs of Abi as a teenager, also completely out of context, making her appear as a drunken slut. And, worst of all, they'd completely fabricated the story that Abi herself had put Natasha in the children's home. Where they dredged that idea up from, Simon had no idea. His blood ran cold as he imagined Gideon's reaction to the article.

He ran a sweaty hand through his curly hair and debated his best move. He still hoped the article would sow even a tiny seed of doubt in Gideon's mind, and in his own rather twisted and deeply disturbed mind he could still visualise a situation where Gideon would welcome him back into the band, possibly even as a saviour. He decided to cling to that thought, and in the meantime he would let the dust settle for a day or so and go and visit his mother. He had attempted to call her twice but had had no reply, so he'd decided he would just turn up and surprise her. He still couldn't remember what it was she was pissed with him about, but he shrugged and told himself she would have forgiven him after such a long time. He'd racked his brains but couldn't remember exactly when it was he'd seen her last. A tiny part of his still rational brain shouted a warning to him that maybe it was time to take stock of his lifestyle and cut down the drinking and drugs, but he conveniently managed to ignore it as he crammed his belongings back into his bags in preparation for the visit to Berkshire.

Chapter 16

Half an hour after Chris had woken them so unexpectedly, Abi and Natasha were dressed, packed, and ready to go. So far no suspicious-looking vehicles had appeared in the vicinity, and they decided they were safe to leave.

"I'm surprised no one has turned up here yet," Abi said with a frown as they loaded the back of the 4x4 with enough clothes and food to last them for several days. "I really thought we would have seen someone by now."

Chris flicked his hair back. "Do they maybe think you're in London with Gideon?" he hazarded.

"Shouldn't think so." Abi shook her head. "He's been on the news several times already, obviously never with me. Maybe they're not coming. Maybe we don't need to run at all."

She glanced up the track towards the main road, shielding her eyes from the morning sun. As she did, two large vehicles approached from the direction of Penzance, slowing as they reached the end of the track. They both turned down, pulled into the first passing place, and turned their engines off. Almost immediately a third vehicle appeared at great speed along the main road, screeched to a halt as it passed the turning, reversed rapidly, turned down the track, and joined the first two in the passing place, pulling well up onto the grassy verge.

Abi glanced at Chris and raised her eyebrows. "And so it begins," she muttered with a slight grin.

Chris sprang into action, his eyes sparkling. "I have a plan, sweetie," he said at once. "I learnt well from Judy last time. You two get in the car and get ready to go. As you'll see, I brought my own vehicle," he indicated his red estate car parked beside Abi's 4x4. "I shall drive up the track directly behind you and then park across it to prevent them from getting out, and you can drive off towards Penzance as fast as you can!"

"Impressive!" Abi laughed, locking the house behind them and ushering Natasha into their car. "But that would really only work if they parked where they have. How did you know they would?"

Chris grinned and tossed his head. "I had no idea, darlin'," he said, with a twinkle in his eye. "I just made up the plan on the spot. But it should work, so get ready to drive fast once you get past them."

He jumped into his car and started the engine. Abi followed suit, and the two cars drove slowly up the track, keeping close together. As they approached the parked vehicles, several reporters appeared, cameras flashing and microphones at the ready. They peered into the 4x4, getting far too close for Abi's comfort. A microphone was thrust towards her window, and the weathered face of a seasoned reporter appeared behind it.

"What d'you think of the news, Abi?" he shouted. "What does Gideon think? Is Natasha his, or are the rumours true? Where is Gideon?"

Abi put her foot on the accelerator, the wheels spun some small stones up at the reporter, and he stepped backwards hurriedly. Natasha leaned over and pressed the button to open the window.

"Of course Gideon's my dad," she yelled, sticking two fingers up at him. "You leave us alone. Go and bother someone else."

Abi quickly raised the window again and sped up.

"Tash, don't let them get to you," she muttered through clenched teeth, watching in the mirror as Chris closed the gap between her car and his. As he passed the parked cars, he turned his wheel hard to the right and immediately pulled across the narrow track, blocking it completely while Abi floored the accelerator and shot off to the left onto the main road, with a loud toot on the horn as she went. Natasha turned round in her seat and waved enthusiastically at Chris. She laughed and turned back to her mother.

"He's done it!" She giggled. "They're all shouting at him to move, and he's just sitting there."

"I hope he's okay," Abi murmured, glancing in the mirror. "They can get pretty nasty sometimes."

Natasha twisted round again and strained to see the road block. "He's still there," she said. "They wouldn't dare do anything bad to him."

"I guess you're right," Abi agreed cautiously, "but tell you what: call him and make sure he's okay. Use my phone."

Natasha picked up Abi's phone and dialled Chris's number. She pressed it close to her ear in an attempt to block out the noise of the engine, and waited for him to answer.

"Hello, Chris, are you okay?" she shouted down the phone. Her face broke into a grin, and she mouthed to Abi, "He's fine," before speaking to Chris again.

"How long d'you think you can stay there?...Ooh, really?...Okay, I'll tell Mum. We'll call you when we get there. Bye-bye." She disconnected the call and placed the phone back on the dashboard. "He says they're shouting abuse at him but haven't threatened him at all." She grinned. "He reckons he can stick it out for about another ten minutes, and he wants us to call him when we get there."

Abi nodded, her face serious as she sped along the A30 towards Penzance. "That should give us time to get well ahead," she said. "Then I think we'll cut across country rather than stay on the A30. They're most likely to assume we're going to London to join Dad, or possibly Newbury to Judy or my dad, so they'll probably head up the M5 to Bristol and then across on the M4." She flashed a quick grin at Natasha. "So we'll cut across to the A39 and take the Atlantic Highway along the north coast. It's going to take much longer, but by the time we finally join the M5 the paparazzi should be well ahead of us. You up for that?"

"That sounds cool." Natasha gave a little wriggle of excitement. "This is fun already! So long as we can stop for food."

"Trust you." Abi smiled. "Of course we'll stop for food. Much easier if we go this way."

Natasha grinned at her and bounced on her seat. "Shall I programme the SATNAV?" she asked helpfully.

"Okay, if you like. Tell it we want to go through Barnstaple and Minehead, and see what it comes up with."

Natasha leaned forward and started to input the required data in the built-in satellite navigation system in Abi's car. After a couple of minutes she sat back in satisfaction.

"It's going to take us six hours and fifty-nine minutes," she announced proudly.

Abi wrinkled her nose. "Really?" She sighed. "Let's see if we can shave a bit off that, shall we?" She put her foot to the floor as they sped up along a nice straight stretch of road. "It's going to take us the best part of an hour to get to the A39 turning," she added, "so I need to keep the speed up until then, just in case Chris can't keep them occupied as long as he hoped. Hold tight, Tasha!"

****

The taxi dropped Simon right outside his mother's house, and he leapt out, paid the driver without a word of thanks, and stood for a moment on the pavement staring up at his childhood home. He shuddered at the sight of the old-fashioned red brick monstrosity where his mother still chose to live. It annoyed him that she had made no effort to move to somewhere more salubrious, even preferring to stay there alone after his father had died. Such was his character that it never occurred to him she might be financially strapped and therefore forced to stay put. That he could have bought her a large house anywhere she wanted also didn't occur to him, and with a disgruntled sigh he heaved his bag over his shoulder and walked heavily up the path. He had long ago lost his house key, so he pressed the bell and waited. Nothing happened, so he pressed it again, listening as it pealed loudly in the hallway. Still nothing happened. Simon scowled. She had clearly gone out shopping. He would need to wait. He hesitated for a moment, then walked across the garden, down the side of the house, and round to the back. He stood back and stared to see if any of the windows had been left open, but all were securely fastened and the house had a very empty feel about it. He muttered an oath under his breath and walked back round to the front. He had one last try on the doorbell, ending with a loud knock on the frosted glass panel. Still nothing happened, and he stepped back and stared up at the empty windows, wondering where to go to wait for her. He was just making his way back down the path when a voice halted him in his tracks.

"Simon? Is that you?".

He turned and found his mother's neighbour Mrs. Ellis smiling uncertainly at him from her gate.

He gave a brief nod. "Yes. Hello, Mrs. Ellis. My mother seems to be out," he said, attempting a smile.

Mrs. Ellis shook her head. "No, dear, she's away. On holiday." She beamed at him. "Did you hope to surprise her?"

Simon stared at her in amazement. "On holiday?" he repeated. His mother never went away. "Where has she gone?"

"Spain," came the gleeful reply. "She went with her sister. Should be back this evening, I believe. It will have done her so much good. She really needed a break."

A break from what, Simon wondered uncharitably. All she ever did was housework and shopping. How hard could that be? He sighed and dropped his bag on the ground.

"Right," he said at last. "I'll not be staying here, then." He paused and looked hopefully at Mrs. Ellis. "Unless you have a spare key, that is?" he asked, attempting another smile.

"Ooh, no, dear, she doesn't hand out spare keys. Do you not have one any more? Mind you, I seem to remember she changed the locks not long ago, so it probably wouldn't work if you did have one..." Her voice dwindled as if she had suddenly remembered something, and her face flushed.

"What?" Simon asked suspiciously. "What's wrong? Why did she change the locks?"

Mrs. Ellis pursed her lips and stared at him, her look suddenly a little hostile, and shook her head.

"I really couldn't say," she replied shortly. "Well, I must get on. Sorry you missed her. I'll tell her you called." She turned and walked quickly back up her path and into the house, slamming the door shut behind her.

Simon watched her go, his mouth open in surprise. He frowned. What would have made his mother change her locks? And why wouldn't Mrs. Ellis tell him? A nasty little thought niggled at the back of his mind, but he dismissed it immediately, slung his bag over his shoulder again, and set off up the road towards the town. Since he was here, he might as well check into a hotel for the night while he planned his next move regarding Gideon. Also, Mrs. Ellis seemed to think his mother would be back that evening. If so, maybe he should try and see her the next day. Find out about the lock change issue. As he made his way along the quiet suburban road, he could feel the net curtains twitching and sense the whispered comments passing across garden walls.

He turned into the next road and was just crossing, in order to cut through the park and into town the shorter way, when he heard his name being called. He turned in surprise and saw a middle-aged lady, her untidy blonde hair caught back in a loose bun, beckoning to him from the gate of one of the houses. He hesitated, then started towards her, realising as he approached that it was Mary Cromwell, the mother of Abi's best friend Judy. His heart sank, and he considered ignoring her and going on his way, but she had fixed him with such a fierce stare he felt sure she would follow him if he did, so he turned and slowly crossed back over the road to join her.

"Simon," she said, her voice sharp, "are you anything to do with this?" She brandished a copy of *The National Crier* at him.

He stopped in front of her and attempted to look shocked. "What?" he asked.

Mary thrust the paper under his nose and jabbed her finger at the picture of Natasha.

"This," she said, "as you very well know. There's a scurrilous story about Abi in this disgraceful paper, and I suspect you may have supplied them with the information. They quote from one of Abi's letters to Gideon, and I know they suspect you took those." She stepped closer and scowled at him. "Well?"

"Nothing to do with me, Mrs. Cromwell," Simon stuttered, adding insincerely, "this looks dreadful! Poor Abi."

Mary regarded him suspiciously and snatched the paper back. "Hmm. Well, I'm not so sure. And what are you doing here? Are you visiting your mother?"

"Trying to." Simon nodded sullenly. "But she's away."

Mary stared at him again and folded her arms

across her chest. "So you'll be going back to…where?" she asked, narrowing her eyes.

Simon shrugged. "She's back tonight, so I'll stay locally and see her tomorrow," he said, hitching his bag further onto his shoulder and beginning to edge away from her. As he crossed the road to the park, he was uncomfortably aware of her eyes following him.

****

Judy was humming to herself as she cleared the breakfast dishes off the table and tried to fit them all into the dishwasher. Finally giving up, she piled the excess ones on the draining board and started the machine. Then, wiping her hands on a tea towel, she popped her head round the door of the conservatory and checked on the children.

As usual, Tommy was building a train track, his tongue protruding from his mouth with concentration. Sabrina was busily employed taking all the clothes off her dolls, and little Oliver was sitting in the middle of the playpen surrounded by wooden blocks with which he was attempting to build a tower. Judy grinned affectionately at them all, then moved back into the kitchen, made herself a cup of coffee, carried it into the living room, and sank onto the sofa with a sigh. She was at the feeling-sick stage of her pregnancy, and, curiously, coffee seemed to be the only thing that cured it. She took a grateful sip and reached for the TV remote just as the phone rang. She leaned over and picked it up.

"Hello?…Oh, hi, Mum. Have you heard about Abi?" She paused, took another sip of coffee, and listened, her eyes widening in surprise. "No, I haven't seen it yet. Which paper is it in again?…Mum, that's a dreadful paper! What are you doing with that anyway? Abi called me early this morning to ask if they could borrow the caravan for a few days…Yes, I know. I told her till the weekend…She didn't tell me any details. She said they were in a hurry to avoid the press and would call me later to explain everything. I was going to go and get a paper in a bit. What does it say?" Her eyes darkened as she listened to her mother speak, and she urgently pressed the remote to activate the television. "Mum…Hang on…Did they really suggest that? How could anyone even consider it? Where on earth did they get…" She stopped as her mother continued speaking. She glanced up at the television and selected the BBC News channel. As she watched, a picture of Natasha appeared behind the presenter, followed by a picture of Abi at about fifteen. Judy gasped as she recognised the photo. "Mum…" She interrupted her mother's flow. "It's on the news! There's a picture of Abi from that New Year's party you had. She looks dreadful! Who's done this? Who hates her this much?…" Her eyes widened again as her mother spoke, and she sat up suddenly, slopping some of her coffee out of the mug and onto the sofa. "Oh, my god! Surely even Simon isn't that evil? Oh, Mum, this is dreadful…I'll bet he denied it!…I'm not sure his mother'll be pleased to see him…Well, I guess she may not know anything about what he did, but…" She tailed off again, watching the television as several pictures of Abi cycled past, none of them flattering and all of them making her look like something she wasn't. Judy felt the bile rise in her throat. Cutting her mother off in mid flow, she said, "Mum, sorry, I must go now. I need to get a copy of that…filth, and then try to call Abi. She must be devastated. I think she was too fired up and angry this morning for it really to have sunk in. Speak to you later."

She disconnected the call and laid the phone down beside her.

****

When Charles returned to the flat with a copy of *The National Crier*, he found Gideon deep in conversation on his mobile. His face was thunderous, and his free hand was balled into a white-knuckled fist at his side. Charles raised his eyebrows at him and was rewarded with a ferocious scowl.

"I'm coming down there," snapped Gideon into the phone, then disconnected the call and flung it down onto the sofa.

"We going somewhere?" Charles asked mildly, handing the paper to his friend.

"I am," Gideon growled, running a hand through his hair. "I'm going to kill the editor of that fucking paper. You can stay here."

He glanced down at *The National Crier* and went very still. As he stared at the front page, with its grainy picture of his daughter innocently riding her pony in the New Forest, his already dark face tightened and his startling blue eyes flashed dangerously. He scanned the page quickly, then turned it over, to be confronted by the pictures of Abi. He sank into the nearest chair and read rapidly through the article, his eyes becoming more dangerously narrowed with every word he read. Finally he finished reading, neatly folded the paper, placed it on the coffee table, and sat staring up at the ceiling, his mouth set in a thin line and his brows drawn together.

"I am also," he enunciated carefully, "going to kill Simon. Can we find out where he is, Chas?"

"That's a bit of a teaser." Charles frowned. "If he's in London, he's probably staying at one of the most expensive hotels, but if not, then I've no idea. D'you think he'd go and see his mother?"

Gideon narrowed his eyes. "You were going to stay at The Ritz," he said. "Try there, see if he had the same idea. Doubt he'd go to Newbury. He never cared enough about his parents, even in the early days." He stood up and walked to the window. "Christ, how many of those fuckers are there? Did you get past them all right?"

"Just pulled the hat down and kept walking. But you'd never manage it. Where's your car?"

"I'm not using that." Gideon grinned despite himself. "It's got a personalised number plate. Dead giveaway. Much too flashy, too." He walked to the other side of the room and peered down at the back of the building. "Jesus, there are some round here too! Hmm, that puts the fire escape out of use." He frowned and walked back to the front window. The reporters were all congregated around the front gate, some of them leaning on the wall surrounding the small front garden, some of them by their cars, but all of them closely watching the building. As Gideon's face appeared at the window, several cameras flashed, and he stepped back in annoyance. "Think I might have to get some help with this," he muttered, retrieving his mobile from the sofa and dialling a number. "Dad? Hi, got a problem…Oh, you saw it? Don't get me started… Yeah, I know. Thing is, we're besieged in the flat… Paparazzi are outside, and I need to go out. Can you call someone?" He paused and nodded as his father spoke. "Well, I thought so too. I was a bit surprised they found me, actually. Sorry about that. Can you still call them?" He listened again, his face serious and his left hand clenching and unclenching at his side. "Dad, you're a star...Thanks for that. Are you home yet?... Oh, I'm sorry. Didn't mean to spoil your holiday." He grinned as his father answered. "Did she really? Well, tell her thank you. I could do with her when I go to see that bastard Richard Morrison." He almost spat the words out, and his eyes sparked dangerously. "But thanks, Dad. I'll hang on here, then, until it's sorted. See you in a day or so." He flung the phone back on the sofa and turned to Charles. "Dad's sorting it," he said casually. "They should be gone within the hour."

Charles stared at him impassively, his head tilted back and his eyes thoughtful. "Would you tell me, if I asked you how?" he said eventually.

"No." Gideon shook his head with an apologetic shrug. "He's got connections. They'll only work here at the flat, though. I'll still get mobbed everywhere else." He paused and walked over to the window again. "But at least it means I can get out of here."

He stalked into the bedroom and returned carrying a pair of socks, his leather jacket, and his baseball boots. He sat down on the chesterfield and smiled ruefully at Charles.

"Don't think we're gonna get much recording done today," he said, bending down and pulling on a black sock. "I'm going straight to Canary Wharf as soon as I can leave safely. You try and track Simon down." His face darkened as he thought of his erstwhile friend. "What the fuck was he thinking?" he muttered half to himself.

Charles watched him, chewing on his lip. "If I know Simon," he began, "I reckon he'll come and see you in a day or so." Gideon looked up and raised a surprised eyebrow. "This whole story... Its main purpose seems to be to throw doubt on Natasha's paternity, yes?" Gideon nodded, his face wary. "Well, if his mind's working the way I think it is, he'll be hoping you start to have doubts yourself, and then he'll roll up and be sympathetic, no doubt hoping you'll forgive him for hiding Abi's letters."

Gideon stared at him in disbelief. "You mean he actually thinks I'll thank him for trying to save me from her?"

Charles nodded. "Yeah, I reckon that's his plan. He was definitely odd when I met him in New York. Odd and desperate."

Gideon was silent for a moment, digesting this latest information. Eventually he looked up at Charles, a tiny smile playing around his lips.

"Then I'll play him at his own game," he said, his blue eyes glinting. "I'll let him believe I do have doubts, and in doing so I'll draw him in and eventually get a full confession." He pulled on his other sock viciously, slid his feet into his shoes, and looked up at Charles. "I'm still going to Canary Wharf to kill Richard Morrison, though," he said darkly.

Chapter 17

Judy laid down the phone and sat silently for a moment, staring at the wall. She had finally managed to speak to Abi and had got a better idea of their plans. She arranged to go and join them at the caravan, taking Oliver with her, on either Friday or Saturday, depending on how things went. Abi had still been more angry than upset about the article, and Judy hoped she'd stay that way for the time being. She herself had managed to get a copy of *The National Crier* and had nearly cried when she read the whole story. The sight of little Natasha adorning the front page of such a disreputable paper tore at her heart, and she'd felt an almost uncontrollable desire to do damage to whoever had set the whole thing in motion. The thought that it might be Simon—almost certainly was Simon, she corrected herself—was too much to bear. She'd known he could be vindictive, but this was just plain evil.

She got slowly to her feet and went to make another cup of coffee. The children were being very quiet, and Judy peeped into the conservatory to see what they were up to. Tommy had completed his train track and was sitting cross-legged in the middle, making each of his engines crash in turn. Oliver was fast asleep in the middle of the playpen, his thumb stuck firmly in his mouth. And Sabrina was busy mixing the pieces from two jigsaws together. Judy grinned to herself, then crept back into the kitchen and left them to it. She would sort out the jigsaws later. At least they were all happy.

She went into the living room, switched on the television, and sank down onto the sofa. The news was still reporting the story, much to Judy's surprise—surely something more important had happened in the world—and was showing a shot of a group of reporters crowded around the entrance to a large town house in London. She turned up the sound.

"...although no one has yet appeared out of the flat, reports that Gideon Hawk is inside have been backed up by the sight of someone at the window. The flat belongs to Hawk's father, and it's believed Gideon is staying there alone while he records his new album. The recording studio in St John's Wood confirm that Hawk has not been there yet today." The presenter suddenly pressed a hand to her earpiece, and a look of surprise crossed her face. "Oh, some information just in... It seems the press are all now moving away from the flat. At present the reason is not obvious, although a number of unmarked police cars have arrived on the scene, and some heated discussions seem to be going on."

Judy frowned and sipped her coffee. She was fairly sure Gideon was still in the flat, so why would the press be leaving? She watched as, one by one, the vehicles drove away from outside the flat, and a couple of men in dark suits positioned themselves at the end of the road. The presenter was still talking.

"...with the last of the press vehicles having now left the road. There's still no clue as to the reason for their removal. We'll keep you updated as more information comes in. Our reporter in the South West was also foiled in his attempt to speak to Hawk's wife, Abigail, who was seen leaving her home in Cornwall early this morning with her daughter Natasha. The press were prevented from following their car by an impromptu roadblock, apparently created by a family friend. The whereabouts of Mrs. Hawk is not currently known."

The presenter moved on to the next item, and Judy muted the sound. She considered the curious turn of events. She knew Gideon's father had some sort of government connections, and the only thing she could imagine was that he had somehow managed to get the press called off. She smirked to herself—how nice to have connections. Abi had certainly chosen well there! Her mind flitted back to her conversation with her mother. She had mentioned she'd seen Simon in Newbury, and Judy wondered if she should let either Abi or Gideon know he was in England. She decided she probably should, and picking up her phone she sent a quick text to Gideon.

"Mum saw Simon in Newbury. Thought you ought to know. Hope you're ok. J. x"

She laid her phone down again and finished her coffee. It was certainly never dull being friends with the Hawks!

****

Gideon leapt out of the taxi, thrust a twenty-pound note at the driver, muttering, "Wait here, I won't be long," and then strode into the building, a thunderous look on his face.

He marched up to the reception desk and glowered at the smiling girl.

207

"*The National Crier?*" he barked.

"T-twenty-sixth floor," she managed, her eyes wide with shocked recognition.

Gideon nodded curtly and weaved his way over to join the crowd waiting for the lift. As the doors opened, he moved forward and found himself crushed into the small space with twenty other people, some of whom seemed to have recognised him. A small thin secretary with blonde hair tied tightly back in a ponytail gazed up at him.

"You're Gideon Hawk, aren't you?" she asked, blushing under his ferocious stare. Gideon nodded briefly, his expression softening. The girl smiled shyly and thrust a notebook and pen in front of him. "Can I have your autograph, please?"

Gideon took a deep breath and summoned up a smile. "Sure." He took the pen and scribbled his signature across the page, ending with a kiss.

The girl giggled and held the book against her chest. "Thank you," she whispered.

The lift stopped at the twenty-sixth floor and Gideon squeezed out between the other occupants, nodding briefly to his fan. As the doors closed behind him, he made his way along the corridor towards the well-signposted offices of *The National Crier*. He burst through the double doors and found himself at one end of a large newspaper office. The girl seated at the reception desk leapt to her feet and looked nervously over her shoulder.

"Mr. Hawk!" she exclaimed, panic showing on her overly made-up face.

"Where's Morrison?" Gideon snapped at her, scanning the room. The girl ran round to the front of her desk and stood before him, still looking around her.

"He's not here," she said, shaking her head. "He's...umm...he's had to go out to cover a story."

Gideon raised an eyebrow, pushed past her, and walked rapidly down the huge office towards the glass-fronted room at the end. He could just make out the top of two heads close together behind the glass, and he was fairly sure one of them was Richard Morrison.

"Mr. Hawk, you can't go in there..." The receptionist teetered after him on her skyscraper heels, frantically beckoning to someone across the room. "I told you, Mr. Morrison is out..." Gideon reached the door, glanced briefly back at her, and pushed it open.

The editor was deep in conversation with a hard-faced woman whose hands were gesticulating wildly as she related some anecdote to him. They both looked up in surprise when Gideon burst in. Richard Morrison sighed and indicated to the woman with a toss of his head that she should leave. She got to her feet and sauntered past Gideon with a knowing smirk on her face. Ignoring her, he marched over to Morrison's desk, leaned forward, and placed both hands fist down on the mahogany surface.

"What the fuck're you playing at, Morrison?" he snarled, his eyes as hard as flint. "No one slags off my wife with filthy lies, and no one plays fast and loose with my daughter's photograph." He stood up straight and walked menacingly around the desk until he was towering over Morrison. "Who paid you to do this?"

"I pay people for the stories, not the other way around," Richard Morrison sneered, with an unpleasant laugh. "And believe me, the person who gave me this was very keen that it be made public."

"And who was that?" Gideon asked dangerously, his fists clenching at his sides. Richard Morrison leaned back in his chair and regarded his visitor calmly.

"Oh, Gideon, you know better than that! I'm not going to reveal my sources to you, am I?" he mocked, lifting his legs onto his desk and crossing them at the ankles. Gideon was moving threateningly when the door burst open and two heavily built men in dark suits rushed in.

Richard Morrison glanced up at them. "Ah, Jake, Phil, see Mr. Hawk out, will you?" he said with a grin. "And make sure he doesn't return."

The taller of the two men approached Gideon and took hold of his arm. Gideon shook him off violently and strode towards the door.

"Get your hands off me," he snapped. "I'll go. But you haven't heard the last of this, Morrison. I'll see you and your fucking rag brought down."

He flung the other man aside and strode back down the long office and out the double doors at the end. Instead of going to the lifts, he headed straight for the stairs and began to run swiftly down them. After four flights, his pace slowed, and he paused on the landing to compose himself better. The fact that he'd been prevented from venting his anger physically on Morrison rankled with him, and he felt the need to do some damage. He leant back against the cold stone wall of the stairwell and closed his eyes. He really needed to calm down before he ventured out into society again.

By the time he reached ground level he'd finally begun to unwind. He walked straight back out to where his taxi was still waiting and threw himself into the back seat.

"Back to Belgravia, please," he said shortly, leaning back and closing his eyes. He was extremely frustrated and felt he'd got nowhere. He also realised just how annoyed Abi would be if she knew what he'd just done. He really needed to control his temper a bit better. Not so long ago he would have got himself into serious trouble in the same situation. He would probably have ended up smashing Morrison's office and getting arrested. At least Abi had rubbed off to a certain extent. He hadn't expected the editor to tell him his source, but he was still convinced it was Simon, and he was at a loss what to do next. As he pondered the problem, his mobile bleeped, announcing the arrival of a text. He fished it out of his pocket and peered at it. As he read Judy's message about Simon, his face darkened again, and he punched in a brief reply. *"Thanks, Judy. Useful to know."*

So Simon was definitely in England. He smiled mirthlessly to himself. He would be ready and waiting for him.

****

Arthur stared sadly at the newspaper as it lay on the kitchen table in front of him. His neighbour had taken great pleasure in telling him what was in it, and he'd popped along to the local shop to get a copy for himself, praying she'd been exaggerating in her description of the article. Sadly, she hadn't been, and he sat down heavily and put his head in his hands. Abi didn't deserve that. And to put an innocent twelve-year-old child on the front page was unforgivable. He read the article again slowly, taking in every word, his heart clenching as he imagined how his daughter must be feeling. He found it hard to imagine anyone who hated her enough to print such lies, and he shook his head in disbelief. He could also imagine how Gideon must be feeling. Although he didn't know him very well, he felt extremely sorry for him and dearly wished he could do something to help. He sighed heavily. What could he do to help anyone? He was just a useless old man, beaten down by the years of living with his wife and weighed down by the guilt of his actions towards his daughter.

No, he couldn't help anyone.

****

Abi and Natasha eventually arrived at the caravan site at Llangennith at six in the evening. They'd taken it fairly slowly, after their speedy start, and had included quite a lengthy stop for lunch and a brief shopping trip on the way. As they drove along the narrow road leading to the site, Abi turned to Natasha.

"Made it," she said with a grin. "And I don't think we've been followed."

Natasha stretched her legs out as far as she could and yawned. "Good," she said decisively, "'cause I'm not going anywhere else!"

Abi laughed and slowed down as they approached the entrance. The gate was no longer manned for the evening, so they drove straight through and parked up while Abi ran into the shop to collect the key for the caravan and the remote control that operated the barrier to the caravan section. Judy had phoned ahead and asked them to keep them for her.

Ten minutes later they were parked outside the van, busily heaving their luggage out of the car.

"Mum," puffed Natasha, lugging a large canvas bag towards the door, "just how long are we staying?"

"Who knows?" Abi regarded her solemnly.

"Depends how long the furore about the story goes on."

Her face darkened as she remembered the lies that had been printed about her and Natasha, and she swung the large suitcase containing her mother's memories out of the car viciously. She followed Natasha into the caravan and deposited the case in the middle of the living area. Natasha had put the other bags in the two bedrooms and returned to the car for the boxes of food.

Abi stood and looked around her. The caravan held such memories for her these days. The few days she and Gideon had spent there in November '05 were as fresh in her mind as if they'd happened the week before. During those days her whole life changed beyond recognition, and the memories of that time were almost palpable.

Natasha came crashing in through the door, her arms full with a cardboard box of food. She dumped it on the worktop with a grunt and turned to her mother.

"Am I doing this all on my own, or are you coming to help?" she asked, pursing her lips in annoyance.

Abi guiltily followed her out to the car. Natasha was peering into the next box, a frown on her face.

"Mum, do we really need all this? It looks like we're staying for a fortnight!" she asked in exasperation.

Abi picked up the box with a grin. "Unless you want to live on tinned chilli and crisps, then yes, we do need it," she said firmly, kicking the caravan door open with her foot and depositing her box in the kitchen area. She heard Natasha slam the back of the car shut and struggle in through the door carrying two pairs of green Wellingtons.

"You're very pessimistic, Mum. It's nearly August.

We should be needing our bikinis, not our wellies."

"This is Wales," Abi said, continuing to unpack her box of food. "What d'you fancy for dinner tonight?"

Natasha had gone into the smaller bedroom and was bouncing on the bed.

"Jacket potatoes with cheese and beans," she said promptly, puffing slightly.

"Really?" Abi sounded surprised. "We've got pizza."

Natasha leapt off the bed and joined her mother. "No. I saw the potatoes and have been thinking about them ever since. Is that okay?" she asked, looking up at Abi with big eyes.

"'Course it is." Abi laughed, delving into the bag and pulling out the required ingredients. "I'll get them on right away. It's been a long day. Might be good to have an early night."

Natasha delved into the other box and pulled out some cans of cola. She put them into the fridge, then wandered back into the bedroom to sort out her bed.

"Can we read the next bit of Pauline's diary tonight?" she called.

"Aren't you too tired?" Abi asked as she popped the potatoes into the oven. Natasha's curly head appeared around the bedroom door.

"Nope," she said with a wide grin. "I can't wait to see what happens next. Can you?"

"I guess not," Abi admitted. "Okay, then, just a little bit more. From the sound of the weather forecast, tomorrow's going to be raining, so we can read loads then."

An hour later, both showered and dressed in pyjamas, Abi and Natasha were tucking into their jacket potatoes in front of the television. Natasha flicked through the channels, stopping only when she saw a picture of her mother flash up onto the screen. She turned up the sound.

"…whose whereabouts are not known at present. It is thought Abigail Hawk and her daughter left their home in Cornwall early this morning and travelled to an unknown destination. Gideon Hawk is currently in London, staying at the Belgravia flat owned by his father, Roger. Gideon has also been keeping a low profile today and has been unavailable for comment. Our correspondent James Arnott is in Belgravia now. James, any more news?"

The presenter fell silent as the picture changed to that of a rather damp young man standing on a street corner in London. He pulled the collar of his jacket up, and put his microphone to his mouth.

"No, Fiona, no more news from here, I'm afraid. As you know, earlier in the day the press were moved on from outside the flat, and a roadblock has since been placed at the entrance to the road. It's not known exactly who ordered the roadblock. It's believed Gideon Hawk left the flat for a couple of hours this afternoon, and it's been suggested he went to Canary Wharf, but that has still to be confirmed."

The picture went back to the studio, and the female presenter smiled tightly. "So no more news about the big story of the day, Gideon Hawk and the doubt over the paternity of his daughter Natasha. We'll bring you more news as it comes in. In Edinburgh this morn…"

Natasha muted the sound and tossed the remote onto the floor.

"Why are they doing this?" she muttered, scowling

at her mother.

"I don't think it's a 'they.' " Abi sighed. "I think it's all Simon's doing. If your father went to Canary Wharf like they said, he probably went to see Richard Morrison, the editor of *The National Crier*." She paused and a wry grin crossed her face. "He was obviously thwarted in his mission, or we'd be hearing about Mr. Morrison being dangled from the window, or something equally delightful."

Natasha managed a small smile. "Dad does have a bit of temper, doesn't he?" She giggled. "I bet he's mad as hell."

"He's not the only one," murmured Abi darkly, getting up and switching the television off. "Now, you clear away the plates, and I'll get the suitcase."

Chapter 18

Friday 14ᵗʰ July, 1950

"Pauline, come on!" called Joan impatiently, heaving open the tall wire-covered gate that led to the chicken run. "We've still got all the eggs to collect, and then Aunt Maureen wants us to bake the bread."

The twins had been in Norfolk for three weeks, and Maureen Holmes was working them hard. Joan was actually quite enjoying it, but Pauline was finding it very taxing, and her increasing size was making everything much more of an effort. Maureen was strict and a hard task mistress, but she was kind and made sure they were well fed and had a comfortable place to sleep. In their time off, they were allowed to venture into the village or go for a walk along the beach. So far they'd kept themselves to themselves, but both girls hadn't failed to notice the attention one of the younger farmhands had been giving them. Every time they walked down the lane and he was on the tractor, he would wave energetically to them, and if they came across him in the farmyard, he would give them a cheery smile and greeting. Pauline knew Joan, in particular, was touched by his attention, and she had noted with interest how her sister would flush every time they encountered the young man. As she puffed across the farmyard to join her at the chicken run, she decided to broach the subject.

"I'm here, Joanie," she said with a sigh, brushing her hair out of her eyes with one hand and scooping up an egg-collecting basket with the other. "Let's do this really quickly. Then we can go out later. It's a lovely day, and it would be nice to go to the beach."

Joan, busily removing eggs from beneath disgruntled chickens, grunted her assent, and Pauline joined her. After several minutes of silent collecting, Pauline grinned over at her sister.

"Maybe we'll see that nice farmhand on our way to the beach," she said. "What did Aunt Maureen say his name was?"

"Billy," said Joan quietly, keeping her head down.

"He's nice, isn't he?" Pauline smiled. "I think he's really quite good-looking." Joan's head shot up, and she stared at her sister suspiciously.

"You can't have him," she said sharply. "You're having a baby. You can't have a boyfriend."

Pauline giggled, then relented. "I don't want him, Joanie, but I think you probably do. And I think he likes you too."

Joan turned a bright, unbecoming red and hurried over to the other side of the chicken coop to collect more eggs. Pauline sauntered after her, carrying her full egg basket in both hands.

"That's a good thing," she persisted. "He looks really nice. Shall we try and bump into him this afternoon? Perhaps Aunt Maureen will tell us when his afternoon off is."

Joan turned to face her. "We can't ask that!" she said in horror. "She'll never let us meet up with him. She's been told to keep us out of trouble, and it's obvious what sort of trouble you can get into. She probably thinks I will too."

Pauline chewed on her lip thoughtfully. She had to admit Joan had a good point. Maureen would be sure to report back to their mother if either of the girls so much as looked at a boy. They would need to be very careful. She put down her egg basket and caught Joan by the arm.

"Okay, I see what you mean. But we can still try to meet him by accident," she said, a mischievous look in her eye.

"All right," Joan agreed, smiling. "No harm there, I'm sure. I think he's usually in the long meadow on a Friday afternoon. We can walk that way when we go to the beach."

Pauline grinned, picked up her basket, and tossed her hair back. "Good. That's settled then. Now let's get these eggs inside, and get the bread made."

Together they crossed the farmyard and entered the large, flagstoned kitchen where Maureen was busy scrubbing down the surfaces prior to bread-making. She looked up as the girls entered.

"Good, good. Lots of eggs today then." She nodded her greying head pleasantly, wiped her hands on her khaki overalls, and gestured towards the sink. "Pop them over there. We'll get them washed and sorted later. Need to get the loaves on now if you two want some time off this afternoon."

Pauline glanced at her as they heaved their baskets onto the marble slab next to the sink. "Is that all right, then, Aunt Maureen?" she asked with her most winning smile. "We thought we might walk down to the beach. It's such a lovely day."

"If you get your work finished, the rest of the day is yours," Maureen promised with a nod, her deep brown eyes running shrewdly over Pauline's swelling belly. "Are you still managing the work all right? I don't want you to put your baby at risk."

Pauline felt her face colour. It wasn't often her condition was mentioned, and it made her feel rather uncomfortable.

"I'm fine, thank you," she said politely, washing her hands prior to starting the bread. Maureen heaved the bag of flour onto the enormous farmhouse kitchen table and stood back.

"Right, I'll leave you to it," she said, with one last look around the kitchen. "Once the bread's proving and the eggs are washed, you can get off to the beach. Don't want your mother to think I'm overworking you," she added with a short bark of a laugh.

An hour and a half later, Pauline and Joan had changed out of their working clothes into fresh summer dresses and sandals and were on their way across the fields towards the beach. It was an easy walk of not much more than half a mile, and they had to pass through the field that Billy was working in. Pauline pulled Joan in through the open gate.

"Come on, let's go this way. No reason to keep to the path," she said with a wicked grin.

Joan giggled and followed her, taking care to step over the array of cow pats clustering around the entrance to the field. Billy was sitting on the tractor eating his lunch. He waved enthusiastically when he saw the girls approaching and climbed down from the seat to stand beside the huge wheel.

"Hello," he called, his voice muffled by the large

bite he had just taken from his cheese sandwich. "Where are you two off to?"

"The beach," called Pauline. "D'you want to come too?"

"Love the chance." He laughed ruefully. "I've still got about five hours work left to do. You go and have fun."

The girls stopped just in front of him, and Pauline nudged Joan. Her sister blushed and looked uncomfortable. Pauline rolled her eyes.

"Maybe you could come with us when you have a day off?" she said boldly. "We'd like that, wouldn't we, Joanie?"

Billy looked hopefully at Joan, who reluctantly nodded her head.

"Yes," she whispered. "That would be very nice."

Billy grinned widely at her and held out the rest of his sandwich. "Would you like some?" he asked ingenuously.

Joan smiled shyly, and shook her head. "No. Thank you. Aunt Maureen feeds us very well," she said. "But thank you for offering." She thought for a moment, then asked, "When's your day off?"

"Saturday afternoon, and all day Sunday," he replied at once. "Unless it's harvest time. Then we work every day till it's done. But that's not till next month."

"So we'll see you tomorrow afternoon then," Pauline said decisively. "You can come to the beach."

Billy nodded enthusiastically, and looked at Joan. "If that's okay with you?" he asked, wrinkling his brow.

Joan nodded, a little smile playing on her lips. Billy

ran a large dirty hand through his mop of corn-coloured hair and smiled back at her.

"I'll look forward to it," he said, waving as the girls set off across the field again.

Pauline led the way back onto the path down to the beach, and Joan fell into step beside her.

"Honestly, Joan," she said in exasperation, "you must be more forthcoming. How will he ever know you like him if you don't speak?"

"But s'pose he doesn't like me?" Joan grunted sulkily.

"Of course he likes you!" Pauline sighed. "He offered you his sandwich. Honestly, Joanie, don't you know anything? Now, tomorrow, I think I'll stay home. You can tell him I didn't feel well."

Joan stared at her sister in horror. "I can't meet him on my own!" she gasped. "What would I say?"

"Oh, Joan, honestly!" Pauline rolled her eyes. "I'll talk you through it tonight. You do like him, don't you?"

Joan nodded, peeping at Pauline under her lashes. "Oh, yes," she said at once. "He's really nice. But why would he like me and not you? Boys always like you."

Pauline stopped walking and caught hold of her sister's arms just above the elbow.

"Joan, look at me. I'm having a baby. No boy is going to be interested in me. And anyway, he's not my type. He's a nice boy, much more your type. I'd scare him."

"I hope you're right."

****

Pauline was sitting in the cool shade of the large cedar tree outside the farmhouse when Joan returned from her afternoon at the beach the following day. She looked expectantly at her sister.

"Well?" she asked. "How did it go? Did you have a nice time?"

Joan walked over and sat down on the grass in front of Pauline. She looked up at her and grinned. "It was lovely," she said. "I met Billy in the field and told him you didn't feel too good. He actually seemed to be pleased"—her voice betrayed her wonder—"and we walked to the beach together."

"I told you he liked you." Pauline smiled smugly. "What else happened?"

"Nothing, really." Joan shrugged. "We just talked. He's seventeen, and he's got two little sisters." She looked down at the grass, and picked a daisy. "Oh, and he held my hand on the way back."

Pauline smiled and lay back in her deckchair. "I knew I was right," she said in satisfaction. "When are you seeing him again?"

"Tomorrow afternoon," Joan whispered, looking round apprehensively. "But I think you'd better come too. I don't want Aunt Maureen getting suspicious. Billy won't mind. He understands."

Pauline nodded, and struggled to her feet. "Okay, then. I expect you're right. Now come on, let's go in. I'm starving, and I'm sure it's nearly tea time."

****

Thursday 17th August, 1950

"There'll be thunder by lunchtime," Maureen warned, as Joan picked up the egg basket and headed for the door. "Get them eggs in quickly, child, and lock down the chicken coop." She glanced round to where Pauline was sitting at the table shelling peas into a

223

bowl. "Then you can help your sister with the vegetables. You can both have the afternoon off since it's your birthday." She smiled and carried on kneading the dough.

Pauline looked up in surprise. "How did you know it was our birthday?" she asked curiously.

"Could be the parcels that arrived for you yesterday." Maureen smiled. "The ones that said 'Open on 17th' on them."

"We've got presents?" Pauline gasped in delight. "I never thought we would this year."

Joan opened the door and paused. "Mum would never forget our birthday," she said, "however cross she is with us."

Pauline flushed, and bent her head over her work. She had settled in very well at the farmhouse, and despite her growing size she managed most of the time to forget the reason they were there. Maureen seldom mentioned her condition, although in recent days she'd been giving Pauline much lighter jobs to do in deference to her growing fatigue.

"You just finish those peas, and then you can go and rest," Maureen interrupted Pauline's thoughts, her voice kind.

Pauline looked up at her, her eyes troubled. "You're very nice to me," she said simply. "I thought you'd hate me. Mum does."

Maureen stopped kneading the dough and stared at the girl in dismay. "Your mother doesn't hate you, child," she said at once. "She cares deeply about you. She sent you here so I could keep an eye on you."

"And so our father didn't find out," added Pauline dismally.

Maureen wiped her hands on her apron, walked around the table, and sat down next to Pauline. "Doesn't that show she cares?" she asked gently. "She didn't want you to get in any more trouble than need be. Walter is very set in his ways. He wouldn't understand—or tolerate—your condition. It's better for all of you if you stay away until the baby's born."

"And then what?" Pauline whispered, her eyes filling with tears. "You're going to take my baby away, aren't you?"

There was a slight pause, and then Maureen patted her gently on the shoulder.

"Isn't it better that way?" she asked quietly. "You couldn't go home with it. You couldn't look after it yourself—you're too young. Surely it would be better for it to go to a family who can care for it properly. And you can go back to your life with no one any the wiser."

Pauline sniffed and rubbed her hand across her nose. "But I want to keep her," she said. "She's my baby. No one will love her like I will." She raised scared eyes to Maureen. "Will someone just come and take her? Will I be able to hold her?"

"Of course you will," replied the older woman, taking pity on the girl. "We're not monsters. You can have the baby here; you don't need to go to the nursing home. I know the midwife, so I'll arrange everything. I believe your mother is going to arrange for someone to take the child soon after birth, but I'll make sure you get to spend a little time with it." She hesitated a moment, biting her lip thoughtfully. "If there was any way you could keep the baby, your mother would have found it. Believe me, I know her better than anyone. She's not meaning to be cruel."

Pauline looked at her gratefully. "Thank you," she said. "You're being very kind."

Maureen patted her hand. "Well, you finish up doing those peas, and then you can rest before you get ready for your party," she said, getting up and going back to her bread-making.

"Party?" Pauline looked at her in surprise. "We're having a party?"

"Just the people who work here, and I've even persuaded Mr. Holmes to come in, too." Maureen's husband was a very taciturn elderly farmer, and the girls had scarcely exchanged a word with him in all the weeks they'd been there.

"Thank you." Pauline smiled at her. "That'll be lovely. Is Billy coming?"

Maureen continued kneading the dough and didn't look up. "Yes. Billy was very keen to come. I just hope Joan is behaving herself."

"You know about them?" Pauline asked fearfully.

"I know everything that goes on here. Don't worry. There's no reason why they shouldn't walk out together. Billy is a very nice boy, and I suspect Joan is rather more cautious than her twin." She turned to face Pauline, raising her eyebrows.

"Yes," Pauline said, blushing, "she certainly is. She's much more sensible than me."

Maureen went back to her baking, and Pauline applied herself energetically to her peas, and they were both still hard at it when Joan reappeared with a full basket of eggs.

"They're laying well today, Aunt Maureen," she said with a grin. "They must know it's our birthday." She heaved the heavy basket onto the work surface next to the sink and began to sort through the eggs.

"We're having a party," Pauline told her with a small smile, "and Billy is coming."

Joan carried on with her task. "That's nice," she said. "Thank you, Aunt Maureen."

Maureen paused in her task and tucked a strand of greying hair behind her ear.

"You deserve it. You've both worked very hard. You need a bit of fun." She moved over and laid her hand on Joan's shoulder. "And Billy is a very nice boy. Behave yourselves, and I don't need to tell your mother." And she took off her apron, and went out into the farmyard, shutting the door behind her.

Joan turned to Pauline, horror in her eyes. "She knows! Did you tell her?" she gasped.

"Of course not." Pauline rolled her eyes. "She said she knows everything. She thinks you're more sensible than me."

"That wouldn't be hard," Joan remarked, carefully washing the eggs. "Why is she being so nice?"

"I think she likes us," said Pauline. "She says I can have the baby here. But she said I have to give her up. Joanie, I want to keep her. You will help me, won't you?"

Joan dried her hands and sat down next to her sister. "Pauline, you know I will. That's what we got the money for, remember. So long as they don't take it as soon as it's born, we can manage. Billy'll help."

"We can't ask him. That would be dangerous for him. Maureen promised I could spend some time with the baby before they took her." Pauline looked hopefully at Joan. "Do you really think we can get away?"

Joan put her arm around her sister. "Leave it to me," she said with confidence. "Everything'll be all right. Now, let's get our jobs done and enjoy our party."

****

Tuesday 19th September, 1950

Pauline eyed the midwife with mistrust and lay back on the bed.

"Don't be silly, child. I'm not going to hurt you. Now, lift up your dress. I need to feel your stomach." The midwife stood back and waited as Pauline pulled her dress up so that her swollen belly was revealed. She placed her hands on the bulge, and Pauline gritted her teeth as the cold fingers probed her warm skin. "Hmm… I think you have about six weeks left," the midwife pronounced at last, straightening her back and nodding at Pauline to cover herself up again. "Are you feeling well?"

"Yes, thank you," Pauline whispered. "But I do get very tired."

"Of course you do. You're carrying another person around with you," was the brisk reply. "Unless you have any problems, I won't come again until you go into labour. Mrs. Holmes will call me when she thinks the time is right. Make sure you eat well and get plenty of rest." She picked up her bag and started towards the door.

"Please…" Pauline cleared her throat nervously. "Will it be you who takes my baby away?"

The midwife turned. "No," she said. "A foster parent will come and take it. I don't know who that is yet. You don't need to worry about that." And she nodded to Pauline and left the room.

Pauline stayed lying on the bed, her body feeling

violated by the midwife's prodding and probing, her mind in a whirl. She and Joan had talked about what they were going to do when the baby was born, but they had made no definite plans. Now she knew it would only be another six weeks, she began to panic. In that time they would have to find her somewhere to live. Somewhere her parents couldn't find her. Somewhere she and the baby could live together safely until such time as her father agreed to allow her home. There was a tentative tap on the door, and Joan's head appeared.

"Has she gone?" she asked anxiously.

Pauline nodded and propped herself up on her elbow. "Yes. She was very scary," she said.

Joan grinned and sat on the bed beside her. "That's her job," she said with a shrug. "Are you okay?"

"I suppose so." Pauline nodded. "She said I had about six weeks to go. Joan, we must arrange somewhere for me to go as soon as she's born," she said urgently.

Joan patted her arm. "It's all under control," she said mysteriously. "Leave it to me."

"Why? What have you done?" Pauline eyed her suspiciously.

Joan got up and closed the bedroom door. "I've found you somewhere to go," she said in a quiet voice. "Or rather, Billy has." Pauline gasped and looked expectantly at her. Joan perched back on the end of the bed. "Billy has a cousin who lives in London, in a flat. He says there's a spare flat next to his, and he's going to ask his landlord if you can have it. It's very cheap 'cause it's not very big, but you don't need anything big, do you?" Pauline shook her head, her heart racing. London! She would be living in London! She had never even been to London.

"Is this really going to work?" she whispered, her voice quavering with excitement.

"I think so," Joan said cautiously. "So long as they don't take the baby away the day you have it, then we can get you away as quickly as possible."

Pauline frowned. "The midwife told me I'd have to stay in bed for a week after the birth."

Joan made a face. "Well, I don't think you'll be able to do that. I'm sure you'll be all right." She paused for a moment. "We do need to get stuff for the baby, though. You know, clothes and bottles and stuff," she said vaguely. "I'll ask Billy about that. He has a big family. One of them will have had a baby recently." She caught her sister's hand and gave it a squeeze. "Don't worry, Pauline. Everything'll be fine. You wait and see." And they smiled at each other across the bed.

Chapter 19

Thursday 31st July, 2008

Abi awoke to the sound of rain thundering onto the roof of the caravan and pulled the quilt up to her chin with a shiver. The bed felt big and empty without Gideon beside her, and she sneaked her hand out from under the covers, picked up her mobile, and dialled his number. He answered on the second ring.

"Abi!" His voice sounded a million miles away.

"Hi, you," she said, her voice full of emotion. "I'm missing you so much. Are you all right?"

His reply crackled down the line. "No, of course not. Are you?" He carried on, not waiting for her reply. "I went to see that fucking editor yesterday. They threw me out before I could do anything to him. He wouldn't tell me who gave him the story, but I'm sure it's Simon. Judy told me her mum saw him in Newbury yesterday."

"Really?" Abi gasped. "Wow, I never thought he'd go back there. From what your Mum said, I don't think his mother'll be too pleased to see him." She paused and chewed her lip. "Gid, I was thinking. Shouldn't we do a press conference or something to tell everyone that it's all lies?"

His reply was instant. "Yes, I think so. I nearly did that yesterday, but something Chas said made me hesitate. He suggested Simon might be hoping I'd

231

believe the stories and start to turn against you. We wondered if maybe I shouldn't deny it all until he's shown himself. Until he's been to see me. Maybe trick him into revealing his part in it all by letting him think he's won. D'you think you and Tash could cope for a day or so if we did that? It might be the way to get him exposed for what he is and finally get him off our backs."

Abi took a deep breath. Her first instinct had been to scream "No" down the phone. She couldn't bear the thought that the public might actually believe the lies that had been written about her, but part of her totally understood where Gideon was coming from. It would be wonderful if they could get Simon exposed for the troublemaker he was, and if she could just lie low for a day or so that might actually work. She sighed.

"I guess so," she said reluctantly, "although I do resent being held to ransom by him. You make damn sure he gets what he deserves at the end of this." She scowled down the phone.

Gideon gave a small chuckle. "Thanks, babe," he said. "You're the best. It won't be long. Hang on there. I'll call you later. Give Tasha a hug." He disappeared, leaving Abi clutching a silent phone to her ear. She laid it back on the bedside table and sighed heavily. She felt very frustrated at being unable to do anything to right the wrong that had been done to her family, although she fully understood Gideon's reasons for the delay. She scowled to herself and swung her legs out of bed just as Natasha appeared in the doorway, yawning widely.

"Were you talking to Dad?" she asked, rubbing her eyes. Abi nodded and ushered her daughter out of the room and into the main living area of the caravan.

"He sent you a hug," she said, walking over to the window and surveying the long sweep of Rhossili Bay. The rain was lashing down and beating hard on the caravan windows, and the only life visible on the beach was a number of seagulls wheeling noisily overhead. Abi shivered and wrapped her arms around herself. "Honestly, it's nearly as chilly as it was in November," she grumbled, going over to the gas fire and flicking it on. Natasha sat down cross-legged on the floor and turned on the television.

"Let's see if we're on the news again," she said, flicking onto one of the news channels. Abi took the remote from her and turned it off. "Hey, give that back, Mum! I want to see if we're on."

"Not today." Abi shook her head firmly. "Your Dad says we must wait until he's heard from Simon before we can publicly deny the allegations. I'm finding that very hard to stomach, but I'm prepared to go along with it…but that does mean I don't want to see any more about it on the television. Today must be about getting away from it. Okay?"

Natasha nodded and scrambled to her feet to throw her arms around her mother.

"Sorry, Mum." Her voice was muffled in her mother's shoulder. "I didn't think how you might be feeling."

Abi stroked her hair gently as she rested her chin on Natasha's head. "That's okay, sweetie," she said with a crooked smile. "Let's spend the day getting lost in Pauline and Joan's story, shall we?"

Natasha raised her head and grinned. "Yeah!" she said with enthusiasm. "We're getting close to her giving birth. Then we might finally find out what happened to her."

Abi wrinkled her nose. "It worries me how excited you get about that," she said. "I think we can be pretty sure it's not going to be a happy ending."

Natasha shook back her hair and shrugged. "I know," she said, "but it's a long time ago. It just feels like a story. They don't really seem real."

"I know what you mean," Abi agreed. "But just remember Joan was your grandmother. What really interests me is how such a lovely teenager turned into such a dreadful adult. I guess that's what we're about to find out." She glanced out the window. "Tell you what—the rain has let up for a bit, so let's go for a quick walk along the beach, then come back and get stuck in. Nice idea?" Natasha nodded and skipped back to her room to get dressed.

****

The hotel where Simon had chosen to spend the night had sadly failed to come up to his expectations, and he regarded his breakfast bleakly. He had finally managed to find an establishment that could offer him a superior double room with whirlpool bath and a well stocked mini-bar, but when it came to breakfast, he found that not only was he expected to partake of it in the dining room but that the choice of food was severely limited. He stared at his droopy bacon, greasy egg, and burst sausage with ill-concealed distaste, and turned instead to his waiting cafétière of coffee. Pouring it gingerly into his cup, he added a small amount of milk, then dropped in three large cubes of Demerara sugar and stirred briskly. He tentatively took a sip, then lowered his cup into the saucer with a loud clatter. The two other couples in the room looked round, and Simon pretended to be studying his breakfast. The coffee had proved to be as lacking as the food, and he made the decision to find the nearest decent coffee shop as soon as he'd checked out. He picked up the sausage with his thumb and forefinger and peered closely at it. A drip of fat slid down his hand and landed on the plate. Simon replaced the sausage with a shudder. He sighed, finished his glass of orange juice, then pushed back his chair and headed back to his room.

His plan for the day was to visit his mother before finding somewhere more salubrious to stay until he decided the time was right to make his approach to Gideon. He was heartened to see that no denial of his accusations had yet appeared in the papers or on the news, and he hoped it meant Gideon did indeed have doubts about the paternity of his daughter.

He let himself into his room and immediately brushed his teeth to remove the imagined taste of the greasy breakfast, then rapidly flung his belongings back into his bag and made his way downstairs to reception. The pretty, dark-haired girl behind the desk smiled brightly at him.

"Good morning, Mr. Dean. I hope you had a pleasant night," she said, a slight East London twang sounding in her voice. "Would you like your bill?"

Simon nodded curtly, not bothering to reply to her pleasantries, and fished his wallet out of his pocket. She handed him his account, and he passed over his credit card without reading it. The girl raised her eyebrows but made no comment and passed his card through the machine.

"Are you going anywhere nice today?" she asked politely, while she waited for his card to be authorised.

Simon stared at her. "Is there anywhere nice around here?" he asked rudely, tapping his fingers on the desk. The girl pursed her lips, completed the credit card transaction, and returned his card to him, not bothering to hide her dislike.

"Thank you, sir. Enjoy your day," she said, determined to observe the conventions but moving into the back office without waiting for him to reply.

Simon hitched his bag onto his shoulder and strode out onto the pavement, oblivious to the receptionist's attitude. He glanced around, then headed round the corner to the taxi rank he'd located the previous day. He jumped into the first one in the line, barked out his mother's address to the driver, and then sat back and considered his options for the day. Mrs. Ellis had told him his mother would be back the previous evening, so he should be able to see her, get that out of the way, then find a better hotel to spend the night in.

He just needed to find out why his mother had changed the locks. If only he could remember why she'd been annoyed with him. There was something just on the edge of his memory, but he couldn't quite catch hold of it. He became aware the taxi was slowing and peered out the window. His mother's road looked as dreary as usual, and his heart sank as the vehicle pulled up outside Number 78. He opened the door and stepped out onto the deserted pavement, paid the driver, and then, hitching his bag over his shoulder, walked slowly up the path to the front door. He pressed the bell and stepped back to wait. Out of the corner of his eye he was aware of the curtains twitching from the next door house, and he deliberately turned his back on them. He pressed the bell again, for longer this time, and attempted to peer through the frosted glass. There was still no sound from within, so he raised his hand and knocked hard. A few moments later he heard a door bang from inside and the sound of footsteps coming down the stairs. The door opened a crack, and his mother's face appeared. At the sight of her son, her mouth dropped open and her eyebrows shot up. She pulled the door open slightly further and stepped out onto the doorstep.

"Simon," she said. "I was in bed. I only got home at one this morning." She pulled her pink dressing gown more tightly around her and awkwardly shuffled her feet in their fluffy slippers.

"Hi, Mum. Did you have a nice holiday?" Simon asked politely, his mouth smiling at her.

Josephine Dean looked suspiciously at him. "How did you know I was on holiday?" she asked with a frown.

Simon nodded towards the next-door house. "Mrs. Ellis," he explained. "I came yesterday, and she told me." He paused and looked closely at her. "She said you'd changed the locks."

"Yes," Josephine looked at him squarely. "I have. What are you doing here, Simon?"

Simon felt a frisson of shock run through him at the tone of her voice. "I've come to see you, Mum," he said uncertainly.

"Clearly your memory isn't too good," she regarded him coldly. "I asked you to leave the last time you were here. Do you remember why?" She paused and watched his face. "No, I thought not. You need to sort your life out, Simon. You'd better come in, now you're here. The doorstep is no place to discuss this." She pushed the door open and indicated that he should enter the house.

With a quick glance at the shadowy figure behind the next-door curtains, Simon followed her into the kitchen and took a seat at the table. Josephine sat down opposite him and rested her hands on the table. Simon attempted to lighten the mood.

"You look well. Your holiday must have done you good," he said with an attempt at a friendly smile.

"Don't be ridiculous," his mother said sharply. "I've just got up, I'm in my nightie, and I have no makeup on. Admit it, Simon—you have no idea why I'm not pleased to see you, have you?"

After a pause Simon shook his head. "Did I upset you?" he asked, genuinely trying to remember and failing miserably.

Josephine looked at him in amazement. "Simon, the last time you were here you told me you'd concealed Abigail's letters to Gideon. You admitted you wanted to split them up, and you told me you'd read some of the letters. I surmised from that you still had the letters." She paused and fixed him with a steely glare. "Now an excerpt from one of those letters has appeared in one of the most unsavoury of newspapers. I asked you to leave after you told me about stealing the letters. I changed the locks because I didn't want you to come back here. Have you honestly forgotten all that? Is your brain so addled by drugs and alcohol that you can't even remember a fight with your own mother?"

Simon stared at her in horror as the memory of that last time he'd seen her came flooding back. Of course!

He'd confessed to her about the letters. Now she'd seen the article in *The National Crier* and had rightly deduced he was behind it. He felt his whole body go hot and cold, and his fingers began to tingle. He stared at his mother, trying to formulate the right words.

"Oh, shit," was all he could come out with.

"Is that all you have to say?" she snapped, leaning back in her chair. "You made up some cock-and-bull story about Abigail's past in order to discredit her, and you sit here expecting me to entertain you in my house? Simon, what on earth possessed you? What have you become?"

Simon dropped his head forward and rested it on his arms. He had no idea how to answer her questions. What had he become? Why was he acting this way? He was aware she was speaking again.

"Simon, why are you doing this? Gideon's meant to be your friend. What's your problem with Abigail?" she persisted.

Simon shuddered every time she said the name Abigail, and he found it grated even more than if she'd called her Abi. He reluctantly raised his head.

"She would have broken up the band," he muttered.

"Maybe, back in 1995," Josephine conceded, "although Gideon did that for himself in the end. But now? Simon, what is it you want from them now?" He was silent, and she peered more closely at him. "Simon, is it jealousy? Is it because she took him away from you?" He looked away from her and didn't reply. She reached across the table and tapped his arm sharply. "Simon, answer me. Are you jealous? Are you in love with Gideon? Or with Abigail?"

Simon's head shot round. "No," he yelled. "Of course not! I'm not in love with either of them. But she changed everything. He didn't want anyone else when he found her."

Josephine withdrew her hand and surveyed him thoughtfully. "You're thirty-two years old," she stated, "and you're behaving in much the same way you did when you were ten and Gideon went to the cinema with another little boy to see *Star Trek Four*. You didn't speak to him for a week!"

Simon got to his feet and began to pace the room. "No one understands," he muttered. "She changed everything. While she's still with him, nothing can get back to normal."

Josephine frowned, consternation on her face. "What is normal to you, Simon? What are you expecting?"

He looked at her in surprise. "The band getting back together, of course," he said, "and that can't happen if he's still with her. That's why she has to go." He turned wild eyes on his mother. "Don't you see? I've got to make Gideon see she's no good. Then he'll leave her and take me back in the band."

Josephine stood up and moved towards him. "Simon, I'm not sure that would happen," she began gently. "If Gideon knows you took his letters, then he probably guesses you put the story in the paper, too. Also, he's never going to believe that story. He loves her, Simon. You can't change that." She reached out her hand to him, but he brushed it aside and stalked across the room to the window,

"He doesn't know I took his letters," he said. "He may think I did, but he doesn't know for sure. I'll deny it, of course, and he can't ever prove it." Josephine remained silent, the memory of her encounter with Gideon's parents fresh in her mind. Simon turned to face her. "You're the only person I've told," he said, scowling at her, "and you won't have told him, will you?"

****

The rain was thundering on the roof of the caravan again by the time Abi and Natasha returned from their walk. They burst through the door, water running in rivers off their waterproof coats and pooling on the floor. They kicked off their boots, quickly removed their coats, and hung them to drip in the shower. Abi shook her head violently.

"Phew," she gasped, her wet hair sending droplets of water flying around the room, "that was fun!"

Natasha had grabbed a towel from the shower room and was vigorously rubbing her face and head. She grinned out from beneath it.

"Brilliant," she agreed, continuing to dry herself. "I'm completely soaked despite the coats."

Abi lifted a foot and peeled off her sock, dropping it in the sink. "Don't quite know how these got wet," she mused, bending down to pull the other one off. Then she padded through to the living area, turned on the gas fire, and knelt down in front of it. "Make sure you take off anything that's wet," she called to Natasha, running her hands through her wet hair. Natasha appeared from the kitchen area, dressed only in her underwear and carrying the hair dryer.

"D'you want this?" she asked, holding it out to her mother.

Abi took it with a smile. "Thanks, pet. Now put

some clothes on, or you'll catch your death."

"That sounds like the sort of thing Joan might have said," Natasha remarked with a grimace, disappearing into her bedroom in search of more clothes.

Abi laughed. "Yeah, I guess it is. Sorry about that." She plugged in the hair dryer and proceeded to get her hair to a state in which she could then use the straighteners. Natasha reappeared, dressed in jeans and an oversized check shirt, her wet hair dripping over her shoulders.

"Shall I put the kettle on?" she asked.

"Yes, please. Coffee for me. And dry your hair," Abi ordered.

Natasha rolled her eyes, flicked the kettle on, and picked up the now discarded hairdryer.

"You're so bossy," she complained, turning it on and waving it vaguely in the direction of her head.

"It's my job." Abi grinned and peered into the mirror, deciding her hair would have to do. She unplugged the straighteners and put them away. "Shall we start the next bit of the diary in a minute?"

"Of course." Natasha nodded at once. "It's getting really good now. Pauline should give birth in the next section, I think."

When the kettle had boiled, Abi made coffee for herself and hot chocolate for Natasha, then carried the drinks to the living area and placed them on the coffee table. Natasha was still fighting with her hair, so Abi opened the suitcase and retrieved the next section of Pauline's diary. The extra book Natasha had found lay just beneath it, and she picked it up and flicked quickly through it.

"This is definitely Joan's diary," she said frowning

at the spidery writing. "It seems to cover some of the time they were in Norfolk. It overlaps with Pauline's a little bit." She turned to the end of the book. "It seems to go up to some time in late November. That's the bit that's missing in Pauline's account. Hers goes up to the end of October, then takes up again in the second half of November." She glanced up at Natasha. "We need to read Pauline's up to the end of October first, then Joan's."

Natasha sat on the floor beside her mother. "So Pauline wrote hers up till the baby was born, then?" she mused. "And started it again a few weeks later. Maybe she was too busy those first weeks."

"Makes sense." Abi nodded. "Funny we only have the one bit of Joan's, though, isn't it?" She flicked through the little book again and shrugged. "Oh, well, maybe we'll find out why later. Shall we get started?"

Chapter 20

Saturday 28th October, 1950

The wind howled around the farmhouse, lifting the slates and rattling the windows noisily. Pauline sat at the window of her bedroom staring out into the gathering gloom, watching the leaves being whipped up into a frenzy and spun around the farmyard. She shivered and wrapped her arms around her swollen body. Her baby was due any day, and she was tired, uncomfortable, and very, very scared. She had had no more contact with the midwife since the visit in September, and she was beginning to feel quite alone and abandoned. Joan was still working hard on the farm, and since she'd been going out with Billy, Pauline had seen a lot less of her. She stood up and pressed her hands into the small of her back with a sigh. She didn't know the exact date the baby was due, but she felt sure it was very close. She was hot, uncomfortable, had constant indigestion, and her ankles were permanently swollen. A tear trickled down her cheek, and for the umpteenth time she mentally chastised herself for her foolish behaviour. She would never be that stupid again, but she feared she'd probably ruined her life with her thoughtless actions. She was very pleased to see that Joan was not making the same mistakes with Billy. Their relationship had so far consisted of holding hands and walking along the beach together at sunset. Pauline suspected they may have kissed once or twice, but nothing more serious.

She walked over to the bed and sat down with a groan. Part of her wanted to do something to hurry the baby along, but another much larger part was so terrified of the prospect of actually giving birth that she felt she would do anything to stop it happening. The wind was getting louder and more persistent, and Pauline heard the kitchen door open and close with a bang, heralding the arrival of Joan back from her egg collecting. She could just make out muffled voices below, followed by the sound of footsteps running up the stairs. The door burst open and her sister erupted into the room.

"Guess what!" she gasped, her hair all over her face, having been pulled from its ribbon by the wind. "The forecast is for a storm tonight. It might bring some trees down. Hope you don't start the baby. I doubt the midwife would come out in this." She bounced onto the bed beside her sister, her face flushed with excitement.

Pauline stared at her in consternation. "That sounds dreadful," she whispered. "Suppose the midwife can't get here? Suppose the baby comes and no one's here to help me, suppose…"

Joan jumped up and grabbed her hands. "Pauline, stop worrying!" she said. "The baby hasn't started, and anyway Aunt Maureen has delivered lots of calves and lambs. How different can a baby be?"

Pauline looked horrified. "Very different, Joan!" she snapped, her hand going protectively to her swollen belly. "My baby has two arms and two legs, not four legs and a tail. Don't be so ridiculous. I need a midwife."

"Well, let's hope your baby doesn't have a tail anyway," Joan remarked cheekily, then patted Pauline on the hand. "Don't worry. I'm sure you won't go into labour tonight anyway. Now come downstairs and have some tea. Aunt Maureen has made a fruit cake." She pulled her sister into an upright position and chivvied her out of the room and down the steep narrow staircase.

A delightful smell greeted Pauline as she entered the kitchen, and she breathed deeply. "Ooh, that's lovely," she said, smiling at Maureen, who was laying the table for tea. "I'm actually quite hungry."

The girls took their places at the table and tucked into the wholesome farmhouse fare with alacrity. Since staying at the farm, Joan had put on a little weight, and her rosy cheeks had a healthy glow about them.

Pauline looked over at Maureen, swallowed her cake, and asked, "Joan says the midwife might not make it tonight because of the storm. What will happen if I start the baby?"

Maureen flashed a look of slight annoyance at Joan, then smiled encouragingly at Pauline. "Don't worry. You don't look quite ready to me…another day or so probably. Anyway I'm sure Sister Metcalfe would make it over even in a blizzard. You'll be well looked after," she reassured her.

They finished their meal in silence, and then Pauline pushed her plate aside and leaned back in her chair. "Thank you, that was lovely. I feel really full now." She laid a hand on her belly and rubbed gently. "I haven't felt her kicking so much these last few days," she said, flushing as she mentioned so intimate a detail.

"Do you think she's all right?"

"Yes." Maureen nodded. "She's so big now she doesn't have much room to move about. You'll certainly go into labour in the next couple of days, I'm sure. Now go and put your feet up over by the fire. Joan will help me clear up." She rose from the table and began to gather up the dishes.

Joan leapt up to help her, and Pauline heaved her cumbersome body over to the rocking chair by the hearth. She sat down with a sigh and closed her eyes. The thought of what was to come for her over the next week was almost too overwhelming to consider, and she needed something to take her mind off it. She opened her eyes and glanced around her. There were a number of farming magazines lying on the small table next to her chair, and Pauline picked one up. She started to flick through it, passing over the articles about the best feed for sheep, the advertisements for tractors, and the letters page. She finally paused on an article about a farm in Devon and decided to read it properly. If that didn't take her mind off her condition, then nothing would! Within three minutes of starting to read, Pauline was dozing.

****

Sunday 29th October, 1950—2.30 a.m.

Pauline awoke suddenly, her eyes snapped open, and she gasped. She was aware of a clenching pain in her stomach, and she cautiously sat up. As she swung her legs out of the bed, another pain gripped her body, and she stifled a cry. She felt as though something was trying to punch its way out of her—exactly what was happening. She glanced at her watch. Two thirty in the morning. The wind was still howling outside, and the rain was lashing against the diamond windowpanes. Pauline struggled to her feet and staggered over to the door. She wrenched it open, and another pain caused her to double up and drop to her knees. She cried out, and within seconds Joan had appeared beside her.

"Pauline!" she cried, kneeling down next to her. "Is the baby coming?"

Pauline raised terrified eyes and nodded jerkily. "I…think so…" she managed, clutching at Joan's arm for support.

Joan helped her to her feet and led her back into the bedroom.

"Stay there," she ordered, pressing Pauline down onto the bed. "I'll go and fetch Aunt Maureen." As she finished speaking, the lady in question appeared at the door, her dressing gown clutched around her and her hair contained in a hair net.

"Has it started?" she asked, moving swiftly to the bed. Pauline lay back and gritted her teeth as another contraction gripped her body. She grunted, and her hands clutched wildly at the sheets. Maureen laid a hand on her stomach for a moment, then patted her arm. "Hang on in there, child. I'll go and ring for the midwife." She gave Pauline an encouraging smile, nodded to Joan to take her place by the bed, and hurried downstairs.

Joan perched on the edge of the bed and took her sister's hand. "It'll be okay, Pauline," she said soothingly. "The midwife will come, and everything'll be all right."

"She'd better hurry up," muttered Pauline through gritted teeth. "I feel like I'm about to explode. Joanie, this really hurts." She gripped her sister's hand tightly as yet another contraction shook her body. Suddenly she squealed in dismay and struggled into a sitting position, her hands clutching at her nightdress. "Joanie, I think I've wet myself!" she whispered, her face flaming. Joan edged off the bed, looking down at the growing wet patch that had appeared between Pauline's legs.

"Shall I tell Aunt Maureen?" she asked in confusion.

Pauline stared at her, terror in her eyes. "I don't know," she wailed. "I don't know what's happening. Make it stop!"

"It's all perfectly normal." Maureen had re-entered the room, carrying some towels and a jug of water. "Your waters have broken. That means the baby is really on the way." She sat down on the bed beside Pauline and laid a towel over the girl's lap. "Just lie back and try to breathe deeply. That should help you relax."

Pauline did as she was told. "I'm so glad you're here," she told Maureen. "You're so calm. Is the midwife coming?"

Maureen frowned and looked slightly annoyed. "Unfortunately, the phone lines are down," she said, "so I've been unable to contact her as yet. I was planning to send Mr. Holmes down to fetch her, but I don't think he'd make it in time. Never mind. We can do this on our own." She smiled at Pauline encouragingly.

"No midwife?" Pauline squeaked. "But we need her! You've only delivered lambs. I'm not having a lamb…"

Maureen put her fingers to her lips, laughing.

"Calm down, calm down. It's fine. I know how to deliver a baby, too. In fact, I delivered your little sister Margaret when you and your mother were staying in the village at the beginning of the war, and a healthier child you'll never find. Now, keep breathing deeply and try to relax."

Pauline stared mutely over at her sister, and Joan ran round to the other side of the bed and knelt on the floor next to her.

"I'm here, Pauline. I'll stay with you." She looked up at Maureen. "I can stay, can't I?"

Maureen hesitated for a moment, then nodded briskly. "You can stay," she said. "Normally I wouldn't recommend a child of your age witness a birth, but this is your twin. You should be here for her. You can be my assistant."

Joan grinned at Pauline and squeezed her hand. Pauline panted fast, and her back arched off the bed as her body contorted with another contraction. She screamed out loud and almost twisted Joan's hand off.

"Oh, my god!" she gasped. "That was awful! I can't stand this. How long is it going to take?"

Maureen felt her stomach and shook her head. "It'll be a while yet," she warned. "You mustn't start pushing just yet."

"Pushing? What d'you mean, pushing?" panted Pauline, sweat dripping down her flushed face.

"Pushing the baby out," Maureen replied, wiping Pauline's brow with a towel. "You mustn't start pushing too soon. You need to wait until the baby has room to get out."

Pauline stared at her as if she were speaking Japanese.

"What does that mean?" she wailed, her voice rising to a squeak.

Joan concealed a smile, and gently stroked her hand.

"Your body has to be ready to let the baby out," explained Maureen cautiously. "The hole through which the baby exits needs to get bigger, and I don't think yours is quite there yet."

"How does it get bigger?" Pauline whispered, her eyes wide with horror.

Maureen sighed. "Don't worry yourself about it," she said gently. "Everything will go all right. You just do everything I tell you."

Pauline swallowed nervously and nodded.

Joan glanced over at Maureen. "Can I do anything?" she asked.

"Just what you are doing," Maureen said simply. "Stay with your sister and hold her hand. She's going to need you."

****

By four o'clock the wind had picked up still more, the rain sounded as though it was trying to force its way through the ill-fitting windows, and Pauline was still experiencing contractions every few minutes. She was totally exhausted, and it was taking all Joan's efforts to keep her concentrating on the matter in hand. She wanted nothing more than to sleep, but there was still no sign of the baby, and Maureen was intent on keeping her awake.

"Come on, Pauline," she chided. "Keep breathing deeply, stay with me. You're nearly there. Time to start pushing soon."

Pauline groaned and shook her sweat-soaked head

from side to side.

"I just wanna sleep," she muttered. "Make it stop. Jus' give me my baby and make the pain stop."

Joan squeezed her hand tightly. "Hang on, Pauline," she said as cheerfully as she could manage. "It won't be long now. Aunt Maureen is going to need you to push soon." She glanced enquiringly up at Maureen, who nodded and gently pressed on Pauline's belly. A huge contraction took hold of the girl, and she screamed out loud and grabbed the headboard of the bed with both hands. Maureen lifted the towel that was covering her legs and peered between them.

"Okay, Pauline, time to push. When the next contraction comes, push as hard as you can. Can you do that for me?"

"Does it mean…" Pauline panted, regarding her balefully, "that this will stop?"

"Soon." Maureen nodded.

Pauline looked unconvinced and tried to wriggle into a sitting position. "Can you see the baby yet?" she asked ingenuously.

"Not yet, but it won't be long." Maureen smiled. "Now lie down again and get ready to push."

Pauline lay back with a sigh and glowered at Joan. "I am *never* doing this again," she said distinctly. "And I don't think you should either," and with that pronouncement her body was racked again with a strong contraction.

"Push!" yelled Maureen, still peering under the towel. "Good girl, that was great."

Pauline grimaced and rubbed her hand across her sweating face. She gritted her teeth and prepared herself for the next onslaught, summoning all her strength so she could push harder. As the contraction came, she pushed with all her might, screaming loudly.

"I can see the head." Maureen patted Pauline's arm. "Good girl, we're nearly there. Keep pushing." Pauline fell back panting, and Maureen beamed at her. "The next one should do it. You're doing so well."

Joan moved closer and gently wiped the sweat off her sister's forehead. Pauline opened her eyes. "Nearly there?" she whispered, attempting a smile.

Joan nodded and bending down, planted a quick kiss on her head. "Yes," she said with a smile, "nearly there."

The next contraction came without warning, and Pauline screamed and pushed as hard as she could. Maureen lifted the towel.

"That's it, keep pushing…oh, well done," she bent forward and caught the baby as it slithered out between Pauline's legs. She held it up by the legs and administered a sharp tap between the shoulder blades.

"Don't hit her!" Pauline gasped, holding out her arms.

Maureen turned to face her as the baby gave a short cry. "Just getting her to breathe," she said. "It's a girl, just like you said it would be." She bent down and placed the baby in Pauline's outstretched arms. "Have a quick hold, and then I need to cut the cord and make sure the placenta is out." Pauline looked at her blankly for just a moment before turning her attention to her baby.

"Hello," she whispered to the tiny bundle in her arms. "Hello, Sarah."

Joan sat on the edge of the bed and peeped over at the little girl. She smiled and gently touched the baby's cheek with her finger.

"Sarah's a nice name," she said, smiling at Pauline. Pauline yawned and handed the baby back to Maureen, who finished what needed to be done and then wrapped her in a shawl and laid her in the makeshift crib they'd prepared for her.

"You need to get some sleep now," she said to Pauline. "Joan will help you have a wash after you've had a rest. The baby will need feeding in an hour or two, so we'll have to wake you for that."

Pauline looked at her sleepily. "Can't someone else feed her?" she murmured, her eyelids lowering.

Maureen laughed. "Not really. You're the one with the milk," she said. "Now off to sleep, and we'll wake you when we need to."

****

By midday the wind had dropped to a more bearable level, and Mr. Holmes had been despatched to fetch the midwife to check on Pauline. Maureen popped her head around the bedroom door and smiled at the girl. Pauline was propped up in bed, her blue eyes dark-rimmed in her white face. Her hair was held back from her face with a red ribbon, and she had a shawl around her shoulders. She smiled weakly at Maureen.

"Is Sarah all right?" she asked anxiously.

Maureen stepped into the room and nodded. "Yes, she's fine. Sleeping soundly." In order for Pauline to get some much-needed rest, the baby's crib had been moved into Joan's bedroom. "I'll bring her to you as soon as she wakes again. The midwife is on her way over, too. I'd like her to check you over, make sure you're both fine."

Pauline's eyes registered fear. "She won't take her

away, will she?" she asked, her voice cracking.

Maureen moved over and sat on the edge of the bed. "No, Pauline, she won't take her. That's not part of her job. A foster parent will come for her later in the week. Your mother has found a family that would like to adopt her," she said gently, watching Pauline's face carefully. "You do realise it's for the best, don't you? You could never look after a baby on your own."

"Yes, I could." Pauline wriggled petulantly, muttering, "I won't let them take her."

Maureen watched her silently for a moment, then sighed and stood up. "I'm afraid you may have to," she said at last. "Unless you can find some way of showing you can look after the baby on your own. Then they'll deem it in the best interest of the child." She turned to leave but hesitated in the doorway. "If you want to make sure she's called Sarah, it might be an idea to register the birth as soon as possible," she said. "Maybe Joan could do it for you tomorrow?"

"Register the birth?" Pauline looked at her blankly. "Of course she must be called Sarah. What's registering the birth?"

Maureen smiled, remembering just how young the girl was. "She needs a birth certificate, Pauline. Everyone does. In order to get one, her birth needs to be registered at the Registry Office in town. Anyone can do it, but I expect you'd prefer it to be Joan, wouldn't you?" Pauline nodded emphatically. "Then I'll take her over there in the morning. You decide if she's to have a middle name or not." She smiled encouragingly at the girl and left the room.

Pauline lay back on the pillows and stared at the beamed ceiling. At least they weren't going to take the baby for a few days. That should give Joan time to organise her travel to London. A feeling of panic began to rise in her throat as she imagined being alone in a flat, in a city she knew nothing about, with a tiny baby to look after. At least she had the money Joan had stolen from the factory. That should keep her going for ages. There was a slight noise outside the door, and Joan's head appeared. She grinned at her sister, slipped into the room, and perched on the end of the bed.

"It's all sorted for you going to London," she whispered, her eyes shining with excitement. "Billy has found out the train times and everything."

Pauline sat up and leant forward. "When are we going?" she asked, licking her suddenly dry lips.

"Tuesday morning. Early," said Joan quietly.

"So soon?" Pauline gasped. "I can't get up that soon!"

"Pauline, they're coming to take Sarah away, remember? Probably on Wednesday, from what I heard the midwife say to Aunt Maureen. You have to go on Tuesday." She took her sister's hand and squeezed tightly. "Don't worry. It won't be for long. I shall go home and get them to agree to you coming back to live with us." She smiled with confidence. "They're not monsters. They're our parents; they won't let you live on your own."

Pauline looked doubtful and chewed her bottom lip. "I hope you're right," she said bleakly. "I don't know how I'll manage in London."

Joan moved further up the bed and took her other hand. "You'll be fine," she assured her. "Billy says it's a nice place. His cousin told him all about it. You've got plenty of money, and I'll talk Mum and Dad round as soon as I can."

"I suppose it'll be all right," Pauline said at last, nodding slowly. "But I wish you were coming too, Joanie."

"So do I." Joan grimaced. "But I really have to go home and tell them what's happened. Mum'll be expecting us both back next week, and will expect the baby to have been taken away. I need to go and tell her what's really happened."

Pauline lay back on the pillows and closed her eyes. "I need to sleep," she muttered, "or I'll never be able to go anywhere on Tuesday."

Joan got to her feet and moved towards the door. "Okay," she said. "I'll leave you to it," and she slipped out of the room just as Pauline started to snore gently.

****

Tuesday 31st October, 1950

"Pauline, Pauline! Wake up!" Joan hissed at her sleeping sister in the dark bedroom. Pauline stirred and rolled onto her back. Her eyes opened slowly, and she stared blankly at Joan. "Come on, Pauline, we have to go. The train goes at six thirty," Joan urged, pulling the covers back.

Pauline shivered, sat up, and brushed her hair out of her eyes. "What time is it now?" she asked in a loud whisper, trying to stop her teeth from chattering,

"Five," came the reply, "but it takes over half an hour to get to the station, and we have a lot to do first."

Pauline slid out of bed and searched around for her clothes. "Where are all my things?" she asked frantically, staring around the room.

Joan put her finger to her lips. "Hush, we mustn't wake anyone else. I've packed your things. Look I've just left you some clothes for today on the chair." She pointed to the dark corner of the room, where a navy blue pinafore dress and a white polo-neck jumper were lying on the chair.

Pauline picked up the dress. "This is a maternity dress," she objected. "I've had the baby. I don't need this."

Joan tiptoed across the room. "Yes, you do," she whispered. "Look at your tummy. It's still too fat for normal clothes. Just put them on, Pauline. We need to get going."

Pauline frowned but did as she was told as quickly as her still-weary body would allow, then followed her sister silently from the room and down the narrow staircase.

"Where's Sarah?" she asked staring around nervously.

Joan pulled her towards the back door. "Already in the car," she said, "along with your case. Come on."

The two girls slipped through the door and ran across the cold yard towards a dark shape that was waiting down the farm track. As they approached the black Morris, Billy got out of the driving seat, Sarah in his arms, and opened the back door. Joan flashed him a quick smile, pushed her sister into the back of the car, then ran round and got into the front passenger seat. Billy handed the baby to Pauline, then closed the door and got into the driver's seat. Pauline pulled back the shawl covering her daughter and gently stroked the top of her head.

Joan swivelled round in her seat as Billy started the car and they set off down the track towards the main road. "Billy managed to get you a pram," she said with a smile. "He took it to the station earlier in his father's truck. Sarah will have to sleep in that until you can get a cot."

Pauline looked at her in horror. "How do I get a cot?" she asked, her voice shaking. "I don't know how to get a cot."

"From a shop," Joan said vaguely, biting her lip. "You know, a shop that sells things for babies. There are lots in London." She put her hand in the pocket of her coat and pulled out an envelope. "Here's the money," she said, holding it out to Pauline. "I had to spend some of it on things you need to take, and Billy had to buy the pram, but there's plenty left. You need to get your train ticket when we get to the station, but you should be all right for quite a while with what's left."

Pauline took the envelope and gripped it tightly. She was beginning to feel she had no control over her life whatsoever. Although she desperately wanted to keep her baby, she was seriously beginning to doubt her ability to deal with the situation ahead. She knew nothing about living alone, or shopping, or even cooking, and she had no idea whatsoever about how much things cost. She frowned at Joan.

"Do I have to pay rent?" she asked.

"Yes. Apparently the landlord comes round to collect it every Friday," Joan said with a smile. "Billy's cousin says it's quite reasonable."

Pauline had no idea what that meant, but she decided to trust Billy's cousin and pay what she was asked for. "Will I meet Billy's cousin?" she asked, thinking it would be nice to have a contact already in London.

"I'm afraid not." Joan wrinkled her nose. "He

moved away last month. He's got a job in"—she leaned over to catch Billy's murmured words—"in Liverpool, and he moved there."

"Oh." Pauline sat back and held Sarah tightly.

They travelled the rest of the way to the station in silence, and by the time Billy pulled the car into a parking space near the track, it was very nearly six o'clock. Joan jumped out and opened the back door for Pauline, who struggled out with her precious armful. Billy disappeared around the corner and returned pushing a large black coach-built pram. Pauline gasped when she saw it, but gently laid Sarah inside.

"Oh, she looks so tiny!" she said with a break in her voice.

Joan put an arm around her shoulders. "You'll both be fine," she whispered. "I'll come and see you as soon as I can. Hopefully to bring you home."

Pauline turned and flung her arms around her sister's neck. "Oh, Joanie," she sobbed, her voice muffled by her sister's collar. "I'm going to miss you so much."

Joan held her tightly, and a tear trickled down her cheek. "It won't be for long, Pauline. You'll see," she murmured.

Billy came up behind them and cleared his throat awkwardly. "Sorry," he said, "but I think we should get your ticket. You may have to put your pram in the guard's van. We need to ask the station master."

Joan gently pulled away from Pauline and wiped a hand across her nose. "Here's the address of the flat," she said, thrusting a piece of paper at her sister. "The landlord lives downstairs, and he knows you're arriving today. Don't lose the paper. I put Sarah's birth certificate in your case, too. I thought you'd need it."

Pauline looked down at the paper but didn't unfold it. She put it in her pocket and nodded at Joan. "Thank you," she said, "we'll be fine." Then, taking a deep breath, she followed Billy into the station, calmly pushing the pram in front of her.

Chapter 21

Thursday 31ˢᵗ July, 2008

"What I don't understand," said Caroline, frowning at the newspaper that lay open on the table in front of her, "is why they haven't made a public statement denying the allegations. I mean, surely that would put paid to the rumours once and for all."

Roger looked affectionately at his wife over the top of his glasses.

"Caroline, you really are very naïve," he said with a sigh. "If they do that, they'll be accused of 'protesting too much' and some paper somewhere will print a story saying it's obviously true *because* they denied it. They can't win." He paused and took a sip from his coffee. "I must say I thought they might have said something publicly by now, though. Damage limitation or something…" he ended vaguely.

Caroline stood and pushed her chair back noisily. "Well, I think the whole thing is atrocious. The poor things are prisoners, and not even in their own home. They're not even together. I feel so impotent—Roger we must do something to help them."

Roger narrowed his eyes. "What?" he ventured suspiciously.

Caroline shook her head impatiently. "Well, I don't know," she said, fixing him with a beady stare. "You're the one who worked in Intelligence. You think of something." And she left the room with as close to a flourish as she could muster.

Roger watched her go, a resigned expression on his face. He had no idea what they could possibly do to help the situation, but he knew his wife wouldn't let him rest until he came up with a plan to help their son. He sighed, finished his coffee, slowly pushed his chair back, and stood up. He needed to give the matter some serious thought.

****

Gideon and Charles had managed to get to the recording studio by early afternoon but had failed to do more than lay down a couple of tracks before finding the building besieged by the press.

"Shit." Gideon slammed his fist into the wall and swung round to face his friend. "I don't think I can keep this up, Chas. I have to say something to them. They're going to think it's all true if I don't say something soon."

Charles shook his head and put out a calming hand. "No, hold fast, Gid," he warned. "We need to wait until Simon makes his move. Anyway, if you deny it they'll only twist it and say you would say that. If Abi was here you could at least appear together, but since she's in Wales, you can't even do that."

"Oh, god, d'you think she should have come here?" Gideon's head shot up, his eyes dark.

Charles shook his head again. "Definitely not," he said emphatically. "If this is going to work with Simon, we really need Abi and Natasha not to be here. Just hang on. It'll all work out in the end. If Simon doesn't appear by tomorrow, we may have to rethink, but trust me—he will. That was a desperate man I saw in New York."

Gideon sighed and ran a hand through his hair. "Just until tomorrow, then," he conceded ungraciously, scowling towards the door, behind which he could hear sounds of the security men refusing admittance to the media. "How we gonna get out of here now?"

"Sit it out till they get bored?" Charles suggested with a shrug.

"Yeah, right," Gideon snorted, curling his lip. "That ain't never gonna happen. I can't concentrate on music, though. Can you?"

Charles shook his head. "Not a chance. Maybe there's a back door?" he suggested.

Gideon scowled. "No good. They'll have that covered. I do have an idea, though," and he grinned wickedly. "I'll need your help. You need to make a phone call." He put his arm around his friend's shoulders and pulled him into the corner, speaking quietly. Charles grinned, nodded, and rapidly made a call on his mobile.

"Hi…Yeah, I've got some information regarding the Gideon Hawk story," he said distinctly, speaking with a pronounced London accent. "…Yeah, that's right. No…Not about Gideon. It's about his wife." He paused, listening, then grinned over at Gideon and continued to speak. "Yeah, about Abigail Hawk. She's been seen in London." He fell silent again and rolled his eyes at Gideon as he listened. "Yeah, honestly. She was seen driving into town from the M25 about an hour ago. Looks like she was heading for Canary Wharf… Yeah, that's right. Probably going to *The National Crier* office. Just thought you might be interested." He frowned and listened again. "Dunno, mate. Couldn't say. I just know she was seen driving in…It was a 4x4, I think…Yeah, about an hour ago…Okay, then, no problem. Ta-ra." He disconnected the call and grinned at Gideon. "Okay? Think that'll do the trick?" he asked.

Gideon raised his eyebrows. "Well, might divert them for long enough for us to get back to the flat. Well done. That sounded pretty convincing. It only needs one of them to set off in a hurry and the others will soon follow to see what they're missing. Just like fucking sheep, the lot of 'em," he said damningly, pulling his cigarettes out of his pocket and sticking one in his mouth. As he reached for his lighter, one of the sound engineers tapped on the glass and waved a hand at him.

"Sorry, Gideon, can't light up in here." he said apologetically.

"What has the world come to," Gideon muttered, returning his lighter to his pocket but keeping the unlit cigarette in his mouth. "Could you ever have imagined, even a couple of years ago, recording an album without being allowed to smoke? Unbelievable." He threw himself down into a chair and glowered at the wall. Charles perched on the chair opposite and looked sympathetic.

"Crazy, isn't it?" he said. "Bet Simon's finding the smoking ban really hard. He's been in the U.S. for so long he probably didn't even know about it. Bet he's not sticking to it."

Gideon scowled at the mention of the drummer's name and picked up his phone.

"Guess I'd better warn Abi she's been spotted in London!" he said with a wry grin. "She'll probably see it on the news."

****

"Wow, poor Pauline," breathed Natasha, her eyes huge and round. "She must have been terrified, going to London on her own with the baby. She was so young, and she was really quite stupid, too. She didn't know anything."

"She wasn't stupid." Abi frowned at her. "She was just innocent. Girls didn't know nearly as much about life in those days. It was a very different time. They'd led a very sheltered existence. After all, Pauline didn't really understand about contraception, did she?"

"Even I know more than her"—Natasha laughed scornfully—"and I'm only twelve. Didn't they teach them stuff at school?"

Abi shook her head. "Not that sort of thing," she said. "They would have found out where babies came from in biology lessons, but certainly no one would have told them how to prevent babies from coming." She got to her feet and stretched. "I'll make some sandwiches, and then we can read the next bit, if you like."

Natasha grinned and jumped up. "Ooh, yes," she said enthusiastically. "We can't leave them like that! Is Joan's diary the next one, or is it another one of Pauline's first?"

Abi walked into the kitchen area and filled the kettle. "I think it's Joan's next," she said without turning round. "They do overlap a little, but Pauline didn't write any more until the middle of November. She was probably too busy trying to cope with the baby on her own."

Natasha walked over to join her mother and started buttering some bread. "Were you really scared when you had me?" she asked after a while.

Abi gave a short laugh. "Terrified!" she admitted. "And to be honest, apart from the fact that I did have some painkillers, Pauline had a much better experience than I did. She had nice people with her who cared about her. I had a midwife who couldn't give a damn. It was the most dreadful night of my life," she added, her face darkening at the memory.

Natasha glanced at her, reached up, and squeezed her arm. "I'm sorry," she said quietly. "It must be weird reading about Pauline. It must have brought back really bad memories for you. At least Pauline kept her baby."

Abi glanced down at her daughter. "At the moment anyway," she warned. "But I still don't think this is going to have a happy ending."

Natasha opened the Marmite and began spreading it on the bread and butter. "It might," she said hopefully. "Maybe they live happily ever after in London and Joan goes to live…" Her words dwindled as she remembered that Joan was Abi's mother, and that Abi had never even heard of Pauline. "Oh. I guess it can't be like that, can it? Otherwise you would have known Pauline and Sarah."

"Yes. I rather think we're in for a bit of a depressing read," Abi said sadly. "D'you still want to carry on?"

Natasha looked at her in surprise. "Of course I do!" she exclaimed. "Don't you?"

"Yes, I do." Abi sighed. "I need to know what happened to her. I'm already beginning to understand my mother a bit better. If she saw her sister go through this, and maybe something really bad happens, she probably didn't want the same for me."

Natasha put her head on one side. "Okay," she conceded, "but surely things in 1995 were very different to 1950? I mean, loads of people had babies, and no one really minded, did they?"

"Well, I was a bit young," Abi admitted with a grin, "but yes, you're right, it wasn't nearly so much of a scandal. Well, not to most people anyway. Just to my parents." Her lips set in a thin line as she recalled the dark time.

They carried the sandwiches over to the living area of the caravan, and both perched on the window seat to eat. Natasha stared out at the almost deserted beach.

"Doesn't look much like August," she remarked, managing to get Marmite on the end of her nose. "I like it here."

"So do I." Abi smiled, gazing round the small space. "I have very fond memories of this caravan."

Natasha grinned at her. "I meant the beach," she said. "This is just a caravan."

Abi tutted. "Not just any old caravan," she retorted. "This is where I got to know your father again, where we found out about you, where…" She stopped and stared out of the window, her face turned away from her daughter.

"Where what?" Natasha asked curiously. "You didn't finish."

Abi bent her head to let her hair fall over her face. "Nothing else," she muttered, taking a bite of her sandwich.

Natasha stared at her for a moment. "Ewww! No, too much information!" she said, wrinkling her nose. "You mean you and Dad…here in the caravan? Oh, that's gross!" She shook her head in an attempt to rid herself of the image.

Abi smiled. "There's nothing wrong with it," she protested mildly. "It meant we loved each other."

Natasha raised an eyebrow but said nothing. At that moment Abi's mobile trilled, and she snatched it up quickly.

"Hello?" she said, grinning as she realised it was Gideon. "Uh-huh. We've been avoiding the news today...Really? Why would they say that?" She took a bite of her sandwich as she listened, her eyes widening in surprise. "Oh, Gideon, you didn't! And they believed him?...Well, I guess that's pretty clever. Did they go away?" She listened again, indicating to Natasha to turn on the television. "So are you back at the flat, then?... Good, yeah, we're okay. Been reading more diaries. Pauline has just given birth...I know. We'll tell you all about it when we see you. D'you think you can get down here anytime, or should we come to London?" She paused and wrinkled her nose. "Okay, we'll wait. I hope he does it soon, though. I'm getting fed up with this. Talk to you later." She disconnected the call and laid her phone on the table.

Natasha had turned on the television and flicked through to Sky News. Abi crawled across the floor to join her and turned up the sound. As they watched, a picture of Abi and Gideon appeared behind the presenter, and she began to speak.

"We've just heard on good authority that Abigail Hawk, wife of rock musician Gideon Hawk, has been seen driving into London in the vicinity of Canary Wharf. Abigail was the subject of an article in *The National Crier* yesterday, and it's possible she's on her way to their offices. Our reporter Sean Manning is at

Canary Wharf. Sean, any sight of Abigail yet?"

The dark, thickset young man huddled against the driving rain at Canary Wharf shook his head. "No, not yet, Susanna. Apparently she was spotted entering London from the M25 about an hour ago and was later seen heading this way. Nothing to report yet, but I'll keep you posted."

Abi turned the sound off and grinned at the puzzled Natasha. "Dad got Chas to phone the BBC and tell them I'd been spotted entering London. It was just a story, in order to get the reporters to leave them alone and go looking for me. Apparently it worked, 'cause they managed to get out of the recording studio and back to the flat with no real problems."

Natasha giggled. "That's brilliant! Good old Dad. No sign of Simon yet?"

"Not yet." Abi shook her head, getting to her feet and carrying her plate to the kitchen. She picked up her phone off the table on her way past and glanced at it. "My battery's getting very low," she said with a frown. "Did you happen to notice where we packed the chargers?"

Natasha shook her head and scrambled to her feet. "No idea," she said. "I s'pect mine needs charging, too."

She followed her mother into the big bedroom, and together they rummaged in the various bags they'd brought. Ten minutes later they stared at each other.

"We didn't bring them," announced Abi flatly. "Well, that's a bit of a bummer. I don't think mine'll last for another call. How about yours?"

Natasha fished her phone out of her pocket and peered at it. "Oh," she said blankly, "it's run out completely."

Abi frowned and picked hers up again. "I should have just enough to send a text," she muttered, her fingers flying over the buttons.

"Very little battery left. Forgot chargers. Call campsite shop in emergency. Please let Judy know. x," she wrote, then sent it to Gideon.

She looked up at Natasha. "Oh, well, can't do much about it, I suppose. Let's hope no one needs us in a hurry." She grimaced. "Very stupid to have forgotten to pack them. I s'pose it was because we left in such a hurry. I'll have to try and call your dad from a payphone."

"I've never used one of those," Natasha said curiously. "Do they still have them?"

Abi looked at her and tutted. "Of course they do!" She laughed. "Not everyone has a mobile, even these days. So what would you like to do now?"

"Read the next bit," replied Natasha promptly, dropping to her knees in front of the open suitcase. "Joan's bit next, yeah?"

Abi nodded and squatted down beside her. "Yes. That seems to cover the time they were in Norfolk and most of November." She reached out, picked up the notebook and flicked quickly through it. "The bit we need to read starts from when they see Pauline and the baby off on the train."

"Come on, then, no time to waste." Natasha grinned at her. "I can't wait to see what their parents say when Joan goes home without her."

Abi got to her feet and carried the notebook over to the window seat. "I can't imagine their father—my grandfather—was very impressed," she remarked, making herself comfortable. "He didn't even know Pauline was pregnant. It seems very strange calling him my grandfather. He was dead before I was born. I never really knew anything about him. In fact, the only grandparent I ever knew was my father's mother, and she was pretty scary!"

"You never knew Janet, then?" Natasha asked curiously. "I meant to ask you before."

"No." Abi shook her head. "I'm not sure when she died, but it must have been before I was born. She can't have been very old, actually. Not even seventy."

Natasha put her head on one side. "Maybe the stress of Pauline and the baby weakened her?" she suggested.

"Maybe." Abi shrugged. "Shall we read on and find out what happened?"

Natasha nodded and joined her on the window seat. She took the book from Abi's hands and flicked through until she came to the end of October.

"This is the day Pauline left to go to London," she said, frowning at the faded writing. "Let's start there."

Chapter 22

Tuesday 31st October, 1950

Joan and Billy stood side by side, close but not touching, as they silently watched the train pull out of the station and puff steadily off towards London. They had settled Pauline and the baby in a corner seat, and the guard had stowed the pram safely in his van, promising to help Pauline when they arrived at Liverpool Street Station. As the train disappeared from sight, Billy took Joan gently by the hand and led her back to the waiting car. They sat together in the dark, neither knowing quite what to say. Eventually Billy broke the silence.

"Will you have to go back to Luton now, then?" he asked sombrely.

Joan glanced sideways at him and nodded. "Yes," she said, so quietly he had to strain to catch her words. "I have to tell my parents what Pauline's done." She swallowed and stared out of the window at the dim lights of the station office. "I have to get them to agree to let her come home."

"When will you go?" Billy asked gruffly.

"Soon, I expect." Joan shrugged. "I doubt if Aunt Maureen will let me stay now. She'll be very angry." She glanced at Billy. "But I won't tell her you helped us. I won't let you get in trouble."

273

Billy smiled in the darkness. "I'm sure she'll guess," he said. "But don't you worry about me." He paused for a moment. "Will I see you again?"

Joan turned her head away and rested it against the cold glass of the car window.

"I don't know," she answered truthfully. "I hope so. I'll try and come back to see you when we get it all sorted. But it may be a while."

Billy nodded philosophically. "I can wait," he said. "You're worth waiting for."

Joan felt her face flame, and glanced shyly back at him. "So are you," she whispered with a smile.

The sun had fully risen by the time they arrived back at the farm, and Joan was greeted by an extremely flustered Maureen.

"Joan! Where on earth have you been?" she cried, emerging from the kitchen, her hair on end and her jacket buttoned askew. "And where are Pauline and the baby? She shouldn't be out of bed yet."

Joan stood in the middle of the farmyard, and the enormity of what she had just been a party to suddenly hit her. Her face drained of colour and her knees began to buckle beneath her. Maureen leapt forward and caught her arm just as she was about to crumple onto the cold ground.

"Good heavens, child, let's get you inside at once." She propelled the girl through the door and into the early morning warmth of the farmhouse kitchen. The range was lit, and Maureen pushed Joan into a chair at one side of it. She took the seat opposite and stared at the girl intently. "What's happened, Joan?" she asked again. "What have you done?"

Joan raised huge, dark-rimmed eyes and stared

mutely at her. She swallowed, then sniffed, and a solitary tear trickled down her ashen cheek.

"Pauline and Sarah have gone to London," she whispered, "so they can't take the baby away from her."

Maureen sat back with a sigh. "Oh, I should have foreseen you'd do something like this," she muttered, clearly annoyed with herself. "Have they got somewhere to stay?"

"Yes." Joan nodded. "A flat in a big house. B— Someone we know has a cousin who lives there," she said, flushing.

Maureen looked at her in exasperation. "I know Billy helped you," she said sharply. "I saw the car drop you off. Don't worry, I shan't sack him. But I just wish you'd talked to me about this."

"We couldn't," Joan said in surprise. "You'd told us someone was coming to take Sarah away on Tuesday or Wednesday. We couldn't risk waiting any longer. You would have stopped us going."

Maureen leaned forward and took one of Joan's hands. "Of course I would," she said patiently, "but I would also have tried to intervene on Pauline's behalf. Maybe see if there was some way she could keep the baby."

Joan stared at her in consternation, unshed tears swimming in her eyes.

"D'you mean we didn't need to send them away?" she asked, her voice wavering. "They could have stayed here safely?"

Maureen shook her head. "I couldn't have promised anything," she admitted. "But I would have given it a try."

Joan stood up abruptly and paced the room in agitation. "Now I have to go home and tell my parents," she said shakily. "Pauline wants to come home and bring Sarah with her." She turned to face Maureen, her arms wrapped tightly around her body. "Does Mum know the baby is born?" she asked. "Did you telephone her?"

"Yes. I did that on Sunday morning." Maureen nodded. "Your mother was…" She paused. "Well, she was relieved that Pauline and the baby were both all right. She was concerned that Pauline shouldn't get too attached to the child, though. She thought that would make it even harder when she was taken away."

"But you let her look after her," Joan looked surprised. "Surely that would make her get more attached?"

Maureen got to her feet. "I wanted the child to have some time with her before they were separated. Now, come along, Joan, the chickens won't collect their own eggs." She picked up two baskets and held one out to Joan.

The girl took it and followed her out into the farmyard, her heart feeling empty at the thought of her twin all alone in London.

****

Saturday 4th November, 1950

As the train pulled into Luton station, Joan took a deep breath, straightened her hat, pulled on her gloves, and picked up her suitcase. She had already spotted her mother and Margaret waiting for her on the platform and was dreading the moment when they realised she was alone. She made her way towards the door and stepped down onto the platform behind a large man wearing a camel coat and trilby hat. Being hidden behind him for a moment gave her time to study her mother and little sister from afar. Margaret was holding her mother's hand and hopping up and down in excitement, her curls bobbing on her shoulders. Janet stood straight and silent, her eyes fixed on the train, her mouth set in a firm line. Joan swallowed nervously and started towards them. Margaret spotted her first and pulled hard on her mother's hand, pointing down the platform.

"Joanie!" she cried, and pulling her hand free she sped towards her sister and flung her arms around her waist. Joan smiled and put her suitcase down. She bent and put both arms around the little girl, holding her close.

"Hello, Maggie," she whispered, rubbing her face in the child's hair. "It's so good to see you."

Margaret wriggled free and stepped back a pace. "Where's Pauline?" she asked with a frown, peering round Joan and looking down the platform.

Joan bit her lip. "She's gone to London to see a friend," she said at once. "She'll be home soon, I hope."

Margaret nodded and caught Joan's hand, pulling her towards their mother, who had remained standing in the same spot.

"Hello, Mum." Joan stopped in front of her and set her case down again. Janet leant forward and gave her a quick peck on the cheek.

"Joan," she said guardedly, "where's your sister?"

"She's gone to see a friend in London," announced Margaret, her eyes wide. "Can I go to London, Mummy? I've never been there. Can I go too?"

`Janet frowned at her and stared at Joan. "Alone?"

she asked.

Joan shook her head, her heart thumping uncomfortably in her chest. Without another word, Janet turned and led the way back to where the car was parked. Margaret clambered into the back, and Joan joined her mother in the front.

"Mum, she wants to come home," she murmured, as Janet started the engine.

"Not now, Joan," came the brisk reply. "We'll talk at home."

The journey back to their house seemed interminable to Joan, but she managed to answer as many of Margaret's questions as she could without having to mention Pauline very much at all. She avoided all mention of Billy, as well, knowing the reaction that would get from her mother. When they arrived home, she was relieved to see her father's car was not in the driveway. She got out, retrieved her case from the boot, and followed her mother up the path to the front door.

"Go and unpack and get changed, Joan," Janet ordered. "Then when you come down we'll talk. Margaret, go to the sitting room and read your book for school."

Margaret opened her mouth to protest but, seeing her mother's face, closed it again and scuttled off in the direction of the sitting room.

Joan unpacked swiftly, changed from her travelling clothes of dark green skirt, cream blouse, and brown cardigan into a pair of pale blue slacks and a dark blue polo-necked jumper. Then she checked her hair in the mirror and made her way down to the kitchen. Her mother was at the stove and gestured to Joan she should take a seat at the table. Eventually she turned, placed two steaming cups of tea on the table, and sat down opposite her daughter. Her expression softened as she looked at Joan's ashen face and red-rimmed eyes, and she reached over and patted her hand.

"Now, tell me what happened, Joan," she said. "You're not in trouble."

Joan took a deep breath and licked her lips. "I think I might be," she began. "Pauline didn't want to give up her baby, Mum. She loves her so much, and she couldn't bear to be parted from her." She paused, watching her mother's face. "So I helped her get a place to stay in London, and on Tuesday they both went there by train. She really wants to come home and bring Sarah with her. Please, can you persuade Dad to let them?" At the mention of the baby's name, Janet's eyes flickered, and Joan could see she was considering her daughter's information. Eventually she sat back and looked at Joan.

"He'll never agree," she said bluntly, "and I'm not sure I should even ask him."

Joan's face went even whiter, and she leaned forward urgently. "But Mum, she'll never give her up. If she can't come home she'll have to stay in London, and you'll never see her again." She burst into tears and rested her head in her hands.

Janet sucked in her breath. "Pull yourself together, Joan," she said sharply. "I'll have to discuss the matter with your father. This is very unfortunate. I had hoped he need never hear of this. I should have realised Pauline wouldn't give up her baby so easily. How on earth is she going to manage in London? Where is she staying? Does she have any money?"

Joan lifted her head and wiped her hand across her eyes. "She has a flat in a big house. She has enough money to keep her going until you let her come home," she said, desperation sounding in her voice.

Janet sighed again. "Joan, however much you and Pauline want this, I'm very much afraid your father will say no. He'll feel she's disgraced the family, and he probably won't want her to come home even without the baby."

Joan bristled. "Her name is Sarah," she stated. "Oh, and Mum, she's so sweet! Don't you even want to see your grandchild?"

An indecipherable emotion passed across Janet's face before she got to her feet. "One day I'll be ready for grandchildren," she said firmly, "and that time will be when one of you girls is married and old enough. A grandchild born from a sordid encounter with a married man is not what I had in mind. They weren't even in love."

Joan opened her mouth to object, then changed her mind and compressed her lips together. She looked appealingly at her mother. "What will you say to Dad?" she asked. "Can I be there too?"

"I don't think that would be wise." Janet shook her head, her eyes full of the fear she herself was feeling. "I think it would be best if you took Margaret to the pictures this evening. I'm sure there's something suitable showing at The Odeon." She delved into her handbag and pulled out her purse. "Here's five shillings; that should be plenty. Your father should be home in about half an hour, so I suggest you go before he gets here." Joan scrambled to her feet and took the proffered coins. "And Joanie, I'll do my best, but please don't hold out too much hope."

Joan smiled a watery smile, slid past her mother, and walked out into the hall. She could hear her little sister reading aloud to herself in the sitting room, and she ran upstairs and into her bedroom, where she closed the door and flung herself down on the bed. She could tell from her mother's demeanour she'd been moved by the thought of her grandchild, and Joan was confident Janet would do all she could to persuade their father to let Pauline come home. However, Joan also knew how strict her father was, and she didn't really hold out much hope for success. She sat up and ran her hand through her curls, then fished up her sleeve, pulled out her handkerchief, and blew her nose. Margaret must not suspect anything was wrong. She would of course, eventually find out what was going on, but for now Joan needed to behave as if everything was normal. She got off the bed, slipped her feet into a pair of flat black court shoes, picked up her black winter jacket, popped the five shillings into her pocket, and went back downstairs. She opened the door to the sitting room and smiled at Margaret.

"Would you like me to take you to the pictures?" she asked.

Margaret jumped up with a squeal. "Yes, pleeease, Joanie!" she said, her book flying off her lap and landing on the floor. "That'd be such fun!"

Joan laughed. "Come on, then, put your book somewhere safe and come and get your coat and shoes on."

As the girls reached the corner at the end of the road, Joan turned and glanced back at the house just as her father's car pulled into the drive. She hurried

Margaret round the corner towards the town centre, mentally crossing her fingers for her mother.

****

Thursday 9ᵗʰ November, 1950

Joan stared out of the window dismally. The rain was pouring down and the wind was howling in the gables. Since her mother had informed her father about Pauline and the baby nearly a week before, Joan had been confined to her room. Walter Forrester had been so angry he had wanted to turn Joan out of the house as well, for her part in aiding and abetting her sister, but on the intervention of Janet the punishment was commuted to two weeks confined to her bedroom. Janet had tried to appeal to his softer side, but Walter had remained adamant that no daughter of his would be tolerated in his house with a bastard child. He had gone further and said he would no longer have her name mentioned in the house and that as far as he was concerned she was dead. Janet had pleaded on behalf of herself and Joan and Margaret, but he would not be moved. Joan was to be kept in her room for two weeks, and then she was to start work at the factory, and none of it was ever to be mentioned again.

She stood up and walked into the middle of the room, frustrated and desperately upset that she had let her twin down so badly. She hadn't even been able to write to her during her period of confinement and was very worried about how she might be coping. A knock at the door heralded the arrival of her mother with a tray of food. Joan watched as Janet placed the tray on the dressing table, then turned to go.

"Mum," she said tentatively, "can you help me with something?"

Janet glanced at her, pity in her eyes. "I don't know," she said honestly, taking a step back into the room and closing the door.

"I need to write to Pauline," said Joan. "Please, will you post it for me?"

Janet hesitated for just a second, then nodded. "Yes, I will," she said. "I'd love to know if she's all right. If *they're* all right." She paused and bit her lip. "Joan, I don't agree with what your father's doing, but at the moment I'm powerless to oppose him. If I did, he could cause a lot of pain for the whole family. But that doesn't mean I've given up. Trust me. I just need a little time."

Joan stared at her silently. If her mother was on her side—on Pauline's side—maybe there was still hope.

She smiled. "Thank you. I'll write to her now. Please, can you post it today?"

Janet nodded again, smiled at Joan, then left the room.

Joan hurried to her chest of drawers and pulled open the top left-hand drawer. She took out a sheet of notepaper and an envelope and carried them over to her bed, where she sat down cross-legged and began to write.

"Dear Pauline, I miss you so much. I really hope you and Sarah are all right. I'm so sorry I haven't written before, but Dad has me locked in my room at the moment. I've just now got Mum to agree to post this to you for me. As you'll gather from that, Dad's not being very helpful. He's adamant you can't come home…" She paused in her writing, wondering whether or not to mention her father had also banned all mention of Pauline's name. She decided not. *"but Mum is still*

trying to persuade him. I told Margaret you're staying with a friend in London, but she keeps asking for you. I'll keep trying, and I'll also try to come and see you soon. Please write back and let me know you're all right. Dad never collects the post, so it's quite safe. You could also try to phone during the daytime when he's at the factory. He's making me start work next week, but don't worry. I'll still manage to come and see you. Do you need me to bring you anything? I love you, Pauline. Give Sarah a kiss from me. All my love, Joanie."

She laid down her pen and read through what she'd written. Then she folded it carefully and slid it into the envelope. She sealed it and wrote the address clearly, adding her own address on the back in case it didn't get delivered for some reason. Then she hopped off the bed and investigated the lunch tray Janet had brought her. As soon as she heard back from Pauline that they were all right, she'd be able to relax a little. Until then, each day felt like a life sentence.

****

Tuesday 14th November, 1950

By Tuesday, Joan was beginning to make plans to escape down the drainpipe and was agitatedly pacing the room when her mother came hurrying in. She closed the door behind her and beckoned to Joan.

"You've had a letter," she said in a hushed voice, feeling in the pocket of her apron and producing a white envelope. Joan was across the room in seconds, tore the single sheet out, and unfolded it.

Janet hovered behind her. "What does it say?" she asked urgently.

Joan quickly scanned through it, and her face fell. "Shall I read it out?" she asked, sitting down on the bed. Janet nodded and sat down beside her.

"Dear Joanie, Thank you for your letter." Pauline's writing was untidy and obviously hurried. *"Sarah and I are all right. thank you. although we would like to come home now. She doesn't really sleep much—except in the day. Not at night at all. Then she just cries all the time. I'm very tired. and I don't seem to have enough milk for her. The flat is okay but very small, and the landlord seems fair, I think. I don't think the money you gave me is going to last very long. Everything is very expensive in London. My rent is ten shillings a week. That seems an awful lot. What do you think? And they made me pay three months in advance. That took six pounds all in one go. When you come maybe you could bring me some more money? We're all right, though. I'm getting very good at changing nappies. I haven't really seen any of my neighbours. I think they all go out to work all the time. It's a pity Billy's cousin doesn't live here any more. I'm really missing you and Margaret and Mum. Please persuade Dad soon. All my love, Pauline."*

Joan laid the letter down on her lap and turned to her mother. "Oh, Mum, she's not all right, is she?" she said, a break in her voice.

Janet picked up the letter and scanned it again. "She will be tired," she commented sadly. "It's hard work looking after a newborn baby, especially if you're little more than a child yourself." She frowned and sighed. "I'm not getting anywhere with your father, I'm afraid. In fact, he refuses to discuss the matter any further. I think the best thing would be if we could find somewhere nearer for her to live, for now at least. Then we could help her look after Sarah."

Joan smiled as she heard her mother use the baby's name. "That sounds like a good idea," she said enthusiastically. "How can we do that?"

"I'll give it some thought." Janet smiled at her. "You write back to her and say you'll try and visit soon. I'll give you some money to take to her." She stood up and started towards the door, then paused and turned back to Joan. "By the way, who's Billy?"

Joan felt her face begin to flush and bent her head forward to cover it. "He's a farm hand at Aunt Maureen's farm," she whispered. "His cousin found the flat for Pauline. He used to live there."

Janet looked at her closely, then nodded and left the room. Joan watched her go, then grabbed another sheet of writing paper from her drawer and sat down to reply to Pauline.

"Dear Pauline, I'm so sorry you're so tired. It must be really hard looking after a baby. I'll try and visit you as soon as possible, and Mum says she'll give me some money to bring you. I have to start work at the factory on Monday, so I probably can't come next week, but I shall try and make it the week after. I shall tell Dad I'm ill or something. Mum will help. Mum says maybe we can find you somewhere to live round here— like a flat or something—so you're nearer to us. She's going to keep trying with Dad, though, too. I'll see you very soon. All my love, Joanie."

She sealed the letter in its envelope and put it to one side for her mother to post.

****

Friday 24th November, 1950

Joan let herself in the kitchen door and put her bag down on the table. Her mother was at the stove, busy stirring a large saucepan from which wafted the delicious smell of beef stew.

Joan sniffed appreciatively. "Mmm," she said, "that smells good. Is it nearly ready?"

Janet turned and smiled at her. "Nearly," she said, wiping her hands on her apron. "Get your coat off and then come back to talk to me. I have something to tell you."

Joan looked at her curiously but ran upstairs, slipped off her coat and shoes, slid her feet into her slippers, and went back down again. Janet indicated she should shut the kitchen door, then gestured to her to sit at the table.

Joan looked at her. "What is it?" she asked. "Has Dad agreed to let Pauline come home?"

Janet sighed. "I'm afraid not," she said, "but this is about Pauline. I have a friend who has a rooming house in Caddington, and she's agreed Pauline and the baby can rent a room from her." Joan's eyes lit up, and Janet went on, "It would only be a room, with use of a bathroom, but it would be better than her being all that way away in London, and it will do until I can sort out something more permanent."

Joan nodded enthusiastically. "Shall I write and tell her?" she asked.

"I thought we'd go and tell her"—Janet smiled—"and bring her back with us."

"Oh, yes, please! When can we go?"

"Tomorrow," Janet replied, pulling out a chair and sitting down facing her daughter. "I've arranged for Margaret to go to a friend's house for the day, and your father has already told me he has to go in to the factory all day even though it's Saturday."

Joan bounced on her seat. "Ooh, this is very exciting! Are we taking the car or going by train?"

"Since we're hoping to bring Pauline and the baby back, I think we should go in the car," said Janet. "I take it you have the full address?"

Joan nodded and got to her feet. "Thank you, Mum," she said, giving her mother a quick hug. "Maybe everything will turn out all right in the end after all."

Janet looked a little doubtful but returned the hug and turned back to her stew. "Supper will be ready in ten minutes," she said. "Go and make sure Margaret's ready, will you?"

****

Saturday 25th November, 1950

The drive to London was conducted mostly in silence. Janet needed to concentrate on her driving, and Joan was almost too excited to speak. She was clutching the address of Pauline's flat in her hand, and her mind was going over and over what she would say to her sister when she saw her. She was fully prepared that Pauline might look rather ill and tired, but she was confident that, between them, she and her mother could get her back to Bedfordshire and installed in the nice cosy room Janet had found. It was about three miles from their house to Caddington, where it would be very easy for Janet to keep an eye on her daughter and granddaughter.

Joan wriggled in her seat in excitement. In about an hour she would be reunited with her twin, and by the evening Pauline would be back where she belonged. Or very nearly. Joan glanced at her mother. Janet's face was serious as she concentrated on her driving, but she caught sight of Joan out of the corner of her eye and smiled.

"Excited?" she asked. "If all goes according to plan, Pauline will be back close to home by this evening."

Joan nodded and clutched the address tighter in her hand. Pauline would be so pleased to see them. She thought for a moment, then turned to her mother.

"Mum, d'you mind if I go and see Pauline on my own first?" she asked. "She won't be expecting you to be with me, and, well…" She didn't want her mother to feel offended.

Janet smiled again. "That's fine, Joan. A good idea, actually. You can prepare her for what's to happen. After all, the last time she saw me I wasn't very nice to her, I'm afraid. She may be nervous if I arrive with you."

Joan smiled and settled back in her seat.

Chapter 23

Friday 1ˢᵗ August, 2008

Gideon laid down his guitar and took a long swig of lukewarm coffee. He pushed his hair impatiently out of his eyes and glowered at the sound engineer.

"Take a break," he barked, and turned his back to stalk to the far corner of the room and sink down onto the floor, resting his head on his knees. Charles wandered over, his bass still slung around his neck.

"You're really in a mood this morning, Gid," he remarked mildly, squatting down beside his friend. "Could this have anything to do with the fact that you haven't spoken to Abi today?"

Gideon glanced up at him and had the grace to look slightly abashed.

"Maybe," he conceded. "How could she be so stupid as to forget her charger? It's almost impossible to contact them now." He sighed and ran his hand through his hair. "And I'm half expecting Simon to show up today. I need a fag and more coffee." He jumped to his feet and strode over to the door that led into the back room.

Charles sighed and followed him. "I think you've probably had enough coffee," he said with a grin. "Maybe some chamomile tea would be better?"

Gideon snorted and continued to pour himself

another mug of strong coffee, adding three large teaspoons of sugar and stirring vigorously.

Charles laughed. "Okay, then, if that's the way you want it. Pour me one, will you?" and he held out his nearly empty mug. Gideon obliged, and the two of them carried their drinks over to the window and stared out onto the busy road below. "I think you may be right about Simon," added Charles, leaning against the windowsill. "If he thinks the way I believe he does, then today is the perfect day for him to carry out his little plan."

Gideon turned abruptly and threw himself into one of the armchairs, slopping coffee over the rim of his mug. "Yeah, that's what I was thinking. Not sure I can pull this off, though, Chas." He looked up at his friend. "Trying to get him to believe that I believe the lies— not sure I can do it. I'll just want to rip his fucking head off." He drained his mug and slammed it down on the coffee table with a crash.

Charles perched on the arm of the chair opposite and leaned forward. "You must try, Gid," he said earnestly. "If you can win his confidence, even for a few minutes, we can get him to give himself away. Stay strong! It'll be worth it."

Gideon raised a sardonic eyebrow. "It's easy for you," he said, flicking his hair over his shoulder. "It's not your wife and daughter who are being maligned. But you're right. I need to do it. Just hope he hurries up if he is coming." He lay back, stretched his legs out in front of him, and closed his eyes.

Charles watched him curiously. He could sense a huge build-up of tension in his friend and was quite concerned for Simon's welfare, should he show up at the studio. He sipped his coffee thoughtfully.

"Maybe I should talk to him first?" he suggested after a moment.

Gideon opened his eyes and stared balefully at him. "Like hell," he muttered. "No, Chas. You're welcome to be there, but I need to deal with this." He paused for a moment, then grinned. "You need to be there to stop me from killing him."

Charles rolled his eyes. "Hmm. That's what I thought. Well, just remember…" He broke off as one of the technicians appeared at the door.

"Someone to see you, Gideon," he said. "Shall I send him in here?"

Gideon glanced at Charles and sat up straight. "Who is it?" he asked. "Is it Simon Dean?"

The technician was new and very young, and he shrugged. "Dunno," he said. "He didn't say his name. Fat dude with curly blonde hair."

"Simon," Gideon and Charles said as one. "Yeah, send him in," continued Gideon. "We may as well get this over with."

He stood up and walked over to the window, where he leaned nonchalantly against the glass. Charles joined him, and the two of them watched as a shadow appeared in the doorway. Simon entered the room tentatively and stopped when he saw the two men across the room.

"Hi, guys," he said, apologetically. "I hope I'm not disturbing you too much?"

"What do you want, Simon?" Gideon snapped. "Have you come to gloat?"

Simon looked taken aback. "Gloat?" he repeated. "Why would I gloat? D'you mean about that article in the paper? That was pretty nasty stuff."

Gideon watched him from beneath hooded eyes. "Yeah, it was," he said. "Sit down, then. If you haven't come to say 'I told you so,' then why are you here?"

A gleam appeared in Simon's bloodshot eyes, and he perched on the edge of the chair. "You think it's true, then?" he asked cautiously, watching Gideon's reaction.

Gideon pushed himself upright, ran a hand through his hair and glowered at Simon. "God knows," he snapped. "It's certainly brought up some issues." Charles moved across the room and positioned himself between Gideon and Simon. Gideon took a deep breath and sank down into the chair opposite Simon. "You never liked her, did you?" he asked, trying to keep his voice neutral. "You never trusted her."

Simon's already ruddy face flushed still more. "Well…that's maybe a bit strong," he said, "but I always thought she'd cause the band to break up if you stayed with her."

Charles watched as Gideon's hand balled into a fist at his side, not visible to Simon. He moved closer and glanced at Simon.

"So you think the stuff in the paper could be true, then?" he asked.

"Probably." Simon shrugged. "It would explain why she didn't tell Gideon before he left that she was pregnant." Gideon made a strange sound and jerkily crossed his legs. Simon, thinking he was agreeing with him, carried on. "Printing that letter she sent you was a pretty cheap trick," he said. "Not that you ever got it, did you?" Gideon shook his head, not trusting himself to speak. "It wasn't quite accurate, but it certainly painted her badly, didn't it?" Simon went on blithely, completely failing to notice his slip-up.

Gideon exchanged glances with Charles, then held up his hand. "What was that, Si?" he asked, his voice deceptively calm. "What did you say about it being accurate?"

Simon, his confidence riding high, shrugged again. "Well, they didn't print the whole letter, did they? But it didn't really matter. She should have told you before you left, if it was really your baby."

Gideon got to his feet and hovered menacingly over Simon. "How d'you know they didn't print it all, Simon?" he asked. "How could you have known that unless you've already seen the real letter?" Simon's face fell, and sweat began to bead on his forehead. He opened his mouth but no words came. Gideon stepped closer. "You stole those letters, didn't you, Simon?" he said, his voice ominously quiet. "You stole them, and then you sold them to that rag." Simon got to his feet and backed away across the room, cornering himself against the pool table.

"No—no, Gid, you've got it all wrong. I wouldn't do that. I'm your friend. I love you, Gid. I wouldn't do anything to hurt you."

Gideon advanced towards him, his hands balled at his sides.

"Don't fucking lie to me, Simon," he warned, his face dark with fury. "What the fuck did you think you were doing? How dare you drag my wife and child through the gutter press? What have they ever done to you? I know you stole my letters back in '95—I almost understood that. I couldn't forgive it, but I could begin to understand. But this…this total betrayal? I can't believe I ever called you a friend." He paused and watched as Simon attempted to gather his thoughts, to form some words to defend himself. "Chas told me you wanted me to re-form the band. Well, I *am* doing." He stared at Simon. "I *am* doing, and Chas is going to play bass again. You, on the other hand, are to come nowhere near us."

Simon cowered back against the window, the sweat pouring down his face and soaking the collar of his shirt. He realised he had completely lost control of the situation, but he made one last-ditch attempt to redeem himself.

"But, Gid, I didn't give them the letter or the pictures," he blustered. "I did steal the letters back in '95, and I regret that, but I didn't sell the story to *The Crier*. You have to believe me. Someone else must have done that."

Charles gave a short laugh and stepped forward. "Yeah, right, Simon. And who could that have been? You were the only person who'd ever read those letters. Unless you showed them to someone else, that is."

"No, no, of course I didn't." Simon shook his head. "No one knew I had them. I never told anyone…except my mother. But that wasn't until after the band broke up. And I didn't show them to her." His face, by this time almost puce and shining with sweat, took on a haunted look. "Look, Gid, I didn't sell them to the paper. Why would I do that? I want you to have me back in the band, not alienate you forever."

Gideon stared at him from across the room. "You did sell them, Simon," he said, his voice hard. "And you did it to discredit my wife. To try to make me believe she was a lying cheat. To try to break us up. In your twisted little mind you thought that if we broke up then I would welcome you back into the band." He paused, a mirthless smile playing about his lips. "But you really don't know me, Simon, if you thought that would work. We were expecting you to turn up today. We planned it that I'd pretend to believe the stories in order to catch you out. And it worked." His brows came together, and he advanced a couple of steps towards the cowering Simon. "Now get the fuck out of here before I kill you! Don't ever contact any of my family again—*and* I expect you to go to the media and withdraw all allegations made in that shit of a paper. I'll be calling a press conference to put them right, too."

Simon swallowed and ran a chubby hand through his now sweat-soaked hair. "All right, I'll go," he stammered, edging towards the door. "But think about it, Gideon—How d'you know you can trust her? She was just a kid. A kid who wanted you to stay with her. She wanted to break up the band even back then…" He fled through the door as Gideon advanced towards him, fury in his eyes. Charles caught Gideon's arm and restrained him.

"Let him go, Gid," he warned. "You don't want the police to get involved, do you? I think he'll leave you alone now. He knows now he'll never get you to think ill of Abi."

Gideon, staring at the door as it banged shut behind Simon's retreating figure, growled under his breath, "He's gone too far this time."

Charles pulled him away from the door and reiterated what he'd said. "He's gone now. He knows he can't win. Let him go, Gid. You go to the press and put things straight, then put Simon behind you forever."

He grinned. "He'll never dare come near you or your family again."

Gideon slumped down in a chair and ran his hands distractedly through his hair. "God, Chas, I really wanted to kill him," he muttered through clenched teeth. "That he could say those things about Abi... I can't let him get away with it. I'm going to expose him when I give the press conference."

Charles looked doubtful. "Talk to Abi first," he advised. "That might seem a good idea in the heat of the moment, but it probably won't serve any real purpose."

Gideon raised dark-rimmed eyes. "I'd talk to Abi if she had a sodding phone," he growled. He leapt to his feet. "I'll call the campsite and ask them to get her to call me." He strode across the room to retrieve his phone from the table and punched in the number of the campsite. They waited in silence while the call was connected, and then Gideon frowned in annoyance. "It's engaged," he muttered and slammed the phone back on the table. "I'll try again in a bit. Shall we lay down some more tracks while we wait?"

****

When Simon left the recording studio, he headed straight for the nearest hotel and ensconced himself in the bar. He ordered a pint of lager and a whisky chaser and retired to a dark corner to brood. That the morning had not gone according to plan was something of an understatement, and Simon was feeling a mixture of annoyance, fear, and disgust. The look in Gideon's eyes when he advanced towards him had been, quite frankly, terrifying, and Simon felt quite hard done by. He had only been trying to show Gideon what his wife was really like, hadn't he? He'd been trying to help. Surely anyone would see that.

He downed his pint in one long gulp, then emptied the whisky down his throat. He wasn't going to give up. If Gideon really couldn't see what a bitch he was married to, then it was up to him to show him. He'd been very shocked to realise Gideon and Charles had rumbled his little plan so easily, and he also realised it would do no good at all to attempt to approach Gideon again. Simon's eyes took on a wild look as he puzzled over what his next move should be. It never once occurred to him to admit defeat, to admit the bond between Gideon and Abi was not only too strong to be broken but that it *should* not be broken. Simon still felt sure that without Abi Gideon would be his old self again, the self who would welcome Simon with open arms. He smiled to himself. Well, if Gideon wouldn't do anything, then he'd have to go directly to the problem herself. If it meant he had to somehow remove her from the picture, that's what he'd do. Gideon would thank him in the end.

****

Abi was struggling to keep her hood on as she fought against the strong wind on her way to the campsite shop. The weather forecast had predicted periods of rain, sun, and strong wind, with the possibility of thunder, and Abi was beginning to get fed up with it. She arrived at the wooden cabin that served as the shop and hurried inside out of the rain and wind. The young man behind the counter looked up and smiled at her.

"Hi, Abi," he said in his lilting Welsh accent. "Nice weather, isn't it?"

Abi rolled her eyes, and pushed the hood of her waterproof back. "Hi, Gareth, perfect for August, eh?" she said with a grin. "Any chance I could use your phone? I forgot my charger, and I told Gideon I'd try to call him this morning."

Gareth wrinkled his nose and shook his head. "Sorry, Abi, no can do. The lines are down. It's this awful wind, you know. Happens all the time." He saw her face and took pity on her. "I'll come over and tell you when they get fixed, shall I?"

Abi smiled at him. "Thanks, Gareth. That'd be great. When does Caitlin get her A level results?" Abi and Gideon had first met Gareth and his girlfriend Caitlin when they'd visited the caravan together in '05.

Gareth flushed. "Oh, in a couple of weeks," he said with pride. "She's predicted to get two As and a B. That would mean she could go to Cardiff. Not too far away."

"That's great." Abi smiled and turned to pick a couple of bars of chocolate off the shelf. "And how's your degree going?"

Gareth rang up the items and popped them into a bag. "Well, thank you. Only one more year to go, now. That'll be one pound twenty-two, please."

Abi paid, then waved a hand and headed back to the caravan, where Natasha was busy preparing some brunch. They had both slept late but were very keen to carry on reading Pauline's story, so to save time Natasha had volunteered to do the food while Abi phoned Gideon.

Abi burst through the caravan door, bringing a swirl of wind with her.

Natasha gasped. "That looks really horrid out there," she commented, carefully pouring hot water into two mugs. "Now come on, let's get on with the story. Did you speak to Dad? Is he okay?"

Abi shook her head, shrugged off her waterproof, and kicked her boots into the corner. "No. The phone lines are down. Gareth said he'd let me know when they're mended." She padded into the living area and smoothed her hair down with her hand. "Phew! It really is like winter out there. Apparently there's supposed to be some sun later, but I find it hard to believe."

Natasha stared out the window across the bay towards Worm's Head. "It would be nice to walk to the end of Worm's Head while we're here," she commented.

Abi joined her at the window and nodded. "Yes, it would. Maybe tomorrow'll be better. I checked the tide table, and we should be safe to cross the causeway from about ten past ten tomorrow. Then we'd need to be back over by three o'clock at the latest."

"That gives us loads of time." Natasha grinned.

"Should do, although you sometimes don't get quite that long. It depends on other weather conditions and stuff," Abi said vaguely. "If we reckon we need to be back by two thirty, then we should be all right."

Natasha turned away from the window and sat down cross-legged on the floor. "Can we look at the next diary now, Mum?" she asked, her blue eyes glinting.

Abi turned and grinned at her. "Okay, okay. Let me fetch my tea. What food did you do?" she asked, walking back into the kitchen area.

Natasha jumped up again and skipped over to join her. "Cheese on toast," she said proudly. "And loads of crisps."

Abi laughed, picked up her mug, and bent to drop a light kiss on her daughter's curly head. "Sounds lovely," she said, "and I bought some choccy from the shop, so we should be fine. You bring the food through; I'll bring the drinks." She went back to the living area and made herself comfortable on the window seat. Natasha plonked the food onto the coffee table, then squatted down on the floor again, pulling the suitcase towards her.

"Right," she said with satisfaction. "That was all of Joan's, wasn't it? I wonder why she didn't write any more after that? Or maybe she just didn't keep them." She rummaged around and pulled out the next volume of Pauline's diary. "Here we go. This one starts on Friday 17th November. That's about a week before Joan's ended." She looked expectantly up at her mother. "Are you ready?"

Abi nodded and slid down onto the floor beside her daughter. "This might not be so nice," she warned. "Please don't expect a happy ending."

Natasha nodded, her young face serious. "I know," she said with a sigh, "but we have to find out."

Chapter 24

Friday 17th November, 1950

Pauline covered her ears and closed her eyes tightly. Sarah had been crying all night and was now demanding to be fed yet again. Pauline had come to know which cry meant food, and she got wearily to her feet and shuffled over to the tatty secondhand cot that stood in the corner of the room. To describe her abode as a flat was something of an overstatement. It consisted of a large high-ceilinged room, sparsely furnished with a single bed, a plain wooden table, two wooden chairs, an old wing chair covered in unidentifiable stains, and a small two-ring gas cooker that resided on the top of a work surface that also housed a sink. Pauline had added the cot, and a wooden airer on which she was attempting to dry a large number of nappies. The only heating in the room was a very small gas fire set into one wall. They had access to a shared bathroom on the landing below.

She took a deep breath and reached into the cot to pick up the screaming baby. Sarah was still very tiny, and Pauline was quite worried she wasn't getting enough to eat. She had taken her to the doctor's, but when she tried to register at the reception desk, they started asking all sorts of intrusive questions about her marital status, and she had lost her nerve, made an excuse, and left. Apart from her landlord and the postman, she rarely had any contact with anyone else unless she went out to the shops. She tried to keep those trips to a minimum because Sarah wouldn't stop crying and people stared at her.

With the baby in her arms, Pauline walked over to the wing chair and perched on the edge of it. She glanced around, then shyly uncovered her left breast and encouraged Sarah to suckle. After a moment or two the baby latched on and began to suck. Pauline winced as her cracked nipple was pulled on, and her arms clutched the baby tighter. She had no concept of the time of day and glanced towards the window to see if it was still daylight. She hadn't drawn back the curtains for days, but she could just make out the hint of sunlight in the gap between them. She leant back in the chair and tried to relax. When she'd received the letter from Joan nearly a week before, she'd begun to think that maybe help was at hand, but she'd heard nothing since, and her determination was failing. She really couldn't carry on like this. She was cold, hungry, tired, and—what was even worse—so was her baby. She looked down at the tiny child suckling at her breast and bent forward to place a kiss on her forehead.

"I love you," she whispered. "I'll make all of it all right soon."

As she spoke, she became aware of footsteps running up the stairs outside her door. She quickly pulled Sarah free from her nipple and covered herself up, then lifted the now screaming baby into her arms as she stood up and faced the door. The expected knock came, loud and abrupt. Pauline hurried over and opened the door a crack. Her landlord stood outside, an unpleasant smile on his greasy face.

"'Lectric day," he said, pushing the door further open with his foot.

"What?" Pauline asked, puzzled.

He rolled his eyes and bent closer to her, making her recoil from his beery breath. "Time to pay for your 'lectric." he repeated impatiently.

Pauline stared at him in consternation. "Surely that's included in the rent?" she said, her eyes wide.

"What d'you think I am? A bloody charity?" The man sneered unpleasantly. "Na, 'lectric is separate. Five bob."

"Five bob?" Pauline gasped in horror, stepping backwards. "Every week?"

The landlord shook his head. "Ev'ry fortnight," he said. "You got it?"

Pauline nodded and moved over to the table, where her purse lay next to her bag. She awkwardly fished out two half crowns while balancing Sarah with her other arm. The baby was yelling lustily, and Pauline felt her head begin to pound. She went back to the door and held the coins out to the man. He snatched them from her and nodded.

"Right. I'll be back for the gas money next week," he said with a nasty smile.

"And how much is that?" Pauline sighed.

"Half a crown," he said, turning to go. As he reached the top of the stairs, he turned again, holding out a white envelope. "Oh, yeah, this came for you."

She snatched it from him, retreated back into her room, and slammed the door shut. She ran back to her chair, unhooked her blouse, placed Sarah at her nipple, and then looked down at the letter. It was in Joan's rounded handwriting, and Pauline breathed a sigh of relief. Maybe this would be good news. She ripped the envelope open and removed the single sheet of white notepaper. She unfolded it and began to read, her whole body beginning to relax as she took it in. Joan was coming to see her. Her mother was on her side and was going to try and find her somewhere to stay! Only her father remained a problem. Pauline leaned back and smiled to herself. Things were going to be all right after all. She just had to keep going until Joan came to see her.

****

Friday 24th November, 1950

Pauline closed the door behind the landlord, having just handed over the half crown for the gas. She sighed and walked over to the cot. For once Sarah was sleeping, lying on her back, her little arms up on either side of her head. Pauline mustered a smile. She was so tired. They'd been up all night and all the night before, without much break in between. She realised she ought to take advantage of the respite and get some sleep herself. She walked over to the tiny mirror that hung over the gas fire, peered at herself, and made an attempt to tidy her hair. Ever since she'd received Joan's letter she'd been making more of an effort with her appearance and had managed to keep her hair washed and tidied most of the time. She didn't want her twin to arrive and find her in too bad a state. She wanted her to think she could cope. She went over to the bed, kicked off her shoes, and lay down. Within seconds of closing her eyes she was sleeping soundly and dreaming about playing with Sarah on the farm in Norfolk.

Four hours later Pauline was awakened by the

piercing sound of Sarah's cries. With a groan she struggled up and rubbed her eyes. She could see through the gap in the curtains that it was dark, and a glance at her wristwatch told her it was nearly eight o'clock. She got to her feet and went to the cot. The cry was a dirty nappy cry, and she picked up her daughter and laid her on the floor in front of the fire. She retrieved an almost dry nappy from the airer and dropped to her knees beside her. Smiling at the tiny child, she then removed the dirty nappy, cleaned her as best she could, and then fastened on the clean one. She pulled the rubber pants over the nappy and dressed the child in a clean vest and flannelette nightdress before carrying her back to her cot and putting her down. Within seconds the baby was screaming again. Pauline identified it as the hungry scream this time and picked her up again. She positioned herself on the wing chair and allowed Sarah to latch onto her breast. Her nipples were becoming almost too sore to bear, but she had still not plucked up the courage to return to the doctor's surgery, so she was having to cope with it as best she could.

As Sarah sucked, silent for once, Pauline felt the familiar panic begin to rise as she approached the night hours. Each night from ten until the following morning Sarah would scream. Whatever Pauline did made no difference. Sarah would scream nonstop. It had been a week since Joan's letter, and despite her attempts to remain clean and tidy, Pauline had almost given up hope of ever being rescued from the hell she had found herself in. The days and nights all merged together, and when she did get a moment to herself, all she wanted to do was sleep. She had even fallen asleep with Sarah attached to her nipple on more than one occasion. She looked down at the baby and sighed. How different her life would now be had she been more careful. How could she have been so stupid? Here she was, barely sixteen years old and with a tiny baby, struggling to survive all alone in a dismal room in a city she knew nothing about. And if she'd only been more sensible, more like Joan, she could have been safe at home now, starting a new job, earning money, going to the pictures—and sleeping each night.

She leaned back and closed her eyes. She didn't think she could take another night of the screaming. It went right through her, right to her core. On and on and on. It never seemed to end. And there was nothing she could do to stop it. Yet she was the mother; she ought to be able to stop it. Pauline's eyes filled with tears. She was even failing as a mother. She couldn't stop her baby from crying. She was useless. Sarah stopped sucking and gave a little whimper. Pauline froze. Surely she wasn't going to start now. She stared down at her. Sarah's face was red from the exertion of sucking, and her blue eyes were focusing on Pauline's face.

Pauline managed a smile. "Hello there," she said softly, touching the baby's cheek with her finger. "You're not going to cry tonight, are you? I don't think Mummy can take another night of it. Please, darling. Please don't scream tonight."

Her voice shook as she uttered the words, and the little girl latched back onto her nipple and started sucking again. Pauline breathed a sigh of relief, her whole body shuddering. So long as she continued to suck there could be no screaming.

****

Saturday 25th November, 1950—4.30 a.m.

"Hush, Sarah, hush, please hush," Pauline pleaded with her baby as she paced the room, the screaming child in her arms.

As on every other night, Sarah had begun to scream just after ten, and Pauline had been pacing the room with her ever since. She had changed her nappy, fed her several times, sung to her, bounced her on her knee, winded her, and simply just walked around with her. But all to no avail. She was desperately tired, desperately unhappy, and her head was pounding endlessly. She walked over to the cot, picked up Sarah's shawl, and wrapped it around the baby just in case she was cold. The screaming didn't stop. Pauline, her legs aching from the pacing, walked over to the bed and lay down, cradling Sarah next to her.

"Mummy needs to lie down, darling," she murmured. "Please try and stop crying. Mummy's so tired."

Sarah continued to scream, her little face bright red from the effort and her tiny body quivering with the sobs. Pauline screwed her eyes tightly shut and tried to block out the sound. Even the bed was shaking, and she thought her head was about to explode. A sudden hammering on the ceiling above them alerted Pauline to her neighbour.

"Shut that sodding child up!" shouted a disembodied voice from above them, and Pauline's face flushed a fiery red.

"Sarah, you must be quiet," she hissed desperately at the baby, picking her up and holding her tightly. She got to her feet and began the interminable pacing again, clutching Sarah tightly, the child pressed into her chest, the shawl pulled over her head. As she paced, Pauline muttered over and over again, "Please be quiet, please be quiet, please be quiet," until after a while she realised the screaming had stopped and Sarah lay quiet in her arms. With a sigh she sank down onto the wing chair and loosened her hold on the baby. The shawl fell back from her face, and Pauline tensed in shock. Sarah's tiny face was tinged with blue, her eyes were closed, and she didn't appear to be breathing.

"Sarah?" Pauline quavered uncertainly, pulling the shawl back further. "Sarah, why aren't you crying?" She pulled the shawl all the way off and dropped it on the floor, then picked Sarah up and held her in front of her. "Sarah—no— Sarah, please cry. Please cry, Sarah. Mummy needs you to cry," and she shook her gently.

The baby's head flopped back, and Pauline uttered a strangled cry. She got to her feet, looked around her in panic, then ran over to the cot and placed Sarah in it lying on her back. Then she picked her up again, shook her once more, and pressed her cheek to the baby's head. She put her ear to Sarah's mouth in an attempt to discern if she was breathing. She wasn't.

Pauline took a deep shuddering breath. She'd killed her baby. While trying to stop her crying she'd smothered her baby. Moving like an automaton, she gently laid her back in the cot and covered her with the shawl. Then she pulled a blanket off her bed and, wrapping it around herself, sat down in the wing chair and waited for morning.

****

Saturday 25th November, 1950—9.00 a.m.

Pauline was still sitting silently in the wing chair when she heard a knock at the door. She didn't move, or even turn her head.

The knock came again, then a voice called out, "Pauline? Are you in there? It's me. Let me in." Pauline tensed at the sound of her sister's voice but remained in the chair. "Pauline? Can you hear me? Let me in."

This time her gaze moved over towards the door, but she still didn't get up. "It's open," she managed to call through dry lips.

After a moment the door opened a crack, and Joan's nervous face appeared. It broke into a wide smile when she saw her sister in the chair, and she pushed the door open and stepped into the room.

"Pauline!" she cried, running over and flinging her arms around her twin. "I've missed you so much." She pulled back and studied her carefully. "You look very tired. We've come to take you home."

Pauline turned her face away. "It's too late," she muttered, almost inaudibly.

"What did you say?" Joan frowned and leaned closer.

Pauline shook her head and pointed to the cot in the corner of the room. Joan got to her feet and cautiously approached it. As she got closer she saw the raised lump in the middle, covered by a grubby white shawl. With her heart in her mouth she tentatively reached out and pulled back the corner of the shawl. A quickly stifled cry caught in her throat when her eyes fell on the body of the dead baby, blue, cold, and already stiff.

Her hand clasped firmly over her mouth, Joan stepped backwards, transfixed by the scene in the cot. Behind her, Pauline began to speak quietly and slowly as if totally disconnected from what she was saying.

"She cried every night. Every night from ten till morning. Last night she cried. The person upstairs banged on their floor for her to be quiet. I was so tired. So very tired. I asked her to hush. I begged her to hush. I wrapped her up in the shawl and held her tightly and walked and walked and walked…all around the room… and finally she stopped crying." She raised her eyes and looked directly at her sister. "But she hadn't stopped crying. She'd stopped breathing. I killed her. I'd smothered my baby, Joanie. I killed her."

She stopped speaking and continued to sit in the chair, her hands clasped on her lap, her eyes vacant. Joan moved over and squatted down in front of her, taking her hands and speaking urgently, her blue eyes swimming with tears.

"It wasn't your fault, Pauline," she whispered. "It was an accident. You didn't mean to hurt her."

"I didn't hurt her," Pauline clarified. "I killed her."

Joan took a deep breath and stood up. She took off her hat and coat and laid them on the bed.

"Okay," she said briskly, "we'd better get you tidied up before the doctor gets here. I take it you haven't called him yet?"

Pauline looked at her uncomprehendingly. "The doctor?" she echoed. "Why would the doctor come?"

Joan moved around the room tidying things away. "If someone dies, the doctor has to see them," she explained, "and I think he should see you, too. You look dreadful."

Pauline frowned and stood up, her eyes beginning to come alive. "No," she said emphatically. "No, Joanie. No one must know. You can't call the doctor."

"But Pauline, you have to," Joan soothed. "I know

311

you're in shock, but we have to do things right. And I need to go and get Mum."

Pauline stepped forward and grabbed her sister's arm. "Mum?" she gasped. "Mum's here?" Her voice was a mixture of horror and relief, and she caught at the table to steady herself.

"Yes, she's waiting round the corner in a Lyon's Tea Shop. I said I'd fetch her as soon as I'd told you the news." She glanced at the cot. "But I don't suppose…"

Pauline stared at her with enormous eyes. "News? What news?" she asked faintly, her voice puzzled.

Joan swallowed, holding back tears. "Mum has found you a place to stay near Luton. A place for you and Sarah to be safe."

Pauline's head fell forward, and a solitary tear rolled unheeded down her pale cheek. "If only you'd come yesterday," she whispered. "If only you'd come yesterday."

Joan sniffed and rummaged in her pocket for a handkerchief. She blew her nose, wiped her eyes, and turned back to her sister.

"I'm so sorry, Pauline," she said, "but right now we need to be practical. I'll go and get Mum, and we'll call the doctor. You stay here and tidy yourself up. I won't be long," and patting her sister on the arm, she turned to leave the room. With an anguished cry, Pauline sprang into life and leapt in front of her.

"No!" she cried. "No, you can't tell anyone. I'll get into trouble—I'll go to prison. Joanie, you can't tell anyone."

"Oh, Pauline, I have to." Joan stared at her. "You can't just ignore it. We want to take you home. You won't get into trouble. They'll understand what happened. Let me go now. It'll be all right."

She moved towards the door again, but still Pauline barred her way.

"No, Joan. I said no," she repeated, a desperate look in her blue eyes. "I can't let you tell anyone. Please, listen to me." She pushed her sister further into the room, back towards the table.

"Pauline, please, listen. You won't be in trouble. We can tell them Sarah just—died—in the cot. No one need know what happened," Joan begged, backing away from her sister.

"They won't believe that." Pauline shook her head vigorously, her eyes blazing. "We need to hide her. We can't tell anyone."

"But Pauline, what about Mum?" Joan sounded fearful. "She's waiting for me. She'll come and look up here if I take too long."

Pauline shook her head again. "No, you can't tell her. Tell her…I don't know…tell her I've gone away. Tell her you couldn't find me."

She stood firm in front of Joan, her strength returned in full force. Joan glanced at her nervously and moved forward, edging towards the door.

"Pauline, you don't know what you're saying," she began, when Pauline lunged at her and grabbed her arms.

"No, Joan!" she yelled desperately. "You're not to tell anyone, d'you hear?" and she gave her sister a shove to emphasise her point. Joan stumbled as her heel caught in a hole in the worn carpet, and she fell backwards, her arms flailing out towards Pauline. She landed with a crash, the back of her head slamming down on the corner of the table before she fell to the floor in a crumpled heap and lay still. Pauline froze to the spot and stared at her.

"Joan?" she quavered. "Oh, Joan, I'm so sorry! I don't know what came over me. Joan?"

There was no answer, and Pauline moved forward and dropped to her knees by Joan's side. She touched her shoulder and shook it gently. There was no reaction, and she leant over and carefully moved her twin's head. There was a damp patch beneath her hair, and Pauline pulled her hand away, staring in horror at the deep red blood that covered it. She quickly put her ear to Joan's mouth to try and detect breathing, much as she'd done with Sarah a few hours earlier. She could detect none. With an anguished moan, Pauline shoved her hand inside Joan's blouse and tried to find her heartbeat. She couldn't. She sat back on her heels, her mind in total confusion. A few hours ago she had accidentally smothered her baby. Now she had accidentally killed her twin sister.

Chapter 25

2008

Abi and Natasha stared at each other in consternation.

"But Joan can't be dead," gasped Natasha. "She's your mother. She's Nan. She can't be dead!"

Abi stared down at the book in her hands again. "Well, Pauline seems pretty sure," she said, shaking her head in mystification. "I suppose she could be mistaken, although she knew when Sarah was dead."

Natasha crawled across the floor and sat down next to her mother. "This is really horrible," she said in a small voice. "You said it might be."

Abi put an arm around her and pulled her close. "I was afraid it would be," she admitted, kissing the top of Natasha's head. "I rather expected Sarah to die…but obviously not Joan." She frowned, her mind doing somersaults in its attempt to make sense of what they'd just read. "Go and make some more tea, Tasha, and then let's find out what really happened."

Natasha scrambled to her feet and padded over to the kitchen area. "It's really not been Pauline's day, has it?" she asked with a grimace, attempting to make light of the story.

"Not really," Abi agreed, getting to her feet. "What a lot for a sixteen-year-old to cope with, even assuming she's mistaken about her sister. To lose her baby like that…" She remembered the feelings she'd experienced when she too had thought her baby was dead. And she hadn't had the additional horror of being the cause of the death.

She joined Natasha in the kitchen and rummaged in the cupboard until she found a packet of Oreos. She emptied them out onto a plate and carried them into the living area. Natasha joined her with a mug of tea and a mug of hot chocolate, and the two of them sat on the window seat together for a moment.

"Poor little Sarah," commented Natasha after a while. "She didn't have much of a happy life, did she? She was cold and hungry and cried all the time."

"Yes. A very sad little life. It's hard to believe she was my cousin." Abi frowned. "She cried so much. I wonder if she had something wrong with her or whether Pauline was just too young to know what to do."

Natasha wriggled closer and held her mother's hand. "It sort of explains why Nan didn't want you to keep me, doesn't it?" she said thoughtfully. "She probably thought she was acting for the best."

Abi looked at her with pride. "Yes, she probably did," she agreed, "and that's very mature of you to see that."

Natasha shrugged and grinned. "That's me," she said smartly. "I'm very mature."

Abi laughed and ruffled her hair. "Well, shall we continue?" she asked. "We can't leave them like that, can we?"

Chapter 26

Saturday 25th November, 1950

Pauline felt the tears welling up behind her eyes, but she held them back and summoned all her inner strength. There was nothing she could do to help either Sarah or Joan now, and in her mind suddenly everything became clear. She jumped to her feet and locked the door, then pulled her dress over her head and dropped it on the floor beside her sister. With intense effort, she knelt beside Joan again and began to undo her skirt and blouse.

"I'm so sorry," she whispered, as she worked. "Oh, Joanie, I'm so sorry. But I have to save myself. You do understand, don't you? I have to do it for Mum." She pulled the skirt down over Joan's legs.

With a lot of pulling and tugging, she managed to remove the blouse also, only to find it was stained with blood on the back. She almost panicked, then pulled herself together and remembered she had a very similar one. She delved into the box where she kept her clothes until she found the plain cream-coloured blouse. She quickly put it on and buttoned it up, then pulled on Joan's skirt. Once dressed, she gently pulled her discarded frock up over Joan's body, careful to avoid touching her head. Luckily the dress fastened at the front, so she did the buttons up, fumbling a little, and made sure Joan was lying in the same position she had landed in. Biting her lip, Pauline rearranged her sister's body so that it was covering the patch of blood, and made sure it was obvious she'd tripped on the carpet. Joan's shoes were dark brown, with small heels, and since they were crucial to the accident, Pauline couldn't remove them. She racked her brains to see if she had anything similar and finally remembered a pair of slightly lighter brown shoes that would serve the purpose. She grabbed them out of the box and slipped her feet into them. Then she put on Joan's overcoat and hat and checked her appearance in the little mirror. Her hair was completely unacceptable, so she removed the hat, brushed her hair into submission, fastened it with a green ribbon, and replaced the hat.

She looked as much like Joan as she ever would, and she crossed her fingers that she could fool her mother. As young children the twins had often swapped identities for a lark, and Pauline hoped that this time it would work for real. She emptied her own handbag out onto the table, took the few things she really wanted to keep, which included Sarah's birth certificate, then transferred them to Joan's bag after stuffing in the blood-stained blouse at the bottom. Finally, she knelt down once more next to her sister, gently kissed her on the forehead, and whispered, "I love you, Joanie. I'm so sorry. I'm going to miss you forever."

When she stood up, she took a deep breath and walked over to the cot. She picked up her now-cold baby, cradled her for one last time, kissed her on the head, and placed her on her tummy in the cot, with her face on the pillow. She tucked the shawl neatly around her, gently stroked her back, and then walked out of the door, taking care to let it lock behind her. Still just managing to hold in her tears, Pauline crept down the stairs and out onto the pavement.

She stood for a moment savouring the fresh November air, then set off in the direction of the Lyons Tea Shop where her mother was waiting.

She saw Janet sitting in the window as soon as she rounded the corner. It took all her will power not to break down in front of her and tell her everything, but Pauline knew she needed to stay strong, both for her sake and for her mother's. If not, then her mother could lose both daughters on the same day, and there was no way Pauline was going to let that happen. Everything that had happened so far had been her fault, and for the rest of her life she would try to make things right again as far as she could. She opened the door of the tea house and walked over to her mother's table. Janet looked up in surprise.

"Joan," she said, peering over her glasses at her, "you were a long time. Is everything all right?"

Pauline sat down opposite her and rested her hands on the table in order to stop them from shaking. "Not really," she said with a frown. "I couldn't get an answer when I knocked at the door. I think they may be out."

"Oh, dear," Janet sighed, removing her reading glasses and slipping them into her bag. "I hope they haven't gone far. It's very early to go out. Are you sure you knocked loudly enough?"

"I think so." Pauline nodded. "But we can go back and try again. Will you come too, this time?"

"Of course," Janet agreed at once. "We can't wait all day for them." She waved to the waitress, paid her bill, then gathered up her bag and followed Pauline out of the shop. They walked together the hundred yards to the large red-brick building that housed the flats.

Janet stared up at it with distaste. "The sooner my girl is out of here, the better," she said.

Pauline glanced at her, her head spinning. Why had they not come just one day earlier? She led the way up the steep narrow staircase and stopped at the top opposite a wooden door with peeling cream paint.

"This is it," she said, knocking loudly on the door.

There was no reply, and Janet leaned forward and tried. Still nothing happened. Janet put her mouth close to the door. "Pauline," she called. "Pauline, it's your mother, please open the door."

"Something wrong?" asked a rough voice behind them.

Janet turned and stared at the untidy man who stood surveying them with a sneer on his face.

"We can't get any reply from my daughter," she said haughtily, peering down her nose at him. "And you are…?"

The man leant against the newel post and stared at her insolently. "I'm the landlord," he said. "Noisy kid your daughter's got. You taking her away? I'll be glad to be shot of 'em." Pauline stiffened and half turned towards her mother. The landlord peered at her curiously. "Hey, you look just like her in that flat. You her sister or what?"

Pauline nodded. "Her twin," she replied in a whisper.

"We can't get a reply." Janet frowned. "Do you have a key? Maybe we could go in and wait for them."

The landlord considered for a moment, then nodded and plunged his hand into the pocket of his grey trousers. He pulled out a bunch of keys and quickly located the one he was looking for. Pushing past Pauline, he inserted the key into the lock, turned it, and pushed the door open. Janet moved to step past him, but he stopped short and swore loudly.

"Shit! What the fuck's 'appened 'ere?" he cried, entering the room and edging over to where Joan lay half under the table.

Pauline stifled a cry and pressed her body back against the wall, trying to keep her eyes averted from the cot in the corner. Janet ran into the room and knelt beside Joan. She reached out a hand and pressed her fingers on her neck, feeling for a pulse. Her face paled and her hand began to shake. She got unsteadily to her feet and turned to face Pauline.

"Your sister... Your sister is...is...dead." She swallowed and attempted to compose herself before looking around the room. "Where's the baby?" she asked, her voice shaking with emotion. "Joan, where's the baby? Look for the baby!"

Pauline didn't trust her legs to hold her and remained leaning against the wall, her face ashen and the long-held-back tears beginning to fall. Janet saw the cot and shot over to it. As she peered in, a strangled cry left her lips, and her gloved hand covered her mouth. Very gently she reached down and pulled the shawl up to cover the baby's head. Pauline had sunk to the floor and was sobbing uncontrollably. Janet turned to the landlord, who was hovering in the doorway, a terrified look on his face.

"Call a doctor," she ordered, waving a hand at him. "Call the doctor. We'll wait here for him."

"What 'appened?" he muttered, backing away.

"Why're they dead? Did someone kill them?"

Pauline's head shot up and she stared at her mother through her tears.

Janet shook her head. "No," she said, "no one killed them. The baby suffocated in her cot. My daughter…my daughter seems to have tripped and fallen, maybe on her way to see to the baby." She paused and took a long shuddering breath. "It was all an accident. Now, please, fetch the doctor." She sat down on the edge of the wing chair, her hands in her lap, and looked over at Pauline. "Come over here, Joan." She held out a hand, and Pauline crawled across the floor and sat at her mother's feet. Janet put her hand on her shoulder and pulled her closer. "I'm so sorry you've had to see this," she murmured. "This is not a scene for the eyes of a child."

"I'm not a child." muttered Pauline between sobs.

"You are," Janet said firmly. "You both were. I feel very responsible for this. We should have come sooner."

"You should have come yesterday," whispered Pauline, resting her head against her mother's knee.

Janet bent her head to catch the words. "What did you say?"

"*We* should have come yesterday," repeated Pauline, correcting the pronoun. She looked up at her mother. "We should have come yesterday."

Janet stared down at her daughter, an inscrutable look on her face.

"You look very tired," she said quietly, stroking her hair.

Pauline rested her head against her mother's knee. "I am," she said her voice breaking. "We should have come yesterday."

Janet bit her lip thoughtfully and frowned down at her daughter's head.

"I know," she said. "We should have come yesterday." Pauline stiffened at her tone, and looked up at her fearfully. Janet continued to stroke her hair. "But what happened here was clearly an accident. Or rather, two very sad accidents. No one was to blame." She looked down at her daughter. "Remember that, *Joan*. You must remember that."

Pauline nodded, her mind in a whirl. Did her mother realise what had happened? Did she know that she was Pauline? She knew she must never ask her. Janet stood up, pulling Pauline to her feet as well.

"I can hear someone coming," she said, attempting to compose herself. "Dry your tears, my love. We must deal with the doctor now. Time for grieving later."

****

Friday 1st December, 1950

Pauline sat on the window seat in her bedroom and stared out at the light flurry of snow that had just started to fall. The family had just returned from the joint funeral of Joan, now buried under the name of Pauline Forrester, and baby Sarah. They'd kept the affair completely private and had returned to the house immediately after the service. Walter Forrester wanted no more mention of his wayward daughter or her bastard offspring, and Janet, Pauline, and Margaret had been forbidden from ever mentioning her name again. He informed them the family needed a new start and they would be moving down to Berkshire to open a new branch of the factory. No one must ever hear of the shame Pauline had brought to the family.

There came a gentle tap on the door, and Pauline turned to see her little sister's curly head appear in the gap.

"Come in, Maggie," she said kindly and held out her hand to the little girl.

Margaret came in slowly, her face red from crying and her black dress crumpled and already covered in crumbs of some sort. She ran over to Pauline and buried her face in her lap.

"I miss Pauline," she said with a sob, "an' I never got to meet Sarah. That's so sad. Are you sad, Joanie?" She looked up at her sister with red eyes.

"Yes, darling. I miss her dreadfully. I expect I always will. But we'll have to get used to it." Pauline's gaze wandered around the room. She was sleeping in her old room rather than in Joan's room, explaining to her mother she would feel closer to her sister if she slept there. She hadn't been able to go into Joan's room since she'd arrived home. It held too many memories and made her feel so guilty.

Her father had begun to mention her going back to work at the factory, but Janet had intervened, saying she had suffered such a trauma in London, and with the loss of her sister and niece it would be better if she didn't start work again until they moved to Berkshire, and then it might be better if she found some other sort of work rather than the factory. Walter had argued with her, but for once Janet had held firm, saying she wasn't sure her daughter was suited to that type of work and should be allowed to choose her career for herself. Pauline had been extremely grateful to her mother and couldn't help wondering once again whether Janet had guessed at the deception.

Margaret wriggled onto her lap. "Joanie," she said slowly, "you've been different since you came back from London."

Pauline looked at her in dismay. "Well, I've been very sad," she said at once, putting her arms around the little girl.

Margaret shook her head. "No, it's not that," she said. Clearly she was puzzled. "It's sort of like you're Joan *and* Pauline. All in one." She looked innocently at Pauline. "Does that happen with twins when one dies?"

Pauline dipped her head forward so her hair fell in front of her face. "Maybe it does," she said, trying to hold back her tears. "Maybe it does."

Margaret cuddled up to her. "I'll look after you now, Joanie," she said seriously. "I'll be your new twin."

Pauline buried her face in her sister's hair, and the tears began to trickle down her cheeks. "Thank you, Maggie," she whispered. "Thank you."

The two girls were sitting together watching the first of the snow start to settle on the cold pavement below when a quick tap on the door heralded the arrival of their mother. Janet slipped into the room, a strange look on her face.

"Joan," she said, biting her lower lip, "a letter has arrived for you. From Norfolk." She tentatively held out a white envelope to her daughter.

Pauline froze and stared at the letter in horror. "Who's it from?" she whispered. "Is it Aunt Maureen?"

Janet shook her head. "No. I know Maureen's handwriting. This is from someone much younger." She looked closely at Pauline. "Could it be from Billy?"

Pauline went pale, and her hand flew up to cover

her mouth. "Why…why would he write to…me?" she stuttered, reaching out to take the envelope.

"He was a friend, wasn't he?" Janet said gently. "He helped you find a place for Pauline to stay. Maybe he's heard what happened and wants to express his sympathy. Open it, child."

Pauline stared at her. "But it's not—"

"Just open it, Joan," Janet said firmly. "You'll need to reply to him."

Nervously Pauline slit open the envelope and pulled out the sheet of folded paper. She opened it out.

"Dear Joanie," she read. *"I heard what happened to Pauline and the bubby. I'm so sorry. You must be so sad. If you're ever in Norfolk again, I would love to see you. Yours, Billy."*

She lowered the page and stared at her mother. "What do I say?" she asked in bewilderment.

Janet took the letter and scanned it quickly. "You must reply, of course," she said at once. "Thank him for his concern and tell him we're moving house to get away from the memories." She paused and watched Pauline. "Tell him you won't be coming to Norfolk again because it would be too sad for you. He'll understand."

Pauline nodded and laid the letter on the window seat beside her. "Yes. I'll do that," she said. "Billy was kind."

Margaret leaned against her and looked up. "Was he your boyfriend?" she asked, wide-eyed.

Janet tutted and snapped her fingers at her. "Margaret! Curiosity killed the cat. Downstairs now. It's time for tea." She ushered the little girl out into the hallway. Before she closed the door, Janet turned to

Pauline. "You'll know what to write. Be kind to him." Then she left and followed her youngest daughter down the stairs.

Pauline took a deep breath. She'd not even considered the problem of Billy. She knew Joan would have told him she'd keep in touch, and maybe they'd even made plans to meet up again. She had to let him down gently. She really wished she could tell him the truth, but that would probably cause him even more distress than if she just told him they wouldn't be able to meet again. With a sigh she got up, fetched some notepaper from her desk, and sat down on the bed.

"Dear Billy," she began. *"Thank you for your letter. Unfortunately I won't be able to come to Norfolk again. The memories would be too sad. We are also moving house to another part of the country for the same reason. Thank you so much for the help you gave us in Norfolk."* She paused and chewed on her pen for a moment. *"Maybe one day when we're very old we can meet again and I can explain properly why I couldn't see you again. Until then, look after yourself and have a happy life. Love, Joan."*

She laid down her pen, folded the letter in half, and popped it into an envelope before she could change her mind. She scribbled the address, then carried it downstairs and laid it on the hall table.

She turned to go into the dining room and paused for a moment to watch the rest of her family: Walter, seated at the head of the table, his face as stern as ever, and Janet opposite him. She was carefully pouring a cup of tea ready to pass to him, and Margaret was sitting quietly with her hands in her lap, but Pauline could see her feet swinging under her chair. She took a deep breath. She had to go through with the deception for everyone's sake, but especially for Joan's. She owed it to Joan to live her life as she would have done.

Pauline closed her eyes briefly and made a vow, to live a good and healthy life, to follow the dreams Joan had had, and never to have another child. She opened her eyes, smoothed her hair down neatly, just as Joan would have done, and walked into the dining room to join her family.

Chapter 27

2008

Natasha turned to Abi, tears running unheeded down her cheeks. "Mum, that was awful," she wept, rubbing ineffectually at her eyes with her arm. "That was so sad and so…just awful."

Abi leaned back against the window seat, her mind spinning. She stared down at Natasha, her face white and her eyes huge. "Tash," she said, "d'you realise what this means? Pauline was my mother. Not Joan." She paused and tried to get her head around the shocking information they'd just read. "And Sarah was my sister. No wonder my mother acted the way she did. She was terrified I'd run off on my own with my baby—which I would have done—and then…" Tears swam in her eyes.

Natasha sniffed and rubbed her eyes again. "Why did she have you?" she asked at last. "She vowed never to have another baby."

"Well, I always knew I was a mistake." Abi grinned wryly. "She told me that often enough. She was forty-four when I was born."

Natasha shuffled across the floor on her bottom and sat next to her mother. "But she could have had an abortion," she mused. "That was legal in 1979, wasn't it?"

"Oh, yes, it was legal," Abi said slowly, "but my guess is I was a menopause baby and she didn't know she was pregnant until it was too late."

"What on earth is a menopause baby?" Natasha asked in surprise.

"A baby that's conceived when a woman is going through menopause… Do you know what that is?" Natasha nodded. "At that time her periods are very erratic, and she could well not realise she is pregnant until she's several months along."

"No wonder she wasn't very nice to you," said Natasha sadly. "She must have been so unhappy all her life. She must have felt guilty all the time. D'you think she could ever forget it?"

Abi shook her head. "How could she? She'd accidentally killed her baby—that's enough to tip anyone over the edge—and then she helped to cause her sister's death. And spent the rest of her life living a lie. There's no way she could have forgotten it—ever."

"D'you think Janet knew?" asked Natasha, picking up the diary again and flicking through it.

"Oh, yes." Abi nodded at once. "I'm sure of it. A mother will know her twins apart even if no one else does. She obviously decided not to speak of it because then she might have lost them both." She paused, and a tear trickled down her cheek. "I think she felt partly to blame for not rescuing Pauline sooner. She thought she owed her something."

"It seems so weird." Natasha wriggled uncomfortably. "And your father didn't know about it?"

Abi sighed. "Apparently not," she said, shaking her head. "She's wasn't really very likely to tell him, was she? You know, 'Oh, pleased to meet you, call me Joan, but by the way I'm actually Pauline and I killed my baby and my sister when I was sixteen and then took her identity.' That wouldn't be likely to induce my father to marry her, would it?"

Natasha grinned. "You make her sound like a murderer," she objected. "They were both accidents."

"I know," Abi agreed, "but still very hard to explain. Especially when she'd kept the secret for so many years." She glanced at Natasha. "He knows now, of course; he read the diaries before he gave them to us."

Natasha leaned forward and rummaged in the suitcase again. "I wonder if there's anything else from after that?" she asked, pulling out papers and envelopes and glancing at them.

Abi joined her, and almost immediately they found something of interest.

"Look," she said, holding up a small spiral-bound notebook. "This is in her handwriting too. Maybe it's another diary." She opened the book, and her eyes flicked down the pages. "Hmmm, it is, sort of," she said with a frown. "Listen to this— there's no date or anything: *Today I found I was pregnant. I vowed never to let this happen again. I thought I was too old now. I want to get rid of it, it brings back too many memories, but the doctor says I'm too far advanced. And Arthur seems pleased. Maybe it will be all right, although I think I'll find it very hard to love the baby. I'll have to try. I don't deserve to have another baby. But most important, if it's a girl, which I sincerely hope it's not, then I'll have to make sure she doesn't make the same mistakes I did. I couldn't let that happen to another person. I shan't let my child ruin her life like I*

331

did."

Abi stared at the writing, a huge lump forming in her throat. She was beginning to feel so sorry for her mother. For all her foolishness, she had not been a truly bad person. When she'd visited Natasha in the children's home she had obviously been trying to make up for it in some way. Abi was sure her mother had wanted her to find Natasha eventually.

"I wonder what happened to Billy?" Natasha was rummaging again. "D'you think he died of a broken heart?"

"If Pauline managed not to, I doubt he did!" retorted Abi, tossing the spiral notebook to one side and peering into the suitcase again. "He'll be an old man now. I hope he found a nice girl to marry and had lots of happy kids."

"I wonder if Pauline ever managed to see him again and tell him what happened?" mused Natasha, her eyes looking dreamily into the distance.

Abi shook her head. "I very much doubt it," she said. "She died too soon for that. I think she meant when they were really, really old."

"Or maybe when she knew she was dying she went to see him, to confess," suggested Natasha.

"Maybe she did." Abi stared at her thoughtfully. "That would make sense."

"Can we go and find him?" asked Natasha suddenly. "Take him that bit of Joan's diary that we have? Then he'd know she loved him."

"Don't you think that might make him sadder?" asked Abi. "If he's had a nice life and married a nice girl, then wouldn't it be better to leave him with his memories of that time with Joan rather than let him know any more?"

Natasha sat back on her heels. "That depends on whether or not Nan went to see him before she died," she said sagely. "If she did, then he already knows Joan is dead. If not, then no, we shouldn't tell him. Unless he's sitting at home waiting for her, thinking she's still alive!" she added in horror.

"I doubt if he's doing that." Abi smiled at her. "This all happened nearly sixty years ago. He was seventeen and she was sixteen. He'll just remember her as his first love. Most people don't marry their first love."

Natasha stared at her. "You did," she pointed out. "And you waited ten years for him."

Abi flushed and looked away. "That's different. And that was only ten years. I didn't have time to find anyone else."

Natasha raised an eyebrow at her. "Ten years is plenty of time," she said briskly. "You were still in love with him and didn't want anyone else. Maybe Billy was like that."

Abi stood up and stretched. "Don't worry about Billy," she said, glancing down at Natasha. "I think we have enough to think about with the rest of the story. My mother was not the person I thought she was. She had led a whole secret life. It takes a while to get one's head around something like that." She frowned in annoyance. "I wish I could call your dad. I'd love to talk this over with him." She glanced down at her watch. "You know, we really should have gone to Swansea today and bought a new charger. I didn't think of it until just now. The shops'll be shut now. We must do that tomorrow."

Natasha looked up at her in dismay. "I thought we were going to walk to Worm's Head tomorrow?" she said plaintively.

"Hmmm…yes, we were." Abi wrinkled her nose. "If we get up early we could pop to Swansea first thing, then leave the phone charging while we do the walk. How does that sound?"

Natasha scrambled to her feet and nodded. "Okay," she said with a grin. "And Judy's bringing Ollie tomorrow, isn't she? I can't wait to see him."

"Oh, me too!" Abi said with a sigh. "I've been missing him so much that I've been trying not to think about him. Judy said they'd arrive mid afternoon—we have to be back over the causeway by three, so that should be fine."

Natasha was rummaging in the kitchen cupboards. "What shall we have for supper?" she asked, peering into a packet of mashed potato.

Abi joined her and put an arm around her shoulders. "Dunno," she said with a grin. "Let's see what we can find."

****

Simon stood in the trees watching the house intently. After a lot of trouble he'd finally managed to track down where Gideon's parents lived and had arrived there around four o'clock. He was fairly sure that was where Abi and the children would be hiding out, and he'd positioned himself where he could observe the house safely without being seen. During the three hours he'd been in position, he'd watched Roger and Caroline arrive home, unload their shopping, then park the Range Rover in the garage, which as far as Simon could see contained only an old estate car, certainly not a car he imagined Abi would drive. An hour later, Roger had gone out again, this time on foot, and returned after a while carrying some eggs. Since then the house had been quiet, the only activity being the occasional turning on or off of lights.

Simon came to the conclusion he'd been mistaken about Abi and swore under his breath. If she wasn't there, he had a couple of other options to consider. One was that she was staying with Judy in Berkshire, which posed a problem to him because he had no idea where Judy lived; or she may have gone to the campsite in Wales where they'd got married. He knew the name of the site, the papers having been bombarded with pictures of the wedding, and although it was two years ago he could remember it perfectly. He shivered as a few drops of rain fell off the leaves above him and ran down his neck. He glanced at his phone to check the time and decided to head in the direction of South Wales and find a place to stay on the way. That way he would be able to arrive fairly early in the morning. If he set off immediately, he could find somewhere decent to stay near Bristol and get there in time for dinner.

****

"That does it. I'm going to Wales tomorrow." Gideon slammed his phone down on the table, his dark brows drawn together.

Charles glanced up from his magazine. "Still can't get through?" he asked unnecessarily, leaning back and crossing his legs at the ankles.

Gideon scowled at him. "Still that sodding message saying there's a fault with the line." He glanced at his friend. "You up for a trip to the caravan tomorrow?"

Charles raised his eyebrows. "Really? Don't you

want to be alone with Abi and Tasha?"

"I won't be." Gideon stood up and yawned. "Judy's going down tomorrow too—taking Ollie with her. It'll be a full house. May as well take one more."

"Cool. Sounds fun to me. D'you want to leave early?" Charles grinned, taking a long swig out of his can.

Gideon walked to the window and peered down into the gathering gloom.

"Not too early," he said with a laugh. "Mid-morning'll do. I'd go now if I hadn't already had too many drinks, but since I have, let's get stuck in, shall we?" and he strode into the kitchen and returned with an armful of lager. "Stick some music on, Chas, and let's pretend we're on tour."

Charles laughed and got to his feet. "What d'you wanna listen to?" he asked, squatting down in front of the collection of CDs that filled the lowest shelf of the mahogany bookcase. "These belong to your Mum and Dad, don't they?" he added after a slight pause.

Gideon grunted. "Yeah. Guess the choice is not what we might have wanted. Are there any of ours there?" he asked.

"Christ, Gid, really?" Charles chuckled. "You want to listen to us? There isn't any anyway. It's mostly classical, bit of jazz, some early blues—and—Elvis Presley!"

Gideon groaned. "So my own father doesn't have any of my music?" he muttered. "Stick on some jazz, then. I need to have words with him."

Charles popped a CD into the machine, pressed play, and wandered back to the sofa. "This is only his London flat," he pointed out fairly. "He's probably got your stuff at the house in Hampshire."

Gideon raised an eyebrow at him. "Don't you be so sure," he muttered darkly. "Parents just don't appreciate you. You check *your* parents' collection when you go home. Bet they haven't got any, either."

****

Caroline peered out of the landing window into the misty drizzle and frowned. She rubbed the glass where her breath had steamed it up, and peered again.

"Roger!" she called. "Roger, come here!"

The sound of footsteps creaking up the stairs heralded his arrival, and he stood behind her, a slight smile on his face.

"What is it, Caroline?" he asked patiently, leaning forward and peering out of the window with her.

"I think there's someone out there," she said at once. "Over there, in the bushes." She pointed vaguely in the direction of the forest.

"Where?" Roger demanded, moving closer and opening the window.

"Over there," she said again. "Just to the right of the gate. In that thicket. I'm sure I saw something move."

Roger stared into the gloomy evening. "Can't see anything," he said at last. "Probably a pony."

Caroline stared at him in exasperation. "Roger! I know a pony when I see one," she said in annoyance. "No this—person—was smoking. I saw the glow of a cigarette."

"Well he—or she—has gone now," said Roger dismissively, closing the window and pulling the curtains across. "Who on earth would stand out there in this weather anyway?" He glanced at his wife and paused as he saw her face. "Hey, you look really worried. I'm sure it was nothing important. No one casing the joint or anything," he said with a laugh. "But if it'll put your mind at rest, I'll ask around in the morning, see if anyone saw anything suspicious."

Caroline looked slightly mollified and started down the stairs. "Well, all right," she conceded. "But if we get murdered in our beds tonight, it'll be your fault." And she marched into the kitchen with a toss of her head.

Roger grinned to himself and followed more slowly, making a mental note to make sure the burglar alarm was set before they went to bed.

Chapter 28

Saturday 2nd August, 2008
Belgravia—9.00 a.m.

The sound of his mobile ringing finally broke through Gideon's dream, and he groped on his bedside table. He knocked the phone onto the floor, swore under his breath, and retrieved it.

"Hullo?" he muttered thickly, attempting to sit up and push his hair out of his eyes. "What...Oh, hello, Dad. Bit early, isn't it? Is something wrong?" He listened, wriggling into a more comfortable position. His brows came together, and he pushed back the covers. "What did you say?" he bellowed. "He was doing what?" By this time he was out of bed and searching urgently for his jeans. "But Dad, how do you know...Oh, right...So it was definitely him?...Yeah, I'm sure he was. Okay, I'm going to go straight to Wales, then." He paused in his attempt to pull on his jeans with one hand. "No, her phone is dead, and the landline to the campsite was down yesterday. I'll try again before I leave...Well, that would be nice. Are you sure you want to?...All right, but I can't come all the way to Boldre to get you..." He paused. "Really? Well, okay, if she doesn't mind. I guess that would work. Don't be late, though. We'll be leaving in about ten minutes." And he disconnected the call, grabbed the rest of his clothes, and burst into the spare bedroom.

"Chas, Chas, wake up, man," he said loudly to the snoring mound in the bed. "Chas, we got to leave for Wales now."

Charles groaned and pulled the covers more tightly over his head. "Fuck off, man," he muttered. "My hangover hasn't even got going yet. You said mid-morning."

Gideon hopped over to the bed, one leg in his jeans, and pulled the covers back. "Abi and Tasha may be in danger," he said, scowling. "We've got to leave now."

In seconds, Charles had scrambled out of bed and was searching for his clothes. "What d'you mean?" he gasped to Gideon's retreating back. "What d'you mean, in danger? From what?"

"Not what, who," came Gideon's voice from the kitchen, where he was knocking back two paracetamol and a glass of orange juice. Charles stumbled in, wearing boxers and a T-shirt, his jeans and shoes in his hands.

"Who?" he demanded, his eyes squinting against the morning sun flooding in through the window.

"Simon," Gideon replied shortly, pushing past him to hurry around the flat, thrusting his belongings into a bag. "Mum saw someone watching the house last night. Dad didn't think anything of it until their gardener came this morning and told him he'd seen a man lurking in the bushes just by their gate." He turned to Charles, a dark look on his face. "That man fitted Simon's description to a tee. Dad reckons he was checking the house to see if Abi was there, and since she wasn't, there's a good chance he'll try the caravan.

We need to leave now, and Dad's coming with us. I can't afford to waste the time driving all the way to the New Forest, especially on a Saturday in August, so Mum's going to drive him to meet us at Membury Services on the M4. We'll need to take his car to Wales; there's no room in mine." He paused for a moment and frowned. "Which means my mother'll have to drive home in mine. Not sure about that."

Charles raised an eyebrow. "Or she could come with us, and we leave your car in the car park at the services?"

Gideon stared at him as if he'd gone mad, and shook his head violently.

"I'm not leaving the Mercedes at a service station!" he gasped in horror. "Even my mother driving it's preferable to that." He zipped up his bag, then picked up his phone and dialled the campsite office again. "Still out of order," he muttered savagely, thrusting his phone into his pocket.

"But Simon would never hurt Abi, would he?" asked Charles doubtfully, attempting to gather up his scattered belongings and fill his bag.

"I think he might," Gideon growled darkly. "He got nowhere with me, did he, and he still seemed pretty set on getting back in the band. I think his twisted little mind might be working on the idea that if Abi was out of the picture altogether, then I'd still have him back." He paused and glowered at Charles. "I think he's gone over the edge, Chas. I can't take a chance on this."

Charles finished putting on his shoes and disappeared into the bedroom.

"You know I have to fly back to the States on Monday, really early, don't you?" he called as he gathered up the last of his luggage.

"That's fine. We'll get you back in time. Unless you don't want to come to Wales? I'll understand if you don't." Gideon's dark head appeared around the door, his eyebrows raised.

"Try and stop me!" grinned Charles, slinging his bag over his shoulder and scooping up his phone and headphones from the bedside table. "Won't your dad be mad we've left the flat in such a mess?"

Gideon waved a hand dismissively. "I'm coming back next week," he said. "Bringing Abi and the kids. They can tidy it," and with that somewhat unreasonable remark, he picked up his bag, set the burglar alarm, and ushered Charles out the door.

****

Near Weston-super-Mare—9.00 a.m.

Simon flung his bag into the boot of the car and slammed the lid shut. He had spent the night in a large hotel just outside Weston-super-Mare, and had managed in the short time he was there to alienate almost all the staff. He scowled back at the tall building he'd just left and slid into the driver's seat. He programmed his destination into the hire car's built-in SatNav and groaned inwardly when he realised he was still nearly two hours away from Llangennith. He had not formulated any real plan for the day but had decided that once he located Abi and Natasha something would come to him. He glanced at the black case that lay on the seat beside him, and his stomach did a minor flip. He was beginning to realise he may have bitten off more than he could chew, but his determination was such that he managed to squash the feeling and remind himself that what he was about to do was for the good of the band and ultimately for Gideon. He nodded to himself as he pulled out onto the A370 and headed north. Yes, he was doing this for the good of the band. Gideon would thank him in the end.

****

Caravan Site, Llangennith—10.00 a.m.

The trip to Swansea to replace the phone charger had gone according to plan, and Abi and Natasha were back at the caravan by ten o'clock. Abi turned off the car engine and smiled at her daughter.

"Right, let's get this thing on charge so we can get off on our walk." She gathered up her bags and got out of the car. "I'm really looking forward to this, aren't you? I thought we could have a good natter about the Joan and Pauline story."

Natasha bounded up to the caravan and unlocked the door. "Yeah," she agreed, nodding with enthusiasm. "I still can't get my head round it all." She glanced over at her mother. "It must be even weirder for you. I mean, your own mother wasn't who you thought she was." She paused and frowned. "In fact, she was actually a murderer."

Abi tutted, and chivvied her into the caravan. "Not a murderer," she corrected. "Both the deaths were accidents, remember? But I think she considered she was a murderer. I suspect it completely dominated her life, actually." She dumped the shopping on the counter and pushed her hair back off her face. "I feel really sorry for her. Which is a very strange feeling."

Natasha skipped into the living area and bounced down onto the window seat. "It's easy to see why she was so horrid to you, now that we know her story," she commented. "But if she'd told you what really

343

happened to her you would have understood, wouldn't you?"

Abi wandered over and stood in front of her, staring out onto the long sweep of the bay. "Yes, of course I would. But how could she tell her own daughter something like that? Something she'd kept secret for thirty-odd years? By the time I was born, she must have been so used to being Joan she probably couldn't have told anyone. After all, my dad didn't know. She'd managed to get married and live as Joan for so long…"

"I know some of the story was really, really sad," Natasha said, looking up at Abi, "but it's really quite exciting to have a grandmother who lived a double life."

Abi gave a wry grin. "Add to that your spy grandfather, and you have quite an interesting genealogy," she said. "Now let's get this phone on charge, and then I can try and call your dad before we go out. He must be so pissed off with me for forgetting the charger." She walked over to the kitchen counter and rummaged in the shopping bag, finally pulling out a small box containing the new charger. She plugged it in and attached her phone. "Hmmm. This must be really flat—it's not registering it yet. We may have to wait a few minutes before I can use it. Let's get some provisions ready for our walk while we wait."

Fifteen minutes later the two of them were fully prepared, dressed in shorts, T-shirts, and hooded sweatshirts, with trainers on their feet. Abi had insisted they put the waterproof jackets in their backpacks, along with water bottles and lots of chocolate.

"Do we really have to take the waterproofs?"

Natasha objected, attempting to stuff some crisps into her overflowing bag. "The sun's out."

"Yes, we do. The forecast for this afternoon is for heavy showers and possible thunder. We need to be prepared. We'll probably be back before then, but just in case."

Natasha grinned in delight. "Thunder?" she echoed. "Brilliant. That'd be ace. I really hope we get caught in a thunderstorm."

Abi rolled her eyes. "Hmm. That'd be wet," she said, peering at her phone, "and probably not as enjoyable as you might think. My phone's registering a charge now. I'm going to try and phone Dad." She picked it up and dialled Gideon's number, only to listen while it rang and then cut to voicemail. With a sigh, she ended the call and laid the phone back on the counter. "He's not picking up," she said in annoyance. "Probably still in bed. I'll send him a text to say where we're going, then call him when we get back." She rapidly typed a message to Gideon. *"Hi, babe, just bought charger. Tash and I are going to Worm's Head, will call you when we get back. Leaving phone on charge while we're out. Love you. xxxx."*

She laid the phone back down and grinned at Natasha. "Right. Let's get going. Otherwise we won't have enough time to get all the way to the end. Ready?"

Natasha picked up her backpack and headed for the door. "Yeah, let's go." Then she paused and turned back to Abi. "What about Judy? Should we leave her a note in case we're late back?"

"I thought we'd tell them in the shop to pass a message on if someone calls looking for us. Judy'll have to go to the shop to ask them to open the barrier.

Gareth won't mind doing that." She opened the door, and they walked down the steps to the car. As Abi started the engine and pulled away, the phone plugged in on the kitchen counter began to ring.

****

Membury Services M4—10.30 a.m.

Gideon and Charles made very good time once they got out of London, and they pulled up in the car park at Membury Services at exactly ten thirty.

Gideon looked around impatiently. "I can't see Dad's car," he muttered under his breath, eventually parking his Mercedes in a corner position well away from other cars. "I hope they hurry up. I have a feeling the traffic might get pretty bad once we get near Bristol."

He opened the door and stepped out, his sharp eyes scanning the cars entering the car park in a steady stream. Suddenly he spotted his father's Volvo and waved frantically. As his father drew up beside them, Charles clambered out of the Mercedes.

"Gid, you just got a text, and it looks like you have a missed call, too. We must have lost the signal back there." He held Gideon's mobile out to him.

Gideon snatched it off him and peered at the screen. "It's from Abi!" he said, relief sounding in his voice. "She must have got a charger." He scanned the text, and his brows came together. "They're going to walk to Worm's Head," he said, "and leaving the phone charging. That means I still can't contact her. Maybe they haven't left yet…" He dialled her number and pressed the phone to his ear. After a moment he swore under his breath and thrust his phone back into his pocket. "Voicemail," he muttered, his face dark. "Come

346

on, Dad, we need to leave now. Hi, Mum."

Caroline climbed elegantly out of the Volvo and smiled at Gideon and Charles. "Hello," she said. "Nice to see you again, Charles. Are you well?"

"Yes, thank you, Mrs. Hawk," Charles said with a smile. "Nice to see you, too."

Gideon walked to the back of the car, where Roger was checking his tyre pressures. "Now, Dad? Really?" he asked in exasperation. "Couldn't you have done that before you left?"

Roger carried on with what he was doing. "No time," he said calmly. "We left as soon as we'd spoken to you. I rather thought we might get here first, but no matter. This won't take long. Did I hear you say you'd had a message from Abi?"

Gideon nodded and ran a hand through his hair in frustration. "Yes, she and Tash have gone to Worm's Head and left her phone on charge at the caravan. So I still can't contact them. Now, please hurry up, Dad!"

Caroline laid her hand on his arm. "Calm down, darling," she soothed. "If Abi and Tasha have gone out, then Simon won't be able to find them, will he?"

"Well...maybe," Gideon conceded, glancing at her, "but I really don't want to take a chance. This is too important, Mum. Abi's life may be in danger."

Caroline looked worried. "I really can't imagine Simon hurting her," she began doubtfully, "but then I wouldn't have imagined he would have sold that disgusting story to the paper either..."

"Exactly," said Gideon impatiently. "Now, we really must go. Dad. Hurry up."

Roger appeared from behind the car. "Calm down, old chap," he said. "Morning, Charles. Nice to see you.

347

Right, Caroline, we'll keep you posted, and you let us know if by any chance we're wrong and Simon turns up back at our house."

Reluctantly, Gideon handed his car keys to his mother. "Mum, this car is nearly as precious to me as Abi," he said with mock seriousness. "I shall be calling every hour to check on it. No one else has ever driven it."

Caroline took the keys and reached up to kiss him on the cheek. "Don't worry, darling. I'll take good care of it. Now off you go, and I hope everything goes fine. I'm sure Abi and Tasha are all right." She turned to slide into the car, then paused and called to Roger, "Don't forget to give them the lunch, darling."

Roger grinned and waved her off, then turned to Gideon. "Shall we get going, then? Would you like to drive?"

Gideon nodded and took the proffered car keys. "Thanks, Dad. What was that about lunch?"

"Oh, your mother has packed some sandwiches and cake." Roger chuckled. "Thought we might get hungry."

"Mum and her cake!" Gideon snorted, shaking his head with a grin and sliding into the driver's seat. Roger got in beside him, and Charles slid into the back to find he was sharing the seat with a large bag of food.

"Leaving now, we should get to Rhossili by about one forty-five," announced Roger, consulting the SatNav as Gideon rejoined the motorway. "That's assuming no holdups, of course."

****

Rhossili—10.50 a.m.

Abi and Natasha drew up in the large car park at

Rhossili just before ten to eleven, slipped their backpacks on, and set off in the direction of the causeway that led to Worm's Head. Abi had done the walk many times, both in her youth when holidaying with Judy and also several times since she and Gideon had reconnected. They had taken Natasha with them once, and the child was very excited to do it again.

"Are we going to climb over those really spiky rocks again?" she asked, her blue eyes shining.

"If we want to go all the way to the end, then that's the quickest way. Otherwise we need to climb down and go across that flat rocky bit, remember? And that's only accessible if the tide's right."

Natasha skipped along beside her. "Oh, that bit's fun!" she said. "It's got rock pools and stuff to look at. Maybe we can come back that way?"

Abi shrugged. "Yeah, maybe we can. Let's see how the time goes, shall we? We've still got nearly a mile to walk till we reach the causeway. It should have been open for about forty minutes by now, so we need to get a wiggle on if we're going to have plenty of time to explore."

They walked on together, passing through the gate that was just after the National Trust shop and following the Gower Way, which led to the lookout station and the start of the causeway. The day was warm and sunny, with light clouds scudding across the sky, propelled by a strong breeze. Abi's hair whipped in front of her face as she turned to Natasha.

"Do you feel better disposed towards Nan now that you know her story?" she asked with interest.

Natasha paused for just a second, then nodded her curly head. "Yeah," she said. "I do, but I still think she behaved badly. She kept us apart, and that's still unforgivable. Just 'cause I understand why she did it doesn't make it any better."

Abi nodded in agreement and gave Natasha's hand a squeeze. "I know, darling. I feel the same. I just wish she'd told me. Things could have been so different." She stared off ahead, her eyes sad. "I actually think we could have been good friends if she'd told me the truth. She was very like me as a teenager."

Natasha looked up at her solemnly. "One thing does puzzle me," she said, wrinkling her nose. "Why did she hide Dad's letters to you? Why did she want to keep you apart? She didn't even know about the baby when she started doing that."

Abi sighed and brushed her hair out of her eyes. "I've been thinking about that too," she said, "and all I can think is it was because of Jimmy." She looked down at Natasha. "Jimmy was eighteen, the same age as Gideon, and he abandoned her. I think she thought Gideon was going to abandon me once he went on tour, and she didn't want me to get hurt like she did." She paused and shrugged. "Or something like that. I don't really think her mind worked quite logically when it came to relationships. I'm pretty surprised she ever married my dad, actually."

Natasha hoisted her bag further onto her shoulders and frowned. "Surely when he kept writing to you she could see he wasn't going to abandon you. And when she found you were pregnant, surely she could see that it would have been better if he knew about it?" she suggested.

"No, she wouldn't have done that." Abi shook her head. "After all, Jimmy left her *because* she was pregnant. There's no way she would have thought Gideon would have stood by me. Her whole life was coloured by that incident...that and the baby and her sister." She paused and gave a small smile. "I still keep having problems remembering she was actually Pauline, not Joan." She looked down at Natasha again. "We can never tell people, you know, except Dad, of course. We'll have to keep her secret for her."

Natasha smiled and nodded. "I know. In a way that's kind of exciting. Now, come on! We need to get to the causeway." And she skipped a few steps to encourage her mother to hurry.

****

Caravan Site, Llangennith—11.00 a.m.

Simon made good time, and after following the directions of his SatNav as far as the village of Llangennith had managed to ask a local the way to the campsite. As he approached along the very narrow single-track road, his heart beat faster and his mouth became unexpectedly dry. He mentally shook himself as he drew up at the entrance and wound down his window.

"I'm just visiting someone who's staying here," he said to the lady at the gate. She charged him for a day's car parking and waved him over the cattle grid.

Simon had no idea where to find Abi and Natasha, so he parked outside the shop and took stock, getting out of the car and staring around him. To his right and down a steep slope was the campsite—four fields of tents and motor caravans lay spread out below him, reaching to the edge of the sand dunes that bordered the beach. In front of him was a large low building that announced itself as an all-day café, and to the left were the ranks of static caravans, approached via a barrier. Simon paused for a moment, then turned and walked into the little shop. It was fairly busy, with barefoot youngsters buying ice creams and harassed-looking mothers stocking up on tins of beans and bottles of wine. Simon joined the end of the queue that was waiting to pay and attempted to remain calm. He felt beads of sweat beginning to form on his forehead, and he wiped them away impatiently, running his chubby fingers through his fair hair as he did so. When he reached the front of the queue, he summoned up his most affable smile and addressed the young man who was serving.

"I wonder if you can help me?" he said. "I'm visiting some friends who are staying here, but we didn't arrange where to meet. Would you be able to help me locate them?"

"Possibly." The young man shrugged. "Who is it you're looking for?"

"Abigail Hawk," Simon murmured, leaning forward so only the young man heard him.

The youth's eyes opened in surprise, and he broke into a grin. "Oh! You're one of the band, aren't you? You're Simon Dean."

Simon cursed silently and put his finger to his lips. "Yes, but please don't spread it around," he said, still keeping his voice low. "I don't want any publicity."

"Oh, I understand. Abi's the same." the boy nodded, proudly showing off the fact that he knew her. "I do know where they're staying, but they've gone out for the day."

Simon looked at him in dismay. "Oh," he said inadequately. "Umm, maybe I could wait for them?"

"They've gone to Worm's Head," said the boy. "They only left about half an hour ago. They said they were expecting some visitors later. If you went now you might catch up with them. The causeway is open till about three today."

Simon stared at him in non-comprehension. "Causeway?" he asked, confused. "What causeway? Where's Worm's Head?"

The boy laughed at him. "You need to drive to Rhossili," he explained kindly. "Then you need to walk to the causeway and cross over to Worm's Head. The causeway's only open a few hours a day. Otherwise it's an island. If you go now you should meet them somewhere." Simon nodded his thanks and started towards the door. "Don't get caught by the tide, mind," called the boy. "It's very dangerous to try and cross once the tide's coming in. It'll tell you the safe times at the lookout station just above the causeway."

As he drove out of the campsite again and back towards Llangennith, Simon began to come up with the germ of an idea which formed as he travelled.

****

The Causeway, Worm's Head—11.20 a.m.

"It says the causeway's open until five past three," read Natasha from the board outside the lookout station.

Abi stood beside her, fishing in her backpack for her water bottle. "Yeah," she said, after taking a long swig, "that's the latest time. Sometimes because of the wind, or other stuff, the tide comes in faster. I suggest we aim to be back over by half past two, at the latest." She glanced at her watch. "That gives us just over three hours. Should be enough if we don't dawdle. Ready?" They grinned at each other and set off down the path

Rachael Richey

towards the causeway.

The wind was behind them, and by the time they reached the start of the rocky path across the sea, both Abi and Natasha were feeling very exhilarated and full of energy. The causeway was busy with a variety of travellers, some making the full trek to the end of Worm's Head, some equipped with fishing rods and possibly planning to strand themselves overnight, and some who were just planning to potter in the rock pools on the causeway for an hour or so. Abi led the way across the rocks, leaping nimbly over the pools and patches of slippery weed. Natasha scrambled along behind her, puffing as she attempted to keep up.

"Hey, slow down, Mum," she called eventually. "You're too good at this! I keep slipping on the weed."

Abi paused on the top of a large rock and turned to face her. "Sorry, sweetie," she said with a grin. "Forgot you haven't done this as often as I have. Once we're over the causeway, it's easy walking until we get to the spiky rocks, as you call them." She reached out a hand and pulled Natasha up onto the rock beside her. "All right now? I'll slow down a bit so we can walk together."

They walked in silence for a while, stopping only to investigate the huge anchor that lay half buried in the sand.

"How d'you feel about your grandfather now, Tash?" Abi asked at last. "Do you think you can ever forgive him?"

Natasha didn't answer for a while, but then she stopped walking and gazed out to sea. "No," she said. "No, I can't. He didn't have the excuse Nan had, yet he still let her take me away from you. And he didn't come

354

and see me. He could at least have done that. He's a very weak man, and I don't think I'll ever like him." She peeped up at her mother through her lashes. "Sorry."

Abi shook her head. "Don't be," she said at once, taking Natasha's hand and leading her on across the rocks. "I'm not sure I can forgive him either. He let me down when I really needed him, and, like you say, he didn't have the excuse that she did. I can't believe he knew she was visiting you and yet he never said a word, or even tried to go with her." She paused and looked sadly at her daughter. "You're right. He's a very weak man. It makes me wonder what else he did that I don't know about." They'd reached the land by that time and scrambled up onto the grassy top of the Inner Head and flopped down on the ground for a rest. Natasha lay back on the grass and closed her eyes.

"This is fun," she said, wriggling to get more comfortable.

Abi grinned down at her. "Don't get too comfortable," she warned. "That took us longer than I thought it would. We need to get going fairly soon if we're going to make it all the way to the end."

Natasha opened one eye and looked balefully at her. "Hmm. Well, all right, but I need some chocolate first." She sat up again and delved into her backpack, pulling out a bar of nut chocolate and ripping off the wrapper to sink her teeth into it hungrily. Abi laughed and took a swig out of her water bottle.

"Don't eat it all at once," she advised. "You may be glad of some more later."

Natasha looked up at her, her mouth brown with chocolate. She licked her lips. "We'll be back home in just over three hours," she remarked, "so unless you're planning on us getting stranded here all night, I think I'll eat it now."

"Don't say I didn't warn you." Abi shrugged with a smile, popping her bottle back in her bag and zipping it up. "Now, come on. Let's get going again. I don't much like the look of those clouds gathering over there." She pointed at the horizon, where a bank of dark cumulonimbus clouds were building up.

Natasha jumped to her feet and struggled into her backpack, wiping her sticky fingers on her shorts. "Okay, then, lead on. Oh, I do hope it thunders!" And, laughing, they made their way along the Inner Head towards the Low Neck—the spiky rocks, as Natasha called them.

****

Rhossili—11.30 a.m.

Simon parked the car at the far end of the car park and jumped out impatiently. He realised he must be at least half an hour behind Abi and Natasha, and if his plan was going to work it was imperative he catch up with them while they were still on the island. He pulled his jacket on, slipped his phone into his inner pocket, and opened the black case that had travelled on the seat beside him. He placed the contents in one of his outer pockets. Then he locked the car, slid the keys into his trouser pocket, lit a cigarette, and set off in the direction of Worm's Head.

The path was crowded, and Simon walked quickly, dodging between the dawdling tourists and arriving at the beginning of the causeway just before ten to twelve. He paused briefly to read the safety instructions on the board outside the lookout station, then glanced at his watch, did a quick calculation, and set off down the path to the causeway. If his plan worked, he wouldn't be back on dry land until well after dark, by which time he would have accomplished his mission. He smiled grimly to himself as he began to pick his way gingerly across the slippery rocks.

Chapter 29

Saturday 2nd August, 2008
Judy's House, Berkshire—12.15 p.m.

"Now, you will ring as soon as you arrive?" Robert watched his wife as she carefully strapped little Oliver into his car seat.

Judy flashed him a smile over her shoulder. "'Course I will," she promised, "and don't worry. I've done the trip loads of times." She straightened up and closed the car door. "I'm going to miss you and the kids, but I'll be back tomorrow."

Robert caught her wrist and pulled her to him. "I'll miss you too," he murmured, kissing the top of her fair head. "We could all come, if you want."

Judy shook her head and stood on tiptoe to kiss his nose. "No, it would be too crowded," she said. "Specially now I've found out Gideon and Charles are going to be there too. There won't really be room for me!"

"What was it Gideon said in the text?" Robert asked with a frown. "Something about Simon?"

"Yeah." Judy grimaced. "Some strange story about thinking Simon was going to look for Abi at the caravan site, so Gid wants to get there to protect her."

Robert looked serious. "But surely he wouldn't hurt her, would he?" he asked. "I don't know the chap, but he's not violent, is he?"

"Didn't used to be. But after his strange actions lately, who knows. I doubt he'd hurt anyone, though. Probably wants to talk to Abs. Try and get her to leave Gideon," she added.

"Fat chance of that." Robert gave a short laugh. "They're besotted with each other. What's his problem with them anyway?"

"Abi and I both think he's in love with Gideon," Judy said, her eyes twinkling.

Robert raised his eyebrows and shrugged. "Well, he *is* very good looking…" He watched Judy out of the corner of his eye.

She chuckled and slapped him on the arm. "Oh, not you too!" She giggled. "Now come on. I must go, or I'll never get there. Look after the kids, and I'll see you all tomorrow evening."

She leaned forward, kissed him briefly on the lips, then slid into the car and fastened her seatbelt. As she reversed out onto the narrow lane, Robert bent down and called through the window, "Call me if there's any trouble. Keep me posted," he said, his face serious.

Judy waved a hand in acknowledgment and set off up the lane, watching in the mirror as her husband disappeared from view.

****

The M4 near Bristol—12.30 p.m.

"This is ridiculous!" Gideon slammed his hands down on the steering wheel and glared at the queue in front of them. They had been almost stationary in a line of traffic approaching the junction of the M4 and M5 in Bristol for almost half an hour, and it showed no sign of speeding up.

Roger looked up from his phone. "There's an accident just before the junction," he said, squinting back at the tiny screen. "They've closed two lanes. We'll get there eventually. No point in getting stressed, son. We can't do anything about it."

Gideon growled under his breath and shifted angrily in his seat.

"Can't we turn off? Take a back road?" suggested Charles, leaning forward and peering over Roger's shoulder.

"Afraid not." Roger shook his head. "This goes right up until the next exit. Just got to sit it out." He glanced at his son. "Don't worry, Gideon. I'm sure they'll be fine. How's Simon going to find out where they've gone anyway?"

Gideon grunted and continued to stare out at the seemingly never-ending stream of almost motionless traffic, his mind playing out a variety of scenarios, none of which ended well.

****

Worm's Head—12.30 p.m.

The rain had continued to hold off, although by the time Abi and Natasha reached the Low Neck the sky was a threatening dark grey and the wind was whipping the surrounding sea into a mass of swirling white horses. Natasha slumped down on the springy grass and stared at the rocks in front of them. She pushed her windblown curls out of her eyes and squinted up at her mother.

"Okay, shall we do it, then?" she asked, sniffing as the wind made her nose start to run.

Abi squatted down beside her and nodded. "Yes, we'd better press on. It's nearly twelve thirty, and with this wind I definitely don't want to chance getting back across the causeway any later than two thirty." She stared across the rocks to the far side, her eyes narrowed against the wind. "In fact, I think we may need to turn around almost as soon as we've crossed the rocks."

Natasha screwed up her nose in annoyance. "Oh, can't we just go as far as the Devil's Bridge?" she pleaded. "We've come this far."

Abi glanced at her watch again, then nodded. "All right, just that far, then, but only if we start across now."

She pulled Natasha to her feet and led the way along the path to the start of the rocky section.

Ten minutes later Abi was nearly at the other side and Natasha was struggling bravely on, taking her time on the jagged and sometimes slippery rocks. Abi paused on a relatively flat rock and peered back at her daughter.

"Are you okay?" she called, the wind almost carrying her voice away.

Natasha looked up and gingerly waved a hand in acknowledgement, then put her head down and continued to slide on her bottom down a particularly deep crevasse. When she had nearly reached the bottom she stopped and, stretching her leg out in front of her, pulled herself over the chasm and started to scramble up the next set of rocks. When she reached the top she paused and took stock. She was nearly there. She could see Abi just reaching the far side, scrambling nimbly up onto the tufts of springy grass. There was just one more up and down to negotiate, and then she could join her. She leant forward, grasped the nearest rock in one hand,

and lowered herself carefully down.

When she finally joined her mother, who was stretched out on the grass with her eyes closed, she dropped to the ground with a loud sigh.

"Made it!" she said triumphantly, grinning down at Abi.

Abi opened one eye and shielded it from the watery sun. "Well done. And you didn't need any help. Much faster than last time, too," she said with a nod. "I thought we could go back the other way. What d'you think? It gets a bit boring if you have to do that all over again so soon."

Natasha wriggled out of her backpack and pulled out her water bottle. "Yes, please," she said, opening the top and taking a long swig. "I like the other way. You get to look in all the rock pools. And we get to go over the Devil's Bridge first." She lay down on the grass and rolled onto her tummy. "Do we need to start right now, or can we have a rest?"

Abi glanced at her watch. "Well, it's twelve forty-five now. I suppose if we don't dawdle on the way back we can have a little rest here for ten minutes. We managed that last bit quicker than I anticipated." She sat up and rummaged in her backpack. "I fancy some chocolate. Have you got any left?"

Natasha looked up at her under her lashes. "No. I ate it all. Can I have some of yours?" A cheeky grin flitted across her face.

Abi laughed and broke off a few squares. "Go on, then," she said, holding them out. "I knew you'd do that. You'd be hopeless on a trip up Everest. You'd eat all the provisions before you left the base camp."

They sat together, happily munching on the

chocolate, with Abi pointing out items of natural or geological interest, until it was time to continue on their way.

Abi got to her feet and pulled her backpack on. "Come on, then. Devil's Bridge, and back across the flat bit." She tucked a straying strand of hair behind her ear.

Natasha scrambled up and grinned at her. "Let's go," she said, heaving her backpack over her shoulder before turning and leading the way towards the narrow natural rock bridge that joined the Inner and Outer Heads.

****

Simon had made good time across the causeway, and by twelve forty-five he was rounding the bend on the Inner Head and coming into view of Natasha's spiky rocks. He paused to catch his breath and scanned the land ahead of him for any familiar figures. To his delight, he was rewarded with the sight of Abi scrambling up the final rock and jumping agilely onto the grass at the far side of the rocks. He screwed up his eyes and looked around for Natasha. He finally spotted her small figure heaving herself out of a deep chasm and onto the top of a flatter rock. The child paused and looked around before continuing on her way towards her mother. Simon smiled grimly to himself. Now they'd crossed to the Outer Head, his task might be a little easier. He started down towards the rocks, then pulled up again and considered his position. He could see from the other walkers that it was possible for the girls to return by a different route—a lower one, over flat rocks at sea level, and he really needed to be sure which route they were going to take before he took further action himself. He moved off the path and positioned himself on a grassy slope that commanded a view of both routes and of the high bridge-like natural stone arch that joined the two portions of land together. Once he knew what the two were going to do, he would make his next move.

After about ten minutes, his patience was rewarded. He watched intently as Abi and Natasha got to their feet and set off in the direction of the bridge. He watched as they tentatively made their way across it, keeping close together, then headed off in the direction of the far end of the promontory. He stood up in order to keep them in sight and noted with satisfaction when they veered to their left and started the descent to the flatter rocks for their return. He glanced around at the other walkers in the area. The vast majority of them were already passing him on their way back to the causeway, with just a small number making their way laboriously back over the rocks, or picking their way across the rock-pool-dotted lower level. He could make out no figures further away than Abi and Natasha, so he sat down again and decided to remain where he was until they got a little closer. By the time he confronted them, he wanted no witnesses remaining.

****

"Mum, look!" called Natasha, bending almost double in order to peer into a rock pool. "This is full of anemones. They're lovely!"

Abi joined her daughter and squatted down to get a better look.

"They are pretty," she agreed with a smile. "It's amazing what you can find in these rock pools. Keep a look out for starfish. I always liked finding them."

Natasha straightened up and pushed her hair out of her eyes. "I'm glad we decided to come back this way," she remarked, shielding her eyes from the watery sun and staring out to sea. "Those rocks are hard enough to do once!"

"You need more practice." Abi laughed and stood up. "P'raps we should do this again tomorrow?"

"We'll have Ollie then," Natasha objected. "He can't come."

"Mmm, well, maybe we'll come back again later in the holidays—after Dad finishes recording?" Abi suggested, adjusting her backpack and glancing over at the sea. "I guess we should press on now, though. The tide turned about forty-five minutes ago. We mustn't risk getting cut off."

Natasha looked up at her imploringly. "Let's just explore for a little bit more. We've still got time. Look, it's only quarter past one. Please, Mum, this is so fun." She looked at Abi under her lashes. "It's helping me forget about that horrid newspaper story."

"Clever girl." Abi grinned, reaching out and ruffling her hair. "You know how to work me, don't you? All right, then, just a few more minutes. We can always run across the causeway."

Natasha looked at her doubtfully, then realising she was joking, grinned and hopped across a small rock pool and knelt down beside another larger one. "Thanks. You know you want to stay longer too," she called back to Abi. "Let's see what's in this one. Come on."

Abi joined her, and they spent the next twenty minutes happily pottering around the numerous pools, spotting varieties of fish and shellfish that Natasha had never heard of before.

Eventually Abi straightened up and glanced around her. "Looks like everyone else has headed back to the causeway," she remarked with a frown. "I think we really had better get going now, Tash. Look, that man over there on the grass is the only other person in sight."

Natasha looked up from her rock pool and squinted in the direction Abi was indicating. A lone figure was sitting on the grassy slope overlooking the area they were currently exploring. She screwed up her eyes and held her hair back against the wind. "I think he's watching us, Mum," she said at last. "D'you think he's paparazzi?"

Abi sighed and looked back at the man. "Oh, I do hope not," she said wearily. "We came here to escape them. I don't want *them* spoiling our day." She shielded her eyes from the glare of the sun and chewed on her lip thoughtfully. "Too far away to see him clearly. He's probably just looking at the view. He still has plenty of time to get back to the causeway." She paused and grinned. "At least I hope he does. Otherwise we're in trouble, because it'll take us about ten minutes to reach where he is."

Natasha picked her way over to Abi's side and caught her mother's hand in hers. "Mum, I don't like the look of him," she said in a small voice. "Can we go back a different way?"

Abi glanced down at her in surprise. "Why, darling? Does he frighten you?" she asked in concern.

"Yeah. A bit." Natasha hesitated. "He looks...scary," she ended lamely.

Abi glanced over at the solitary figure again and

frowned. "Well, I'm sure he's just a tourist," she said, "but if he scares you we could loop round nearer the rocks and come up to his right. Then, if we have time, we could go over the top of the Inner Head instead of round the edge." She looked down at Natasha and raised her eyebrows. "Would you like to do that?"

Natasha nodded. "Yes, please. And keep watching him in case he starts to follow us."

She started to lead the way away from the sea's edge towards the higher rocks. Abi paused for a moment, stared at the lone watcher again, then followed her daughter thoughtfully. It wasn't often Natasha was scared in that way, and Abi wondered if the newspaper business had upset her more than she'd previously admitted. She caught up with her, and together they began to make their way towards the grassy slopes of the Inner Head.

****

Simon watched the two figures as they veered away from the sea and started to make their way towards him by what seemed a very tortuous route. He got to his feet and watched as they moved inland until they were almost up against the higher rocks, then turned and started back in his direction. He had been watching them impatiently as they'd pottered around the rock pools for what seemed like an eternity, and now he was confused as to their intentions. He knew they'd be making their way back to the causeway in order to cross to the other side by three o'clock, and based on his own calculations they were beginning to cut it rather fine. He sat down again and decided to wait. They would have to pass by him on their way back. He contented himself with the knowledge that all the other walkers had already passed him on their way back and as far as he could make out he was alone with the girls. He smiled grimly to himself and sat back. If his plan worked, then all his troubles would be over. He could rejoin Gideon in the band and everything would be how it was meant to be. He nodded contentedly, keeping his gaze firmly fixed on the progress of his prey.

****

"This is taking longer than I expected," muttered Abi, puffing as they scrambled across the slippery rocks. "I don't think we'll have time to go over the top, Tash. We'll just have to hope the man has moved on. Can you still see him?"

Natasha, who was leading the way and was on slightly higher ground than her mother, paused and stared up at the grassy slope. "He's still there," she whispered. "I don't think he's moved at all."

Abi joined her and strained to see the figure stretched out on the grass. "I don't think he's looking at us," she murmured. "I still think he's just a tourist who's cutting it fine with the tides. Like we are now," she added with a frown. "Come on, we must keep moving. I really don't want to spend the night here with no phone."

"Oh, gosh, yes! Judy's coming, and she wouldn't know what happened to us. Come on, then," Natasha gasped, springing to life and scrambling across the rocks again towards the Inner Head.

Abi paused for a moment and stared at the lone figure. When he suddenly moved and turned to face them, she caught her breath and felt her whole body turn cold with fear.

"Tash!" she hissed urgently. "Come here, quick," and she dropped to her knees, holding out her arm to the approaching child.

"What is it?" Natasha asked, fear in her voice as she saw her mother's face. "What have you seen?"

Abi pulled the girl down beside her and pointed up at the figure. "I think it's Simon," she said quietly.

"Simon?" Natasha echoed in horror. "Why is he here? Surely he'd want to stay away from us after what he did."

Abi was silent for a moment, then licked her lips and turned to her daughter.

"Maybe he didn't get the result he wanted from the newspaper article," she said, her mouth going dry. "Maybe he's come to finish the job."

"What d'you mean?" Natasha stared at her blankly. "How can he do anything here? How did he know where we were anyway?"

"Luck on his part that he guessed we'd come to Wales, and bad luck on my part that I left a message in the shop for our visitors. I didn't tell Gareth who the visitors were. He would have recognised Simon and thought he was who I meant." Abi raised her head and peered over at the grassy slope again. Simon had got to his feet and was gazing across in their direction, clearly looking for something. "He can't see us here," she murmured pulling Natasha a little further back against the rocks. "He's searching now. We need to move— get hidden somewhere he can't get to."

"But what can he do here?" persisted Natasha, obediently following her mother across the rocks into a concealed inlet.

Abi looked at her, chewing on her lip. "Tash, I

don't want you to be too scared, but it's possible he means to hurt us. Or me, anyway." She paused while Natasha digested the information. "So we need to keep out of his way for as long as possible. It's unfortunate we have so little time to get to the causeway and get across, and to be honest I'm beginning to doubt we'll make it now. We need to come up with a plan."

Natasha's face had gone pale, and her blue eyes were huge. "Hurt us?" she whispered. "Why would he hurt us? Does he hate us that much?" Her voice shook, and her lower lip began to tremble.

Abi moved closer and put her arm around her. "He's not behaving rationally," she said firmly. "The newspaper article showed that. Since that hasn't worked—his plan obviously being to split your dad and me up and get back into the band—then maybe, just maybe, he thinks he needs to get rid of me permanently. In his diseased little mind he thinks Dad will then welcome him with open arms."

Natasha shivered and leant against her mother. "That's sick," she commented. "He must be mad to think like that." She pulled back a little and scowled. "And if he tries to hurt you, he'll have me to answer to."

Abi nodded and gave Natasha a quick squeeze. "Likewise, if he tries to hurt you," she said, her eyes glinting dangerously. "Now, come on. We need to find somewhere to hide where we can see him but he can't see us."

She caught Natasha's hand and pulled her even nearer to the high rocks. They ducked into a narrow inlet, and Abi struggled out of her backpack.

"Put your waterproof on," she ordered Natasha,

pulling hers from her bag.

"Why?" asked Natasha with a frown. "It's not raining yet."

Abi glanced at her as she slipped her arms into her green jacket. "Camouflage," she murmured. "We'll be much less conspicuous in green jackets than in brightly coloured hoodies," and she nodded at Natasha's vivid red top.

Natasha scrabbled in her backpack and pulled out her waterproof. "Wow, this is quite exciting!" she said with a grin as she struggled into it.

"Hmm. You won't be saying that when we get stranded here all night with a lunatic drummer," Abi remarked. "Now, come on. Let's see if we can get onto the Inner Head without him seeing us. Clamber up between those rocks and keep your head down."

The two of them edged their way along the rocks, taking care to keep as low as possible, hoping to remain out of Simon's line of sight. Abi's mind was spinning through the possibilities they faced. She was well aware it was already after two o'clock and they would need to move very quickly if they were to get across the causeway before three, let alone two thirty as she would have preferred. In order to stand any chance of getting across on time, they would have to pass right by where Simon was sitting, and as far as she could see there was no way around that. If they went up and over the top of the Inner Head, they wouldn't have enough time, but if Simon was planning what she assumed, then he would prevent them from passing by his way anyway. She came to a decision and called quietly to Natasha.

"Tash, I think we need to make our way to the causeway over the top, in order to avoid Simon," she said. "Then if we've missed the tide, which we almost certainly will have, we can ring the emergency bell to alert the lookout point that we're stranded."

Natasha looked impressed. "Will they send out a boat to pick us up?" she asked hopefully.

"No, They won't do that, but it will mean the people on the mainland will know we're stranded, so hopefully that'll stay Simon's hand. He can't risk doing anything if the coastguard know we're here." She patted Natasha reassuringly on the shoulder. Of course he could push them into the sea and make it look like they drowned trying to cross too late, but she thought she'd keep that idea to herself. They continued to scramble across the rocks towards the grassy slopes of the Inner Head, Abi keeping one eye in the direction of Simon in case he suddenly located them.

****

Simon was getting very frustrated. He'd lost sight of the two girls once they'd reached the higher rocks, and he was beginning to wonder if they'd seen him and were attempting to keep out of his way. He got to his feet and stared over at the rocks, shielding his eyes against the watery glare of the afternoon sun. As he watched, a large dark cloud drifted across the sun and the temperature fell by several degrees. Simon shivered and took a few steps towards the rocks. He glanced up at the sky and cursed under his breath. He could see the rain had already started out at sea, and he realised it wouldn't be long before they were engulfed in a downpour. He quickened his pace and moved rapidly towards where the rocks joined the inner head. He climbed to slightly higher ground and stared intently at the area where he'd last seen Abi and Natasha.

Eventually his diligence was rewarded, and he caught sight of a dark curly head bobbing down between two high, sharp rocks. So they were trying to keep out of his way, he mused to himself, narrowing his eyes speculatively. He had been hoping they wouldn't recognise him and he could take them by surprise. He sucked in his breath and sat down on a grassy hummock out of sight of the girls while he thought out a new strategy. Glancing around, he sussed out the lay of the land and realised the girls would have two options when they finished crossing the rocks. They could either go back the way he had just come from, or they could climb up and over the top of the Inner Head. He calculated that if they went over the top, they stood no chance of catching the causeway before the tide, but if they went on the lower path, they still stood a very slim chance of making it. He was fairly sure they wouldn't be keen on the idea of getting stranded for the night with him, so he surmised they would probably attempt to make it back in time by taking the lower route. However, he also realised they wouldn't attempt that if he was in their path. He looked around again and finally selected the perfect hiding place from which he would be able to see exactly which way they decided to go, and either way he would be well placed to cut them off. He positioned himself in a grassy hollow behind a large lichen-covered rock and settled down for a prolonged stay.

****

Abi raised her head cautiously and peered towards the grassy area where they'd last seen Simon. There was no sign of him, and she slid back down the rock and crouched next to Natasha.

"He's not there," she whispered. "But I doubt he's gone. He's probably hiding somewhere to watch which way we go."

"So what do we do now, then?" Natasha shivered, her voice shaking.

"Well, don't worry for a start," Abi said, smiling at her. "Whatever happens, we can look after ourselves. We can outwit Simon any day." She paused and grinned. "I know this place like the back of my hand, while, to the best of my knowledge, Simon has never been here before. We have a distinct advantage." She raised her head again and scanned the hillside. After a moment she spotted a slight movement behind a large rock half way up the slope. She screwed up her eyes and concentrated. The movement repeated, and this time Abi was able to identify it as that of a person. She ducked her head down again and grinned at Natasha. "Okay," she whispered. "I can see him. He's hiding behind a rock. If we're very careful, we may be able to sneak up and onto the higher ground over to the left. Then we can go over the top and make our way to the causeway."

Natasha nodded her head vigorously. "Okay. Will we be in time to get across?" she asked.

Abi glanced at her watch, and grimaced. "'Fraid not," she grunted. "It's gone two thirty. There's no way we could get across safely now. Our best bet is to go and ring the bell to alert them we're stranded. Then we'll just have to make the best of it and keep out of Simon's way."

"Wish I hadn't eaten my chocolate now," Natasha muttered crossly.

Abi gave a short laugh. "Told you," she said with a

fond look at her daughter. "Don't worry. I've still got some. We're not going to starve." She stood up again and peered over towards where she'd located Simon. "Hmm. He's still there. Now, this isn't going to be easy, but we need to give it a go. Are you ready? Follow my lead."

With an encouraging smile she cautiously began to climb up out of their hiding place and around the last of the rocks that led to the Inner Head. They moved quietly and carefully, Abi keeping one eye on Simon's rock. When they reached the start of the grass, she dropped to the ground and lay flat on her stomach. Natasha wriggled along and joined her, pulling her hood up over her head.

"Has he seen us, Mum?" she whispered.

"Don't think so," Abi murmured, her eyes never leaving the rock. "Now comes the really difficult bit. We need to get up onto the slopes and make our way uphill." She paused and glanced at Natasha. "If he sees us and starts to follow, I'm fairly certain we can outrun him. He was never very athletic, and from what I've heard he's really let himself go. Again, follow my lead."

With that she began to edge her way, still on her stomach, towards the start of the slope leading to the top of the Inner Head. Natasha wriggled along behind her, hardly daring to glance over towards where Simon was hidden. As they reached the beginning of the slope, the first of the rain began to fall and a distant rumble of thunder sounded out over the sea. Abi got to her feet cautiously and gestured to Natasha to follow her. As they began the steep ascent, Abi was aware of movement to her right. As she looked, a figure

375

appeared from behind the rock and stared directly at them. Abi stopped moving and dropped to her knees. For a long moment she and Simon stared at each other across the hundred yards that separated them, and then Abi turned to Natasha.

"Run!" she shouted, and took off up the hill with the agility of a mountain goat, Natasha leaping along behind her.

Chapter 30

Saturday 2ⁿᵈ August, 2008
Rhossili—3.00 p.m.

Gideon finally swung the car into the car park at Rhossili just on three o'clock and stopped impatiently at the ticket office. He handed over his two pounds, then drove through the rows of cars looking for Abi's vehicle.

"There it is," said Roger, pointing to the large 4x4 parked at the far end of the car park. Gideon pulled up beside it and leapt out. He peered in through the windows, then turned to the others.

"Yeah, they're still here," he said unnecessarily. "We should meet them walking back from the causeway." He paused, locked the Volvo, and tossed the keys to Roger. "You look after these," he said, striding off towards the path. "I checked the tide table, and the causeway will be closed now, so they should already be back over." Anxiety was evident in his voice, and Charles glanced at Roger with a raise of his eyebrows.

"They'll be fine, Gid," he soothed. "We'll meet them coming back any minute now. We don't even know that Simon's here, remember."

Gideon didn't answer and squeezed through the gate that led to the path, striding ahead with his head down.

"Pity we don't know what Simon's driving," observed Roger, strolling along behind his son. "That would be really useful."

"He's here," announced Gideon shortly without turning round. "I know he is. He's here, and he's come to kill Abi."

Charles' eyes opened wider, and he glanced over at Roger again. The older man shrugged and quickened his pace to move alongside Gideon.

"He wouldn't do that, Gideon," he said. "That would just be one step too far, don't you think? I mean, the newspaper stuff was one thing, but murder? Surely not."

Gideon glanced at him. "Dad, he's not thinking straight. He's unhinged. I just don't trust him. We need to hurry." And he sped up and headed out across the large grassy stretch that led to the causeway.

By the time the three men reached the lookout station, they hadn't encountered Abi and Natasha, nor Simon, and it was nearly three fifteen. Gideon walked straight to the edge of the cliff and stared out over the now partially covered causeway. The final few stragglers were making their way up the long steep path towards him, and he quickly scanned them but failed to locate the girls. He stared out across the causeway, panic beginning to rise in his throat, but no figures were visible.

Roger moved over to speak to the NCI man who was watching the last of the walkers climb back up the slope.

"Good afternoon," he said with a smile. "My daughter-in-law and granddaughter were over on

Worm's Head today, but they don't seem to have returned yet. I was wondering if we had somehow missed them. I don't suppose you'd remember all the people who pass by, would you?"

The elderly man shrugged. "I remember some," he said. "What do they look like?"

"Tall, long dark auburn hair, late twenties, and twelve with long dark curly hair," Roger said at once.

"I think I remember them from this morning," the man said at last. "They stopped to have a drink before they crossed over. Haven't noticed them coming back, but obviously I don't see everyone." He indicated the causeway. "No chance now, I'm afraid. If they haven't made it back yet, they'll be stuck till the next tide. There's a bell over the other side we ask people to ring if they get stranded. No one's rung it yet."

Roger bit his lip. "You see," he began, "we have reason to believe someone may have followed them over there— someone who wishes them ill. Is there any way to get over there by boat?"

The man looked shocked and shook his head. "Not now," he said at once. "It's not the easiest place to take a boat to. Especially when the tide's like it is now. And with this storm that's coming in—no chance for a landing this afternoon, I'm afraid." He frowned and leaned towards Roger. "What sort of ill d'you think he means them?"

"I think he wants to kill them." Gideon had joined them, fear clearly evident in his eyes.

"You need to call the police," said the man at once. "They may have some way of getting over there. Not sure what, though."

Gideon pushed his hair out of his eyes impatiently

and swung round to stare out across the causeway again. "So how do we get out there?" he demanded. "Dad, think of something, please."

****

Caravan Site, Llangennith—3.15 p.m.

Judy drove slowly over the cattle grid and drew her car up outside the shop. Since Abi had the remote control that opened the barrier to the Caravan Park, she would need to ask them to activate it from the shop. She left Oliver in the car and stepped into the small building. Gareth was behind the counter, and he looked up as she entered.

"Hello, Judy," he said with a smile. "Have you come to see Abi too?"

"Too?" she asked warily. "Who else has come to see her?"

Gareth beamed. "Simon Dean. The drummer of NightHawk," he added in case Judy didn't know who he was. "He arrived about eleven this morning, just after Abi and Tasha had set off for Rhossili."

Judy felt her heart come up into her mouth. "What did you tell him? Did you tell him where they were?"

"Umm, yes I did," he said, a frown creasing his forehead. "Was that wrong?"

Judy swallowed and took a deep breath. "No, no, don't worry. I'm sure it'll be all right," she said, unconvinced. "Can you open the barrier for me? I'll go and wait at the caravan—or should I go to Rhossili…?"

Gareth emerged from behind the counter and stood looking down at her.

"Judy, what's wrong?" he asked. "Should I not have told Simon where they were?"

Judy glanced at him and sighed. "There's been

problems between them," she said, "and now Gideon thinks Simon might have followed her here for some…some not very nice purpose," she ended rather tamely.

Gareth's face flushed, and he stared at her in horror. "You mean he wants to hurt her?" His Welsh accent became stronger as his agitation grew. "And I told him where she was—Judy, we must go and save her!"

Judy chewed on her lip thoughtfully, then shook her head. "Not sure what we could do," she admitted. "But Gideon's on his way down. I'll text him and tell him what you've told me. I've got little Oliver in the car. I don't want to take him into possible danger."

She pulled out her mobile and quickly located Gideon's number.

"Simon knows Abi's gone to Worm's Head," she wrote. *"I'm at caravan site with Oliver. Shall I come to Rhossili or stay here?"* She pressed Send, then took a deep breath and glanced up at Gareth. "Don't blame yourself," she reassured him. "There was no way you could have known Simon was a possible threat. He was the one who sold that disgusting story to the paper."

"That's dreadful! How could he do something like that? What's Abi ever done to him?"

"Long story." Judy sighed. "But it's all in his mind. I'm going to go to the caravan, at least until I hear back from Gideon. Please, can you open the barrier for me?"

****

Rhossili—3.20 p.m.

As Gideon stared at his father in desperation, his mobile bleeped. He snatched it out of his pocket and peered at the screen.

"It's from Judy," he reported. "She's at the caravan. Apparently Simon does know Abi and Tasha came here." He slammed one fist into the other palm. "I knew it! I fucking knew he'd try something. Dad, we have to act fast." He paused and stared out across the causeway into the heavy rain falling over the island. "Why have they not come back over? Has he already found them? Are we too late?" His voice rose, his agony apparent.

Charles took his mobile from him. "Does Judy say anything else?" he asked, glancing at it. He read the text, then sent a quick reply.

"Thanks, Jude. Stay where you are for now. Keep your phone on. Chas."

Gideon turned back to his father, saying, "Dad, what can we..." and stopped short when he realised the older man was deep in conversation on his mobile. He moved closer and listened.

"Yes, Laurie, that's right. I know it's a huge thing to ask, but...Really? You wouldn't mind? That's fantastic. I'm sure you understand our worry...Okay, thanks again, see you in about ten...fifteen minutes? ...Bye."

He disconnected the call and slipped the phone back into the pocket of his Barbour jacket. Gideon raised his eyebrows at him.

"What was that?" he demanded. "Who were you talking to? Is someone coming with a boat?"

Roger shook his head and gave a slight smile. "No, a boat would be no use. He's coming with a helicopter."

Charles gasped, and Gideon stared at his father in surprise. "A helicopter? You can just call someone and they promise you a helicopter? How the hell...?" He shook his head in amazement.

"Just an old friend from the...from work." Roger grinned. "He happens to live near here and keeps his helicopter at Swansea Airport, which is only a few miles up the road. I explained the situation and he was only too happy to help. He's going to come now and will need to land here." He looked hopefully at the NCI man, who nodded his assent. "Then he'll fly you over to look for them. There's apparently only one place you can land a helicopter on Worm's Head. The first bit you reach when you cross the causeway. With any luck, Abi and Tasha will be waiting there anyway, but if they're not, you'll have to go and search for them."

Gideon stared at his father, speechless for once, and Charles chipped in. "Can I come too?" he asked. "Two searchers will be better than one."

"I'm afraid not." Roger shook his head. "The helicopter only takes four, and you must leave room for the girls."

Charles nodded, and Gideon looked up at them. "I need to do this myself," he said curtly. "I need to rescue my wife and daughter and deal with Simon myself."

Roger looked at him with narrowed eyes. "Careful how you deal with Simon," he warned. "Remember his state of mind. He might be armed." He paused, then reached into his inner pocket and pulled out a small revolver.

"Dad? You carry a gun?" Gideon stared at him in surprise. "Is that legal?"

Roger shrugged. "Well, you know," he said vaguely. "I still have it. It comes in handy sometimes. Take it just in case, but please only use it to threaten him. Don't shoot him—that would take far too much explaining."

Gideon grinned despite his desperation and took the proffered weapon. "Thanks, Dad," he murmured, slipping it into his pocket. "I won't do anything silly."

At that moment the distant sound of a bell carried across the water towards them. Gideon's head shot up, and he frowned at the NCI man.

"What's that?" he asked.

The man smiled. "That's the emergency bell. We ask people to ring it if they get stranded. We can't rescue them, but at least we know they're all right and that they're there. I expect that'll be your wife."

Gideon stared out across the sea, but his view was hampered by the rain. He glanced at Roger and Charles. "Looks like we may be in time," he said, relief sounding in his voice.

Roger smiled. "Of course we are, son. Of course we are."

****

Worm's Head—3.30 p.m.

Abi let go of the bell rope and caught Natasha by the hand. "Come on, Tash," she yelled above the sound of the torrential rain. "We need to find somewhere to hide. Simon can't be far behind us."

They started to run back the way they'd come. The storm that had started as they began their run up the hill had gathered momentum, and both girls were now soaked to the skin despite the protection of their waterproof coats. Their hair was drenched and hanging limp, and their legs and feet were cold and sodden. As they started back towards the higher route, Simon appeared around the lower path, panting loudly. He stopped a few yards from the girls and glowered at them.

"There you are," he gasped, attempting to wipe the rain from his eyes. "I've been looking for you."

He stepped menacingly towards them, and Abi caught Natasha's wrist and pulled her towards her. "What d'you want, Simon?" she yelled above the noise of the thunder and rain. "Why did you follow us?"

Simon smiled unpleasantly and took another step towards them.

"I think you know what I want," he said through gritted teeth. "I want my life back." He took another step forward, and Abi pulled Natasha around to the right and up onto the grass. "I want my sodding life back, and it's your fault I can't have it."

Abi pushed Natasha in the direction of the higher path, hissing, "Run! He can't follow both of us. It's me he wants. I'll catch you up." Natasha hesitated, and Abi gave her another push. "Go, Tash! Go and hide. I'll find you."

Natasha gave her one last look of desperation, then turned her back and ran as fast as she could through the grass towards the higher path. Simon took a step towards her, then stopped and stared at Abi.

"Clever girl," he sneered. "But you can't save yourself. The kid's not important— at least not as important as you." He stopped and stared at her again.

She took a step backwards. "Simon, it's not my fault you haven't got what you want," she began, attempting to keep her voice reasonable. "Gideon left the band because he'd had enough. He won't take you back because you treated us so badly. What did you expect?"

While she was speaking, Abi's mind was working

overtime in an attempt to formulate an escape plan. Simon moved towards her again, his eyes narrowed against the driving rain.

"It *is* your fucking fault," he hissed. "Gideon's been obsessed with you ever since that stupid school dance. I never stood a chance." He paused and wiped a chubby hand across his wet face again. "We could have been great together, we could still be out there being adored, being noticed, being famous. But he had to find you. You ruined him. You ruined what he could have been. You ruined everyone's lives."

Abi stared at him, her eyes wide. "Simon, you can't decide who people fall in love with. Gideon fell in love with me. You kept us apart for ten years— isn't that enough? If you love him like I think you do, then surely you want him to be happy. Hate me as much as you like, but don't make Gideon sad. If you hurt me or Natasha, then he'll be really sad and really, really angry. With you." She took a step towards him. "Simon, he's never going to let you back in the band if you hurt me. Can't you see how wrong this is? You're not thinking straight." He watched her silently, and she had one last try. "Stop this now, Simon. Come back with me when the tide's right, and we'll all talk. If you stop trying to hurt us, trying to split us up, then maybe we can all be friends again. Surely you'd like that? That would make Gideon happy."

She said the words as though she was speaking to a small child, and attempted a smile at him. Simon continued to stare at her silently, his hands balled into fists at his sides. Cautiously she took a few steps to her right and glanced up at the hill to see if she could see her daughter. Aware of a sudden movement, Abi swung back to face Simon, only to discover he'd moved right up to her. She stared him straight in the eye.

"You don't want to do this, Simon," she repeated. "It can only lead to heartbreak."

He thrust his face close up to hers and sneered at her. "Yeah, for you and your family. I've already had all the heartbreak I can take. It's your turn now." He reached out and caught her by the wrist, yanking at her roughly. "You've ruined my life. I'm nothing because of you. You have to pay for that."

Abi forced herself not to flinch as she felt his breath on her face. She kept her eyes firmly fixed on his. "Simon, if you hurt me, you're hurting Gideon. I don't think you want to do that. You love him, don't you, Simon? That's what this is all about, isn't it?"

Simon sucked in his breath and closed his eyes briefly. "You stupid bitch," he spat out. "Of course I love him. He's my best friend. But it's not about that. It's about you, Abi, you. You ruined everything—you took him away from me, you ruined the band. You made him hate me." He paused and stared at her with intense hatred. "You made him hate me, and I planned to make him hate you." He exhaled sharply. "That hasn't worked. So...I need to use my other plan." He looked her in the eyes, his own wild and unfocused. "He'll soon see how much better life is without you. He'll thank me. When he realises how much more fun he can have with me. With the band. With no ties holding him down." He smiled, a strange, twisted smile. "Then everything will be back to normal. Back the way it should be. How it was in '94. Surely you can see that, Abi? Surely you understand it's for the best?" Slowly Abi began to edge away from him, her wrist still firmly gripped in his hand. She tugged at it, and he gripped tighter. "Now, now, I can't let you go, can I?" he chided, shaking his head at her. "We need to finish this little game. I rather think you might have started back across the causeway a little late. You and that kid. Very believable, really. After all, who wants to get stranded here overnight? It would be perfectly natural to take a bit of a chance with the tide. I'm sure it happens all the time." He paused and looked behind him up the hill. "We just need to find that child, and then it's into the sea with you both."

He smiled at her with his mouth, his eyes remaining flat and unemotional. With a swift movement he pulled Abi round to his side and began to walk up the hill, dragging her behind him. She stumbled against him as she lost her footing on the slippery grass, and her free arm flailed out, catching him on the back of the head. He swore loudly and slapped her hard across the face.

"Walk properly, bitch," he snapped, dragging her upright and catching her arm with his free hand. Abi stared up the hill in front of them and stopped walking.

"Tasha!" she screamed against the noise of the storm. "Hide! Don't let him find you."

Simon loosed his grip on her arm and slapped her across the face again, his eyes flashing with anger. "You fucking whore!" he yelled at her. "There's nothing you can do to save her or yourself. I've got you now."

With a swift movement Abi aimed a kick at Simon's shin, at the same time lifting her wrist up to her mouth and biting down hard into his hand. With a strangled cry he wrenched his hand away and hopped backwards, thrown off balance by the kick. He fell back onto the wet grass with a grunt. Abi took her chance and ran as fast as she could in the direction Natasha had gone. By the time Simon gained his feet again, Abi was half way up the hill, moving fast. She glanced behind her just as he struggled up and began to follow. The rain was thundering down on her as she dodged up the hill, slipping as she ran, her breath coming fast and ragged.

"Mum!" she heard a shrill voice come wavering out of the noise of the rain, and she turned in confusion, attempting to locate it. "Mum!" it came again, and this time Abi turned towards the sound and saw her daughter's head peeping out from behind a large rock. She stumbled across the slippery grass and slid round behind the rock to join her. They clung together for a moment, and then Abi kissed Natasha quickly on the head and grabbed her hand.

"We can't stay here," she whispered, her mouth close to her daughter's ear. "He's not far behind me. Come on." She caught her hand and pulled her out from the hiding place, veered round to the left, and began the descent to the lower path.

As they slipped and slithered down the grassy slopes, Abi tried to formulate a workable plan. Whatever happened, they were stuck on the island until the next tide and would have to find a safe place to conceal themselves. From what she'd seen so far, Abi was convinced Simon was not going to give up the chase, and she had to keep Natasha safe. If she'd been on her own, things would have been very different, but with Natasha to protect Abi was determined to find a safe haven. As they landed on the lower path, Simon suddenly came into view from the direction of the causeway.

"Shit," muttered Abi under her breath. Catching hold of Natasha's hand, she pulled her in the direction of the Low Neck and the spiky rocks. She glanced round at her daughter and saw that tears as well as rain ran unheeded down her cheeks, and her wide eyes were filled with fear. Abi squeezed her hand and managed to summon up a small smile. "Keep going, Tash. It'll be okay," she encouraged, pushing the child in front of her as they came to a very narrow bit of path. Natasha ran ahead, her feet sliding on the wet ground, while Abi brought up the rear, constantly aware of Simon hot on their heels. As they rounded the bend that brought them into view of the low neck, she realised she could no longer hear his heavy footsteps following them. She slowed and half turned to look behind her. There was no sign of Simon—the path behind her was empty. She slowed to a stop, calling to Natasha. "Tash, wait. He's not following us any more."

Ahead of her, Natasha slowed and turned to face her, her long hair plastered to her head, and her breathing ragged. "Where's he gone?" the child cried, panic sounding in her voice. "Did he fall off the path?"

Abi spun round and surveyed her murky surroundings.

"No," she said with a shake of her head. "I doubt it. He must have veered off. Come here and stay close."

Natasha slithered over to her and caught hold of her mother's arm. Her face was streaming with a mixture of rain and tears, and her eyes were wild.

"I'm scared," she whimpered, pressing close to Abi. "Make him leave us alone."

Abi glanced down at her, her mouth set in a thin line. How dare Simon terrify her child like that! She put her arm around Natasha and gently urged her along the path.

"We need to find somewhere to shelter where he won't find us," she muttered. "I think he may be trying to cut us off, so we need to be quick." Together they ran round the bend and started to dodge down to their left, towards the now sea-covered lower levels. Natasha was scrambling down ahead of Abi and had just reached an outcrop of rocks perched above the swirling incoming sea when Simon appeared between them.

Abi pulled up short and called to Natasha, "Keep moving, Tash. Get behind those rocks and stay there."

The child threw a frightened glance over her shoulder, then slid behind the rocks and pressed herself hard up against them, her body racked with sobs. Further up the slope, Abi stood facing Simon, the rain beating down on her already soaked body. He had positioned himself about ten yards ahead of her, barring her way and preventing her from joining her daughter. His fair hair was plastered to his head, and his thin jacket and trousers were drenched and clinging to his bulky body. Abi squared up to him and pushed her dripping hair out of her eyes.

"Go on, then, Simon. Do your worst," she challenged him. "I'm not scared of you."

Simon sneered at her and gave a short laugh. "No, but your kid is," he remarked, glancing behind him to where Natasha was cowering behind the rocks. He took a step towards them, one eye on Abi. She moved towards him, her eyes flashing dangerously.

"You keep away from her," she shouted. "It's me

you want. Leave her alone."

He turned and took a menacing step towards her. "Oh, I don't want you," he said harshly. "I've never wanted you. That was the problem. No one really wants you. Gideon only came back to you because of the kid. He doesn't really want you. He'd be much better off without you. Then everything will be back to how it should be."

He reached into the pocket of his jacket as he spoke. To Abi's horror he pulled out a revolver and pointed it towards the rocks where Natasha was sheltering. She jumped towards him with a cry.

"Tash, stay where you are! Don't come out, stay there!"

Simon laughed wildly and spun round to face Abi, the gun waving towards her. "I don't want her," he said dismissively. "It's just nice to see you squirm." He paused and steadied his hand. "No, Abi, it's you I want. Just like you said. It's you I've come to get."

She stood her ground and stared transfixed as he lined the weapon up to point directly at her. She swallowed and took a hesitant step backwards.

"Simon, you don't really want to do this," she said, her mouth dry. "You're not thinking rationally. Please, just put the gun down, and we'll talk." She held out her hand towards him and inclined her head.

Simon took a step backwards and shook his head. "No, Abi. No, you're wrong. I do want to do this. I've wanted to do this for thirteen years." He took another step forward and aimed the gun with both hands. "Thirteen years I've waited to do this," he repeated, his eyes gleaming wildly as he stared at her.

At that moment Natasha poked her head around the

rock and took in the scene before her. She screamed and stepped out onto the grass.

"Mum! No! He's got a gun!"

Abi remained rooted to the spot and called desperately, "Get back, Tasha, get back now!" never taking her eyes off Simon and the gun. At the sound of their voices, Simon's arm began to shake, and his face suffused with fury.

"Shut up!" he screamed. "Shut up, shut up, shut up!" and on the last word he fired the gun wildly in Abi's direction. She moved to the side and the bullet skimmed across the top of her arm and came to rest in the soft hillside behind her. With a squeal of pain she jerked backwards and clasped at her arm with her other hand, losing her balance and falling heavily onto the muddy ground. Natasha screamed again, and at the same moment Gideon appeared, racing around the bend on the path above them, howling with rage. With a single bound he left the path and landed next to his wife as she lay on the wet grass, clutching at her arm.

"Abi, Abi, speak to me!" he gasped, sliding his arm beneath her shoulders and raising her up.

She gasped as his hand touched her injured arm and managed to utter, "Go to Tasha. Keep her safe. I'm okay," pointing with her good arm in the direction of the rocks. Gideon looked doubtfully at her for a moment, then jumped to his feet and advanced on Simon, where he stood with the gun hanging from his hand and a look of dazed confusion on his face. Gideon stared over towards the rocks that Abi had indicated.

"Tasha?" he yelled. "Tasha, where are you?"

He moved towards the rocks, keeping his eyes fixed on Simon. Natasha appeared from behind them, tears pouring down her face.

"Dad," she stammered. "Dad, he's got a gun. He shot Mum…"

Gideon strode across and pulled her to him. "She'll be all right," he said, his gaze never leaving Simon. "And I've got a gun, too. Go to your mother." He gave her a gentle push towards where Abi was now sitting up, her face contorted with pain. He turned towards his erstwhile friend and advanced on him with menace. "What the fuck have you done?" he demanded through gritted teeth. "You nearly killed my wife! Simon, have you gone completely mad?"

Simon raised unfocused eyes and stared at him. He looked down at the gun in his hand and then over at Abi and Natasha. With a sudden movement he turned and slithered down the grassy slope. With a cry of frustration, Gideon slithered after him, arriving on the edge of the land just in time to see Simon disappear over the edge and fall towards the sea. He crawled forward and peered over. The spray and the rain made it impossible for him to see clearly, and he called loudly, "Simon! Simon, are you there? Simon…" He moved forward as far as he could and peered down. There was no sign of Simon, and Gideon realised he needed to get Abi back to dry land as fast as possible. He stood up, scanned the water one more time, then ran back up the slope to his wife and daughter.

Ten minutes later, the three of them were safely strapped into the helicopter and waiting to take off back to the mainland. Abi, her arm now tightly bound up with a strip from Gideon's shirt, reached out and tapped him on the shoulder.

"Are you all right, Abs?" he asked shakily. The

memory of seeing her fly backwards as the bullet hit her was still fresh in his mind.

She managed a small smile and nodded. "Fine. Gid, what about Simon? We can't just leave him."

Gideon grinned. "You want to rescue him?" he asked in surprise. "After what he did?"

Abi nodded and raised her eyebrows at him. "Of course I do," she chided, "and so do you. Whatever he's done, he was still your friend for twenty-odd years. He wasn't in his right mind, Gid. Can we look for him?"

Gideon sighed and leaned over to speak to the pilot. The older man nodded and, as they took off into the cloudy skies, flew towards the place where they'd last seen Simon. As he circled over the area, Gideon and the girls scanned the sea and surrounding rocks for any signs of life.

Gideon twisted round to face Abi again. "Abi, we can't see anything from here. I'll call search-and-rescue when we get back, but I rather think he went in the sea."

Abi nodded sadly and lay back against the seat. For all the trouble he'd caused her, she still didn't like to think Simon might be dead. Natasha leaned against her and took a long shuddering breath.

Abi looked down at her. "Are you okay, Tash?" she asked gently.

Natasha shook her head and snuggled closer. "No." she said in a small voice. "I thought you were dead. He shot you."

Abi put her good arm around her and pulled her even closer. She dropped a kiss on the top of her wet head. "I'm so sorry you had to see that, darling, but I'm fine. It's just a graze."

Natasha looked up at her. "Well *I* hope he's dead."

****

Simon watched as the helicopter circled above him and pressed himself further into the cleft in the rocks. He hadn't landed in the sea when he fell but had managed to scramble into a gap in the rocks and remain hidden until they'd left. His next move would be to keep out of sight until the causeway was open again, and then blend in with the tourists and make it back to the mainland without being discovered. He leant back against the rocks, closed his eyes, and patted the pocket of his jacket. He smiled. The gun was still there.

Epilogue

Monday 4ᵗʰ August, 2008

Gideon stood at the window, gazing blankly out at the drizzly scene below him. After a night spent in hospital in Swansea, Abi had been released into his care, and his father had insisted they all go and spend a few days in the New Forest with them to recuperate. Gideon turned and stared down at the bed in which his wife lay sleeping peacefully, her bandaged arm lying on top of the covers. As he watched, she began to stir, and her lips moved in a silent protest. She moved her head on the pillow, and a strand of hair fell across her face. Nose wrinkled, she attempted to blow it away in her sleep. Gideon smiled and moved a little closer to the bed. As the errant hair persisted in tickling her nose, Abi's eyes fluttered open and stared right at him. She summoned a sleepy smile and wriggled into a more comfortable position.

"Morning," she murmured. "Are you all right?"

Gideon moved over to the bed and perched on its edge, staring at her. "No," he said emphatically, "no, I'm not, and I don't think I ever will be again." He took her good hand in his. "You can't witness your wife being shot by your—friend—and come out of it unscathed." He ran an agitated hand through his hair and shook his head. "Abi, that was the worst moment of my life. As I came round that corner and he fired the gun…" He turned his head away.

Abi gently squeezed his hand. "But I'm okay, Gid," she murmured. "He missed anything vital. I don't think he meant to fire at me, really. I think he was just trying to scare me."

Gideon scowled at her. "Abi, he nearly killed you, whether he meant to or not. When he fired and you fell to the ground, I…" He couldn't finish his sentence, and his eyes filled with tears. "Abi darling, I thought I'd lost you. I thought— I couldn't bear the thought— I just wanted to kill him, and then kill myself."

Abi struggled into a sitting position, concern on her face. "Gideon, don't talk like that," she chided. "I'm fine. You know you don't mean that. Think of the children." She paused and took a deep breath. "How *is* Tasha this morning?"

"Gone riding with Dad," he said dismally. "He's trying to take her mind off it." He stared at Abi. "She was quite traumatised, and she's still very angry."

`"I know." Abi shook her head. "Yesterday all she could say was that she hoped he was dead."

`"So do I," said Gideon immediately. "No one gets away with nearly killing my wife and terrorizing my daughter."

Abi frowned and shook his arm. "Gid, no! You don't mean that. You don't really want him dead, do you? He wasn't in his right mind. He was doing it all for you, because he loves you. He didn't really want to kill me."

"Abi, you amaze me." Gideon stared at her, raising his eyebrows. "How can you be so forgiving? If I hadn't been so worried about you, I would have made use of the fact that I had a gun with me and shot him myself."

"You had a gun!" Abi shrieked. "Where on earth did you get that from? You can't just carry a gun!"

"Dad gave it to me," he muttered, looking at her under his lashes. "For protection. He did tell me not to use it, actually, just to threaten him with it."

Abi fell back onto the pillows with a frustrated grunt. "Good god," she said, covering her face with her hand. "What's wrong with you Hawk men? And what was Roger doing with a gun anyway?"

"You may as well ask what was he doing with access to a helicopter at a moment's notice, too." Gideon gave her an apologetic smile. "You know Dad—don't ask too many questions."

Abi sighed and shook her head at him. "You're dangerous," she said. "Have you given the gun back?" He nodded, and she went on. "And do you know if they've found Simon?"

Gideon shook his head. "No, and they've called off the search this morning. They think he fell in the water and his body got washed out to sea. It'll probably never be found."

Abi looked at him. "And what do you think?" she asked at last.

"Dunno," Gideon looked away, "part of me hopes that's the case, but part of me—the part that's known him since he was eight—hopes…" He tailed off and smiled at her. "That doesn't tie up with wanting to kill him, does it?"

Abi smiled and sat up again. "'Course not." She reached over and stroked his face. "I knew you didn't really mean that." She paused and looked at him.

"Unfortunately, I think Natasha *does* mean it. Can you have a word with her?"

Gideon nodded and leaned forward to kiss her on the lips. "I'll try," he said, "but you know what she's like."

There was a quiet tap on the door, and Caroline's head appeared. "Oh, you are awake." She beamed at Abi. "I'll bring you a cup of tea. Gideon, stop fussing round her. She's fine." She shook her head at her son. "Natasha's gone riding with Roger, and Oliver is helping me bake a cake."

Abi laughed. "Good luck with that," she said. "His idea of helping is interesting, to say the least."

Gideon rolled his eyes. "You and your cakes, Mum. Don't you think eighteen months is a little young to be baking?"

"It's never too early to start learning," Caroline retorted. "I'll bring your tea, Abi, and then you can get up when you're ready." She flashed a smile at them and disappeared again.

Abi leaned back against the pillows, laughing. "I love your mother," she said fondly. "She tries so hard to make everything normal, doesn't she?"

"And yet my parents are very far from normal themselves." With a wry smile, Gideon stood and walked to the window. "Are you up to coming up to London in a day or so?" he asked tentatively. "Now Chas has gone back to New York, we could have the flat to ourselves. Or do you just want to take the kids home again?"

"Of course we'll come to London!" said Abi in surprise. "We always planned to do that. Why should now be any different?"

Gideon turned, his face serious. "I think everything's different now," he said simply. "I don't want to be parted from you for a single second, let alone a whole day."

"That's fine by me," Abi said comfortably. "But what are you going to do in London? If you're reforming the band and Chas has gone away for a bit, what can you do on your own?"

"Find a new drummer," came the prompt reply, "and I think, given the circumstances, that you and Tasha should help choose him." He moved over and sat down on the bed again. Reaching out and taking her hand in his, he looked at her very seriously. "And you are *never* going anywhere on your own again."

Abi put her good arm around his neck and buried her face in his shoulder.

"That's fine by me," she said smiling to herself.

If you enjoyed *Rhythm of Deceit*, you'll want to read the next book in the series:

Cobwebs in the Dark

by

Rachael Richey

The NightHawk Series, Book Three

Chapter 1

Saturday 18th April, 2009

"Dear Natasha,
Your letter has been passed to me by the son of
Maureen Holmes, who herself sadly passed away some
years ago. I believe my brother is the 'Billy the farm
hand' you refer to. I vaguely remember some story back
in my childhood about twin girls who stayed at the farm
one summer, and my brother made friends with them. I
also remember he was very sad for a time after they
left. I never knew the reason why. It was fascinating to
hear that these twins were your grandmother and great-
aunt. Yes, my brother is still alive, but unfortunately he
emigrated to New Zealand back in 1955, and I haven't
seen him since. Obviously we still keep in touch with
Christmas cards, but that's all the contact I have with
him. He married out there and had quite a large family.
His wife died about two years ago. Maybe you would
care to write to him, so I have enclosed his address at
the end of this letter. It was lovely to hear from you, my
dear, and I hope you can tell him some more about his
old friends..."

Natasha lowered the sheet of notepaper, her eyes
shining. She had finally found Billy. She glanced down
at the bottom of the letter to make sure the address had
been included, then folded it carefully, replaced it in the

envelope, and laid it on her bedside table. Giving a little wriggle of excitement, she skipped over to the door and made her way noisily down the polished wooden staircase. At the bottom she turned right into the large bright kitchen, where her mother was sitting at the long pine table sipping tea and chatting to a smiling blonde woman with a scattering of freckles on her nose.

"Judy! I didn't know you'd arrived." Natasha beamed and ran over to give their family friend a hug.

Judy laughed and planted a kiss on Natasha's cheek. "Hello, pet. Yes, I arrived about twenty minutes ago. Abi and I are having a good catch-up."

Natasha's mother grinned over at her friend. "A well overdue catch up," she said, nodding to the other side of the room. "Have you looked over there, Tash?"

A Moses basket was lying on the floor in front of the large window, and Natasha gave a little squeak and ran over to peer inside.

"Oh, she's gorgeous!" she breathed as she gazed down on the latest addition to Judy's family, four-week-old Miriam. "Can I hold her?"

Abi laughed. "Not now, Tasha, she's sleeping. Which according to Judy and Robert she doesn't do very much. Let's wait until she wakes up."

"Oh, yes, please don't wake her yet." Judy sighed. "This is the longest she's slept since she was born. The Cornish air must be good for her."

"Are Tommy and Sabrina in the conservatory with Ollie?" Natasha asked, standing up and moving towards the door.

Judy shook her head. "No, they decided to go outside and help the men put up the marquee. They might appreciate your help."

Natasha giggled and disappeared through the door with a bang.

Abi grinned over at Judy. "Oh, Judy, this is wonderful. I've missed you so much. It's been far too long. I'm so glad you could make it for the party."

Judy reached across the table and gave her hand a squeeze. "I wouldn't have missed it for the world," she said firmly. "It's not every day your best friend turns thirty." She glanced over at the window. "And it looks like you might be lucky with the weather, too. It only needs to hold off raining until midnight…"

"One thirty, actually," interjected Abi with a grin. "I was born at one thirty in the morning, so technically I won't be thirty until then."

Judy tutted. "You can't put off the evil moment," she said with a laugh. "You'll still get the bumps at midnight."

Abi squeaked in horror. "No way," she stated. "I am not having the bumps! No one's done that to me since I was twelve."

Judy shook her head knowingly. "Well you'd better take that up with Gideon—I believe he has plans."

Abi's husband Gideon was the lead singer of the grunge band NightHawk, who were just about to start their comeback tour. In a couple of weeks they would be heading off to Australia and New Zealand and had managed to fit Abi's birthday party into a break in the rehearsing. She sighed and sat back in her chair.

"I can't believe I'm this old," she moaned, pushing her long, dark auburn hair back over her shoulders. "Do I look it?"

"You still look fifteen to me," Judy giggled, with a

whimsical smile, "and if you're anything like me you probably still feel it."

Abi grinned. "I think I've grown up a bit since then…" she objected. "At least I hope so. Just hope Tasha doesn't make my mistakes. I hate the fact that she's a teenager now."

Judy looked serious for a moment. "Abi, Tasha is nothing like you in that way," she said earnestly. "You have nothing to worry about there. She might look like you, but she's got more common sense in her little finger than you ever had in your whole body. She suffered because of your mistakes just like you did; she's not going to repeat them."

Abi frowned. "Steady on," she said with a wry grin, "you make me sound completely dreadful. I was just a bit high maintenance and…"

"…and cocky and strong willed and a complete nightmare," Judy finished with a laugh. "But don't worry: you've matured nicely!"

Abi picked up a tea towel and threw it at her. "Hey, you're supposed to be my best friend," she objected, trying not to laugh. "I'm lovely now. A paragon of virtue."

Judy chuckled and threw the tea towel back. "Hope not. That sounds far too boring," she retorted, getting to her feet and stretching. "Shall we go and see how the guys are doing with the marquee? I need to make the most of the time Miriam's asleep."

The large garden overlooking the long sweep of Sennen Cove was a hive of activity, and Abi and Judy stood in the doorway of the conservatory watching in amusement. A huge marquee was being erected in the centre of the garden under the direction of both Gideon and Judy's husband Robert, who were beginning to appear slightly harassed by the unsolicited help supplied by the younger generation. Abi's two-year-old son Oliver was holding tightly to his father's leg and attempting to climb onto his foot, and Judy's older two children, six-year-old Tommy and four-year-old Sabrina, were swinging around one of the supporting poles singing lustily. Natasha had just joined them and was almost doubled up with laughter at the sight of her father's face.

Abi grinned and leaned towards Judy. "Shall we rescue them, or leave them to their fate?"

Judy chuckled. "Leave them to their fate," she said at once. "It's your birthday—or nearly—so you shouldn't have to help. Let's go and open the wine."

****

"Caroline, if we don't leave right now we're not going to arrive in time for the party," Roger Hawk called to his wife, drumming his fingers impatiently on the roof of the Volvo. "What on earth are you doing anyway?" He tailed off and stared as his wife appeared at the front door, several large tins balanced precariously in her arms. With a sigh he darted forward and relieved her of the top one just before it toppled onto the driveway. "Really?" he muttered, frowning at her. "More cakes? Surely they'll have enough?"

Caroline bustled past him and deposited her armful on the back seat. "You can never have too many cakes," she replied, sliding gracefully into the front passenger seat. "Now come on, let's get going. We don't want to miss the start."

With an incredulous glance at his wife, Roger pulled their front door shut and climbed into the car.

Caroline had made herself comfortable and was already making inroads on the tin of boiled sweets they kept in the glove compartment.

Roger grinned at her. "Caroline, you're impossible," he stated affectionately.

"You wouldn't want me any other way." she said, settling back in her seat with a smile.

Their journey from Hampshire to Cornwall progressed uneventfully, and when they finally crossed the border into the county, just east of Launceston, Caroline frowned and turned to Roger.

"What d'you think happened to Simon?" she asked, apropos of nothing. "Really, I mean, not the official story. Do you really think he got washed out to sea that night?" She shivered as her mind flashed back to the dreadful day the previous August when Simon Dean, the unhinged former drummer of Gideon's band, had attempted to kill Abi and Natasha in South Wales.

Roger glanced at her in surprise, his eyes narrowed. "Whatever made you think of him, and what do you mean, 'really'?" he asked.

Caroline shifted in her seat impatiently. "You know very well what I mean," she said sharply. "It was reported that he drowned and got washed out to sea, but I think we both know that may not be the case. Whenever we see Gideon and Abi I think of him, and I just wondered what you really thought."

Roger was silent for a moment. "I think he's alive," he said finally. "I'm not sure how he did it, but I believe he managed to cross the causeway on the next tide without being spotted, and he's been lying low ever since." He glanced sideways at his wife. "Gideon thinks the same."

Caroline pursed her lips. "Hmmm…so where can he be now?" she mused. "It could hardly be possible for him to leave the country. He'd be spotted." Roger didn't respond, and Caroline turned to him. "Roger? How could he leave the country? I'm sure the police were alerted to watch out for him."

"There are lots of ways," Roger said at last. "I suspect they're not keeping quite as close a watch now because the main consensus of opinion is that he drowned, but he could always be using a false passport and a disguise."

Caroline peered suspiciously at him. "You know something, don't you? Roger, what d'you know? If that man is still at large, Abi and Tasha could be in danger…"

Roger put out a hand and gently patted Caroline's arm. "He won't do anything else," he said firmly. "He couldn't possibly risk that. But you're right, I do know something. Someone fitting Simon's description was seen to enter Seattle some months back." He paused again as Caroline caught her breath. "He wasn't travelling under his own name, and of course my informant may have been mistaken, but I think it's safe to say he's probably still alive."

"Does Gideon know?" Caroline asked, her face anxious.

"Yes." Roger nodded. "I thought he should be told. Apparently both he and Abi have never believed Simon drowned, so he wasn't very surprised. Angry still, and very keen I should try and keep tabs on him, but not surprised."

"Honestly, Roger, you might have told me," Caroline complained, leaning back in her seat. "Don't you think I want to know these things too? When my family is in danger…"

"They're not in danger now," Roger interrupted her firmly. "I told Gideon because it was his wife Simon tried to kill, and anyway, you know I'm not really supposed to talk about information I get from my government contacts. You didn't really need to know."

Caroline fixed him with a baleful stare. "Anything that involves a member of my family getting shot at is something I need to know," she said firmly. "In future, Roger, you will tell me everything you find out about Simon…even if you risk getting into trouble over it," and she folded her arms and stared out of the window.

Roger smiled to himself and let her fume in silence.

****

Abi sighed, kicked off her very high heels, and slumped down onto the sofa. She closed her eyes and wriggled into a more comfortable position.

"That was the best party ever," she said in satisfaction. "Even having the bumps was fun." A giggle made her open her eyes to find Natasha curled up in the chair across from her, grinning. "Are you still up?" she asked, smiling back. "Aren't you shattered? It's nearly four o'clock."

Natasha wriggled forward in her seat. "I'm not going to bed till you and Dad do," she stated firmly. "This is the first grown-up party I've ever been to, and I plan to make the most of it. Besides, even Grandma and Grandpa are still up." She nodded towards the conservatory, where Roger and Caroline were deep in animated conversation with Charles and Justin, the other two members of NightHawk.

Abi peered at her suspiciously and attempted to muster up a 'responsible mother' tone. "You haven't been drinking, have you?"

"'Course not!" Natasha said indignantly. "Well, just some of that fruity punchy stuff. Earlier. Justin gave me some. Is that okay?"

Abi rolled her eyes. "Hmm. Apart from the fact that it's full of vodka? I shall have words with him."

"Words with whom about what?" asked Judy, bouncing down onto the sofa next to her friend.

Abi smiled sleepily at her. "Justin," she said, glancing over at him. "Apparently he gave Tasha some punch. Are all drummers not to be trusted?"

Judy giggled and kicked her shoes off across the room. "If that's the worst thing he does, then he's fine in my eyes," she remarked.

Natasha sat forward in her chair and frowned at them. "Justin is very nice," she said. "And he is *nothing* like Simon." Her voice broke as she mentioned the name of the band's erstwhile drummer. Natasha had been badly affected by the experiences of the previous summer, and she suddenly got to her feet, squeezed herself onto the sofa between Abi and Judy, and cuddled up to them. "He's quite different," she reiterated. "You can trust him."

Abi glanced down fondly at her and dropped a light kiss on her curly head.

"I know, sweetie," she said. "I know he is. He seems very nice. But you still shouldn't be drinking alcohol."

Judy chuckled and squeezed Natasha's hand. "Don't listen to her, pet," she teased. "One drink won't hurt you. It's a special occasion. Not many thirteen-year-olds get to see their mother turn thirty."

Abi tutted, reached over, and slapped Judy's hand. "Stop undermining me," she protested mildly. She looked down at Natasha, adding with mock severity, "Don't make a habit of it, okay?"

Natasha looked up at her under long lashes and nodded demurely. "'Course not. I'm not stupid," she replied with a little smile. She wriggled a little closer to her mother and bit her lip. "Mum…can I tell you something?"

Abi looked concerned at her change in tone. "Of course. What's wrong?"

"Nothing's wrong…" Natasha shook her head. "It's just that, well, I've found something out." She paused, and Abi looked down at her inquiringly. "It's about Billy. Billy the farm hand," she added for further clarification.

Abi frowned. "Billy the farm hand?" she asked puzzled. "Who d'you mean?"

Natasha rolled her eyes, then glanced sideways at Judy, remembering they were not alone. "Doesn't matter," she muttered. "I'll tell you tomorrow," and she jumped to her feet and skipped into the conservatory to join her grandparents.

Abi stared after her, a slight frown creasing her forehead. After the first moment, she'd realised what Natasha was talking about and wondered what she'd found out.

Judy put her hand on Abi's arm. "Was that something secret?" she inquired curiously. "Tash clammed up when she remembered I was here."

Abi sighed and glanced round at her. "Yeah, I guess," she said. "Well, she thinks it is, anyway.

Something to do with that stuff we found out about my mum last summer."

Judy nodded. "The stuff you shouldn't have told me," she said with a smile. "Doesn't Tash know that I know?"

"Well, I may have mentioned it in passing." Abi grimaced. "She probably wasn't listening. She ought to know I tell you everything, though," and she giggled like a teenager. Judy joined in, and when Gideon came in a few minutes later, the two friends were almost rolling on the sofa in hysterics. He stared at them in surprise.

"That punch must have been strong," he remarked, catching his wife by the hand and pulling her to her feet. She swayed and fell forward to lean against him. He looked down at her and grinned. "Happy birthday, babe," he murmured as he bent his head and kissed her roughly on the lips. She snaked her arms up around his neck and pressed her body closer to his.

"I love you, Gid," she whispered, "and thank you for the best party ever."

Behind her, Judy struggled up from the sofa as the distant sound of a crying baby reached their ears. "There she goes. Not too bad tonight. At least I'm still up," and she gathered up her shoes from beneath the coffee table and headed off in the direction of the spare bedroom.

Gideon grinned at Abi. "What were you and Judy laughing at?" he asked quizzically, pulling her down onto the sofa and putting his arm around her shoulders. `Abi slithered down, laid her head on his knee, and curled her legs up onto the cushions. "Dunno, really…" She closed her eyes and tried to remember. "Oh, yeah… Well, it started 'cause Tasha said she'd found something out about Billy. Billy the farm hand…" She looked up at Gideon. "You know from the diaries?" He nodded. "Then she realised Judy was there and went off, and I was just telling Judy that I thought Tasha knew that *she* knew, and for some reason we got the giggles." She wriggled her head on his knees and looked up at him solemnly. "It's good to laugh."

Gideon grinned at her and leant forward, his long dark hair swinging over his shoulders. "It certainly is," he agreed, tweaking her nose with his thumb. "Don't ever stop. So you don't know what Tash found out, then?"

Abi shook her head. "No," she said with a slight frown. "I thought we'd decided not to pursue him. The less people who know the whole story the better, but I know Tasha has always had the romantic idea that he's been pining for my aunt Joan for the last sixty years…" She shrugged. "I don't want to think about it now. It's four thirty on the morning of my thirtieth birthday, and all I want to do right now is go to bed. With you," she added with a smile.

In answer, Gideon gently rolled her off his knee onto the floor and stood up.

"Come on, then. I'll tell the rest of the guests to fend for themselves, and I'll see you in the bedroom."

He strode into the conservatory, where the remaining half dozen guests were congregated, chatting quietly, while Abi scrambled to her feet, retrieved her shoes, and scurried upstairs to wait for him.

A word about the author...

Rachael Richey writes Women's Fiction. She lives in Cornwall, England, with her husband, son and daughter. You can visit Rachael's website at:
http://rachaelricheybooks.weebly.com/